Shapiro

To Lynn
May it
all happ
Doris Hun
04/17/07

SISTER KATIE

By

Doris Hunt-Jorden

This book is a work of fiction. Places, events, and situations in this story are purely fictional. Any resemblance to actual persons, living or dead, is coincidental.

First published by AuthorHouse 05/11/04

ISBN: 1-4184-5871-6 (e-book)
ISBN: 1-4184-4015-9 (Paperback)
ISBN: 1-4184-4016-7 (Dust Jacket)

Library of Congress Control Number: 2004105314

Printed in the United States of America
Bloomington, IN

This book is printed on acid free paper.

For my family

ACKNOWLEDGEMENTS

Many thanks are due to Randy Albers, John Schultz, Betty Shiflett and the staff at Columbia College, Chicago who taught me as much about life as they did writing. To the Austin Branch Public Library staff for all the assistance they have given me with my research. To the Illinois Arts Council for its support, and to my loving family whose love and untiring morale boosting kept me afloat.

"Behold, I send you forth as sheep in the midst of wolves....

St. Matthew 10:16

PRAYING

It was said time after time when it rained and the sun still shone brightly in the sky that the devil was beating his wife. But there was no explanation known for the hail storm that suddenly descended on the town of Bennettsville one hot July afternoon, carrying balls of ice the size of hens' eggs on its crest—ice pitched from clustered smoked-gray clouds, and plummeting to the ground with showering clatters of dread. Open doors slammed, windows banged, and people who only moments before had been casually strolling up and down the busy streets now desperately sought shelter of any kind. In a few seconds the streets were deserted except for a sleek, black sedan that cruised down Main Street and came to a halt in the front of Rosie's Cafe.

A tall man in a light gray chauffeur's uniform emerged and, like a trained soldier unaffected by the storm, pushing through the door of the cafe and staunchly presented himself to Rosie, the red-headed woman at the bar. He had come for Katie, he said in a voice that told Rosie he was not a man to be put off. Katie summoned from her kitchen duties and still garbed in the white baker's apron and standard hair net, had no choice but to go with him. Even Rosie insisted that she leave. She was escorted through the white section of the cafe to the sedan and driven to the rambling split-level house on the hill to pray for a man that she had had dealings with two times in her life—each time when it was thought he was dying.

Harrison Townsend-king of Bennettsville County, builder of its schools, churches, and movie houses, owner of most of the land thereabouts, and supplier of jobs throughout the town—lay in his giant, four-poster bed, with only his trembling, silvery head visible above the covers, fighting for his life. The skin on his face was sheer—translucent, and alabaster white. His waxy, blue eyes roamed about the room, watching something that only he could see, and periodically he would clutch the covers to his chest and violently shake his head. Clara, his loving wife of thirty-five years, knelt facing him, her oval face filled with worry. She whispered words of encouragement, assuring him that Max would return shortly with Katie. His children, Junior and Dellie Kay, huddled outside the threshold that led to the master bedroom, their eyes wide. Dellie's were struck with petrified terror over the possible loss of her father, while J.T.'s (as he was called) were filled with conspicuous anticipation of stepping into his daddy's big shoes. J.T., a thin-faced young man in his early twenties, mechanically stroked his teenage sister's long, auburn hair as she buried her head in his chest. He watched his father's struggle with cold, black, unsympathetic eyes.

Downstairs, Earline Simpson, the Townsend's maid, swung the front door open, her black silky face filled with sweat, and greeted Katie. "Thanks the Lord you is here, Sister Katie."

Katie's reputation as a faith-healer was known all over Bennettsville County and farther—God walked with her folks said—and the inside of Townsend's house was not unfamiliar to her. She visualized the location of the master bedroom, nodded in Earline's direction, indicating she could find her way, and climbed the thickly carpeted stairs; she remembered her surprise at its softness the first time she was brought to the house two years ago. Nothing seemed to have changed—the winding staircase lined with countless Creeping Myrtle sprigs rooting in crystal vases that sat on the floor at the top of the landing, and even Townsend's children in the same spot they had been standing on her last visit. J.T. pulled Dellie back against the wall as Katie neared the door, allowing her entry into the bedroom, and Katie walked past them without saying a word. She entered the bedroom with a mental picture of J.T.'s dark eyes following her every move while he pretended to console a brown-haired snip of a girl in a loving embrace. A picture that did not, Katie thought, portray his true character, because everyone knew J.T. was selfish and uncaring; even his own father was once overheard to say that dealing with J.T. could be a bitter experience—like drinking rank water.

Although Katie knew what was expected of her on these visits to Townsend's—something close to the resurrection of Lazarus—she never feared she would be threatened in any way should things not work out. Yet she wondered, if the situation were reversed, would Townsend come to her assistance? Probably not. But here she stood, the "white nigger" of Bennettsville, label so because of her mixed blood-line and her white skin, among them—the elite—at a time when only family members and loved ones should be present. Her black hair was disheveled from the hurried removal of the hair net. A white apron was folded and doubled around her tiny waist, stained with cake flour and butter smears, and her gray eyes slightly lowered in an effort to avoid making direct eye contact. She removed the apron, laid it on the chair near the door, and stepped into the large room, where the frail, gray-haired man lay wasted to the bone. His face was taut as a dried rubber band, his soul straining against its last fiber before snapping and flying away. A flicker of light registered in the old man's eyes as soon as he saw Katie, a light that registered hope, and the shaking ceased. Perhaps a sign, perhaps not. It didn't matter if they were all practically strangers, for all they really knew about each other were names and needs which were very similar—needs so similar it wasn't necessary to discuss them. They all understood—except for J.T.—that they were gathered to fight for Townsend's life until he had either drawn his last breath or had risen from the bed on his own.

At once Clara came to her feet, the blood rushing to her cheeks, her pale blue eyes shining with gratitude at the sight of the Negro cook who had come to their rescue again. "Katie," she cried out, the urgency in her voice caused it to ring high, like that of a young girl.

"Miss Clara," Katie replied and crossed the floor, stopping at the foot of the bed. Clara, a foot taller than Katie, looked down, wrung her hands, then anxiously watched as Katie gazed about as though measuring the space. The room was what Katie imagined a small hospital would look like. Bottles of medicines lined the gleaming oaken-wood bed stand. Heating pads and numerous, exquisitely-designed quilts (probably from Europe) lay on the floor near the bed for extra warmth, should they be needed, along with a humidifier, equipment to assist in breathing, and needles filled with clear liquid solutions to kill the pain that constantly racked the frail man's body. And the space behind her that stretched across the huge bay windows and on to the wall where his children stood within the recess of the door could surely accommodate fifty sick people lined side by side.

Clara stood rigidly, her back as straight as a board, her hands clasped and drawn up against her chest, as though movement or even small talk would somehow interfere with the process of Katie interacting with her God. And Katie, sensing the tenseness in the room, inhaled deeply to slow the racing of her heart. She stood, one hand pressed against her forehead, her gray eyes flitting back and forth, searching for the way to begin. Suddenly, she dropped her hands to her side, tilted her head to the right, and softly, as though to smooth the way to Jesus or ease heavy hearts, began humming the old spiritual, "Jesus is Mine." The song had lain heavily on her mind all morning, from the moment she opened her eyes. And she now recalled that it was Townsend's favorite hymn—Miss Clara had informed Katie on that hasty arrival last year about the song, stating how it gave her husband spiritual strength, especially when sung by Negroes. She moved slowly towards the huge bed, humming in a deep, vibrating contralto, and rocking her head to a beat as though a great band was hidden behind a heavenly backdrop. When she reached the bed stand, she stopped humming—the silence filling the room with a charged expectancy—and passed her hands over the syringes then moaned as if she had been stabbed. She could feel the anger rising from the needles and knew that Doc Smith had tossed them there, probably after Miss Clara had told him to go. This is what had happened in the past when Doc Smith had given up on Townsend. And everyone in town knew that Doc Smith was only allowed at the Townsend's when the specialist from St. Louis could not be reached in time.

Standing with her back to Clara, Katie closed her eyes and sang out loud. "Jee-zus is mine. Jee-zus is mine, all mine. Everywhere I go. Everywhere I be. Jee-eee-zus, so glad He's mine." She turned slowly, glanced over at Clara and immediately Clara joined in; their voices blended, becoming comfortable as two old shoes. It affected Harrison so, he strained against the covers, attempting to rise, even though the death rattle thundered in his chest. Katie turned and looked across into Townsend's radiant eyes—hope shone like a tiny beacon. She nodded her head indicating that she approved, for she had many times seen hope beat death. She had seen hope make death vanish at the end of a song or in the blink of an eye. She walked the few steps to the bed and gazed down on Harrison. Slowly, he dropped his head to the pillow and watching her, waited. Her eyes roamed over every blotch, every wrinkle in his skin, the white fuzz about his bony chin, the cracks in his lips, the hollowness of his eyes, the throbbing pulse in his temples, the broad forehead that pinched the tight skin together, making it pucker around the white stand-away eyebrows and rise like tiny hills, and finally rested there penetrating—as if they bore through his skull and into the tumors that lay behind his forehead. She moaned, her eyes rolling towards the ceiling and shook her head like she had seen the great beasts of hell. Flinging her hands in the air, she cried in a raspy, preachy voice, "I said Jesus is Mine!" Beads of sweat lined the bridge of her thin nose and her eyes stared somewhere into the beyond. Clara eyed Katie curiously and slowly knelt at the foot of the bed. Suddenly, Katie laid her hand on Townsend's forehead, snatched it away as if, she'd touched flame, and knelt quickly on the quilts by the bed. Taking her cue from Katie, Clara clasped her hands tightly, bowed her head, and waited for Katie to being the dialogue with her God that had worked so effectively in the past. Everyone took the same cue. Harrison rocked his head from side to side, Dellie pulled away from J.T. and dropped to her knees at the door, J.T. sighed and rested his head against the frame of the door.

The sunlight leaned heavily against the windows, painting Katie's face with a rosy glow and childlike innocence. Her breast rose and fell in a slow uneven rhythm. She clasped her hands together, propped her elbows on the edge of the bed, and rested her chin atop her hands. Time stood still for everyone as she sought courage to speak. "Father, this is your faithful and devoted servant, Katie, calling on you this dark Monday afternoon…" She finally said, her voice strong and filled with powerful desperation. "I wouldn't interrupt you while you is 'bout your work except it's a matter of life and death, and you said anyone, no matter how small they think they might be, you said that all they had to do was to call on you in their hour of need. You said it didn't matter what time of night or day it might be, all they had to do was call on you, and you would be there beside them. I know I don't have to tell you who I am, cause my credentials have already been put in my file in heaven. I know it ain't no surprise to you, the reason I'se here calling on you. I know I don't have to tell you the reason. So I'se jest down here begging you to consider this plea for this man in Jesus' name, cause I know you have always been partial where he was concerned. I know, before his coming home to be on high with you, he told his disciples that the only way to the Father, was through him. So I know that even if you turned a deaf ear to my request, if I call on Jesus long and hard enough, you will at least listen for his sake—this I know.

"So I ask you in the name of Jesus to hear me out. Hear me out, Lord!" she repeated in a thunderous voice, as though her knowledge of proper protocol gave her the right to demand an audience. She slumped back, rocking on her knees, then stretched her hand across Harrison's body, moving it back and forth like a blind person searching for the door. "Heal!" The word echoed through the room and Clara, absorbing strength from Katie's presence, raised her head and stared at her husband. J.T., infuriated with the scene before him turned a scarlet red and snatched his head away, wishing Doc Smith would return and pronounce the old man dead—he wanted these nigger rituals to end.

"I'se asking you to consider this poor soul whose own flesh is his enemy," Katie continued. "I'se asking you to consider this man called Harrison Townsend. A man whose commitments have been many to this here town, a man who has given much to this town, a man that practically built this town with his bare hands, a man whose education was wide and yet a man that still doubts the workings of the Lord, especially when death hovers near, though he has known only your goodness. Yes, Lord, he's a man with many advantages, a man blessed with a humble and faithful wife and love from his fellowmen—and still, he was not satisfied." She emphasized the words and waved her hands in the air, gasping loudly as if she had swallowed a foreign substance. Regaining her voice, she continued, "I'se asking you to consider this here town and the poor folks in it that needs him, the Negroes and the whites. I'se asking you to give him one more chance to redeem himself in your eyes, Lord, before you calls him home to judgment. I knows you said the sinner's prayer would be mocked, that's why I'se intervening Lord, this ain't no sinner calling on you at this hour, Lord. This is your servant, Katie, a servant that would walk through the fires of hell to be by your side, a holy servant, father, filled with the Holy Ghost and the Fire of your spirit, a servant that ask nothing in return for herself except a home in heaven. I ask you to consider the shell of a man laying here at my side and spare him. I ask you this in Jesus' name, the Holy Ghost and the Fire, amen." She removed her arms from the bed and rocked back and forth on her knees, mumbling, "Heal, heal."

Suddenly the old man, blind with fever, tossed back the many quilts from his malnourished body and sitting up, grabbed the edge of the mattress and twisted his body around to the edge. His paper thin legs dangled over the side of the bed, his pajama bottoms twisted about his legs and his naked chest looked like a twelve year-old boy's. He looked around at Katie who had pushed away from the bed, and remaining on her knees watched as he grabbed the bed post, opened his mouth, and quite clearly and unmistakably, howled like a wolf. Katie, shivered, and advanced on her knees until she was beside him—her body slowly moving across the carpet. The hair on the back of her neck rose, prickling her skin and she cried out "Jesus is Mine." She reached Townsend, quickly placed her hands on his forehead, and in a voice filled with hate cried, "Get thee behind me, Satan! There ain't no room for you here in this house! Leave in the name of JESUS!" Townsend seemed to become very agitated at this command, and his body began to shiver, even though perspiration rolled down his thin face. His eyes were almost black as he crawled away from Katie on now-steady knees heading for his wife. His mouth continually working up and down as though to say something urgent, he crossed the space and stopped a few feet from his wife. He continued to work his mouth, but no sound was audible. Suddenly, his eyes disappeared into the back of his head. His frail body jerked as though someone was shaking him, arched, and spilled out onto the carpet at his wife's knees. Reaching him, Katie realized it was over. She touched his shoulder gently—he was dead.

Dellie rose from her knees, her eyes wide with fear as she rushed over to gaze down on her father. She stood over her mother, breathing heavily with her hands pressed against her cheeks and her fingers covering her eyes. J.T. stood on Dellie's right with his arms hanging loosely at his sides, looking down on the two women. Harrison's body stretched across the floor where his wife, Clara knelt to its right, and Katie to its left. They stared at each other long and hard, neither saying a word. They both understood the meaning of Harrison's death. With the exception of a few, the entire town would be subjected to a new king—J.T.—and the knowledge of this made them resist believing the evidence that lay sprawled between them, the body of Harrison Townsend.

"Katie's he's gone," Clara said in a shaky voice.

"It's all over this time, Miss Clara, the Lord done called him to judgment," Katie replied with a solemn face.

J.T., trailing slowly behind Dellie, stopped two feet in front of the body. He watched the two women on the floor, and bending over his mother's head, he could see the white hairs in his father's nose. He watched his mother, with tears streaming down her face, push herself up, wipe her eyes with her hands, and dash in the direction of the hall telephone to call Lloyd, the undertaker. He saw Katie, the last one to move from the floor, pull up by the mattress, with tears in her eyes, and head towards the chair for her apron. And he saw Dellie suddenly collapse to the floor near their father's body, her black eyes glazed with fear, her head trembling.

The uncanny scene he had witnessed had a strange effect on him. He had never before seen a white man die; and though he felt no remorse for his father's fate, he had chilled when his father threw back his head and howled. He had feared his father at that moment, even more than when the old man was up on his feet and in the prime of health. He couldn't bring himself to turn his head for fear of meeting his mother's eyes—afraid she would see the joy that lay behind them. That same feeling of elation had swept over him when he heard his father send Max to the restaurant for Katie—because she was never sent for unless there was no other recourse. And now that he was in control, now that the old man was finally out of his way, it was hard for him to pretend to be sad. How could he be sad, when doors that had been closed to him all his life would now be open? He would make decisions—major decisions—that would affect mostly all of the fifteen-hundred residents in Bennettsville County. He looked down at his sister sitting on the floor with her head buried in her hands, crying. He would even have control over her misguided life.

He was king now. Gone were the days of sunshine and roses—the loving relationship that Dellie and his father had had—he would treat her differently, and he couldn't help but feel a tinge of satisfaction spreading through his body. Now she would realize what it meant to be like him—isolated from his father's warmth. He hated everything that his father had loved. "Dellie," he called to her, "git on out of here. Go on, I said," He glared at her until she feeling his authority pushed up from the floor and tore down the stairs, bawling.

Alone in the room, he listened to his mother and Katie who had now moved to the staircase. They spoke of the "great man" who lay on the floor, and of their concern for the future of Bennettsville. He walked over to the huge bed, removed the plush red quilt, and draped it across his father's body. A tinge of pity passed through him as he stared at the shell of a man on the floor—a man he could barely recognize, but it was him—the long scar on the back of his hand was proof enough. He shook his head and wondered could this be the same man who had tossed him out of their fishing boat when he was eight years old to sink or swim? That ordeal had terrified him so much that he had hidden from his father's sight for nearly a month. Could this be the same man who had sneered in disgust when Doc Smith informed him that his only son was an epileptic and "would be having them fits." Could this be the same man who had to fight off three burly, black, angry levee men when he panicked and ran away. He had been seventeen and his father was teaching him how white men handled Negro whores when something went awry and she yelled out for help. He had seen the men approach with bottles and bricks and he had never been so afraid in his life. Jumping from the car, he had fled to the safety of his home. And after his father re-cooperated from the beating, there was nothing left between them but the pretense of family closeness for the sake of appearances, and the scar on his father's hand which served as an almost daily reminder of his dastardly actions on the levee that night.

A car door slammed. He heard Max's deep voice whispering to someone outside. He knew it had to be the undertaker, for Lloyd was known for his promptness.

THE RESTAURANT

No matter what occurred or how important the event might have been, there was no escaping the enclosed cubicle—the kitchen of Rosie's Bar and Grill. Earlier this afternoon, a human being had drawn his last breath and fallen dead at her feet; yet here Katie stood back at work, slapping hamburgers on the sizzling black grill as though it had never happened. She flipped the meat automatically and mashed it with the heavy spatula until all the blood oozed out, her thoughts wandering back to Townsend crawling across the floor and wondering what was the significance of the blood-chilling howl. She only looked up when one of the white waitresses would burst through the swinging door with more orders to be filled.

Katie, born Kate Melissa Younger, had milk-white skin, and it wasn't until you were standing in front of her that you realized she wasn't all white. It wasn't the startling, wide, gray eyes, or the long, thick black hair that gave it away; in fact, you just couldn't put your finger on what it was. Up close, you could see a hint of thickness to her rounded lips and a minute flattening of the bridge of her nose, marking the African descent, but even then you still weren't sure. She was thirty-five years old, five-feet-three in her stocking feet, but she always squared her shoulders, held her head high, and stepped down the street as if she were as tall as the trees. Katie's mother, nee Sarah Sturdivant, was a tall, black, uneducated woman with an uncanny natural instinct for nursing the sick. She met Robert Younger, a tall, white man from Indiana, who had been traveling the river boat circuit—gambling—and who had decided, after winning big, to try his hand at farming, in Hattiesburg, Mississippi. They were married, had three children, Addie, Robert Jr., and Katie, then moved to New Hope at the turn of the century. Katie resembled both her parents: she had her mother's high cheekbones and her father's teacup-shaped ears, which some folks said was a sign of stinginess. When Katie was sixteen, her mother disappeared in the middle of the night; her sister married and moved to Tennessee; and after many lonely days and nights, she married James Dunson, a tall, jet-black man, who folks called Jabo. They remained together almost a year before Jabo deserted her—he was running from the High Sheriff the last time she saw him, and he never saw his daughter who was born two months after his flight. When Katie was eighteen, two significant events occurred—her brother married and moved away to Chicago, and her father was lynched. Although heartbroken, Katie stayed and raised her daughter who just recently turned eighteen. And during those years, she became a devout Christian; she joined the Sanctified Church of God in Christ whose tenets held that all their members were Saints, living without sin. It was during this time that she discovered the power to heal the sick through prayer and the laying on of hands. And for the past five years, Katie had worked at Rosie's as head cook.

Katie scraped a clean area on the grill, lined it with hamburgers buns, and wiped her forehead with the tail of her apron. She wondered if she had dreamed going to Townsend's house earlier. It seemed to her that she had just stepped outside the door for a moment and was now back in the kitchen—the place where she spent twelve hours a day, except on Sunday. The kitchen, the heart of the restaurant was always spotless. It was a squared-off area with gleaming floors, shining pots, a giant double oven, and various utensils necessary for Katie's use as head cook. Katie and Alice, the short order cook, worked side by side preparing food, raking dirty dishes, washing them, stacking them again with mounds of food, and sticking them through bins in the wall for pick-up. To the left of the kitchen, facing the alley, was another boxed room, just as spotless, where the Negroes were served. A huge sign hung above the door:

"Coloreds Only." To the front of the kitchen, facing Frank Street was a much larger room, just as spotless, where the whites were served. An even larger sign hung above the door: "Whites Only."

If old man Townsend hadn't died earlier, it would have been the usual Monday routine—people coming in for the Blue Plate Special, fried catfish with okra, ham and eggs, ham butt sandwich with hot peppers, chicken platter, barbecue beef with mashed potatoes, hamburger with everything, or a side order of dumplings. But Townsend's death had filled the town with the dread of dealing with J.T., anxiety over the possible loss of jobs, and excitement that normally follows the shock that no one lives forever.

On the day Townsend died, the talk around Bennettsville was pretty much the same as usual: cotton, beans, and regrading the levee. Bennettsville was a flat stretch of land that extended out to and stopped at Highway 41. Its unique feature was the tall, man-made levee that twisted about the town like a humped-back snake. Although certain sections of the levee sloped and circled like the lip of a cup, creating a natural spillway, the land was rich and fertile—ideal for farming. And rumors that Bennettsville would boom attracted many. The only cultured characteristic it bore was its name, derived from the refined, grand old lady, Clarissa nee Bennett of Richmond Virginia—Harrison Townsend's mother. Townsend had come to the area when it was called "New Hope"—a handwritten cardboard sign was tacked to the big oak tree on the outskirts of town. It was 1908; he was thirty years old, married, independent, and his pockets were filled with one hefty sum-his inheritance. He bought up most of the land thereabouts, and set out to make his name as big as the Bennett's in Virginia. Under his guidance, the town had grown in importance and had begun supplying cotton, soybeans, pecans, and other produce to various southern states and southern Illinois. The gins hummed throughout the night; stores, churches, schools, and a movie show were opened.

And today, although the talk still centered around the activities of the town, it was with less enthusiasm, for if Katie did not pull Townsend through this time, they would all be under the thumbs of J.T.—Townsend's inexperienced and power hungry son.

Off and on all afternoon, Rosie, caught up in the excitement, had been giving a blow-by-blow account of the events leading up to

Townsend's passing—her own version, of course. Rosie knew for sure was that he had died—for it w principles to discuss how, and in what manner the maker. She was a missionary of God, and that p common gossip. How would it look, a missionary o afflictions of the sick and the dead to call attention to herself? It would be much worse than the funeral director who discusses with his friends the deformities of some poor soul's body when he went to claim it. Much worse. And today—upon her return-even though Rosie had planted herself firmly by the grill and stood with plump arms folded across her chest and piercing brown eyes that searched Katie's face for answers—Katie had held fast to her principles. But every now and then, Rosie's crisp voice would rise above the usual chatter and the song on the jukebox in the white section and float back to the kitchen. Katie would hear Rosie talking about Townsend's death as though she had first-hand knowledge. "Yes, it's true, died this afternoon. Is hell got fire, and heaven got angels? Sure I know what I'm talking about. I ought to, since it was me personally who sent Katie up to the house to pray for him…Around one-thirty and, well, you know that's my busiest time of day, but I told her to go. Hell, if it had been me, I would want somebody like her to be at my side. So, by God, I sent her, and it was terrible, just terrible…"

A coldness enveloped Katie's body every time she heard Rosie repeat this story, for only she had heard the chilling wolf howl, and only she had seen those eyes—black as midnight when Townsend crossed over. Rosie had not seen Clara's face filled with indecision. Katie thought to herself, one more hour of this and someone would have to come and pray for her, for she would surely lose her temper and lash out at anyone who happened to be near, especially Rosie. Only a slackening in the orders put her in a better frame of mind. She could now start the preparation of the apple pies for tomorrow's special, a chore she welcomed, for this occupation always placed her outside the realm of Rosie's sharp, droning voice—she lost herself in her work.

Big Jim Davis, Prosecuting Attorney of Bennettsville and its neighboring counties, pushed through the door at seven o'clock p.m., his usual time. His broad frame would fill the doorway, his khaki uniform crisp and official, his white straw hat pulled over his d, shading his eyes. He would stand in the doorway, his dark , scanning the back corners of the cafe until they adjusted to the uish, smoky haze of cigarettes coming from the bar—the left side of the lunch counter—then he would cross the narrow aisle in three long strides, hang his hat on the silver pole by the table, and look about the room as if he were searching for a fugitive. He would sit in the center of the booth, facing the long dining tables, after making it known that he wanted to be alone—the noncommittal gestures, a not-too friendly wave suggesting tiredness, an almost cordial greeting, a half-smile. He would wait for Rosie, no one else, to take his order—one of those unspoken rules—his usual: a huge hamburger burnt on the edges and raw in the middle, mashed potatoes loaded with dark brown gravy, four slices of whole wheat toast, and plenty of creamy butter. Afterwards, a slug of apple pie. He chose this spot by the window because it was the only booth on this side of the room, and because it gave him an overall view of everyone coming and going—it isolated him from the people inside, and yet he was close enough to hear most conversations, and those he could not hear well, he could easily determine from the gestures and actions of the people. Usually, most of the conversations were about the weather, or fishing on the river for cat, but tonight he had heard Townsend's name the minute he stepped inside the door.

He watched Rosie clip an order to the wire rack above the counter, pull a beer from the cooler beneath the counter, and slide it down the bar with a poised left hand. A loud roar went up at the end of the bar when a man with a thick mustache caught the beer in one hand. She turned, a broad smile on her face, and seeing Jim, nodded and playfully flung her hand at the crowd at the bar indicating it was time for her to get back to work. Rosie Dixon was a pale-faced woman with freckled cheeks, and wide, dreamy eyes that some men said could charm the thunder away from the lighting bolt. She was tall, plump in the right places, and had fiery-red hair that bounced with every step she took. She pulled the cooler door to, picked up an order pad, and eased through the open end of the counter.

'Evening, Jim," she said, approaching the booth, still smiling, the pad and pencil in her hands.

"Evening, Rosie," he answered in a husky voice.

"I reckon you done had one hell of a day with Townsend dyi and all..."

"That's for shore. But that was just the raisins in the bread pudding, as my ma used to say. Still gots plenty yet to do." he grinned and scratched behind his ear.

"Lord Almighty, I know it's the truth." She tossed her hair and holding the pencil over the pad asked, "You want the usual?"

He inhaled, leaned back against the booth, and stared at her for a long second. "Yep. Only have Katie serve me tonight, it's important that I talk to her," he said, his voice calm, but demanding. A quick scan of the crowded dining area gave Rosie reason to wonder if this was the proper time for Katie to be coming and going through the white section—the lamps were turned up high, the overhead electric lights were ablaze, and the crowd was moody. Young Roy Larkin and his rowdy bunch, known to try almost anything just as long as it was wild and went against all virtuous principles, sat with their backs to Jim at the lunch counter. The Reverend Augustus Mack, minister of the Baptist Church, and several dignified members, a crowd known for setting standards for others to follow, occupied the center table. And the wealthy Richards from over at Kewanna Bank, a group known for opening and closing doors of finance, sat at the long table on the left. And the front door steadily opened and closed with people coming and going.

"It's all right," he whispered softly, reading her mind, "just let it be heard that I have to see her. I guarantee there won't be no trouble."

Rosie jammed the order pad in her apron pocket, whirled on her heels, and walked quickly up the aisle through the open end of the counter until she faced the bar. She flipped back the hinged counter top with a loud bang and disappeared through the swinging door leading into the kitchen. The lights blazed in the ceiling and the heat from the grill and ovens slapped her in the face like a desert gust. While the constant roar of the single fan droned in her ears, Alice and Katie looked up from the work in unison. Alice, a plump jovial woman the color of tobacco, stood at the sink peeling potatoes, while Katie dished out soup from the huge blue pot on the stove. They both had perspiration dripping from their faces, and the kitchen had the appearance of many different things going on at once. The sink was rrots, potatoes and onion peels; they lay near a bowl of s soaking in vinegar and hot peppers. The grill was all kinds of meats—burgers, ham, sausage, bacon, even hot dogs. Long blue platters filled with turkey slices lined the counter, with matching soup bowls steaming at their edges. "Katie, git Big Jim something to eat and carry it out to him. He wants to talk to you about something," Rosie said, her brow knitted in a frown.

"Talk to me 'bout what, Miss Rosie," Katie hesitated. Holding the ladle in mid-air, she watched Rosie out of the side of her eyes; a feeling of dread forming in her stomach. Her mind raced, focusing instantly on her runaway husband, Jabo. Was he dead? What had he done this time to bring the law into her life?

"He didn't say, Katie, but he's waiting," Rosie answered impatiently, one hand on her hip, the other hanging loosely at her side.

Carefully, Katie eased the ladle down to the table, reached for a platter and, facing Rosie, asked, "He want the usual?"

"Yes, the usual." Rosie turned her attention to the short, fat woman. "Alice you're gonna have to work the orders by yourself for a spell."

"You sho is the center of activity today, Katie," Alice chirped as soon as the swinging door closed behind Rosie.

"First, being called up on the hill to pray for Townsend. And now the Proscutor wants to talk with you. What you reckon he wants with you? I bet you it's got something to do with your old man, Jabo. What else could it be?" Alice rattled on and on while Katie grilled the special hamburger and piled the beige platter with mounds of potatoes and gravy. Katie didn't answer. How could she, when the words Alice spoke freely twisted like a knife in her chest? She set the platter down and changed the stained apron for a fresh one, folding it in half and tying it tightly around her slim waist. She re-arranged her hair net and checked her face in the small mirror on the back door. She was concerned about what Big Jim wanted, and she was concerned about the white folks reacting to her sudden appearance—the same white folks who were friendly to her in their homes but would just as well pass her by without speaking on the streets. Alice made a dreadful clatter with the plates and Katie looked up to see Ruth, a tall, skinny, white girl with glossy black hair, breeze though the kitchen, her face flaming red, and head for the Negro section. "I reckon Miss Rosie done tole Miss Hankty to serve the Negroes," Alice chuckled. Katie turned, pulled the pie from the cooling rack, picked up the black-handled knife, sliced a huge piece, and set it on a plate.

"You know that's 'bout right," Katie answered in a shaky voice and setting the pie on the tray, dropped the knife on the table. Even though she had been up front many times to clean when the cafe was closed, she dreaded going in the front now as much as Ruth did coming back to serve the Negroes. Katie knew every inch of the white section from the L-shaped booths that lined the wall behind the bar, to the red, cracked tile that lay just inside the front door jamb. She had stepped over that very crack earlier today, passing by straining necks, bulging eyes, and faces that snarled like rabid dogs. Hideous faces that had frozen, then melted, and were miraculously reshaped to polite smiles at the sight of the stern-faced white man, Townsend's chauffeur, taking Katie's arm, guiding her through the cafe like she was a lady being escorted to dinner. And now, she was told she would have to suffer through that again, but this time alone. She cast a knowing look at Alice, picked up the tray, took a deep breath, and pushed through the swinging door. She walked quickly past the blur of red faces, flushed from sour mash that floated from the Early Times whiskey bottles on the bar, and on past Rosie standing midway the counter nervously chewing on her bottom lip. She cleared the circle, stepped through the open end into the aisle—the tray seemed heavier that usual—and looked about for Jim. Three long dining tables sat to the right of the aisle, and behind them twelve booths lined the wall. An orange and red juke box was crammed next to the two booths on the end; a silver fan, about the size of a kettle drum was wired to the wall above the jukebox and circulated the hot air. Jim sat to the left of the aisle on the far end of the booth; and, from the end of the counter, all Katie could see was his spit-polished shoes. She swallowed, lowered her eyes, and forced her wobbly legs to move towards Jim's table.

The clatter of kitchenware and the familiar sounds of voices filling the air in the white eating area all ceased in one split second. The hush was deafening. All heads turned in her direction, some immediately, some a bit slower. In that split second, one hundred eyes focused simultaneously on her small frame. Eyes that burned through her clothing, eyes set deep into hollow faces with twisted mouths and with deep furrowed scowls etched across their brows. The only face, the only one filled with contentment, was that of Reverend Mack, who didn't bite his tongue when it came to religion. He simply hated her religion, often came right out and said, "Sanctified folks ain't nothing but heathens with clothes on." His glare she understood, for they were old enemies and she welcomed it as an honest dispute. She realized that his stare today was because Townsend, at the hour of his death, had sent for her and not for him. She neared the table just as young Larkin rose from the stool and yelled, "What's that nig—?" But before he could complete the word, Rosie pushed him down to the stool so hard he nearly lost his balance.

"Jest you shet your mouth, Roy Larkin, and don't you go no where," she hissed. She tossed her red hair and, in a rough voice loud enough for everyone to hear, said, "Now Big Jim sent for Katie and what Big Jim wants, he gits. Stop acting like a green tomato. You know darn well when Big Jim works a case, he'd as soon as go up your daddy's crack if he had to."

"That's for shore," Marmy Braswell thundered, and slapped the counter top, his receding hairline evident under the bright lights. "Hell, Roy, don't you remember last spring when Big Jim was looking for the gun what killed that old nigger, Boswell: He went and dug his hands clean to the bottom of Mr. high-and-mighty Lyles' biscuit jar."

They all laughed, and Katie breathed a sigh of relief and placed the tray in front of Jim. Slowly, the noise resumed, a clattering of knives and forks and casual talk, and Katie relaxed somewhat, but not completely. She said a silent prayer and dared to peek over her shoulder. It was just as it had been this afternoon when Max had stared them down—they were people again. She wondered why they made such faces and put on airs about coloreds and whites mixing, when all it seemed to take was someone to demand they change their rules for them—someone whom they respected or feared.

'Sit down, Katie," Jim said, pointing to the seat across from him with the fork. She eased into the seat happy that no one could see her face, and folded her arms in her lap. Uncomfortably, she faced the white man who was not much older than her thirty-five years, a man known for putting criminals behind bars for long periods of time, and watched his large hands busy cutting into the meat. Seeing those hands, Katie remembered playing games with Jim as a child. He had been like a brother to her until she turned thirteen and his mama ordered him to "Stop playing with that nigger." She had never been able to forget that day, for that was the day when she realized that her pappy was white and her mother was black. Before then, she hadn't noticed the difference between them—they were just Mammie and Pappy.

Jim, though, wasn't always in agreement with his mother. He enjoyed his freedom away from the orderly house, and away from her constant reminders on the proper behavior and social relationships for a young, bright, white boy with ambitions of becoming the High Sheriff. Frankly, he wasn't interested in much that she had to say, but he was fascinated by her definition of what the law represented—power, respect and concern for humanity. He had dreamed of becoming High Sheriff since he was seven when he had watched the sheriff and his deputies ride through parade banners on Main Street on jet, black snorting horses. He would often evaluate his qualifications at obtaining that position by his fastidious tracking skills. He would track animals on the run, mostly coon, when he was hunting with his dad, and once he even tracked his friend Buster as far as Kewanna when Buster tried to run away. He would swell with pride whenever he discovered clues to some information that confirmed his suspicions about people, especially something that uncovered a part of their lives they considered to be secret—like the time he tracked old man Jenkins behind the levee and found the whiskey still.

When Jim's father would haul timber across the states, Jim would often be found down the alley at Katie's house, either questioning her pappy about hunting dogs, or just watching her mammie's dark face. Most of the time he spent at the Younger's house was with Katie, arguing. They would argue about the weather, what time of day the sun was the hottest or coolest, why the dirt was red and not black, why chickens always scratched in the dirt, and why they didn't like each other. But these arguments never got out of hand, in fact, they were seemingly a prelude to touching of some kind. Katie would bend her head down, her two plaits swinging, and Jim would blush red, push his lips out, and peck her on the cheek. As the years passed, the pecks turned into full-blown kisses that often left them breathless.

Jim's mother, a persistent woman, eventually wore Jim's resistance down. He unwillingly severed his relationship with Katie and her parents, and for a long time avoided talking to his mother. He would lie awake at night remembering the ugly sneer that twisted his mother's mouth when she talked about Negroes marrying whites. "It's a sin for Negroes to marry whites," she would say—it was never whites who married Negroes, always the other way around. And he wondered how that was possible. All her talk, however, never stopped him from caring for Katie, but he realized there was some truth in what his mother said—there were obvious limitations to this kind of relationship. He resolved to stay away. At fifteen, Jim pushed thoughts of Katie into the background, and began concentrating on becoming the man his mother had described as proper. But always out of nowhere, like today, Katie would somehow step back into his life, her haunting gray eyes peeping through him, and he would become confused. His emotions would catch him off guard, and he would find himself wondering what would it be like if they were married. But he would stop and think about his career, and of how afraid he had been for Katie when her father was lynched right here in town. He would resign himself to the only relationship they could possibly have, that is, if Katie approved, one that remained behind closed doors, that was sure to be discovered by town locals and classified as "stepping over the fence at night." And on these occasions he would hide behind a mask of authority.

Big Jim took two spoonfuls of potatoes, pulled a long white envelope from his shirt pocket as he chewed, and laid it on the table facing Katie.

"You read, don't you, Katie?" he asked.

"Some," she replied, stunned. Why would Jim call her away from her work to ask her a silly question like that? Instantly, her guard went up; and although she didn't know why, suddenly all her thoughts about Jabo disappeared. As far as she was concerned, most white folks was foolish. Plain downright foolish. Didn't want Negroes eating with them, but it was fine to have them cook their food, tend their young, and beseech God on behalf of their welfare. She could not imagine what he wanted from her, the only thing that concerned him deeply was a case, and what could she possibly have to do with one of Big Jim's investigations? He swallowed a mouthful and said, "Katie, do me a favor and read the name on that there envelope."

She picked up the envelope carefully. She fully expected it to snap shut on her fingers like a mouse trap. "Mr. Jim Davis," she stammered.

"No, Katie, I mean the name at the top."

"Mr. Harrison Townsend Sr.," she replied.

"Now, Katie," he said, leaning over and staring into her eyes. "It is my understanding that you was over to the house today, that you was there when he died. Is this true?"

"Yes, I was there up until he died," she admitted, slowly raising her eyes to meet his.

"Well," he said, pushing the plate aside; the fork still in his hand. "While you was over there, did you happen to see this envelope?"

"No, I weren't concerned with nobody's mail, only Mr. Townsend," she replied, wondering where the conversation was heading.

The restaurant had begun to get even more crowded. From time to time, Katie would look up when the door opened and closed. It probably had to do with Townsend's death, she thought, for the numbers exceeded the usual Monday crowd. And seeing Rosie cross the floor several times, Katie felt as though she was being timed.

"I see," he continued and glanced up to see Buddy, Rosie's son, carrying plates in from the kitchen. "Did he tell you anything that maybe might seem kind of strange to you?"

"No, he didn't say nothing to nobody whiles I was there."

"Well, did he try to say anything?"

"Seems like he was trying to say something, but he only worked his mouth up and down. No words come out."

"You mean he was trying to say something, but couldn't"

"I can't swear to that, but it sho seemed like he wanted to say something, only…"

"Only what, Katie?"

"Only nothing come out of his mouth, except…" She stopped, leaving the sentence hanging. Wringing her hands, she was afraid to go on, not because she thought he wouldn't believe her—everyone knew her word was like the Good Book—but afraid her answer might appear to be the ramblings of an insane person filled with delusions.

This was one time she wished Miss Rosie would call her back to work.

"Except what?" he stopped chewing and stared into her face.

She leaned toward the table. "A wolf howl was the only sound that come from his mouth," she whispered.

The fork fell to the table, making a loud thunk. "What?" he said in a half yell-half whisper and narrowed his eyes to mere slits.

"A wolf howl," she repeated softly, for everyone in the cafe had turned around to investigate his outburst.

"A wolf howl?" he questioned again, and turned and gazed across at the other tables. He turned back and faced her, his eyes probing for an answer.

"Yes."

"Are you sure of that, Katie?"

"I'se a woman born and raised in the country all my life. You knows that to be a fact, since you stayed just 'round the bend, and I definitely knows a wolf howl when I hears one." Her breast swelled with indignation.

"Katie, I believe you," his voice softened, "but only because it's you telling me this and not someone else. A wolf howl. Well, I'll be damned. No wonder Clara and J.T. looked so blank." Shaking his head, he leaned back and slapped the envelope across the palm of his hand. "Do you want to know what's in this envelope?"

"Why should I? It ain't addressed to me," she answered without thinking.

"But it's about you, Katie," he said, tapping the envelope against the edge of the plate. "It's a provision Townsend had the lawyer put in his will before he died that you get some money—quite a bit, I might add."

"Me?" Her face turned red. Her hands automatically went to her throat. "Why in heavens name me?"

"I thought you might know. That's one of the reasons I asked to see you; the other is that if what Lloyd suspects is true, Townsend might not have died...well naturally."

This time she narrowed her eyes and glared at him, her tongue was sharp when she answered. "And you come running directly here to question me! Well it ain't natural that the man ain't even in the ground, and you is traipsing about in his papers, the ones about his money."

"Now hold on, Katie," Jim said, firmly pointing and shaking his finger as though he didn't know quite where to aim it. "I came here to find out if you knew in advance about this here money, and if you did, jest what. It's my right—it's the law. Now as far as the will being opened, that was the family's decision, not mine."

"Family, my eye! You mean J.T., don't you?"

"Yes, as a matter of fact, yes. And you can be sure he'll fight you every inch of the way about that money," he said, pushing himself back in the booth.

She squirmed in the seat as though she was sitting on something hot and in a slow, deliberate voice, filled with conviction, she replied, "He won't have to fight me, cause I'll simply refuse it. I don't want no parts of money tainted with Negro sweat and blood—I don't want it!" She had forgotten about Rosie and the other white folks.

"You can't refuse it, Katie," Jim informed her, a smug look on his face.

"And jest why not?" she asked stubbornly.

"'Cause it ain't for you. It's for your daughter, Margaret, to be used for her education, and only she can refuse. You're just the guardian over it—to see that it's used properly. You and Margaret best be there at the house come Friday, when the will is read. Now if you don't have a way, I'll pick you up." He leaned toward her, waiting for an answer.

She had heard the triumph in his voice and realized that for some reason, it was important to him that she got the money. She cut her eyes at him, letting them wander over his face, and said, "I reckon I can afford a cab, but we ain't taking no money, and that's final. I'll go on back to work, if you is finish. Alice is by herself." He pulled back quickly, stunned, and stared curiously as she rose from the table.

By now the crowd had gotten so large it spilled out into the aisle. Katie had to weave her way around them to reach the end of the counter. She sensed that the people in the restaurant had either accepted her presence or were too hungry to care, for no one seemed to notice her—except for Roy Larkin. His icy, brown eyes lingered on her face a few seconds, then quickly turned away. The jukebox had begun to thump, softly at first, but now was spitting out a loud country song. Rosie's son, Buddy and one of the white waitresses, were practically shoulder to shoulder in the aisles of the dining tables. They piled dirty dishes on top of one another and raked change from the tables. Red-faced men stood side by side, shouting farewell toasts to Townsend and gulping whiskey at the bar, while dense smoke clouded above their heads until the fan's rotation made a complete sweep and pushed it towards the kitchen. Rosie clipped orders to the wire rack above the counter, stopping only to nod anxiously at Katie as she walked around the counter. Katie pushed through the swinging door and stopped. Her body was alive with fear that ran up and down her spine like white smoldering heat. She could hear the din Alice made with the pots, and the Negroes, from the adjoining room, shouting orders at Ruth, but it was no more than a familiar roaring in her ears—like water running in a sink. All she could think of was Margaret and the awful things she might have to say to her—about what being a Negro meant, the very ugliness she had taken such pains to keep Margaret from learning. And even after all of that was said, she knew that Margaret would still fight. Margaret was not afraid of anyone or of anything. She was at that dangerous age for Negroes—the transition from childhood to womanhood when freedom to make your own choices was as vital as sunshine and made compromise unthinkable! Yes, Margaret would fight her tooth-and-nail over that money. She would stomp her feet, and yell, and afterwards begin to quote the great philosophers. And that would be just the warm up-Margaret knew how to fight. Margaret would see the money as a great opportunity, while Katie knew all they would get is a battle from Junior Townsend—one that could lead to death. Margaret had never seen a lynching; Katie had. Unlike Katie, her daughter had never met fear on a lonely road, that hot fear that makes your insides bubble and choke. Katie remembered how it felt to be whole, defiant, and sure of yourself, and she never wanted her daughter to lose that feeling. In agony, she held her hand to the ceiling, closed her fingers one by one until she had formed a fist, and holding it like she had the Almighty by the collar, cried out softly, "Father, this is your servant, Katie." And as though a giant ruler swung through the clouds and rapped sharply across her knuckles, her fingers flew open and she waved her hand in the air and whispered, "Let your will be done."

The news of Townsend's death was passed down the rows of every cotton and bean field and delivered orally, like a singing telegram, with the afternoon mail. It reached Charlie Hudnall just as he tossed his hoe to the ground and dropped wearily on the bottom step of his front porch—he and Luther Dawson, his young assistant usually weeded Charlie's garden between jobs. M.B. Ehlerson, Charlie's old running buddy, braked the new pick-up truck in front of Charlie's yard, leaned out the window, and shouted it from the road. "Dead, you say," Charlie said, coming to his feet and heading towards the road. But M.B. waved him away, promising to return later—his sow was expected to farrow anytime and he had to head home. It was typical of M.B. to seek Charlie out and deliver the message and go. M.B. was not one for long conversations. The two of them had been through what they coined as "hell and high-water"—the hell they shared happened the night Charlie's wife, Anna Mae died when they learned that sometimes it was more terrible to live than die, and the high-water they shared happened during the flood of 1908 when New Town, the lower end, and where M.B. lived now, was washed away. They waded in water that came to Charlie's neck and M.B.'s chest until the relief folks came with boats, corn meal, canned pork, and soft red apples. It was only a few months after the water receded and the earth was dry again that Townsend came to town and bought up all the land he could—everything but this section. Because this land sat too close to the Spillway, it was considered a high risk.

Charlie was a small-framed man, average height, and skin the color of roasted pecans. His broad nose lay too close to his thin face, and made his dark, round eyes appear mean. He walked with a limp—the result of a bullet from a white intruder's gun—and the aid of a cane. Occasionally, Charlie wore slacks and a short sleeved shirt, but most of the time he wore bib overalls, a wide straw hat, and short boots with round toes. He worked as a landscaper, or as he called it, "Yardkeeper" for Townsend three days a week, where he and Luther, who worked for him, would plant trees, mowing and shaping the land and the plants according to the formal garden Townsend had requested. M.B. was the opposite; he was tall, lanky and easy-going. His skin was a smooth as an olive and as black as pitch. He had a long face, a slender nose, and dimples—some called him a ladies man because of his good looks. And like Charlie, most of the time he wore bib overalls, but always with a pair of slacks underneath. A cap with the initials "M.B." was always pulled down across his forehead, and a pipe was always clenched between his teeth. Although he was ten years younger than Charlie, he was better off financially. From the sell of his hogs, he had been able to keep an old truck around. This was the first year he had been able to buy a new one.

Charlie and M.B. worked to keep the land, partly because they didn't know how to stop or even slow down. Charlie had obtained a government loan that secured his mortgage, and still he worked as though he had twelve children to feed. In addition to working the yards, he raised vegetables on his and on Katie's property in Monther's Alley. He paid Luther to plow, plant, and tend the soybeans on both places, and to help him with the upkeep of the white folks' yards who employed him. M.B. raised vegetables, soybeans, and bred livestock. He worked along side his hired hands in the fields, but tended the hogs himself. With the aid of an assistant, he slaughtered the hogs with deftness and precision—he was experienced with the process and used a knife much better than most. They worked as if they expected everything they owned to disappear over night and they would be forced to hustle like they had at the beginning of the Depression. During those times, Charlie and M.B. found many ways to keep food on the table and pay the taxes on their property. One year they picked pecans behind the levee, and sold them to stores in town and over at Kewanna Bank. Another year they worked their land and hired out two days a week to Townsend, where they chopped and picked cotton, chopped beans and pulled corn. And once they had sold catfish door to door—fish they caught at the down slope under the Spillway. Every cent was considered before it was spent—was it necessary of just whim? They fished for pleasure, then sold their catch; they drank to get drunk—to forget everything—and visited Miss Wade, a respectable whore, because there was no charge to get their pipes cleaned. When M.B. sold his first two sows, he bought his first used pick-up, and they would make frequent trips to Huntsville, a small town eight miles out of Bennettsville, to buy cheap corn whiskey. On one of these trips, they got hold of some bad whiskey and nearly died—the moon shiner, so they found out later, had erected his still from an old gas tank. Later, when they bought corn, they only went to one place. But they had mellowed; it had been two years since they bought corn. M.B. attended Sunday Services at the Baptist Church, and Charlie drank Southern Comfort, visited with Katie and Margaret, and brooded—he had come to realize that he was more dependent on them than they on he.

Charlie had lived in Monther's Alley, about two hundred yards from Katie, for as long as Anna Mae had been dead—thirty years. He had witnessed Katie's growth from a string bean of a girl to the striking woman she was now. Over the years they had bonded, becoming like family and he had assumed the role as head of the household even though he lived in his own home. She stole into his aching heart when she was just a snip. There was something behind those intense, gray eyes that pushed his pain aside and reached into his heart. He had playfully called her a man's child because she had had little to do with her own gender. She shot marbles with her brother Robert Jr., played hide-and-seek with Jim Davis, and would trail behind her father from sun up to sun down if he would allow it. Over the years, as she grew, mystery and tragedy surrounded her life. One night, her mother disappeared and was never found. Katie retreated into a shell. She later blossomed into a young lady when Jabo Dunson, a tall, black man from Tennessee asked for her hand in marriage. But she faded away like the print in an old dress when he deserted her, leaving her heavy with child. And shortly thereafter, her father was lynched, and she shriveled up like an old woman, dying from the inside out. That's when Charlie stopped watching and stepped in—he replaced the father figure she needed

He took over, made her decisions, and little by little by little, prodded her back to life. Finally, she began to smile again. Then, he wasn't quite sure when it happened, her demeanor drastically changed—she was calmer than he had ever seen her. "Something wonderful has happened," she told him. She had found God or rather God had found her. She had joined the Holiness church and on one Sunday delivered a powerful prayer that became the talk of the town. The Saints spread the word, telling all how Katie had risen from her knees, her face aglow, and laid hands on one brother Jacobs's neck and the large fleshy tumor that had made it impossible to fasten the neck of his shirt disappeared.

Charlie never discussed God with Katie, or what the Saints had said. He dealt only with things he could see, such as the fact that she was pregnant, ignorant of business, and alone. He advised her how to run the business—whom to hire and when to sell to keep from losing all the land. He was there when Margaret was born, telling Katie the disadvantages of a child carrying the name of a shiftless, thieving, no-account. Through the years he had helped to make many decisions, some as recent as last week—Margaret attending college.

THE INCUBATED CHICKEN

God was silent: Katie fasted and prayed to the Almighty two days straight without receiving any sign on how to tell Margaret about the money. It was early Thursday morning and come tomorrow they were expected at the reading of Townsend's will. She sat at the kitchen table sipping strong black coffee and listening to the soft clucking of the chickens—the back door was open. She wondered how she could convince Margaret that they must not accept this money.

She drained the cup, stood up, and looked out the door past the chicken coop at the weak sunlight breaking through the gray clouds. "It might rain," she thought—good, it was needed. She was dressed for work, the standard white uniform that Rosie provided, and her hair was braided and wrapped around her head to form the shape of a crown. Mechanically, she placed the cup in the dishpan, then turned and crossed the floor of her bedroom to open the door which separated Margaret's side of the house from hers. The light from Katie's bedroom splashed across the floor ahead of her and the soft light of day pushed upon Margaret's window, seeping around the sides of the window shade. She peeked into the dimness of the room until her eyes adjusted and she located the hump under the covers facing the wall. A silk nightgown was swirled in a heap at the foot of the bed. Katie's eyebrows rose as she realized that Margaret was e again. Her long black hair covered the pillow, re pulled up to her neck. Katie's eyes drifted up he far corner of the room where Margaret's track from a hook over the mirror of the small dresser. e of them, the size of nickels, swaying gently as the morning floated through the window, occasionally lifting the shade and splashing the floor with light. She smiled and let her eyes follow the light to the trunk on the floor—the sun danced about the metal clasp, making it twinkle like the eye of a cat. Margaret's treasures, she thought, and sighed—the trunk, Margaret used as her hope chest, the medals, Margaret won at her high school's track team competition. She won three years straight. Katie frowned as she realized these scant treasures were Margaret's world, and now… Katie walked around to the side of the bed, sat on the edge, and gently shook Margaret by the shoulder. "Wake up, child, the birds is singing, the sun is gonna be up, raring to go soon, and you'll still be here in the bed with your head buried in the pillow."

"What time is it?" The sleepy Margaret inquired and, turning to face Katie exposed her bare shoulder. Her eyes focused on the gown at the foot of the bed, and instantly she was awake. She avoided looking in her mother's face as she pulled the covers tightly around her neck.

"Eight o'clock," Katie answered dryly. She turned her head away from Margaret and stared at the chair filled with Margaret's clothes, and shook her head that way mothers do.

"Eight o'clock. But you're supposed to be at work," Margaret declared, still not looking at Katie. Her wide eyes flitted back and forth in fear of discovery.

"I told Miss Rosie last night I had to tend to important business and that I would have to be late," Katie answered, a trace of concern in her voice.

"Miss Rosie, Miss Rosie," Margaret mimicked, sleep still in her throat. "Why do you call her Miss? She's the same age as you—she's not your elder."

"Let's not start that same old mess this morning," Katie snapped, and turned her full gaze upon Margaret's face. "Git up and put some clothes on while I start breakfast. We've got some important business to discuss."

"Why do I have to dress to talk, Mama? And what in the world could be so important that you had to be late for work? I can't ever remember you being late for work. Must be something special happening at the church."

"I ain't used to talking business with people laying flat on their backsides," she mumbled and clutched the collar of her dress. "What we gots to talk 'bout ain't got nothing to do with the church. What I gots to say is strictly between me and you, leastwise for the moment. You understand?" Katie said, dropping her hands in her lap and resigning herself to the confines of the small bedroom and the semi-darkness—she could feel herself losing already.

"Well, what in the world is it?" Margaret asked impatiently, a strain to her voice as she pushed the nightgown with her foot until it fell to the floor behind Katie's vision. Then propped herself up in a sitting position, clutching the sheet to her throat.

"Well," Katie stammered, leaning on her arm and bringing her face closer to Margaret as if to whisper. "You remember the other night I told you that I went to pray for old man Townsend the day he passed."

"He didn't pass, Mama. He died. Is the word so hard to say? He died," Margaret blurted out with an exaggerated toss of her free hand.

"Margaret Younger, sometimes you makes me want to glue your mouth shut and let it stay that way for the rest of your born days," Katie said, exasperated, her bosom rising up and down like she had been wounded.

"I'm sorry, Mama," Margaret said quickly. "I promise to listen without any more interruption. Tell me what it is that's important." Amusement danced in her dark brown eyes.

"Well, as I was saying, I told you 'bout his passing over, but what I didn't tell you was later that evening Big Jim come to the cafe. He told me that Townsend had left some money to us in his will."

Margaret gasped and smacked her thin lips. "Us?" she yelled, flinging her arms, the cover almost falling away. "You mean me and you, Mama" That's our dream come true. How much did he leave us, how much?"

"Hush now, ain't no need telling the whole town 'bout it," she said looking around the room cautiously. "And besides I don't know how much. Big Jim didn't say, jest that it was quite a bit. But since we ain't gonna accept it, don't matter how much it is," Katie said, and braced herself.

"What?" Margaret shrieked. She pulled away from the pillow; she could feel the air on her naked back, but that was not important now. "We're not going to accept this money? Am I hearing you right?"

Katie coughed and pulled her arm to her chest. She could feel Margaret's gaze upon her face. She waited for Margaret to catch her breath before she continued.

"That's right, we ain't gonna accept it, even if it is for your education, and that's a mighty important issue in this house. But not even to git ahead will we take money tainted with the sweat and blood of others. No sir, never," Katie vowed.

The room brightened and began to take on a rosy-orange glow. The two women sat very still; the glow made Margaret's honey-colored skin appear painted like a picture of an Egyptian princess, while Katie's appeared sunburned. "Mama, you mean the money is for my college education? Do you realize how much money that is? Why, we could pay off a lot of bills, and with the scholarship I won, we won't have the headaches we expected, the worry of where the next penny would be coming from. I could really apply myself in school. I could even do better than we had hoped. I could become the teacher that I've dreamed about since I was a little girl. What are you saying, we won't take the money? My God, why not?"

"Now, don't go using the Lord's name in vain," Katie said softly, while tugging at the collar of her uniform with both hands. She let her hands drop into her lap and looked towards the ceiling, her face solemn. Slowly, she lowered her head and faced Margaret. "Surely, you don't think them white folks gonna let us jest walk up and take all that money and don't have nothing to say 'bout it?"

"What do you mean, Mama? Margaret asked, leaning closer to her mother, her dark eyes scanning Katie's face.

"First of all, child, Junior is gonna fight us 'bout that money, and everybody, excepting you, knows how he fights. Then, if by some miracle we win him over and git the money, where we gonna put it? The bank of Bennettsville certainly ain't gonna go against one of its more important customers like J.T. They jest won't take the money, and we sho can't keep it here in the house now, can we?"

"But Mama, if necessary we can move to another city, we can do that, we don't…"

Katie flinched, then smiled as she realized Margaret had no idea of the struggles of her parents to keep the land—no idea of how she had struggled to keep what was left of the land, or even why. "Ain't nothing or nobody gonna make me move off my pappy's land, and that's that!" she said without anger.

"Mama," Margaret stated and squirmed against the pillow. "Junior ain't nothing but another redneck hill-billy, nothing to be afraid of. He's just a spoiled brat used to getting his way. I don't believe the bank will turn away good money, hard as times are, just for his sake. I just wish he would try to do something to me or you. I just wish he would." Her eyes glazed over, then flashed with hot anger.

"What you gonna do, child? Whip him with his daddy's strap?" Katie teased, a half smile on her face.

"No, Mama, but I won't let him take nothing from me just because he's white and greedy after money. I won't let him do that." Margaret stressed, angered by the smug look on Katie's face.

"Sure, you ain't afraid, not now, 'cause you is sitting in the comfort of your home, and your mama is close by your side. But what happens when you meet J.T.'s ruffians on a dark road one night? What then, child?"

"I'm not afraid. It's you, you're the one who's afraid," Margaret stated arrogantly.

Katie took a deep breath, tugged at her collar, and turned her head towards the window. "Yes, ma'am, you is right, I'm scared down to my bones, 'cause I knows these people much better than you. Somebody gotta be scared," Katie snapped, and turned to face Margaret, her gray eyes glaring. "You see, I'se got sense enough to be scared, but you, Margaret, sometimes you reminds me of one of them incubated chickens that stands out in the rain hollering, when all he gots to do is walk inside the coop. He stands in two inches of water hollering until he drowns, 'cause he don't have no knowledge of death."

A humid breeze flitted through the room, and Margaret became aware of the outside world. She could hear the chickens clucking and the crunch of gravel in the distance. Here she sat very close to her mother, their arms almost touching, and she had felt her mother's warm breath on her face; but it was evident that their minds wrestled with different points of view, and that they were each searching for a language that would make the other understand.

"But what is a person to do, give up?" Margaret asked, shaken by the fire in the older woman's eyes. "Are you supposed to let anyone take what belongs to you and do nothing?

"Well," Katie replied and turned away from Margaret's innocent stare, "jest what is yours in the first place? Certainly not that money. It belongs to other Negroes, the ones that sweated and was deprived of food and other comforts so that Townsend could earn all the money. I say first you got to know what's yours, and if you knows that, then maybe the fight is worth the bloodbath."

"I don't understand you, Mama. That's precisely one of the reasons we should take the money, you said yourself that it belongs to other Negroes. Then we Negroes should be the ones to use the money to better ourselves, not J.T."

Katie folded her arms around her breast, hugging herself as if she were cold and sighed. "That may be true. Maybe we have more right to it than he does, but that don't mean we should take it. We is supposed to earn our way in this world and that don't mean tangling with Junior; that ain't nothing but fighting over something that even Mr. Townsend didn't rightfully own. Believe me, child, you always feel better 'bout something when you done sweated for it than when it's handed to you on a platter."

Margaret frowned and slightly shook her head. She turned and faced the wall and sighed. "Well," she said, twisting her head back to face Katie, "If you have already made up you mind we are not to take the money, why are you discussing it with me?"

Silence hung heavy in the room, only the sound of their breathing, deep and regular was heard. And Katie rocked herself on the side of the bed like she had not heard the question. Finally, in a soft whisper she said, "Because." She heard Margaret stir under the cover and knew her eyes were upon her, waiting. "Because," she repeated, clutching the collar tightly, "the way I understands it is that I'm jest the guardian over this here money. Only you can refuse it."

"You mean you don't have any say-so over the money at all?"

"No, I don't mean that, 'cause I got say-so and always will have say-so over whatever you do, Margaret!"

"But you can't refuse the money without my being there, without me actually saying I don't want the money, is that right?"

"That's what Big Jim said," Katie conceded, her jaw set firm.

"Mama," Margaret said softly, almost in a whisper, and scooted to the edge of the bed, dangling both legs over the side, the sheet clasped between her hands at her throat. "Listen for a minute and don't interrupt. We can use that money, and you know it. Just look at this place. It hasn't been painted in years, inside or out. The floors pop and make all kind of noises, there's no running water, the cook stove doesn't draw air, and you have to practically have prayer meeting to get a fire going, not to mention those window shades that have to be fastened with clothespins to keep them up. Just look around you, Mama. These are things we've been wanting to fix for years, and haven't been able to do. But most of all, look at me, Mama. Take a good look at this person sitting beside you, at this girl who has spent all her life with you, all eighteen years. We'll this girl wants badly to become a teacher, something not new to you. And now that way has been opened—a sure thing. No wondering if we will make the payments, or how far I'll be able to go before I have to stop. The way is clear. Perhaps this money is 'tainted' as you say, but if I'm educated, so can other Negroes benefit from my experience. I'll be able to teach other Negro children, pull them out of the darkness of illiteracy. I've never went against your word, but I'm begging you, Mama, don't make me do this. Don't make me turn down this money, the answer to my dream, I beg you." There was a look of helplessness on her face, as naked as her body under the sheet.

The room was silent as the two women sat side by side on the bed, Margaret with her right palm stretched out towards her mother, while the left hand clasped the sheet. Katie sat staring at her hands in her lap. She wanted to burst into tears. Already the money had begun to pull them apart. The only child she bore sat before her, pleading for a future that she deserved. The right to go out and become her own woman was all she asked. Katie stared and said nothing. But Margaret didn't realize the extent of Junior's power. Nor was she aware of the cold blooded murder he had committed. The sight of old Boswell's body lying on the levee bank full of bullets crossed her mind. "Say no more 'bout it, child. We will not take the money, and that is my final word." She stared hard into her daughter's eyes, then pushed up from the bed and stood with her back to the window.

Margaret looked at Katie, her face filled with shock, then dropped back heavily on the bed and gazed at the dingy yellow ceiling, defeated.

Katie turned, rolled up the window shade, clipped it together with the clothespin, and stared out the window at the garden. She watched the sunlight playing above the foliage of the green cabbages, creating a hazy mist of oozing vapors, and listened to Margaret's ragged breathing. A slow irregular sound like that of a frail child recuperating from a powerful blow to the stomach. And suddenly, Katie was not in her home, but in another time. Before her, the face of a young white man. She did not know his name, but would remember his face forever. He and several white men stole onto their land in the early morning and set fire to their barn. He held his head high, and his face was regal and expressionless, like he was the king of Siam. His blue, blue eyes gazed down upon her young, questioning face, and in that instant stripped away all her human qualities. She was suddenly something foul and despicable—a nigger. Being ten years old, she had heard the word many times before, but it had been explained away by her pappy as being nonsense that she was to ignore. But today the word had an entirely different meaning, one that could not be ignored, one that made her feel lifeless and inadequate. She supposed this young man considered himself a true blueblood, righteous in his act to rid the earth of heathens—the scum of the earth, the niggers, and the folks who stood by them as well. He sat proudly on his horse bareback, and in one swift motion bent down, swooped her up in his arms, and tossed her across the wire fence. She fell flat on her face in the mud, which streaked her face and coated her hair. The fall had knocked the wind out of her, and she couldn't get up, no matter how hard she tried.

She lay there and watched her pappy, a giant of a man with fiery red hair and arms as thick as tree limbs, walk up to the young man without saying a word. He stood there calm, as though he didn't have a care in the world, studying the horse like a scientist calculating timed experiments, and with his steel-like fist smacked the horse in its temple with a mighty blow. The horse trembled under the pressure, and its front legs caved in, causing the young man to slide down over the horse's head, and right into her pappy's hands. Pappy grabbed the young blueblood by his collar and shook him. He shook him until the young man's teeth clattered like someone having seizures, until the light in the young man's blue, blue eyes turned to a golden amber. He shook the intruder until he finally tired and then set him firmly on the ground with orders to "Get me my gal and be damn quick about it." The young man scooped Katie up from the mud and placed her gently into her daddy's big white arms.

Katie turned and stared at Margaret. She realized that one day someone would shake up her world, in much the same way that the young white boy had hers that morning years ago. One day, and soon, Margaret would also know the meaning of the word "nigger." She walked from the room, leaving Margaret staring at the ceiling, and closed the middle door. Standing at the edge of her bed, she held on to the post for support. She felt as though she had sinned. It was rare that she denied Margaret anything. She caught a glimpse of the morning sky from the open back door and went out and sat on the crooked steps. With the warm sun bathing her skin, she suddenly felt like a child again. She wondered if she had made the right decision. Outside, everything seemed so calm, as though what had happened between them had gone unnoticed. She needed someone to tell her she had done the right thing, and yet she knew there was no one she could discuss it with other than Charlie, and he was out and about already. She suddenly felt like the small child lying on the other side of the fence and she laid her head in her hands and cried out, "Pappy."

DECISIONS

Margaret Younger lay on her back staring at the dingy, yellow ceiling, crying. The tears rolled down across her high cheekbones, wetting her long black hair and the pillow. She didn't want to go against her mother's word—to do such a thing would shock the residents of Bennettsville into early graves. But how else could she make Katie realize that she was eighteen, grown, and able to make her own decisions about her life. Besides, she needed that money for college. She pursed her lips, frowned, and swore that if she lived to be two thousand years old, she would never understand her mother's way of thinking. Sitting up, she wiped her face and flung the worn housecoat to the floor—a hand-me-down from some white family—and thought about the many things that she and Katie needed just to make do. Her mother's argument that whites weren't gonna tolerate no Negro gitting all that money was simply absurd.

Things were different now, she reasoned. This was 1938. Joe Louis was heavy-weight champion of the world; men of all colors and creeds openly hailed him as the "brown bomber," and women whispered among themselves that Louis was indeed one "fine brown bomber." If a Negro could achieve fame because of the power in his fist, surely, she, a respectful Negro lady, could accept money that had been willed to her by a white man without upsetting the status quo in Bennettsville. Slowly, she pushed herself from the bed and, walking—

naked as a dressed chicken—to the dresser, sat down heavily on the cushioned stool. She propped her elbows on the dresser's edge, shielding her heavy breasts with her arms, and held her head in her hands, staring at the honey-colored girl in the mirror. Her wide brown eyes were red and swollen from crying, and one side of her face was creased with ridges from lying so long on the chenille spread. She resembled a cranky child in need of a long nap. She felt divided—part of her wanted to obey her mother, while the other part of her could not understand why Katie would deny her this chance—the opportunity to attend college without having to struggle with odds and ends jobs. Katie had often told Margaret that if a child honored her mother's wishes, goodness would come to her threefold. Well, she had always obeyed. She had sat in revival after revival, weeks on end, listening to the word of God being delivered by ministers who had traveled from as far as Chicago and those from as close as Kewanna Bank. She had tarried for the Holy Ghost, sat on the moaner's bench and moaned, rolled on the dusty floors in her best clothes. She had stayed out of the juke joints even though the enchanting music beckoned to her. She had even marched down Main Street wrapped in a sheet like a hooded monk to the levee where she was baptized in the unpredictable Mississippi River in the name of the Father, the Son, and the Holy Ghost.

And mostly, didn't she last September get down on her knees and beg forgiveness because her mother demanded she do so to atone for the sin of kissing Johnny Lee Hansen in public? It was the ending of summer, but not quite fall, when death creeps upon the living so quietly that the living are unaware of its presence.

The leaves had been a mixture of flaming orange, honey-nut brown and Christmas green, and the flowers were sunshine yellow and hot pink in their centers while the brown death caressed their petals. It was the time when the scent of freshly-cut wood permeated the air and insects sought the warmth of homes to live out the remainder of their lives. The time for donning light jackets and soft tams, when the sun shone fiercely while the wind chilled your legs above the stocking tops. A time when women were predictable, high-strung, and virgin. It was the time when the sanctified church held its last social of the year and all the other churches in Bennettsville and those that neighbored on its borders were invited. A time of roasted and fried meats and tall cakes of every imaginable color and mixture; creamed and nut-filled pies; tiny and giant fried pies; greens of all sorts from mustards to dandelions; potato salads mashed, diced, pickled, and plain; and mounds of corn bread of every shape from patties to pones to cakes. It was a time of soft hymns praising God in voices that ranged from a shrill soprano to a deep bass, while the sprinkle of tambourines rang through the air like chords of music directly from heaven, chords produced by old, expert black hands. It meant the mingling of all denominations and the exchanging of beliefs—to be precise, it was the time the Saints used to convince the other churches that their religion was the only true route to heaven.

And it was the time that Margaret met and kissed Johnny Lee Hansen, who was down visiting from Chicago, and who, like Joe Louis, was indeed one "fine brown bomber."

The thought of Johnny Lee's taut, muscular body made Margaret flush—tight as a well-mixed cake, hard as a shaft of light penetrating darkness. And suddenly, she could feel his hot breath searing the hollow of her neck. She sighed loudly—the sound echoing through the empty house like the fierce north wind-and pushed the memory away, for on its heels came the memory of her mother's wrath. It had begun when Margaret stepped outside of the oblong white building into the sun, searching for warmth to take away the chill that clung to the rafters of the church like vampire bats—a numbing, biting cold, resulting from a broken damper in the pot bellied stove. She wrapped the sweater about her chest, and tucked her hands under her arm pits. She had decided the sensible thing to do would be to go home, but being a representative of the YPWW (Young People Willing Workers) and sworn to be willing to save souls for Christ, there was no alternative but to stay until the affair was over. At the check-in table, just outside the front door, she spied Zara Lee Dawson and Wilma Ann White staring towards the back of the church, giggling, and acting mighty silly, if one were to ask her opinion.

"What's so amusing?" she asked curiously, walking over to the table where they stood. The three on them were dressed in long white skirts and white blouses of various styles, their hair piled high on their heads, and their skin coloring ranged from soot black to creamed coffee to honey—an ebony rainbow wrapped in white.

"Amusing. Amusing, you say. Honey, this ain't hardly what you'd call amusing," Wilma gasped, smacking her plump lips loudly.

"Well, what are you gaping at?" Margaret yelled over the sudden banging of tambourines.

"Honey, we is looking at one fine brown bomber," Wilma declared, her breathing shallow.

"A fine brown bomber; you've said that at least six times today, Wilma Ann," Margaret responded, unimpressed.

"Well, Miss Prissy," Zara Lee said, rudely pointing toward the small group of Saints gathered at the long table near the back door. "Jest you take a peek yo'self," she added as she bucked and rolled her eyes around in her head like a circus clown. Margaret pushed up on her tiptoes, looked at the tall, lean frame in a blue checked jacket heading her way through the crowd and froze. She responded immediately to the handsome young man who moved with animalistic grace towards them. His light brown eyes sweeping across the many faces, came to rest on Margaret's, and she dropped down from her tiptoes and agreed, he was a fine brown bomber. She became aware of her heart, beating so loudly it threatened to work itself clear through her chest wall. Something strange was happening to her. She could not move or turn way. She was confused. "Excuse me," the soft, husky voice requested. She did not move, only watched, mouth gaped as the rugged shoulders closed the space between them, and Zara Lee and Wilma stepped behind her. Excuse me, Miss," he insisted as the light brown eyes searched her face for a response. She did not move. Instead she began to cough, a dry, rapid cough that quickly evoked from him a familiar reaction of concern—gently he patted her on the back. "Are you all right? May I get you a drink? Perhaps some punch." He asked, a warm smile breaking across his face. She could barely control her head as she nodded her consent. He left quickly and returned with a cup filled with punch, which she carried to her mouth quite feverishly. Her eyes never left the soft concern in his face. He pointed to the nearest chair with long, slim fingers, but she gave a quick, definite shake of her head, and he suggested an alternative. "Perhaps if you got away from the crowd, a walk by the gate maybe… May I?" he said, pointing with his hand.

"Yes," she finally managed to say, even though she knew she should not go without a chaperon or at least without telling her mother. And as they started down the path towards the far gate, she heard a loud gasp and then a spasm of sporadic coughing erupted behind them. She knew it was no other that Zara Lee and Wilma coughing their fool heads off to attract the attention of this good-looking man, and also reminding her that they should stay together. The chink, chink from the tambourines became distant and faint, as they slowly walked across the grounds behind the church towards the gate.

"You're not from around here," she stated in a shaky voice.

He shook his head, stopped, and smiled. "What is your name?"

"Margaret. Margaret Younger," she replied, the words rushing from her lips.

"Johnny Lee Hansen at your service," he said, sticking one hand in hers and saluting with the other, mimicking a soldier. They laughed loudly, but she didn't know why, because it wasn't funny. She was sure if some other boy had done the same thing she would have thought his actions very foolish. "That's my dad over there in the blue serge suit drinking grape soda. He turned and pointed at the tall, slender man at the middle table. "We are down from Chicago for a few days," he added.

"That's my mother standing on his right," Margaret said, suddenly quite proud of the fair-skinned woman who stood, Bible in hand, her face aglow, which meant she could only be spreading the word of God to all who would listen. Nothing else in the world could make her face glow like that. They continued their walk, not realizing the distance they had covered until they heard the faint music coming from the local cafe. The same cafe that for as long as she could remember was described by the Saints as being the devil's house. A song that asked "Whatcha gonna do 'bout me," whispered across the roof tops. They stood with their shoulders pressed against the fence, occasionally looking across the grounds towards the back door of the church and at the indistinct faces of the people in white uniforms and dark suits. They talked about intimate events that had occurred in their lives, like they were old, dear friends. An unusual thing for Margaret, because she had been brought up by the right hand of God—Katie's hand—and knew very well the consequences of stepping outside of those boundaries. She knew very well this conversation should only occur when dating rules had been established and then only after proper introductions—she should be citing scripture. But something was happening to her, something that made her disregard proprieties. It was as though she was under a spell. An ordinary man stood before her, and yet he was not ordinary. His very presence filled the space about them, touching her all over, and even controlled her breathing. He smiled and she could see the tenderness that lay behind his eyes, promising her something—what she did not know. He stepped forward, pulled her gently into his arms, and kissed her hard on the lips. She was overpowered by the smell of him, the feel of him, the all of him. She felt her legs tremble from the strain of his grip, and the movement of his jacket as he pressed in closer. She felt herself getting very warm and lightheaded, like the time she'd fainted from the heat at the baptism on the levee. She wrapped her arms around his neck, leaned her head back, and exposed her neck. She hadn't planned this; but she couldn't bring herself to push him away even though she knew herself to be one of the most sensible persons in this small town.

"You'd better take that kinda stuff back to Chicago, young man." Margaret heard the stern voice of her mother, suddenly upon them without warning. They pulled away from each other, their faces flushed and guilty. And Margaret, suddenly ashamed of her actions, found herself staring at the ground.

"I…" He said.

"Never you mind, git away from my daughter this minute," Katie commanded. And Margaret remembered his confused face as Katie pushed her in the direction of the old house. Every time she slowed her step, Katie, on her heels, would push her again. And once they reached the door that was never locked, Katie, with one mighty hurl, flung her into the hall that divided the front room from the kitchen, a thrust that sent her crashing to the floor—the old house vibrating beneath her, and her skirt flying over her head, blinding her. She lay flat on her back; and before she could sit up, she heard the humming of an angry wasp above her head, which soon landed on her legs and shoulders delivering powerful stings. Instantly, she knew it was the large willow switch that hung on the middle room wall daily, like an ornate object of admiration.

"Git on your knees and pray, girl." The willow singing.

"Mama, please," Margaret yelled, lifting her arms to ward off the blows. "Please, please, Mama, it was just a kiss."

"I thought you said you wanted to be a school teacher. Is them the kind of lessons you gonna give?" The willow singing.

"I do, I do, I mean no, not that, Mama." Margaret waved her arms wildly.

"Can't teach with no big belly, can you?" The willow singing.

"No, no."

"Pray." The willow singing.

"I'm praying. See Mama, I'm praying."

"Pray out loud where I can hears you." The willow singing.

"Lord, dear God, I beg your forgiveness, for I have sinned."

"Pray louder." The willow singing.

"GOD, FATHER, SWEET JESUS, I BEG FORGIVENESS." The willow quiet.

Margaret prayed for the next two hours in silence. She stayed on her knees until they felt like blocks of wood. She prayed that her mother would drop dead on the spot. She prayed the old house that Katie loved would collapse into dust that very night. She prayed that she could go far away from that place, and she prayed that Johnny Lee would come to her and kiss her again and again until she could not breathe.

The next afternoon, a gray day, Johnny Lee came by the house, where he met stony eyes that had haunted him all night. Eyes that told him he was not welcome no matter what he said or did. Katie told him firmly, before he could utter a word, that Margaret was just sixteen and not allowed to receive company. Margaret didn't dare come to the door, and she heard him slowly descend the tall steps, apologizing over and over to her mother and imploring her to let him see Margaret for a few seconds before he left town. She watched his tall frame from the bedroom window, and he suddenly turned around as though he felt her eyes upon him. Their eyes met momentarily through the rain-streaked window pane, and, for a moment, time stopped. Then he turned and walked slowly down the gravel road. She watched, straining every muscle in her body for a glimpse of him, until he was out of sight. Gone.

It was hard for Margaret to return to the routine life that she and Katie shared after the brief encounter with Johnny Lee. He had awakened passions that disturbed her and made her see her mother in a different light. But he lived miles away, and it was unlikely that she would ever see him again. And with that thought, she returned to the old routine—designing and making clothes for the whites, mending and making alterations for the Negroes, and going to church with her mother—but with different goals. She would hit the books even harder, she would win a scholarship, and when she went off to college, if they had the money, it would be with the intention of returning not only as a qualified teacher, but as her own woman—a woman who would settle some place far away from her mother's possessive reach if Katie dared to interfere with her life. The soft clinking of the medals above her head made Margaret look up. The gleaming medals suddenly reminding her of the meet—her aching legs as she crossed the finish line, the presentation of the medals, and the scholarship that followed. Her hard work showed promise.

And now opportunity was there in the form of the money, everything she needed to make her dream come true, and her mother wanted her to toss it aside for the mere whims of Junior Townsend. Never! She tossed her hair, looked back at the face in the mirror and cried out, "No, no, no!" She would not give in this time. She would not refuse the money. But how could she pull it off without embarrassing her mother in front of everyone? For if she let her mother announce that they didn't want the money, and she then stood and claimed it, Katie would be humiliated. She did not want to create an impossible situation between them. She did not want to hurt her mother. But how could she manage it?

And then it struck her like a revelation, like a God-sent vision, and she smiled as she realized how simple but perfect it was. The hot pink dress hanging in Sherman's Department Store window. Yes, that would do it. Why, didn't her mother just last week forbid her to buy it? "That there color dress brings out the animal in men, even respectable men," Katie had said. Margaret clasped her hands in glee. It was perfect to flaunt in the faces of the old, wispy-eyed white men sure to be at the reading. Perfect to show Junior Townsend she was not a woman to be taken for granted, that his position neither frightened nor humbled her—she would take what was rightfully hers. And perfect to show her mother that she was a woman capable of making her own decisions. Incubated chicken indeed! Well, perhaps she didn't have enough sense to be afraid of death, but remaining in Bennettsville for the rest of her life terrified her—it was worse than death! She tossed her long hair and swore she would get that money, and white folks had just better watch out, and Mama, please understand... She rushed to the makeshift closet and pulled out a print dress. She had to hurry. There was a lot to be done before tomorrow.

BACK DOORS

The sun beat down fiercely on the dry, crusty, red earth, driving animals under porches and people inside. Charlie, pushing along on his cane approached the construction site for the new hospital just as the one o'clock whistle, choking under the pressure of the mid-July temperatures, screamed from the Bennettsville Gin, signaling the end of lunch. Negro men, their half-naked bodies glistening blue in the sun, and white men in glaring orange hats, returned reluctantly to laying the foundation for the hospital. This was to be the first hospital for Bennettsville and most people saw it as progress, being that it would eliminate driving the fifty miles to Margestown for medical attention. But Charlie dreaded walking past the building site, for every brick that was laid reminded him of how his wife died for lack of medical attention and made his blood boil.

He made his way across the graveled drive and down the Maple Street entrance to THE BACK, an unusually large block-long alley behind several white businesses and one Negro establishment, a place where Negroes were allowed to gather in large groups for recreation. The heavy coveralls he wore were stained with red, clay mud and hung loosely around his slender middle. The straw hat on his head was crack in several places about the brim and flopped lightly with every step he made.

Every Thursday, for the past five years, Charlie had come straight from Townsend's estate and headed to Rosie's for a hot dinner. At the mouth of the alley, he would pass Mamie's—a run-down shack that leaned towards the edge of the road like a lightning-struck steeple—and wave vigorously to Vernell Boswell, one of Mamie's whores, who could never wave back because she would be hanging soiled bed sheets on the clothesline. There was never much happening this time of day—a few stragglers coming from Rosie's carrying sandwiches wrapped in wax paper, or a couple of thirsty levee men heading to Sam's for hard liquor—and he would not linger. A hurried look at the shiny black screen doors that contrasted sharply with the white stone buildings and he would move on. Once at Rosie's, he would rest his aching feet, spend time talking with Katie, and perform some menial task before leaving. Charlie and Katie would eat lunch and swap news until eventually their conversation would work around to their favorite topic—what was best for Margaret's welfare.

The heat, Townsend's death, Katie and Margaret's names on Townsend's will, all weighed heavily on Charlie today and slowed his pace considerably. He had found himself dwelling in the past all morning, ever since Earline, Townsend's maid, greeted him with the news of how horrible Townsend's dying had been and that he had named Margaret and Katie in his will. He and Townsend had arrived in town with practically the same dreams: owning some land, and building a decent house to raise a family. Only Townsend had succeeded, but, of course, Townsend had the advantage, he was white and he was rich.

Townsend owned the largest estate in Bennettsville, furnished with objects from all over the world; he owned the town and ruled with a firm hand. He married into a rich family and had two children, a boy and a girl. Only part of Charlie's dreams materialized—he managed to hold onto his one acre of land and that only by hiring out to Townsend for the past twenty years. Charlie's house was small, but adequate, and held only the bare necessities. He had no children to leave anything to anyway, and now, he often wondered why he'd worked so hard to keep it.

A gust of wind, like the breath from an oven, sent food wrappers swirling at his feet, and Charlie, absentmindedly knocked them aside with his cane and continued his walk down the back. This place, "the back" ran the length and width of one city block with a man-made path down its center a bit larger than the average car. This was the entrance for Negroes to Rosie's Cafe, Tom's Liquors, Elvira's Cleaners, Sam's Bar, Bill's Tractor Parts, and Mamie's. Charlie stopped and looked around again; he had neared the center of the alley. He squinted hard at the buildings—something was different—a shadow of gray that didn't match the color around it hung above the doors, and he couldn't understand why all the doors had this peculiarity. All of the businesses, except for Rosie's, sat to the left of the path and huddled together like one huge conglomeration with four chimneys and four shiny, black doors. Rosie's, a low, flat building, sat a good forty feet to the right of the path and faced Mott Street. Some twenty feet behind Rosie's back door stood a scrawny pecan tree whose only nourishment, other than the periodical rains, was spilled wine and whiskey, and harked-up phlegm. Four perpetually rusty trash barrels flanked the little tree like sentinels waiting for its fruit—fruit that no one had seen in fifteen years. Had this place been a residential area, "the back" would obviously described five back yards, but no grass grew here because of the constant tramping and because of the weekly sweeping it received from its owners. It was just a big empty space that could easily accommodate two hundred standing people—like a prison yard with defined perimeters.

Charlie approached the pecan tree, stopped, and, looking around, remembered when he was younger what the place was like. He could see Negroes, sweaty and dressed in field clothes, with liquor in hand, going in and out of the back doors as if this place was The Savoy—the now most talked about night club in Chicago. They courted and wooed under the Mott Street lamp which projected their images across the road as shapeless bodies with serpentine legs. The back offered a sense of freedom from the white man's world. Sounds of revelry bloomed in its corners, people coming and going, a constant rhythmic banging of doors, and booming voices. It was a place where down-home blues splashed from the jukeboxes inside, creating such a stir of emotions that women gyrated their hips involuntarily, and men shouted epithets to the air. A place where men fought with switch-blades or broken bottles over a drink, a woman, a word. A place where women ripped the clothes and yanked the hair of their men, where white men, bored with the standard routine at the front of the bars, came to watch the niggers in action and were roughly escorted back where they belonged by the enraged town sheriff, who believed firmly that whites should only be with whites. Where some men and women were billy-clubbed for creating a disturbance, and others strolled hand in hand to make use of Mamie's shack. Somehow at the stroke of midnight, "the back" was always quiet and clear-like the spell of magic had worn away, sending them scattering like brown mice into the streets. He heard a woman's high giggle and looked up to see Alice's broad back in the screen door.

Charlie pushed his way into the Negro section of Rosie's, Alice locking the screen door behind him, and proceeded down the middle aisle, past the booths, two on each side of the aisle, and around the lunch counter—a counter that would have been forbidden to him had this section been open (only Ruth, the white waitress, was allowed behind the counter during these times). But Rosie closed the Negro section at one o'clock every afternoon in order to accommodate the white customers and allow Katie time to complete the supper meal. Rosie's maze of odd-shaped rooms and numerous doors always reminded Charlie of the fancy chicken coop he had once seen, where specific areas were sectioned and closed off for specialized breeding. He shouldered through the swinging door that closed off the Negro section from the squared kitchen and, seeing Katie, paused. Katie stood with her back against the counter, chewing on a sandwich and keeping a watchful eye on the huge black pot on the stove directly across from her. He limped across the floor and stopped in front of the cutting table a few feet to Katie's left. She felt his presence, looked up and eyed him suspiciously. His eyes probed hers and she guessed that someone had told him about the money. That someone could only be Earline Simpson, for she was known to eavesdrop on the white families she worked for and pass the information along through the Negro section of town. She did not speak; instead she continued chewing on the sandwich, as though it was the first bite of food she had had all day. Alice, returning from wiping the tables in the Negro section, breezed by Charlie and humming a loud tune went back to scraping the hot grill. Silently, he turned, walked the few steps to the wall, and hung his straw hat and cane across the metal coat rack. The kitchen smelled of freshly baked apple and sweet potato pies, and of the boiling sweetmeat in the pot. One glance at the stack of pots that lined the sink's counter told him there weren't any left-overs; and he moved quickly to the waist-high cutting table and began pulling the heavy garbage can from underneath.

Although Charlie was not one of Rosie's employees, they had an unspoken agreement; he would perform some menial task like emptying the garbage or loading the front and back coolers with beer in exchange for a meal. He tilted the can on an angle and rolled it through the Negro section and out the door to the trash barrel. Grabbing the can at the end while holding onto the rim, he hefted it and dumped the contents like he was packing cotton in a sack—a little at a time. He emptied the can, pulled out his red, checked handkerchief, and wiped his face and balding head in one stroke. He glanced around again, that same feeling nagging at him, a feeling that something was different, 'out of order' but he still could not see what it was. Rolling the can in front of him, he stepped through the screen door, latched it and returned to the kitchen and slid the can under the table. Without speaking, Katie passed him a wet towel; he wiped his face and hands and hurrying to the Negro section sat in the booth by the swinging doors. As Alice slapped hamburgers on the sizzling grill for the white customers up front, Katie walked out of the kitchen to the booth and set a sandwich and ice cold black tea in front of Charlie. She took the seat across for him, sighed loudly, and immediately folded her arms on the edge of the table. She watched the wrinkles go up and down as he lifted the bread from the sandwich and examined the meat. She smiled, her white skin glistening with perspiration.

"Well," she said, leaning her head against the booth. "I was aiming to tell you myself, but I suppose Earline done beat me to it as usual."

Charlie saw that her black hair was drawn up in a roll under the hair net. She reminded him of her father, Robert Younger—the only white man he ever trusted. They had the same pointed chin and teacup-shaped ears that always turned bright red from the slightest heat.

"Matter of fact," he answered slowly, chewing on the bread crust, a low chuckle in his throat. "Matter of fact, she did mention something 'bout you and Margaret's name being on Townsend's will."

"Matter of fact, my eye," she laughed. "You probably wadn't in that house five minutes before she told you." She nodded her head like she was an authority on the subject of Earline.

"Might say that, and you might not. I recollect it to be 'bout two minutes. In fact, I don't think I had finished knocking on the door when she tole me. He smiled. They both laughed, filling the empty room with a pleasant note that rose above the sizzle of meat frying on the hot steaming grill. As their laughter settled, the rumble of the juke-box up front blended with the noise from the kitchen.

"Yes, it's true. At least that's what Big Jim said, and you knows he ain't one to go round spreading gossip, him being the prosecuting attorney and all," she assured him, a light of mystery behind the gray eyes.

"No, he ain't that kind, and with Earline saying it's so, it gots to be. You knows Earline's ears sharper than any old hound dog's," he said, leaning over his plate, his eyes wide. "Them white folks she works for ain't had no secrets since they hired her. And she don't miss a thang. She even tole me that you and Margaret ain't gonna be 'lowed to sit at the same table with the white folks, even if'n your skin is white as theirs. Said J.T., with his long, slick-headed self, done tole his mama to make sure them niggers don't sit at the table."

"He talked to his mama like that?" Katie gasped and frowned.

"Sho." He nodded his head rapidly.

"So! It's his house already. I should have known. Jest can't wait to step in his daddy's shoes. What did Miss Clara say to that?" she snorted, and rested her chin in her hands.

"Nothing," he said, pointing with the sandwich.

"Leastwise, that's what Earline said. She jest stared at him all white in the face, eyes little and mean like she wanted to scratch his eyes plumb out of his head, and never opened her mouth. But later she tole Earline how much she miss Mista Harrison and that she didn't know what in the world gonna happen to her now that Junior was taking over everythang." He smacked his mouth and leaned his head back against the booth.

"Shoot," Katie said. "That's one of the reasons I quit taking day work altogether. Jest got tired of white folks' mess. And I don't mean cleaning up behind them either. I'm talking 'bout them whining and laying their problems right on top of your'n and specting you to tell them everything gonna be all right. Like you is some relative of theirs. Then clean their house, wash their clothes and tend them spoiled rotten chillen of theirs and be back fresh come morning." Katie twisted in the seat, picked up the edge of her apron and began fanning it in the direction of her face. "But all and all, it's a blessing, a God-sent blessing, that I ain't never worked for Townsend while I was doing day work, 'cause I would have lost my religion on Junior, long time ago."

"Amen to that," he said dryly. He could sense where the conversation was headed—the trials and tribulations of day work, one of Katie's favorite arguments, and one he wanted to avoid today. He picked up the sugar container and poured a tall mound of white crystals on top of the tea. Vigorously, he stirred, the spoon clanking loudly against the glass, until the thick layer of sugar at the bottom of the glass was swirling through the tea like snowflakes, and until Katie, with a sharp cut of her eye, shot him a look of disapproval. He dropped the spoon to the table and cleared his throat. "But tell me," he said, "what is you aiming to do 'bout this here money?"

The apron fell from her hands into her lap, and she stared at him, wondering how to tell him they would not take the money. She lowered her gaze, staring at the crumbs on the plate.

"Probably ain't no need to git all worked up 'bout it," he continued. "Probably ain't enough to spit at. Might be enough to paint your house, though, with a bit left over. That's how them white folks operates—works you near death's door, then leaves you pennies. But since you ain't never worked for Townsend likes I has, I reckon that put you ahead of the white folks for once."

"No, I ain't never worked for Townsend." She sighed and looked into his face. "God jest sent me there to lay hands on him and heal him twice. But that was the Lord working, not me."

"Well, anyhows you was there. Now what you aims to do 'bout this money? And how come Margaret's name on the will, since you the one did all the praying? he asked, picking between his teeth with his fingernail, trying to act nonchalant.

"Charlie," she stammered and twisted about to peek through the thin slats of the swinging door and see what Alice was doing. Turning back to face him, she leaned forward and spoke softly. "Big

Jim told me the other night that the money was left to Margaret for her education, and that it's quite a bit."

His dark eyes widened, his mouth flew open, and he gazed a long second at Katie as though he had frozen to the seat. He reached quickly for the tea and gulped until the glass was drained halfway, his wrinkled, brown hand unsteady as he set the glass on the table. "Jest how much do it take to go to one of them colleges, say for a year?" he said in a shaky voice. "I knows y'all been saving for quite a spell and jest got money enough for a year. Jest how much money is you got right now?"

"We got one thousand dollars stashed away—that is, if you count the five hundred dollar scholarship Margaret won. Jest enough, the way I understands it to pay for one year. That's why me and Margaret been scrimping all this time—eight years now, and some of that money is what I got for selling that back acre of Pappy's land. Now Charlie," she added, pointing a finger at the ceiling and shaking it, "that don't include room and board or books and clothes. Shoot, I reckon if you consider all that, and a little spending money, it probably comes to heap more than that. If you consider all of that, and considering that Mista Townsend did, too—I reckon he did since he done already sent one youngen to college and was aiming to send that there girl, Dellie, next year—I would say that run about five thousand dollars, give or take."

Charlie's head began to spin from the heat and all the talk of money. He suddenly experienced a tremor in his left arm and leg, and the bottom of his stomach seemed to plunge to the floor. It was the same feeling he had experienced when Pete's eight your old son, Willie Lee, was pulled from the river, bloated and missing his privates. "Now hold on there, Katie, jest one minute," he said, his voice hollow and low. "What you is talking 'bout is a whole heap of money. Too much for that boy of Townsend's jest to let y'all walk up and take without him doing something crazy. Who you gots to protect you from that bunch what takes orders from him?"

"I done thought on them very things, Charlie," Katie interrupted. Closing her eyes tightly, she shook her head. But he was somewhere in another time and couldn't stop.

"The only true friends you got is me and M.B. I ain't talking 'bout them Sanctified folks at your church what's gonna start praying for y'all safety. No." He shook his head in protest and laid his hands face down on each side of the plate. His voice was raspy, yet strong, the sound of corn being husked, and his heart ballooned in his chest. "I'ma talking what I knows. Big Jim will do what he can, but even if'n he is the law, he still jest one man, and what can one do when it comes down to dealing with a passel of rats? Besides, he's a redneck, too—a fair one, still… But J.T. ain't gonna hardly mess with nobody but Margaret, 'cause she don't know nothing. I jest wish it was some way y'all could git that money without all the fuss it's bound to start," he said and suddenly became aware of sweat pouring off his face. He dabbed feverishly at his forehead with the crumpled handkerchief, and absentmindedly laid it next to the plate.

She signed heavily and began tapping the base of her neck with her fingertips. "I wish we could have the money too, but only on the account of Margaret's education," she said. "Far as I'se concerned, I don't want no parts of that money, 'cause it's tainted jest like Townsend was. But having to tell Margaret we ain't gonna take it really hurt me bad," she added, her voice small like a child's.

He looked up, a question in his eyes. "Well, I hopes you didn't tell her jest like that, 'cause she's liable to go agin you. I knows if'n it was me, I'd be tempted."

"No, Margaret won't go agin me, Charlie. She'd never do a thing like that," Katie assured him. At the same time, she was trying to convince herself, for she still remembered the gleam of hatred in Margaret's eyes when she left her there on the bed staring at the ceiling. "I told Margaret flat-out weren't no future in taking white folks' money. That it'll only bring trouble down on our heads—trouble like she ain't never seen the likes of."

He pushed the sandwich away from him. It was too hot to eat and Katie's account of her discussion with Margaret lay sour on his stomach. He knew how it felt to have dreams. Didn't his dreams nag at him still, like the bum leg that ached from time to time? Wasn't he an expert on dreams that never materialized, that lay hidden in the cobwebs of his mind for what seemed to be an eternity? Oh, yes, he understood. He hadn't wanted to face the truth either, the stark reality that Negroes didn't count. So he could see the reasoning behind Katie's hesitation. But one thing Katie would have to do if she wanted to save the relationship with her daughter was to sit her down and tell her the truth. Not that Katie lied, she just avoided issues that were painful. She wanted to protect Margaret as long as she could. But he knew that the only hope for these two different beings who agreed on most things and still stood at opposite poles of the earth, was for Katie to sit down and explain to her daughter just what it meant to be a Negro. And as he thought the words, he knew that Katie would as soon as fall from God's grace into Satan's pit as tell Margaret, "Don't dream because there ain't any future for Negroes."

"Katie," Alice called from the kitchen, "better tend this pot. Lawd, Miss Rosie liable to have a conniption you let them crowders burn and they on the special tonight."

Katie scooted to the end of the long seat, jumped up, and hurried through the doors towards the clanging pot on the stove. Charlie stared at the vinyl seat of the booth as though she were still sitting there—as though he hadn't noticed her exit. He didn't believe Margaret would ever come around to Katie's way of thinking, not on this issue. Margaret still believed that she was different from any other person in the world.

He knew what it was like. He had felt that way, too, once. Years ago, he was vibrant and sure of making his mark in life. He knew that he wasn't ordinary, that he too would achieve great things. But what had it come to? An old man with a bum leg who still, after all these years, crawled around in the dirt and pulled weeds for white folks.

An old man who had to adopt another man's family because he had none of his own. Oh, hell, he sighed, and rested his head in his hands. He didn't blame Katie; the truth about how Negroes lived had always been hidden, even from them. Wrapped in a blanket of ignorance, Negroes had wallowed in their own blood and guts and never complained, just like Anna Mae had wallowed in their bed the night she died. Oh, Anna Mae. His heart screamed from the memory of that night. A vivid picture of Anna Mae stood before him. She was smiling and the wind was playing with the tail of the white linen dress. Anna Mae, his third wife, who had stepped into his life when he had settled down and come into his manhood. She was the woman who promised him everything with the mere flutter of an eye-lash and gave him all of herself—never held back. She was the one who haunted his dreams, the one he had understood the least, who had exasperated him into fits of rage, and yet the one he had loved the most of all three.

Charlie had to admit that Anna Mae was plain when it came to looks, but she had an air about her that made his breathing irregular. Perhaps it was her childish way of doing and saying things, she was very rash compared to other women he had known; and she certainly was the most exciting one. But Anna Mae died, because the same Doc Smith who this morning requested him to cut his grass and see what he could do about the peaked-looking Red Hardies in his garden, couldn't be bothered with niggers. It was suddenly that she took sick, and he had to rush in from the fields to see about her. She lay wincing in their four-poster bed, opening and closing her small fists from the pain, and thrashing back and forth across the bed. He stood at the threshold of the door watching her with a knot twisting in his stomach.

"Mae," he said, walking over to the bed and bending down to her face. "I'ma gonna git Doc Smith to come look at you, might be something wrong with the baby."

"No," she cried in a voice that was still musical in the midst of pain. "Stay with me. Git June Bell from next door to go. He knows what to do. "Don't leave me right now," she pleaded, and laid her head back against the pillow. Her eyes were black and sparkling like the dust from coal.

Charlie shook his head and did as she asked. He sent the young boy with the message and returned quickly to Anna Mae's bedside. Each moment they waited seemed like an eternity to Charlie. It was torture to sit there and watch her suffer. And he made up his mind that if Anna Mae lost the baby they would not try again. Having a baby appeared more risky that he had imagined, they hadn't thought about the possibilities of miscarriage.

It wasn't long before June Bell returned, with an adult air about him even though he was only twelve years old. It was an air that instantly set Charlie on edge. The second the barefoot boy, with balls of hair that resembled kuckerbugs, stepped into the room, Charlie sensed trouble. Perhaps it was the way he stood back in his legs, or perhaps it was the dark scowl on his face as he imitated the manner in which he received the message he was about to give. He looked Charlie directly in the eye and repeated it word for word, managing to capture all the emphasis in which it had been delivered. "Doc Smith say tell you, say,' Tell that gal it's too hot to be fooling round with niggers' bellyaches.'"

The pupils of Charlie's eyes became black slits, and his pointed narrow chin fell down upon his chest. Anna Mae saw the dark look on Charlie's face and stopped squirming in the bed. She watched Charlie working his mouth, and then he was off the bed in a flash, facing the boy, whose eyes appeared they would pop out onto the floor. She sensed the old questions creeping into his face as though they were wrinkles that had suddenly bloomed. She could almost hear the words clicking in Charlie's mind—the ones about the treatment of Negroes—and she propped herself up and made a desperate effort to smile, to distract his mind from old wounds. "Charlie," she stammered. But it was no use. Charlie whirled around and faced the wall of the small room, then whirled back to face the boy as though he was about to strike him to the floor. With malice in his voice, as though the ugly words had come from the boy himself, he shouted, "Don't stand there like a dang fool. Run git Miss Josephine," and the boy tore from the room and out of the house.

Miss Josephine, the midwife, arrived at the house in minutes, huffing and puffing from the run, her flowered print dress wrinkled into a thousand cat faces—it appeared to have been slept in—though her face was carefully made up with the special pancake she wore at all times. She ushered Charlie and June Bell outside, and returned to them a few minutes later. "She gonna need a doctor, Charlie," she said, her eyes avoiding his as she spoke. "And quick, or else she gonna be dead come morning. I done seed this kind of trouble maybe two times since I'se been midwifing—the baby ain't in the right place."

Charlie stood there on the porch trying to erase the word "dead" from his mind. He wished he had not listened to Anna Mae and had bought the old pistol. He could use it now to persuade Doc Smith to change his mind about niggers. Well, he wasn't too proud to beg for Anna Mae; he would get down on his knees and kiss that white man's feet if he had to. "I'ma gonna git Doc Smith," he yelled and was off the porch and tearing down the road in seconds. But when he reached the white house with green shutters, he panicked at the sign that hung over the office door. "Gone Fishing" glared at him in bold black letters, and a heaviness attached itself to his feet and legs as he took off in a slow trot towards town, hoping to catch Doc Smith before he got lost on some isolated fish bank.

Every step he took sounded like thunder on the dry gravel, and he kept turning around expecting to see someone—anyone who might help. He went to the sheriff's Office, the General Store, the white cafe, and not taking any chances, he even went to the levee where some respectable white men fished or could sometime be found with women they did not speak to in the daylight. And with every stop, he lost time—Anna Mae lost time—Doc Smith was nowhere to be found; it was as though he had vanished. Charlie remembered wishing that his friend Robert was in town; Robert could have gotten the information he needed—the name and location of the fishing hole. And even though he was not a religious man, he heard himself cry out, "Lord ham mercy on Anna Mae, she jest a little thing."

With no idea of where else to go, and dark had settled around his feet, he headed in the direction of his house, hoping that somehow all of this was the dream it seemed to be, and that when he got there he would find Anna Mae sitting up, smiling. He stopped at the pecan tree about a mile from his house, and smeared sweat across his forehead with the back of his hand. He wondered, what kind of man was he? What kind of man would go back to watch his wife suffer—to watch her die? All at once, he became acutely aware of the beauty of the night—the calmness of the trees, the gentleness of the breeze, the brightness of the moon. The aromatic odor of freshly-cut grass pierced his nostrils, a smell he usually inhaled deep into his lungs until he was intoxicated from its pureness. Now it seemed foul, blasphemous, to him. And he loped down the road gasping for air, his chest heaving up and down, like a berserk, broken spring.

Suddenly, gravel popped, wheels spun, slinging gravel and dust in all directions, and a truck came to a careening halt three feet behind him. Like a wild man, he spun around and found himself looking into the thin, puzzled face of his old friend, M.B.—a black face soaked with perspiration and with eyes the size of saucers that gaped at Charlie from behind narrow, brown-rimmed spectacles. His truck still bouncing from the sudden stop, M.B. leaned forward, clamping down on the stem of his pipe, and swept the sweat-stained cap from his head with one stroke of his hand. The truck was the color of midnight in the darkness; and the basket of tomatoes sitting on the passenger seat looked ominous. "What in tarnation is you doing in the middle of the road?" M.B. stammered. As Charlie fell upon the door and somehow managed, through gasps and broken sentences, to tell him what was wrong, M.B.'s jaw went slack; his eyes moved from left to right in the darkness as though he was searching its depths for an answer to Charlie's predicament. "We better take her over yonder to that hospital in Margestown. Maybe we can git one of them doctors to come outside and look at her," he said, in a calm, take-charge voice. Charlie hopped on the running board on the driver's side, and M.B. gunned the accelerator to the floor.

From the roadside, they could hear her screams within the shadowed house, as Anna Mae's fallopian tube ripped open bit by bit in a zig-zag, like sackcloth tearing under the strain of strong hands, and leaked hot blood into her belly. Hoarse guttural, her screams filled the night air and made them shiver with fright. A large-eyed Josephine, her pancake smeared, met them on the steps, wringing her hands and talking incessantly. "Best do something. Best do something quick!"

Charlie and M.B. marched past her as though they didn't see or hear her. Their faces became solemn—Anna Mae must not see their fear. They ignored her screams by concentrating only on the job they had to do. They were only aware of the pounding of their hearts, and the fumes from the many oil lamps around the small room that burned their nostrils and made them drunk. There were no more shadows around the house. Everything was clear, as transparent as fine crystal. No longer was the fun-loving, Creole-speaking Anna Mae, whom Charlie and everyone else loved, lying in the bed. In her place, was a savage with wild eyes, making animal sounds and thrashing about, kicking at invisible demons. Mechanically, they bent down and wrapped the woman in the quilt. M.B., careful not to look her in the face, focused his attention on the embroidered yellow daisy on the pillow case, while Charlie, astounded by her appearance could not speak as he lifted her feet around the post of the bed. They carried her to the truck quickly, in the same fashion that they had entered the room—marching-their faces solemn.

Ten miles out of town, Anna Mae died, just as Josephine had said she would. For the first time that day, Charlie felt calm. He was numb. And now all these years later, thirty, a hospital with a ward for colored people, was being build in town.

"Where you at, Charlie?" Katie asked, returning from the kitchen, her hands filled with Charlie's straw hat and cane. She placed them on the booth beside him and remained standing. "Huh, I reckon," he said slowly, "I reckon I was dreaming 'bout the past agin."

"What you doing back in the past? she asked curiously, bending over the booth. And as if fire seized him, he became dark and yet hopeful, and he spoke not to her but to the man that used to dwell inside the small frame, he now pushed forward with aid of a wooden stick.

"Cause that's where it all bee-gan. 'Cause," he said bitterly, "sometimes the past helps you to see where you at, and if you had any sense at all you'd tell Margaret to take that money and run as fast as she can until she is so far away from this here town that she can't even remember the name. Never in her life ever set foot or even come near this tainted soil as long as she live." He pushed himself up from the booth with the palm of his hands.

And just as he prepared to vent the anger of his lost dreams and hopelessness upon Katie's slim, frame, Rosie burst through the swinging doors. Rosie always burst through those doors like she resented coming back into the Negro section, like she was trying to tear the doors off their hinges. Her hands jammed down in the white uniform pockets, she went directly to her business. "Katie, is everything gonna be on time?" she asked, tossing her head, and flinging her arm on her hip. "You know how I hate to serve supper late. You didn't have to change nothing, did you? We're still gonna have tom turkey and dressing, sweet fried corn, blue-hull crowders, biscuits and sweet potato pie? And you do have some apple pie for Big Jim, I hope?" She rattled on, not wanting or expecting an answer. When she was satisfied that everything would be sufficient she suddenly noticed Charlie standing quietly by the booth. She faced him, her red hair peeking from the sides of the white hair net, and without changing her pace inquired, "Well, what do you think about it, Charlie?"

"Sounds like a mighty fine meal to me," he stammered.

"I ain't talking 'bout no food, Charlie, I'm talking 'bout 'the back,'" she said, quite exasperated at his answer. Charlie glanced immediately at Katie who stood behind the red-headed woman, hunching her shoulders up and down and holding the palms of her hands open—a signal to let him know that she had no idea what Rosie was talking about.

"It's crazy, plain crazy," Rosie declared. "All the white folks noticed it right off, but not one colored person has even so much as mentioned it in my presence. I mean, just 'cause it was my idea and all," she added, leaning back against the counterstool, "don't mean I'm looking for praise or attention. It always did somehow strike me as being unchristian, them signs hanging all over a decent town like this. I mean, they ain't never been necessary. Everybody here knows their place. Now you take some of them towns in other parts of the country. Maybe they might have a need for them, but not here. So I decided that mine was coming down and Tom and Sam got caught up in the spirit and yanked theirs clean off the wall, and we had us a mighty fine bonfire, even burned some of the trash, cleaned it off a bit. Now don't you think that was a Christian thing to do, Charlie?" Rosie asked, her doll-like eyes so fixed on him that he could not turn away.

"Yes Ma'am." The lie came easy to his lips. "Yes Ma'am, it sho was a Christian thing to do. I best be gitting on home now; 'bout y'all busy time anyhows." He removed the hat and cane from the booth and pushed his bad leg towards and out the door. He strolled down the alley and turned around to look at the shadows above the doors. Sure enough, the signs that once hung over the back doors of the businesses were gone. He knew then what it was that had nagged at his brain earlier. He looked closer now and saw the big, clean, square spot, surrounded by years of dirt on its edges; it stood out like a giant sore that had healed in its middle but left a crusty, infected scab around its body. A sore that would take many, many years to heal completely. Didn't she know? he thought as he turned away and continued his walk. Didn't she know that colored folks never looked at them signs but once, that them signs said Negroes wasn't fit to be nowhere but in the alley? Didn't she know they was too ashamed to ever look at them agin? Didn't she even know that? Maybe she was right about one thing though. Colored folks sure knew their place—that is, everybody but Margaret. Thank God.

The noon rush was finally over and Katie and Alice were glad. The orders from up front would be less demanding and they could finish preparing the supper meal at a slower pace. This was the time they usually took their break.

Rosie's testimony of her so-called Christianity set Katie's nerves on edge. The removal of the signs, designating the entrance for Negroes, might have been misconstrued as an act of kindness, if Rosie hadn't put them up in the first place, but Christian acts mixed with white supremacist demands of "knowing your place" set Katie to focusing on old problems. Suddenly depressed and feeling very much alone, she sat at the long table in the kitchen, listening to the hissing of the pot on the stove and to the soft scraping of the knife against the carrots as Alice prepared side-salads. Katie was reminded of her mother telling her that old problems were the cause of new ones, because all things that happened were a part of something that had happened before. And she recalled her mother telling her about "knowing your place," of how the term had been passed down from the time when slaves had to literally keep to the rut in the road. She had never taught Margaret her so-called "place," because Margaret was not easy-going like Katie had been when she was Margaret's age, and because Katie didn't know how—knowing your place was not something one could easily pin down. There were no ruts in Bennettsville's roads that Negroes had to walk in, unless they were the ones the Negro men followed behind the plow. The definition was only clear when a Negro stumbled upon white folks in the midst of some evil doings and saw something that they should not have seen. That is what happened to her, three years ago, when she came upon J.T. and two teenage boys after J.T. had killed old man Boswell. She knew her place for sure, and even though they did not see her, she had never told a soul but God.

She was doing daywork for Miss Rita who lived on Water Street adjacent to the levee road. She had finished hanging the wash on the line and had gone to find a ball Miss Rita's son had tossed, the day before, in the wooded area behind their house. It was a cool, summer morning, the air heavy with the aroma of burning cedar, and she was angry that she had to stop her duties to fetch for a three year old. The yard was separated from the woods by a chicken wire fence with a narrow wooden gate. She pushed through the gate, taking long strides, her eyes scanning the ground ahead from left to right. The ground was soft and spongy as it always was after a hard rain. She slowed her pace, taking careful steps as the woods were filled with small, furry animals and chuck holes, and she was fearful of running upon a snake—she hated snakes. She was almost to the levee road before she spied the red rubber ball wedged between two flat rocks at the beginning of the watershed. The path that led to the levee embankment. The road was graveled and used mostly by people who didn't want to be seen—hunters and men going fishing, or men with whores, or teenagers using it for a lover's lane. The road was flanked by tall weeds and a wall of small, thin trees that grew so close together that one could not tell where one tree began and the other stopped—a natural watershed. Katie neared the ball just as six gun shots rang out from the other side of the levee. She froze, then dropped quietly to the ground, her ears numb, and stared at the ball which lay an arms length ahead of her. Suddenly a flurry of rocks and dirt rained down the levee embankment, followed by a man who rolled like a barrel, then sprawled flat on the ground a foot ahead of the ball. It was a Negro man dressed in faded dungarees, a white short-sleeved cotton shirt, and black rubber boots with the number 10 stamped on the bottom in red. He lay motionless, his face turned in the direction of the embankment. Instinct told her to stay down, and in seconds rocks and dirt rained down the embankment again; then a rush of pounding feet stumbled down the slope, stopping at the head of the man on the ground. She watched as three white teenage boys dressed in jeans and jackets, wide black hats, and carrying knapsacks used for trapping small game on their backs—the same kind her pappy had used when he trapped rabbit or coon—prodded the body with their guns. They were carrying rifles and that she could not understand, unless they had intended to trap and hunt at the same time as many inexperienced hunters did.

"Damn it, J.T. It's a nigger! You done killed yourself a nigger," she heard one of them say.

There was a long pause and they mumbled words that she could not hear. She lay on the ground listening to the pounding of her heart, her face pressed against the wall of trees.

"I was after coon, wasn't I? Didn't think I was gonna git one this big though," a husky voice said. They laughed, not the laugh of hardened men, but the scared laughter of boys trying to be tough.

And then the ball, as though Satan reached down and flicked it with his pointed fingernail, or it rattled loose from the pounding on the earth, freed itself, and rolled down the path, and came to rest in the middle of the road a few feet ahead of the body. The boys looked at the ball, their eyes cutting back and forth, then turned, facing the wall of trees, their faces white with fright. She could see them clearly through the spaces in the trees, but they could not see her. They stood with the sun in their faces, and immediately she recognized J.T.—everyone in town knew Townsend's son on sight. He had been seen coming to the fields with his daddy, or he had been pointed out as he accompanied his mother through town. They tossed their knapsacks to the ground and headed in her direction, their guns pointed towards the trees and glinting in the sun. She lay there watching them and prayed to God to save her or, if this was her time to go, let it be done quickly. They stopped two feet in front of the trees. She could see the creases and the shine from the iron on J.T.'s jeans, but she could not see their faces from this angle. She would have to roll over on her back to see them clearly, and she was afraid to move—afraid to breathe. God must have answered her prayer, for suddenly J.T. was on the ground thrashing about. The two boys grabbed J.T. by his shoulders and legs and one of them forced something into his mouth; and Katie, having seen this affliction before, knew that J.T. was having one of those spells. She inched backwards slowly, then crawled on her knees until she reached the chicken-wire fence. She crawled through the gate and only then did she stand, snatch the wash basket from the ground, and run inside. She prayed and prayed, asking God what should she do, and during a reverent prayer, she saw her father's bloodless face hanging in the noose. She left it there in God's hands.

"Katie," Alice called. "You aim to boil them sweet po'taters today or what?"

"Huh?" Katie answered slowly, coming out of her reverie, her face flushed as though she had been running.

"I said, is you aiming to tend to them taters," Alice repeated, drying her hands on a towel and taking the seat across from Katie.

They looked at each other for a moment, then Katie as though she thought Alice was reading her mind, lowered her gaze and sighed.

"Don't let what Miss Rosie say git you down," Alice said, a dry smile about her lips. "She thanks she done something hot, taking down them signs and all. The ways I see it, it sho ain't got nuthing to do with being no Christian. She folded her heavy arms on the table and looked toward the open swinging door where she could see down the aisle that led to the front.

"Amen to that," Katie replied in an adamant tone and glanced over at the pile of potatoes lying on the sink. "Alice, believe me, I knows a Christian act when I sees one and I ain't seen one today. But what is it you reckon they wants? I'se been trying to figure out the meaning of them words for a long time." Katie faced Alice, looking into the woman's deep-set eyes.

Alice chuckled, but it was not a happy laugh, more like a person gone mad or about to cry. "You mean Christianity or knowing your place?"

"The last. I knows what a Christian is, didn't I jest say that?"

"Means what it says—Us knowing our place. It's simple as that."

"Simple!" Katie spat the words across the table.

"Yeah. You either knows it or you don't. If you don't, you jest guesses at what's they wont and hopes you can act stupid enough whereas you don't git beat to death when that ain't it. I swears it's a trying thing, puzzling over where you supposed to be, these directions plastered all over the doors and round on the side of the building at the bank and the liquor, but you walks right in the front at the movies, only has to go upstairs. It's enough to plumb wear you out."

"That's true, but it ain't all places, like in slavery time," Katie said, shaking her head.

"What you mean?"

"Them doors jest a part of it." Katie propped her elbows on the table to hold her chin. "Well, I ain't sure how it goes. I'se jest so mad I can't think straight." She shook her head as if to clear her mind. "Listen," she continued. "maybe this is what I mean. Last spring I was in the hardware and old man Phillips told old Elmo to shet up and don't say another word. And when Elmo did liken he was told, Phillips got hot under the collar 'cause Elmo wadn't talking. Told him something 'bout when y'all ever gonna learn. It's heap more than doors and signs. I tell you what it is, Alice." She stretched out her hands and looked at them. "It's white folks poking a hole in the sky and telling Negroes that they place."

Alice's mouth fell open. She let out a long sigh—a gust of air that sounded like the whistle of a tea pot. "That would splain Miss Rosie coming back here all red in the face last week asking me to do something she wadn't sure I'd do."

"Lord, what was it?" Katie asked, her interest keened.

"Well, you was helping Ruth serve in the Negro section, and I was jest setting down to this here table here to eat. She told me—you knows how she talks all fast and everythang—to go over yonder to her house and rinse out a few clothes she had a soaking in the foot-tub. Well, I didn't change a word, 'cause I didn't know what to say, 'cepting I didn't thank that was my job, and I couldn't say that. So's I jest takes my sandwich with me and goes. And guess what I found.

"What?" Katie leaned in closer, holding her breath. Their heads inches apart.

"A tub full of hur bloody draws—I mean the water was plumb red." They give each other a knowing look, and Katie let her arms drop to the table. "I reckon you knows I throwed all them draws in them very trash barrels out yonder on the back, and acted like the craziest nigger this side of the Mississippi when she asked me 'bout them the next day," Alice said, nodding her head up and down.

They laughed, a hearty laugh that filled the room. Then, looking about quickly, remembering that Rosie was right up front, they lowered their voices and snickered like young girls.

They stopped laughing and were silent for a long while. Alice unfolded her arms and placed them in her lap. She spoke softly to Katie almost in a whisper. "What was you pondering on a while back, Katie?"

Katie looked up, a tiny smile on her face. "Jest old problems, Alice. And how they don't never git taken care of. Seems like times you thinks you got one solved, it done come full circle to stare you in the face again."

"You talking 'bout that money Townsend left y'all?"

Katie sighed. "So you done heard it too."

"Sho. Everybody done heard it, I reckons. Luella Carauthers told me yestaday. She overheard Reverend Mack telling his misses the other morning at breakfast. Didn't say nuthing to you 'cause, well, we been so busy ain't had time to talk liken this."

Katie leaned back in the chair and cleared her throat. It was a hollow sound that made Alice flinch with concern. "Well, what you ask me while ago, it didn't have nothing directly to do with the money. But the money is what started it all happening again. And Miss Rosie talking 'bout them signs and that other mess 'bout knowing your place and the likes. It's jest a bunch of things swimming 'round in my head. I wish to God I could git it all off my chest, but I jest can't."

Alice leaned back in the chair, her heavy frame bulging over the sides of the seat. She rocked for a second, her mouth in a pout. "Well, that's that then," she said, smacking her lips and folding her arms around her chest. "You keep on studying on it, something gonna work out."

"Only with the Lord's help," Katie replied and rose from the table. Turning her back to Alice, she headed for the sink to prepare the potatoes.

THE READING OF THE WILL

In the Townsend's parlor, the lights blazed. Ten people—eight whites, two blacks; six men, four women—had been summoned to be on hand for the reading of Townsend's will. They sat in a sterile room filled with books of all sizes that peeked from behind shining glass; a room with light blue walls lined with strange oil paintings, ranging from balmy sea sides to a large bottle of Dr. Pepper soda; a room where a softball, split at its seams, sat in the center of a corner table, next to a small feather duster with blackened tips that obviously didn't belong in the immaculate room. The ceiling fan hummed constantly, but the room was still hot and sticky. Even the open window that brought in an occasional breeze and the scent of assorted flowers wasn't a relief to the tense people who sat around the smooth conference table. The table gleamed from a recent application of red cedar oil polish—there was no mistaking its smell. Above the scent of the flowers and oil, another odor hung in the air, an odor that emitted from the middle of the table. The smell of money hung heavy in the air, the smell of things desired and soon to be possessed—that is, if Townsend had kept his promises and recorded them in the black box that sat gleaming, like a beacon to a drowning person, in the middle of the table.

Margaret, the last person to enter the room, sashayed across the thick blue carpet, ignoring the indignant stares of Reverend Mack and the others. She took the seat next to her mother, Katie, and crossed her legs in plain view of everyone. Margaret and Katie sat directly behind Big Jim at one end of the conference table. The hot pink dress hugged Margaret's wide hips; the high collar, trimmed in white, caressed her olive neck, and exposed her bare flesh through the square opening on the front of the dress—according to the saleslady at Sherman's 'the smart lady's dress.' Shocked at Margaret's appearance and saucy entrance, Katie realized it was the dress she had forbade her to buy and sensed that this display could only mean that Charlie had been right; Margaret would defy her. Katie knew that Margaret could be selfish even when Margaret thought it wasn't so, and that if Margaret was unaware of her selfishness, it was because Katie had given too much—the freedom to attend school and the freedom to chose a job suitable to Margaret's talents. Katie had vowed that Margaret would not work in the cottonfields or for any white folks in their home, and Margaret never had. Katie could feel the tension rising between them and wondered how one day could make such a change in their lives. How could one day sever a relationship that had blossomed for eighteen years?

Katie prayed silently, and as she stared at the dark-eyed girl sitting beside her, a girl Katie hardly recognized, with smooth olive skin now smeared with rogue, a girl who had had in her possession, in her young life, more than Katie ever had in her thirty-five years. Katie wondered where did she go wrong—where had she failed? And now, like one of her troubled visions, her only daughter sat before her dressed like a two-penny whore. Her first impulse was to slap the wide hat out the window as far as the levee bank, and then rip the hot pink dress into shreds so fine, their only use would be stuffing for very soft pillows. But she realized she couldn't do that, not here. Wasn't that how white folks expected Negroes to act? No, Katie would not give them a show—one bandy-leg chicken in the coop was plenty.

The sliding wooden doors rumbled softly as Earline pulled them to a close, and at that moment Katie felt as if there were only two Negroes in the world. Even the knowledge of Earline's presence outside the door didn't alter the feeling that there were no more of her kind around and that she and her child were doomed to confront the sea of white faces huddled around the table alone.

Lee Adkins, owner of two grocery stores in town, a squatty man in a pale blue seersucker suit, occupied the chair at the head of the table, a pitcher of water near his elbow. On his right, Dr. Thomas Smith, a tall, thin man with red hair and bushy eyebrows, who had delivered practically everyone in town; Reverend Augustus Mack, a pie-faced man with a short nose that seemed to act as a sensor sniffing out sin, Pastor of the white Baptist church whose sermons filled their spirit and their lilly white hearts; Lloyd Robbins, a short man with a receding hairline, of Robbins Funeral Home, who buried all the dead with dignity and a long solemn face; Dellie, Townsend's daughter, a young girl with soft eyes and dreams of becoming another Bette Davis; Clara, with pale blue eyes and salt-and-pepper hair, widow of the deceased; and J.T., a thin-faced young man with piercing black eyes, the only son that Harrison sired, who stood to gain the sweat of his daddy's brow, the fruit of his daddy's labor, and the power to make or break the small town within seconds—depending on his inheritance. Big Jim Davis sat on the opposite end of the table across from Lee.

The dreams of these people were locked within the black box on the table, and Katie who wanted no part of the on going situation, looked at Margaret from the wide hat on her head to the low, open-toed sandals on her feet and knew she had no other way out of this predicament but to stand and accept the money before Margaret did. No one must ever believe that she was not in control of her own house. If she didn't stand and accept the money, Margaret would, and so to save face, she had no other choice. She turned away from Margaret, a feeling of despair and heaviness weighing on her breasts—only to face the cold, stony, dark eyes of J.T. He stared at her with such malice it reminded her of the pictures she had seen in the Bible of the sentinels guarding the gates of hell, their evil caught and fixed in time that brought bad dreams even to the holy. She quickly turned away.

Lee rose from the chair, a flush on his cheeks, and pushed his hands out in front of him like he was about to address an unruly mob. "We better git this here reading on with, for you all know that these things sometimes, depending on the wealth and wit of the deceased, can run into an all-night thing. And we know Harrison had quite a bit of both." There was a nervous stirring at the table as heads nodded and strained eyes watched Lee closely.

"And besides," Lee continued, "most of us is got to be up and about our business in the morning, it being Saturday and all. So to speed things up a bit, I'm gonna ask Big Jim to be the gentleman he is and stake his claim first. Lord knows come tomorrow, most of us will be heading to Rosie's looking for some of them golden brown biscuits what Katie magically stirs together," he said, a sheepish grin on his face.

"Might not be necessary to stake anything," Jim said, standing, his eyes fixed on Lee's. "Might not be nothing these folks want to claim," he added, turning to face Katie.

Katie glanced up at Jim, then lowered her eyes. She spoke to the floor. "Mr. Jim. We—I mean, I decided that if'n Mista Townsend left us something he wants us to have, then it might be the best thing if'n we accept." Silence hung heavy in the air, as though they expected someone to object, and Katie braced herself to hear J.T.'s order to remove them niggers from his house; but there was only silence.

Jim smiled, at Katie, then he turned and faced Lee. "Seems like there's gonna be some mighty hungry folks come tomorrow," he said, "as we aim to go by the record and wait our turn."

"Now Jim," Lee whined, you knows perfectly well how the reading of a will operates. First comes the family, then you got the next of kin, then the charities, and I don't rightly know when we'll git to them." He rolled his eyes in Katie's direction. "If that there letter you got is a copy, why don't you jest tell me where to find that particular provision that applies specifically to them, and I can read it first—you know, git it on out of the way. That way…"

"That way what, Lee?"

"Hell, Big Jim, you know what I mean."

"Yes, I know what you mean, and that's why I prefers to go according to the record. Ain't no need to git all riled, Lee. Why don't you take advantage of this opportunity, since you is acting in Tom Nolan's place? Git started on showing us country folks 'round here just how expert you is with the law." Jim dragged his chair towards the table and sat down. A stern look on his face said the issue was closed. Lee fumbled with the small key, his large hands sweating as he tried over and over to insert the metal key into the tiny hole. He stopped, then tried again. His hands still fumbling, every eye in the room fixed on the key as they waited. At last, the top sprang forth, revealing a folded paper with blue ink and embossed seals. The sight of the papers in Lee's hands caused a stir of action from everyone. Reverend Mack coughed nervously and tugged at the bow tie about his neck. Robbins pushed back from the table and began fanning with one of his hand-printed fans, the special ones, the ones with "Jesus Saves" on the front and "Robbins Funeral Home" on the back. Doc Smith shifted his lanky frame and crossed his ankles like a woman sitting in the front pew of church. Clara leaned forward, wrapped her arm around Dellie's shoulder, and lowered her head. Katie bowed her head, and Margaret inched to the edge of her chair. J.T. cocked his head to one side, staring with cold dark eyes at the wall. He sat poised like a statue, staring at the picture of the Dr. Pepper soda.

The comforts available in this grand room now became agents of discomfort. The plush red pillows from Paris that cushioned the high-backed chairs suddenly felt like stone, the brilliance of the neon lamps was suddenly too strong for the human eye, and the ceiling fan from New York hummed liked a giant, pesky bottle fly. But The greatest discomfort to all was Lee, a man described at his best as the death of any party, acting as executor over the will. Lee had been labeled a jack of all trades and master of none, and his latest brainstorm was to open a chain of grocery stores throughout the southern states. The first store of what was supposed to begin the chain had been partially opened for about six months—one side was opened for business, while the other still displayed the grand opening sign in the window. But every time someone went inside the store, they found Lee either leaning on the counter or sitting outside on a crate reading a law book. He often emphatically boasted that "the only difference between me and a real lawyer is a scrap of paper."

Since everyone knew of his latest project, it was a certainty that Townsend knew, for if anyone had the money to invest in his scheme, it was Townsend. Besides, Lee ran errands for Townsend that even school children felt were beneath them, ordering delicacies that ranged from pure corn-fed beef side to rattlesnakes steaks. The idea of Lee acting as executor was a sure sign that the reading would be an all-night event.

Dr. Thomas Smith, sixty years old, was anxious and ready to retire from active practice. He was tired of delivering babies, of sitting up nights with doddering old ladies with imaginary illnesses, and, most of all, looking at backsides. Backsides of all sizes and shapes, white and black, smooth and hairy, dimpled and plain, all afflicted with a common ailment: boils. Dr. Smith watched Lee holding the papers up towards the light for what Lee called a pre-examination of the condition of the papers as to its authenticity, validity, and hoped it would say that the funds to complete his new hospital, now only a structure of twisted iron bars standing south of Main Street on Highway 41 were available. He wanted to be head of the hospital and work within a secure institution that offered benefits. Townsend had seen the rationale in his proposal to build it after the fire at the white school—other than Smith's office, the only medical facility was fifty miles away—Margestown. Smith prayed that Townsend had not left such an important issue to J.T.'s discretion. As Smith watched Lee handling the papers, he held his head in his hands and wished that he had drowned Lee at birth.

Reverend Augustus Mack wanted to be mayor. He was fifty years old and could be seen coming and going, spreading the words of God and a few of his own. He could be heard delivering his messages on the "True Christian" at community meetings every Wednesday at the white school, at yearly graduations at the Negro school, and at neighboring churches when time allowed. He wanted to go on the radio to broadcast on Saturday nights to spread his moral judgments around town. He had asked Townsend for money to build a hall for town meetings where he could broadcast to a radius of fifty miles and still be in touch with the town folk. He often stated that the niggers simply went wild on Saturday nights and even some of the good white folk as well—something that he would remedy should he be elected mayor. He brushed his hair with the back of his hand, a habit of his, especially when annoyed.

Lloyd Robbins, forty years old, was the funeral director and the coroner in town, but limited this service to pronouncing death only when Dr. Smith was not around. Most Negroes, however, chose to wait for Dr. Smith, since they felt sometimes Robbins seemed to mix his occupations and act a bit prematurely—like the time Joe Cassidy was shot and lay bleeding in the streets. When Joe's family arrived, they found his body inside of Robbins Funeral Home and embalming procedures started. Robbins swore Joe was dead, while witnesses swore otherwise. But Robbins was fair when it came to burial policies—he sold two-hundred dollar burials to everyone in town for sixty-five cents a week. He had no idea why he was here—funeral arrangements had already been made—unless Townsend had decided to favor him with the silver limousine, as Robbins had often admired the machine. He sighed and hoped it was something for giving up his time to listen to Lee.

Big Jim was here with a letter requesting him to be on hand at the reading to represent Katie and her daughter. He hoped once and for all that Lee would prove to be the ass that he usually portrayed.

Harrison Townsend Jr., twenty-two years old, had never wanted for anything except the power to manipulate the lives of others. He never had real friends and didn't trust anyone. He was epileptic, a disease defined by most as a mark of insanity. He never like Negroes, not even the ones who worked in his home, and he disliked Katie even more than the others. She was different, a white-skinned Negro that even his daddy had feared. Katie's presence made him uneasy—he hoped the trinket that his daddy had left her would sever all relations and obligations. And Lee, he disliked even more than Katie.

Clara Townsend, fifty-six years old, who had never wanted for anything in her life, other than Townsend, now wanted this house badly. And Dellie, seventeen and starry-eyed—all she wanted was a way out. A way that meant she would never have to come back to this town as long as she lived. They seemed to draw themselves up in a shell when Lee removed the papers from the box.

The document fluttered in Lee's trembling hands as he carefully unfolded it, placed it on the end of the spacious table, and thumbed through the stack like a teller counting new money. He snapped the papers, making everyone jump, to free them of creases and, taking his time, scanned the first four pages. Lee reached for his necktie with his free hand, slid the red-and black striped tie down from the awkward knot, glanced at Clara, and, finally, after clearing his throat three times, addressed the group: "Now, folks, from what I can make out, it appears to be a standard will—a bit odd, but standard nonetheless, until we gits down to page four. Then it seems that Townsend goes into detail to explain what he wants done with Ralston Valley—but everyone here knows Ralston Valley was his prized possession." He bent over and thumbed through the papers again, and a heavy sigh went out across the room. Lee cleared his throat one more time and finally began reading: "I know this is unusual, calling you here so soon after my death; usually, the intentions of the deceased aren't made known until the dirt had been thrown in his face and the grave closed. That's right, it was me, Harrison Townsend Sr., who sent for you, not J.T. I'm sure most of you thought otherwise and that he couldn't wait to get his hands on my money. Well, I know he can't wait, but nevertheless, it was my doing.

"It has never been a habit of mine to surprise anybody. I always was the type to tell it like it was, let people know where I stood—always hated pretenders. And that's why I wanted my will read before my funeral—which I know will be a splendid one, knowing how Robbins loves money." All eyes focused on Robbins, as Lee paused for effect—a method he knew was often used by trail lawyers. Robbin's face turned a fiery red, something no one present had ever seen before in any funeral director. They were always that pasty white color, anemic-looking—even the Negro funeral directors in Margestown. Robbins began fanning so fast the word 'Jesus Saves' became a blur to the eye.

Lee cleared his throat for the fifth time and continued. "I can almost hear the eloquent words that will topple from Mack's tongue as he stands tall in the pulpit with his big arms outstretched towards the ceiling. I always loved to see him do that. It was like God was getting ready to take him in His arms. Mack, I want you personally to invite everyone here to be at my funeral as a special favor to me." It was now Reverend Mack who turned red, but not from embarrassment. He was outraged that Townsend would ask him to invite niggers to his church. He nodded his head stiffly towards Katie, who acknowledge his gesture with a slight bow of her head. After another pause, Lee spoke with a booming voice, "And now to the reading of the will. 'I, Harrison Lyles Townsend Sr., commonly known as and who sometimes appear of record as Harrison L. Townsend Sr., or Harrison Townsend Sr., and being of sound mind declare that this document, dated July 23, 1937, is my last will and testament; and revokes all former wills and codicils by me made'"

J.T.'s head spun around to face Lee, his dark eyes startlingly intense. This was a new will! Not the original he had witness some five years ago, the one he had memorized word for word. Immediately, he sensed that Katie was in some way responsible for this change, and his dark eyes sought hers for confirmation. But Katie's head was bent in prayer. He was convinced that somehow it was all her doing, for ever since she had stepped into their house two years ago, he had noticed a change in his daddy's demeanor. A thin film of perspiration formed above his top lip, and for the first time during this assembly, uncertainty clouded his thoughts. He shifted his icy stare, focusing directly on Lee, as if to command him to retract the words.

J.T.'s stare, so cold, so intense, stopped Lee abruptly, and he looked around the room in a state of perplexity. He came to his feet just as the doors rolled open, and, Max, the chauffeur, hat in hand, entered the room, a sheepish look on his face—he was late. J.T.'s eyes blazed and he turned and snapped, "Max get the hell out of here!" Max waved an arm and stammered, "But, J.T., I'm supposed to be here. J.T. stared at him until Max turned red, his face filled with shame, then left, hurrying past Earline, muttering. Once the door was closed again, and everyone had settled back in their seats, Lee rose slowly from the chair, faced J.T. with an apologetic look and without further hesitation made his delivery, a delivery that surely would make history within this small metropolis and be talked about for decades to come.

Lee's clear, crisp voice cut through the hot, sticky air as he read: "I, Harrison Lyles Townsend, Sr., commonly known as and who sometime appear on record as Harrison L. Townsend, Sr., declare that this document is my last will and testament; and revoke all former wills and codicils by me made. And, as I have taken into consideration the vast wealth of my wife, Clara, and the fact that this state is not a community property state, I do bequeath a somewhat minimal amount of my estate to her. Therefore, I bequeath the sum of fifty-thousand dollars to become hers immediately; the forty acres of land on the southwest junction of Marlin, commonly called 'Witherspoon,' to use for whatever purpose she deems fit—even to plant creeping myrtles; the right to reside in the house at St. Mark and Vandroff

Streets as long as she does not remarry; and, lastly, the title and complete ownership of the black limousine she favored so much. Records and titles of what belongs to me are retained in a safety deposit box at the bank of Bennettsville and available, if need be, for probate."

A low moan escaped from Clara's lips. She had expected Harrison to be his usual self—crude. It was just like him to go out in that style, the shrewd businessman to the end, putting that property in her name, now made her a part of the shady connections that transpired there—rich farming land turned into a cotton patch by using cheap Negro labor. She smiled.

"To my children, Harrison Jr., and Dellie Kay, I bequeath the bulk of my estate. To my son, Junior, I leave the above-mentioned house in ownership and title; the Bennettsville Cotton Gin and its accessories, being named Transorient and Franklin, respectively; the Kewanna Granary and its accessories being named the same as above; one-hundred thousand dollars of which one third shall be distributed to him and become absolutely his on his twenty-fifth birthday. One half of the remainder shall be so distributed when he reaches the age of thirty, and he shall receive the balance when he reaches the age of thirty-five years." Everyone knew Townsend was rich, but just how rich was a mystery even to the head of the bank, Tom Nolan, as stocks and exchanges of funds for Townsend were constantly changing from one figure to another. But most anyone in the room would have moved mountains to receive a legacy such as the one left to J.T. It was a dream of many people to be wealthy and young at the same time, a combination of riches rarely seen. And yet J.T.'s disappointment was evident to everyone. His jaw went slack as though he realized that he was still under his daddy's thumb.

"To my daughter, Dellie Kay," the voice boomed through the air, "I bequeath Ralston Valley. Only to Dellie could I leave my most treasured possession, the haven that I scratched out with sheer will, since only she feels the same about the land as I do. Even though the monetary value exceeds two million dollars, the natural beauty far exceeds that and it is because I believe that only Dellie will strive to keep the land in the hands of the Townsend's, its rightful owners, that I leave it to her care. And upon completion of college, she is to take sole ownership of Ralston valley and reside as well on its premises.

But until that time, decisions required to maintain and properly keep the premises in order of its custom will be made by Tom Nolan, a man I trust explicitly. Also, to Dellie, I bequeath a trust equal to that of my son's but with some necessary differences. Dellie will receive an substantial income for her needs, but there will be no drafts on the principle except at the sole discretion of the trustee, in order to meet a dire need. Upon the death of my daughter, her trust shall continue for the benefit of her children and their children as long as the law permits. No land and titles bequeathed to my son or daughter can be either sold or transferred. Only in the event of death can the land be passed down in the order of their children respectively."

Dellie let out a long sigh, shook her head, and leaned against her mother shoulder. Immediately, Clara folded her arms around the girl.

The 'smart lady's dress,' like a cut rose out of water, had begun to wilt. The high-necked collar was wrinkled from Margaret's constant tugging, and the cuffs that bordered the short sleeves were limp as old lettuce from the pushing and pulling she had given them. Margaret was very uncomfortable, as she had deliberately broken the Pentecostal code of dress, and being subjected to the scrutiny of her mother's cold eye produced flashes of heat all over her body. She wanted desperately to snatch the fan from Robbins' hand—to cool herself, but mostly to shield her face from Katie's roving eyes, eyes that seemed to travel the entire width of the room and somehow always returned to the dress. Come tomorrow, she expected to be the talk of the town. The money she received would probably be stretched into millions by tomorrow evening, and she would have come to the white folks' house practically naked. She expected she would be the subject of Reverend Washington's text come Sunday, and justified her actions as being the lesser of two evils. Had she stood and claimed the money without giving her mother fair warning, Katie's shame would have been far greater than hers was right now. And she was so ashamed that she could not bring herself to look in her mother's face. Margaret pretended to stare out the window, acting as though the proceedings before her were nothing. But not only did she hear everything Lee said, she was quite fascinated by the ugly little man with the bald spot who commanded the attention of everyone with a snap of old papers.

The papers snapped again and Lee announced that the tertiary beneficiaries were next. She held her breath as she realized they should come somewhere in this category. She listened closely as Lee called Doc Smith's name and reported, "Funds reserved for completion of Townsend Community Hospital; funds reserved for operational equipment and its accessories; Doc Smith shall be appointed Chief of Staff for one year and the sole administrator shall be Harrison Townsend, Jr." She watched Doc Smith bend over and hold his head in his hands. The other beneficiaries followed: Robbins would receive title and ownership of the silver limousine. Reverend Mack's deacon board would have to raise one-tenth of the cost to build the town hall before funds would be released from Townsend's trust. A donation of two thousand dollars was on hand to help Lee build the chain of stores whenever he was ready. Max, the chauffeur was to have a life-time job at the family's residence and two thousand dollars. And after what seemed to be an endless list of names or charities she never knew existed, the words she had waited to hear trickled from Lee's mouth like honey. "To Sister Katie Mae Dunson, Missionary of the church of God In Christ, I leave in her trust, the sum of fifteen thousand dollars," Lee looked up in surprise and fingered the top of his head, his face twisted in puzzlement. "I must have made a mistake," he declared sheepishly.

"No, Lee, it ain't no mistake," Big Jim's voice boomed. He rose from the chair, pulled the letter from his shirt pocket and, unfolding it, pushed it across the table. "That's exactly what my copy says, fifteen thousand dollars." The thin spectacles fell down off the nose of Reverend Mack and cracked on the hard table; Dr. Smith's bushy eyebrows went up, forming a perfect upside-down V, Robbins' arm gained momentum and the fan practically disintegrated; Clara's blue eyes widened until they became rivers; Margaret, for the first time that evening, turned and looked directly at Katie and smiled. J.T. stood, his body trembling with outrage, and firmly asked, "When do we go to probate, Lee?" Still in shock, Lee turned, faced J.T. and muttered. "Huh? Hell, I don't rightly know, J.T., but knowing how thorough Nolan is in these matters, I'd say around next week sometime."

J.T. seemed satisfied with Lee's answer and sat back down. Lee's voice cracked like static electricity cutting the air as he continued. "I bequeath the sun of fifteen thousand dollars to Sister Katie Mae Dunson for her daughter Margaret to be used for her education. I made a promise to God the first night Sister Katie laid her healing hands on me, a promise I intend to keep. I vowed for each year I lived after her prayers I would leave her five thousand dollars, and as soon as I got on my feet, after the first visit, I had Nolan set it up. It was not until after my investigation into her character that I found, due to her religious beliefs, she would not accept the money, so I chose to leave it to her daughter for whom she was working so hard to send to college. Sister Katie is to be guardian of the funds. As I said, I intend to keep my promise to God, so I chose to insert a no-contest provision in this will to ensure just that. And this state being a 'gift over' state, if any heir or any other beneficiary contest this gift, their legacy is forfeited and is to immediately become the property of the named person contested against."

The confidence left J.T.'s face; he whirled around in the chair, looking first at Lee and then at Katie. His eyes blazed and he could envision his father standing before him pointing a fat finger, and exposing the long scar on his hand. He glanced at his mother who appeared to be smiling, and he knew there was no way around this tangled web of legality. But there were other ways to deal with niggers, and he knew them all. Only the shuffling of papers could be heard as Lee folded the will neatly and stuffed it back inside the black box. "Now folks," he said, "you will probably receive a letter real soon from Tom Nolan, telling you when and how to go about receiving these gifts." He snapped the lid down hard on the box and locked it with ease.

Lee was the first to leave the room, pushing his heavy frame towards the door, the box tucked carefully under his arm. As if it was a cue, everyone began pushing chairs back from the table. Katie rose, not quite sure of all that had happened, but judging from the radiant beam shining in Margaret's eyes, the money and all the problems they were sure to encounter would soon become theirs. The sliding doors were rolled back, exposing the huge frame of Earline Simpson who stood leaning against the door like an usher, with a glove pointing the way to the outer door. There was a brief exchange of condolences with the bereaved family as each person headed out, and during the pretentious display of grief, Margaret gained J.T.'s attention with an exaggerated bow of her head. The wide hat dipped low to one side, the other side high like an eagle cruising on an angle. A wide smile intended to tease J.T. suddenly diminished into a thin line as J.T.'s black piercing eyes burned through the linen dress and seemed to sear her flesh. A sudden, icy shiver passed across her body, similar to what the old folks said meant "somebody just stepped on your grave," and she stood glued to the spot until Katie, realizing the situation, pulled her away. Quickly, they stepped past Earline, whose jaws were quivering, her mouth twisted like she had had a stroke, but they did not stop. They expected Earline to explode. By the time Katie and Margaret were pulling the covers about them, everyone in town would know what had transpired here tonight at Townsend's house.

As they stepped outside, a cool breeze greeted them, and Margaret removed the hat, holding it down by her side, the heels of her sandals clicking softly on the warm pavement.

"Well, Mama," she said, "what do you have to say about it?"

"I'm ashamed to be walking next to you right now, Margaret," Katie replied dryly.

"I'm ashamed that I had to do this, Mama," Margaret admitted, walking with her head down.

"Well, why did you do it then?" Katie said, stopping under the street lamp.

"Because I didn't want to hurt you."

"Hump, what you call what you did then, child?" Katie said, flinging her arms out before her, her purse dangling around her wrist. "If that wadn't hurt, I don't ever want to feel it, shaming me in front of the white folks like that."

"Shaming you in front of the white folks! Is that all you ever think of is white folks?" Margaret said with outrage and demanding eyes.

"No, I thinks on a whole heap of things, likes why the courthouse, the house what is supposed to give out justice, sits next to the funeral home. And why there is a bullpen in the big jail house, when there ain't no bulls. And why we don't never have enough money to live better than the way we do. And white folks, you right, I do think a lot 'bout them. I often wonders why they hanged my pappy, and how come that there courthouse allowed them to leave free mens."

"What?" Margaret cried. "You never told me that! You never told me Pappy was hanged. You never… Why, Mama? Why didn't you tell me?"

"Lots of things I didn't tell you, Margaret. Lots of things. Why? 'Cause they hurt too bad to talk 'bout em. But I reckon tonight is the time to do just that. If you can dress like that and go against me and the church, I reckon it's time to tell you all 'bout those things that I've been holding back," Katie said, shaking her head and continuing the walk.

"Yes, I would think it was about time you told me every thing. I don't understand why you haven't told me this before."

"It's simple, Margaret, I didn't want to let the air out of you, child."

THE GREAT CRY

Later that night, when the supper dishes had been cleared away and the water brought into the house, Katie's thoughts turned to serious matters: she knew that Margaret would not be put off tonight; and that she would not only have to tell her the details around Pappy's death, but other things that would surely turn up as a result. She removed the white uniform, examined the collar and shook her head from side to side. She would have to wash it before retiring and she was not surprised that it was soaked, as today had been very upsetting. She walked to the tall bed, the uniform draped across her shoulder, the floor boards creaking loudly under her feet. She could hear the old swing bumping softly against the house. Margaret always carried her troubles to the swing, where she would push herself and bump the house until she had either worked it out in her mind or decided talk was the best thing. And Katie knew that soon Margaret would be standing before her with wide, questioning eyes—eyes that would not let her rest until she told Margaret everything. She sat down on the side of the four-poster bed, her face drawn tight, her movements deliberately slow. She looked around the room. The small neat dresser was unadorned. The only items that sat upon it were the tall, slender red can of Mavis Talc, a small hand mirror that belonged to her mammie, and one cut-glass bowl in which she kept her long hairpins. The rest of the room was simple, a plain wooden chest of drawers that didn't quite match the bed and a radio that was never used, on tall, slender legs in the corner of the room. Pappy had built the six-room house with his own hands. Now it was divided equally—Margaret had the three rooms on the far side of the house, and Katie had the other three. They shared the kitchen on Katie's side, because Margaret was not a very good cook and because Margaret used her spare room for sewing to add to their income, which they pooled to share the expenses.

The century had just turned when Pappy built this house and the homes within the area were fresh and new. At least that is what Katie had been told. She remembered Pappy's stories about the move to Bennettsville, about how he had decided this was just the place for his family, and about how rich the land was and sure to yield crops that people could prosper from, not just live off. And how Pappy was buried so far out in the fields that the only way Mammie could get his attention in an emergency was to hang a white sheet on the clothesline. The land was not that vast anymore; most of it had been sectioned off and sold lot by lot to white land-holders. Katie had sold all but five acres, and all the land she kept, excluding the spot off from the far lot where Pappy was buried and the spot where the old house stood, was a source of income. The far lot was worked by Charlie and Luther for a small share of the income from the soybeans. One part she used for breeding chickens—they brought in money all year round. Another part was used for a vegetable garden, a source of food and extra money during the summer months. These five acres she vowed never to sell. Nor would she ever leave them.

The front screen door on Margaret's side of the house screeched loudly and after a few seconds bumped softly against the facing of the door. Katie knew that Margaret had caught the door with the heel of her shoe, a habit of hers especially when something was bothering her. Once, when Margaret had been upset, she had managed to poke her heel through the screen completely. Not entering the room, Margaret peeked her head inside the door to Katie's room. She had scrubbed away most of the make-up, but had missed some of the rouge, and it sat like little half-moons underneath her dark eyelashes. She resembled a small child who expected some kind of punishment for bad behavior, but Katie was not fooled; she had seen that desperate look before, the one that stated quite adamantly that she wanted something and was determined to get it. She strained her neck around the door and asked, "Mama, are you still mad at me?"

"Nope," Katie answered quickly, craning her head around the bed post. "I ain't mad no more. Ain't no need of staying mad 'cause that won't change what done happened." She dismissed her reverie and slid the circular, flesh-colored garters from her slender legs.

"Can I come over and sit with you for a while? I need to talk to you," Margaret begged, with the voice of a very small child.

"I reckon it's all right if you come over; ain't gonna be much sleeping round here tonight anyways. Come on in, child," Katie replied softly. She shook the nylons in the air and watched the fine particles that flew from them. She could see Margaret hugging the bed post from the corner of her eyes, but avoided looking at Margaret as she rose from the bed and carried the nylons and the uniform into the large kitchen where she placed them into the round, white washpan. She grabbed the water bucket from the back of the table, pouring half of the water into the pan, and carrying the bucket to the stove, she filled the kettle. "I'm gonna need more water, and it's pitch black outside," she sighed, as she walked back to the wash table and flicked the wall switch, illuminating the back yard and revealing an aged, rusty pump under the circle of light.

Margaret followed Katie from the bedroom, and grabbed at the opportunity to help her mother, took the bucket before Katie could disagree and, bounding down the rickety step, said, "I'll get the water, Mama." Her gait had changed, she walked upright with firm quick steps which propelled her forward without much body movement—like she had been taught in church, and not like the sassy hussy that had strolled into Townsend's house earlier that evening. Katie lit the stove with a stick match and put the kettle on. One of these days, she thought, I'm gonna have running water, and she suddenly smiled as she realized those were the very words that Pappy often used. But after tonight it might not be just a dream any longer. Money can make drastic changes in a person's lifestyle, especially if that person is poor.

She looked across the space at the well-used ice box and then to the dining table where four mix-matched chairs leaned. It was as though she was unconsciously taking inventory, for in the back of her mind she was sure Margaret would insist upon some changes, such as running water and an indoor toilet. Katie realized it would be hard to refuse Margaret, mainly because she had always been such a practical girl. She wondered if she was making too much out of all of this. Perhaps Margaret was right. Perhaps they would be the exception and be allowed to keep the money without problems. After all, Townsend was a man who planned wisely and had taken steps to ensure that they got the money. But she remembered J.T.'s black stare at the reading and dismissed her wishful thinking. She knew that she could not rely on the wisdom of a dead man.

"Mama, look!" Margaret interrupted her thoughts, setting the bucket on the wash table, her thin mouth in a pout.

"What now?" Katie mumbled. Leaning over Margaret's shoulder, she peeked out the door into the white spot light that fell across the yard to the black earth, making the grass look unreal.

"See, Mama. It's a dog, and a white one at that. See." Margaret pointed towards the black ground.

"I don't see nothing," Katie protested. "Must be your wild imagination, 'cause if'n a dog was in that yard, them chickens would be raising cain." She waved her hand to dismiss further discussion about the dog. But in the back of her mind, she was trying to remember who owned a white dog.

"You got your clothes together for choir rehearsal?" Katie asked, stepping back to the table.

"Yes, Mama, but I'm not going to choir rehearsal tomorrow, and I informed Sister Dunne this morning not to expect me."

"Well, now," Katie stammered, turning away from the table to look at Margaret. "It seems like you'se been doing a lot of changing here lately, ain't you? 'Sputed my word 'bout the money, broke the dress code of the church, teased Junior Townsend to his face—jest asking for trouble—and now you ain't going to choir practice."

"No, Mama. I'm not going, and that's that!" Margaret repeated, slamming the dipper into the bucket, splashing herself with water. She quickly brushed the water spot that darkened the front of her housecoat, inhaled deeply, and let out a long sigh.

"I guess you think you is all grown up now. Don't have to do nothing that don't come up to your standards of thinking. Well, I thank God that I ain't never in my life gone against my mammie or pappy's word. And I'se glad that I can say that up to this day. Can you, Margaret? Can you say that?" Katie challenged, her gray eyes dancing. The water came to a screaming boil. Margaret stepped away from the wash table and leaned against the facing of the back door. Katie removed the kettle, poured the hot water into the pan, and mixed it with the cool water already in the pan, making small circles with her hand. Taking the brown bar of soap from the saucer she began scrubbing the dark line that covered the collar of the uniform. A few seconds passed and Katie looked up from the collar. "Child, close that door," she said, "everything in the world is coming in here." She returned to scrubbing the collar and heard Margaret sigh again, then the soft bump of the screen door as it closed. Margaret leaned against the inner door, watching Katie dip the collar up and down in the water then pick up the soap again and begin scrubbing. Katie suddenly stopped and stared at the soap in her hands as though it had changed before her eyes. "You don't realize how lucky you is to have a mama. My mammie walked off and left us one day. She left me, Addie, and my brother Robert some twenty years ago. But I told you that…"

"No, Mama. You never told me any such thing. All you ever said was you didn't know if your mammie was alive and that Pappy had died suddenly," Margaret said, folding her arms across her chest.

Katie, as though in a trance, didn't seem to hear Margaret and continued. She appeared to talk more to herself than to Margaret, like she was cleansing her soul by trying to fit the pieces together. "She and Pappy had a big argument 'bout a bar of soap. Oh, it weren't no homemade soap like this, but some store-bought kind what Pappy had brung home from one of his trips to town. It was such a silly thing to carry on the way they did, but after the argument she jest walked away and never came back. Deep down inside we all knew her leaving had nothing to do with soap, and I cried many a nights wondering if I might had done something that made her mad enough to walk off. She always seemed to git so upset at every little thing that I did. I was sixteen and didn't know nothing but my ma and pa," Katie spoke to the washpan.

Margaret inched away from the door, walking sideways, her eyes focused on Katie's stooped back. She eased down in the chair at the far end of the kitchen table and stared at the crystal-cut sugar bowl, while she strained her ears to hear every word that Katie said.

"Don't know whatever came of my mammie," Katie continued, in a slow even tone. "Don't know to this day. Pappy looked all over for Mammie, but nobody seed her, or if'n they did, wouldn't say. Folks in them days was too scared to do much talking, excepting maybe a few; but even them what was known to see and hear everything around town swore they hadn't seen Mammie."

"And you haven't heard from her since?" Margaret said, stunned at hearing her mother speak of such things.

"No, not a word, not a scratch," Katie said, standing up, her eyes focused somewhere above Margaret's head, her face blank, like a lost person trying to find his way home. She released the uniform, letting it soak in the brownish water and looked at her wet, wrinkled hands. "It was as though the earth jest swallowed her up and buried her along with all its other mysteries. I never laid eyes on my mammie again, and that was twenty years ago. I spect she's dead by now. You see, child, things ain't always what they seems. Mammie ain't left us on account of no soap. She left on account of other things—bad things. The same kind of things this here money is gonna cause." Katie said, a hollowness to her voice as she cleared her throat. In silence, Katie rinsed the uniform, rolled it inside a large white towel to absorb the water, shook it out until most of the wrinkles were gone, and clipped it to the wire above the open back door.

"Was Pappy a white man or a very white Negro?" Margaret asked, breaking the silence. "Zara Lee said many white folks are really Negroes."

"He was white, ain't no question on that," Katie answered firmly.

"Well, what happened to Pappy?" Margaret asked, turning around in the chair and looking down at her mother as she spread a towel beneath the dress to catch the excess water.

"I told you, they hung him, child," Katie snapped, getting up from her knees, blood in her cheeks from the strain, and surprise in her voice at the direct question.

"Who are 'they,' Mama?" Margaret pressed. It had always been this way whenever she and her mother talked about Pappy's death. Katie seemed to hide her meaning in a cloud of smoke, referring to non-existent people—"they," "them," or "folks." Major incidents were often reduced to one sentence, or a phrase: they killed him, they shot him, they hung him. And always, Margaret was left trying to translate the conversation into language that she could understand.

"White folks—who else?" Katie flung the words across the room at the wide-eyed girl who sat staring at her unaware of the rouge lingering on her cheeks. The buzz of a mosquito seized Margaret's attention, and she clapped both hands above her head, making a loud noise that caused Katie to squeeze her eyes shut and open them cautiously.

Angry from missing the humming pest and from her mother's evasiveness, Margaret, her arms still stretched apart, yelled, "Mama, will you please, for once in your life, tell me what happened?"

The crickets chirped loudly in the night and the neighbor's dogs barked off in the distance. The water trickled from the uniform onto the towel, thumping softly. The mosquito had disappeared. Katie sat down in the chair at the head of the table, a wisp of black hair clinging to her damp forehead. She brushed it aside with her wet finger, and for a moment was quiet. As though the crystal bowl was a magnet, she focused her attention on its glimmering brilliance. She began. "It was the year 1921 and it was cropping time. Folks had worked hard all that year, but now it was crucial that they work even harder to git the crops in. Everybody was busy. Men was hauling beans and corn, starting to scrap the cotton and do the slaughtering; women was canning and smoking meat, making soap—even the chillens was tending the chickens and other stock that was to be kept. It wadn't a minute to lose before the frost set in, and everyone was working hard to put up everything they could before it came. That was all we had to worry 'bout then, hard work and making ends meet. And we was glad of it, 'cause ever since Mammie left, some two years then, the white folks had stopped picking on us. It was almost peaceful. You could tell that by the laughter in Pappy's face. He didn't seem so worried like he used to."

"What do you mean by peaceful?" Margaret probed, resting her chin in her hands and gazing into Katie's eyes.

"I mean, all we had to worry 'bout was doing our work. All of a sudden we didn't have to worry 'bout white folks riding through our crops, setting fire to the barn, and calling us niggers, pickannies, or calling Pappy white trash. Ever since Mammie had gone, they didn't bother us no more; it was like her leaving took some of the evil from their hearts. And I often wondered if—she being the only dark one among us—she figured that's what would happen.

"Well, anyway, we was living without that kind of trouble, and me and Addie had done got married. I married your daddy, James Dunson, who had moved here from Tennessee a year before, and Addie married a young man named Frank Ellison, from over in Kentucky. Pappy was real proud of us, but you could tell it in his face he didn't like the idea of Addie moving so far away. Still, everything had been accepted. And then suddenly it all started up again. But this time it was different. It wadn't jest us the insults was directed at, but at all the Negroes in town.

"And white folks was suddenly keeping to themselves. Even the ones what was working for Pappy all of a sudden quit. We didn't know what to make out of it, until one night me and Addie overheard Pappy and Charlie discussing what was going on. They was talking 'bout a race riot."

"A race riot!" Margaret interrupted, slamming her hands down on the table. "That's impossible."

"Hump, that shows what you know, child," Katie said, tossing her head and looking squarely into Margaret's bewildered face. "There's plenty that happened wadn't put in them books you is always reading. Well, it seems there had been a race riot over in Tulsa, where twenty-one white men and sixty Negroes was killed before the fighting stopped. I never did git the story straight on how it started but I think it was on account of some Klansmen setting fire to some Negroes in a store. Now, this riot had happened three or four months ago, but news was slow in gitting round in them days, and we figured them white folks in town had jest got wind of it from the way they was all acting. We listened as Pappy told Charlie. We had no doubts that Pappy knew what he was talking 'bout, but we also had no idea how this race riot in Tulsa concerned us. We didn't dare ask, 'cause men folks didn't discuss things like that with women, so we cornered our brother, Robert, and got him to explain. Robert said what it meant was that the white folks was mad 'bout some white men gitting kilt, and scared the same thing could happen here. So they was out to get their revenge on the Negroes and even white folks who was sympathetic with the Negroes. Well, colored folks was scared to leave for fear of being caught alone on the roads at night, and scared to stay 'cause they knew something bad might happen. Most of them didn't have no money, and if they left their cropping undone, that meant they wouldn't have no money for a mighty long time. I reckon Pappy was scared, too, but he was the kind that held everything close to his chest, kept everything locked in him. But I reckon that don't matter to nobody."

"Yes, it does matter, Mama. I've often wondered what you were feeling inside and wished you would tell me, but you do the same thing to me that you say Pappy did," Margaret said, looking at Katie.

Katie drew back, her face filled with surprise and suddenly she knew that Margaret was a woman and not a child any longer. An understanding passed between them. Margaret leaned in closer, her face soft with concern, and Katie's voice seemed to lose some of its cutting edge. The white uniform loomed above them; the nylons, forgotten, soaked in the washpan across the room. Katie gazed into Margaret's eyes, but she was back in another time, another part of her life that somehow didn't seem real now—more like a dream. She placed one hand over Margaret's and held it. "I don't like to even think 'bout those days, Margaret, let alone talk 'bout them. That's one reason I never talked to you 'bout it before. Somehow it didn't seem right to bring up so much ugliness. The only way I know to explain the misery folks was feeling is to compare their grief to the 'great cry.'"

"The great cry?"

"The cry that was heard throughout the land of Egypt when God sent his plague of death to all the first-born children. But instead of folks falling dead mysteriously, colored folks was found hanging from trees. Some was taken to the outskirts of town and hung, while others, like Pappy, was hung right in town. He was hung from that big tree right outside of Mr. Cook's Real Estate Office—you know the one. Oh, the office wadn't there then, but it's the same spot," she assured Margaret, nodding her head and clearing her throat again. "You see, they hung people in town when they wanted to make a point, one that everybody, but especially the Negroes, would understand. And they wanted to make a point 'bout Pappy's family. Hall, the ring-leader of the mob, had a score he personally wanted to settle with Pappy. They was old enemies. I can remember it like it was yesterday. Miss Lester walking down the road hollering to the top of her voice that they had done kilt her boy. And me and Pappy run out to help, but her black face trembled like she was having one of them spells, and her eyes got big as saucers with fear when Pappy touched her on the arm. She passed out right at his feet and her body never stopped shaking. Well, we got her home, and that was how we found out that they had started to lynch Negroes in town. But later that evening, Frank, Addie's husband, told Pappy that they better try and leave that night before things got worse than what they was. We still hadn't heard of nobody but Miss Lester's boy gitting kilt. Pappy was dead set against Frank taking Addie over to Kentucky now and told him so. I mean, they had a terrible row, Pappy's eyes blazing like burning coals. But Frank stood his ground and wouldn't give in to Pappy and told him he was scared for Addie to stay; so Pappy, seeing he had no choice, gave in. And we all said our good-byes—I nearly hugged my sister's neck off her body—and they loaded up and left that evening fore it turned dark.

"Later on in the night, the Jenkins' little boy woke us and told Pappy them white men had Addie and Frank up town and was gitting ready to do something awful. They all knowed Addie by sight, so it musta been their way of drawing Pappy out of the house. Pappy dressed and got his gun, and I screamed, 'Don't go, Pappy.' I yelled at your daddy to go with him, but there was a streak in his eyes that said he was a coward, and Pappy seed it too. By that time, Robert run into the room half dressed, almost tripping over his pants legs. He was making to go with Pappy. Pappy with coldness in his eyes as he looked at your daddy, told Robert not to come with him, that he better stay and protect Katie gal."

There were tears in Katie's eyes and she stopped talking to catch her breath and calm her racing heart. She cleared her throat and dabbed at her eyes with her fingers. Margaret's eyes also filled with tears and they streamed down her cheeks, mingling with the red rouge and making it appear that her eyes were bleeding.

"Them was the last words I heard my pappy say, 'stay and protect Katie-gal.'" She shook her head from side to side.

"Charlie brung him home the next morning in the buckboard. His neck was burned from rope marks, and there was a great gash above his right eye. Charlie said that Pappy jest right out and killed Hall. Oh, he didn't tell me, but I heard him talking 'bout it. Said when

Pappy saw they was fixing to hang Addie and Frank from their wagon—had the wagon under a tree and they was tied—he just walked up on that mob firing, not changing a word with nobody until he had got Addie and Frank loose, and sent them hurrying on their way. Charlie said Pappy held that spot until Addie and Frank's wagon was out of sight and it was a spell of quiet before that passel got enough nerve to finish what they had started. Pappy had done made it back to his horse when Hall's brother snuck up on him and hit him across the face with a chunk of fence post. Then the rest of that mob jumped him and wrestled him to the ground. Charlie said it took a heap of them to do it, and I knows that was the truth 'cause my pappy was a big strapping man. By the time Charlie reached them, Pappy was hanging—dead. Charlie was a-watching all of this from the top of the levee. Most of this he seed, except for the times he was running and falling down the levee trying to git down to them. But by the time Charlie got down there, the mob was gone, only Pappy hanging there all by himself. Wadn't a thing left for Charlie to do but cut him down and bring him home. Borrowed old man Cole's buckboard, brung him home. We buried Pappy out back and weren't nobody there but Charlie, Robert, and myself, not even a preacher—excusing Miss Lester who had done buried her boy the day before. She felt guilty 'bout acting scared of Pappy 'cause he was white, and kept splaining over and over that she was jest plain scared, that you jest don't know what white folks to trust in times like them. Your daddy had done slipped off sometime that very night Pappy died, and I was glad, 'cause I couldn't stood the sight of him after that. The last time I saw him, he was in one of the bull pens in the big house, where they hold the colored prisoners till they send them up the road to the penitentiary. That is why I give your last name as Younger—my maiden name—I didn't want you attached to no coward and no thief, even if'n he is your daddy. And here we is in the light again, Margaret, with this here money. It's bound to start up all over again, jest mark my word."

"But, Mama," Margaret insisted, her voice shaky and filled with tears. "We have law now. This is 1938. And besides, the Halls are all dead."

"We had law then, if'n that's what you call it. I can say I ain't seed no difference in the one we got now and the one they had back then. They killed at least ten people, child, and ain't nobody did nothing to them white folks who did it. True, the Halls is dead, but what they stood for ain't. It lives right now in the hearts and minds of folks white and colored."

"What is that?"

"Hatred, child. Plain old hatred," Katie replied, her mouth twisted in anger. "And when poor colored folks hear 'bout this money you is gonna git, you can mark my word they is gonna change towards you. It ain't no need you specting them to be happy for you, 'cause they ain't. Poor colored folks is gonna say you think you is more than them 'cause you got money, and poor white folks is gonna say you ain't good as them and ain't got no business with that kind of money. And evil men like Junior Townsend will die to keep you from having it, even though he would never miss it." Katie raised her hand in the air as though she was about to take the oath. She looked deep into Margaret's eyes. "Look me in the face, child," she commanded. "Look at me hard and long. I wants you to memorize every wrinkle in my face and every blemish mark on my skin. Be sure to look careful now."

"But why, Mama?" Margaret pleaded, terror in her voice, her face a mask of confusion.

"'Cause this face is the only one you is gonna see coming to help you when you gits in trouble, and there is gonna be a mighty heap of trouble when words gits round town 'bout this money. Some of your so-call friends might stick with you for a while, probably to see what they can git out of you; and maybe some of them might have honorable intentions, like Luther, 'cause he genuinely cares for you. But when you really need somebody to depend on, when everybody walk round you like you is the plague, you can bet all them fifteen-thousand dollars, it will be this face that you see standing before you, so take a long hard look, child," she prophesied, as she pointed and shook her finger in Margaret's face. "Now go to bed, child," she commanded and slapped the palm of her hand on the table in time to squash the returning mosquito. She turned her palm over, yanked the smattered bug from her hand, and tossed it in the nearby can. She glanced at the uniform hanging in the open door. The shaded areas told her it would be dry in time for work tomorrow. She decided tonight it would be safe to leave the doors open, but tomorrow she would have Charlie nail all the doors except for the front—there would only be one entrance to the house for as long as it took them to get out of the light again.

Margaret stared at her mother for a few seconds and rising from the table quietly left the room. She wished she could go back to yesterday, where the world was bright and promising. Mama had been right, she thought, the truth was ugly; and for the first time in her life, she wished she hadn't asked so many questions. She slipped off her house coat and fell into the bed, her mind spinning with horrifying sights of Pappy hanging from a tree, and eyes with streaks of cowardliness in them that belonged to her daddy.

Katie remained at the table, staring. She cleared her throat and cried out softly, "Father, I thought it was all over." She then remembered Pappy saying, "We must stay prepared!" She looked about the kitchen for some kind of weapon. She spied the wood-axe sitting in the corner by the kindling box. She would have Charlie sharpen it until it gleamed, even in the darkness. She remembered that Mammie used to tie ropes at the bottom of doors as an added measure even after they had been nailed shut. The windows would have to be nailed also. Only an inch would be allowed to remain open—that's the way Mammie used to do—and all entrances to the house must be checked and double-checked for strength. Perhaps she had better get someone to help Charlie. Her mind was in a whirl about all the things she would have to do. She pushed her small frame back in the chair and slowly massaged the back of her tensed neck with a soothing motion of her hand. A gentle breeze stirred for the first time that evening, and she inhaled the air, drawing it deep into her lungs, savoring the smell of freshly-cut grass that mingled with the aroma of the peach trees and wild honeysuckle. She decided tonight the doors would remain open as usual. She would feel the gentle breeze upon her body. Tonight she would allow herself that pleasure. Tonight and only tonight did she dare.

ALL THINGS IN COMOMON

As Katie and Margaret walked to church on Sunday morning, Katie found herself wishing that she was as black as a lump of coal, not the light-skinned woman born of a Negro mother and a white father. At least if she were completely black, she would only be judged for accepting a white man's money and not the sin of thinking that her white skin allowed her special privileges, as some of the Saints, Katie's fellow church members, had accused her. She glanced over at the brown-skinned, young woman who walked beside her on the footpath, and knew that her daughter was also wrestling with her thoughts. But Katie determined from the fear behind the wide, dark eyes, that most likely Margaret's thoughts centered on her own reckless behavior, and on how Reverend's Washington scalding text at church on this hot morning would certainly be directed at her.

Emerging from the tall weeds through which the path ran, they quickened their steps as they neared the run-down outhouse—leaning as if in prayer—that sat twenty feet behind the church. Its door flapped intermittently with the hot morning breeze. They passed the big middle window that housed the church's only fan, and stepped off the footpath to be greeted by Sister Dunne at the bottom of the church steps. The Church of God in Christ Sanctified looked more like a house than a church—a white framed structure with a slanted roof, two large middle windows on each side, and a small back door.

"Praise the Lord! Sister Katie!" Sister Dunne sang out as she approached Katie and Margaret with an outstretched hand and kissed them each warmly on the cheek. Sister Dunne was a petite woman with long, wavy hair that stood against the brim of her hat with every blow of the wind. Katie and Margaret took turns shaking the stooped woman's hand and placing a kiss on her cocoa-brown cheek. It was the usual custom of the Saints to greet one another with "the kiss of charity."

"Mother Washington wants you to come to her house first, fo' you goes to service," Sister Dunne said, nodding at Katie.

"Praise the Lord! Sister Margaret, jest you gone right inside; service is 'bout to git started," she instructed the younger woman, gently turning Margaret's shoulder towards the church.

Terror sprang to Margaret's eyes, and she snatched her head around to meet her mother's gaze. Katie crinkled up her nose and placed the Bible firmly into Margaret's shaking hands. Margaret stared at it blankly for a moment, then reluctantly ascended the steps leading into the Sanctified Church.

Katie hastily adjusted the straps on the small, box-like purse, then turned sharply on her heels, exhaling loudly. She stared at the house that stood not fifteen feet away, alongside the fairly large church—a typical shot-gun in need of paint and surrounded by a rusty fence covered with Virginia Creeper. The air was hot and sticky to her skin, and her gaze fell longingly upon the pecan trees that lined the roadside. Sun rained through the branches, splashing the red dirt with circles of radiant light. Katie walked slowly up the red clay path, her white, wedge-heeled shoes picking up the red dust, her ankle-length dress swaying evenly around her ankles. Her shiny black hair was hidden under the gray cloth hat that was pulled down on her head as though she expected a sudden frost. She was still a striking woman at age thirty-five, in spite of her constant efforts to appear as plain-looking as she could. She wore no makeup other than a dab of Mavis Talc to close the pores and keep the shine off her face. But somehow this tiny bit of luxury she allowed herself complemented her pale face and shadowed her high cheek bones, making them appear more prominent and refined under the wide gray eyes.

All that morning she had felt the urgency to be among the Saints, hoping to cast out all suspicions about why she had accepted Harrison

Townsend's money. But if Mrs. Washington, the Mother of their church, felt it was necessary to miss service in order to meet privately with her, it could only be about that one thing. She felt uneasy about this hastily called meeting, and when she saw the Porters a few feet away on the other side of Mother Washington's gate, she waved briskly and quickened her step. They walked single file, looking down occasionally at the uneven path. Almeda, sweating profusely, yanked on the arm of the small sunburned child who defiantly walked in the weeds. Zack, all decked out in his black deacon coat craned his neck around Almeda and glared at Katie. Guilt washed over her—Zack's glare confirmed her suspicion that the money had already begun to arouse feelings of hatred among many of the Negroes—and she hastened through the gate, stepping aside briefly to let the Porter's pass. She approached the door of the parsonage and knocked. Helen, Mother Washington's older daughter, let her in with a "praise the Lord" and instructions to make herself comfortable.

Katie stood rigidly, looking about the unadorned parlor. It was like stepping onto hallowed ground. Heavy purple drapes hung from the high, closed windows, blocking out the sunlight and giving the room a stale, solemn atmosphere. The parlor held the bare necessities: a jade green sofa with two matching chairs, a wooden table that stretched the length of the sofa, and a pot-bellied stove. One kerosene lamp sat on the floor and cast its glow up the center of the east wall to a well-preserved painting of the crucifixion.

Katie jerked her head towards the bustle coming from the small bedroom on the left, where three teen-aged girls rushed about, dressing for church. And where a young, angry voice demanded, "Git your tail offa my blouse, Jerline." Walking on her tip-toes, as if she were in church, Katie made her way to the center of the sofa and sat down.

She twisted the straps on the purse into a knot and sighed. She wondered how she could make Mother Washington understand why Margaret had defied her. It wasn't easy explaining a girl like Margaret who sometimes resided in a world so alien to Katie's that at times agreement between them was impossible. Often, sitting at Katie's knee while her mother braided her long, thick hair, Margaret had talked of a changing world, making such bold statements as, "Soon many people will sleep in the nude and won't be ashamed.

Telephones will become a widespread utility, and tuberculosis will no longer exist." At these times, even Katie had been shocked into silence, for she knew any form of nudity was offensive to God, and telephones were for the privileged, and it was obvious tuberculosis would be around until doomsday—why else would the county keep building those little white houses for the terminally ill?

But of all the shocking things that Margaret had said or done, Katie could think of none to compare with the exhibition Margaret had put on Friday evening—showing up at the reading of Townsend's will dressed like Jezebel and acting like the town whore. She had strutted into the white folks house in that low-cut, hot-pink dress and cut-out shoes, and had flung her hips in wild abandon, batted her mascara eyes at every bewildered peckerwood present, and addressing the group in a brazen, lazy drawl, had said, "Glory be! Am I late?" How could Katie convince Mother Washington that Margaret had shamed her into accepting the money?

Through the partially divided curtains, Katie watched Helen stacking the last of the breakfast dishes and issuing orders to the smaller children. A sweet, greasy funk that reminded her of cottonseed cakes drying in the sun lingered in the house—the residue from fried salt pork, Royal Crown Hair dressing, and Mavis Talc. She leaned forward for a better view, hoping to see some similarity to Margaret that she could use to sway Mother's opinion. But as she watched Helen, all she saw was a satiny-black girl engrossed in menial duties, a young woman with manly shoulders and coarse, unruly hair that rolled up at the base of her neck like beads. Helen's dreams, as she had often testified, were focused on marriage, children and a hard-working, God-fearing man; Margaret wanted to step out into the world and cure all that ailed it. Helen accepted everything in stride and took life as it came; Margaret had been planning her life since she was five. It became evident to Katie that Helen and Margaret had nothing in common—that they were as different as bread and water. Katie rose from the sofa. She walked to the threshold and peeked through the curtains that separated the two rooms.

"Anything I can give you a hand with, Helen?" she asked, stepping into the kitchen ablaze with electric lights. The table where

Rosa sat, her head barely visible, was stacked with dishes smeared with sorghum molasses and bits of meat.

"No, thank you, Sister Katie, jest make yo'self to home," Helen replied, while she twisted the hair on the smaller girl's head into a thick underhand braid.

"I reckon y'all is anxious to hear your daddy deliver the word of God," Katie said.

"He ain't gonna talk 'bout God today," Rosa informed her, with big eyes and an air of first-hand knowledge. "He told Mama he gonna talk 'bout…"

"Hush, Rosa Mae! You knows Daddy don't like nobody telling his text," Helen commanded, holding the flat side of the brush inches from the girl's head.

Rosa's sudden downcast face angered Katie. She shook her head disapprovingly and wondered if Mother Washington set store by Helen's heavy hand. She gave Helen a scalding look and returned to the front room. Standing at the end of the couch facing the pot-bellied stove, she nervously tapped her fingers against the back of her neck. She wondered why Mother Washington was making her wait. What could be keeping her? And then she recalled the time that Almeda Porter backslid and stayed away from the church for one solid month—living it up, some said. And how difficult Almeda had found it to be reinstated to her old status in the Sisterhood. Mother Washington had tested Almeda's faith over and over, again and again. She had made Almeda sweat. Oh, yes, Katie thought, Mother Washington knew the power of her position. She knew just where to twist the screw—right where you had the most pride. She didn't hold the position as Mother of the church simply because she was married to the pastor. She was the mother of the church, and all the Sisters were looked upon as her children. She taught them everything from how to escort the elderly to their seats, to recognizing the signal for passing around the collection plates. She questioned their morals, their dress, even the amount of Mavis Talc they used. She addressed herself to any issue that might prove embarrassing to the church, including gifts suddenly bestowed upon her Sisters—especially money.

The sickly sweet aroma of "Mother's Friend"—an ointment used exclusively by pregnant women to ease leg cramps and prevent stretch marks floated through the room, and Katie turned around to face Mother Washington, a middle-age woman whose round, tortured, enormously pregnant stomach had just parted the curtains like a torpedo breaking water. She stood, her jet-black face glistening with perspiration, issuing orders to the three young girls who scrambled before her for a final inspection. Their eyes shone with excitement, their black skirts and white blouses announcing their status as members of the junior choir.

"Now y'all sit down and act like young ladies," the plump woman advised cheerfully, pride shining in her dark eyes.

"Yes ma'am," their voices rang out in unison. "Praise the Lord, Sister Katie," they said, facing her and bowing their heads low.

"Praise the Lord! Katie shouted at them with deep conviction and smiled warmly as the girls swished out the door. "My, them chillens sho is mannerable," Katie said.

"Chillens is supposed to be mannerable; the Bible says 'honor thy father and thy mother,' and in this house we lives by the Bible," the plump woman replied emphatically as she pointed after the children. Katie flinched at the veiled comparison to her house; her smile disappearing suddenly.

From the other room, Mother Ceola Washington turned her full gaze on Katie, staring at her fixedly, and extended a small fat hand. The extended arm wavered back and forth like a divining rod attempting to locate water. To Katie, it seemed that fifteen minutes elapsed by the time the slow-walking woman and the extended hand finally made their way across the room. "Praise the Lord, Sister, sorry to keep you waiting," the older woman panted. She squeezed Katie's hand and placed a quick kiss on Katie's cheek, then quickly turned her head away before Katie could return the kiss.

"Praise the Lord," Katie replied in a puzzled voice.

Mother Washington nodded her head towards the sofa, and Katie walked back to the far end and sat down. Mother Washington sank down heavily into the chair directly facing Katie. Her eyeglasses, held firmly by a long silver chain, rested on her bosom. Her long, brown hair, speckled with flecks of white, was twisted in a ball on the top of her head, revealing stand-away ears. She smoothed the hem of the print dress, focused her round eyes on Katie's, and suddenly assumed an air of dignified superiority.

"Sister Margaret tending the morning service?" she her hands in her lap and squaring her shoulders.

"Oh, my, yes. Margaret ain't one on missing stammered and lowered her eyes.

"Hump," Mother Washington grunted, bucked her eyes and looked at Katie strangely—like she had suddenly turned into a pillar of salt.

Her round eyes traveled slowly from the gray hat on Katie's head down to the white, wedge-heeled shoes on Katie's feet. And slowly they traveled back up the linen dress to stare Katie in the face. The color of Katie's skin annoyed her great deal. And those gray eyes… Mother Washington made all her judgments by what she read in a person's eyes, and for ten years now, she had found Katie's unreadable. She had witnessed Katie's healing abilities and the effect her powerful prayers had on the congregation—prayers so electrifying that the Reverend was often upstaged. She had watched Katie go out of her way to keep her daughter from working the fields like most colored girls in Bennettsville—and secretly disapproved. She had held her peace when Katie converted an unused bedroom into a sewing parlor where Margaret tailored dresses for whites and mended and patched for the Negroes. She saw no sense in building false hope. But now it had been brought to her attention, by a reliable source, that Townsend had left all that money to Katie, for Katie's uppity daughter, because Katie had prayed for him on his deathbed. This Mother Washington had to concern herself with, as it was against the principles of the church—accepting money for doing God's work—unless the money was to be donated to the church.

"I'm glad you could come by so soon, Sister. I realized I didn't give you much notice, but it's mighty important," the older woman said.

"I can always find time for the Mother of my church. I jest regret missing the morning service," Katie answered softly as the lively spiritual, I'm a Soldier in the Army of My Lord, filtered into the house through the open back door. But her thoughts were on Margaret. She imagined the church packed with outraged Negroes and Margaret facing the cold, hard stares that were so typical of people who sat in judgment of others, and her heart ached. However, she reasoned, Margaret had brought this tongue-lashing upon herself;

her sacrilegious display had not only cut them to the quick by attacking the guidelines they lived by, but had also uncovered the demon—Need Mo'—they struggled to keep hidden from each other. And for a sassy gal to receive money for book-learning when they needed basics… Yet, Katie felt responsible for it all because she had so sheltered Margaret from the workings of the white world that Margaret couldn't understand the significance of Katie's argument—that tainted money only brought grief, and that accepting money made from the sweat of others was immoral.

The back door slammed, and Katie and Mother Washington jerked their heads around spontaneously, their eyes focused on the curtain that divided the rooms as they listened to feet scraping against the stoop. And when Helen's bass voice blasted across the yard, "Gal, if you don't git out that there dirt, Ama gonna thump yo' head like it was a watermelon," they turned to face one another, as if to confirm what they had heard, and seeing the shock on Mother Washington's face, Katie quickly looked at the floor.

Mother Washington smoothed the hem of her dress again and turned her gaze back to Katie. "I ain't rightly sure you'd enjoy service this morning. The Reverend is taking his text from Acts, about Ananias and his wife Sapphira. You remember the scripture 'bout the man what took money intended for the church and kept it for himself?" Mother Washington questioned Katie with a raised eyebrow.

"I knows the text well," Katie replied, looking up, and crossed her ankles. A pick-up truck rattled up the road and squeaked to a stop in front of the church. A man's gravelly voice told someone to "go on in and quit fooling 'round," and for a moment Katie and Mother Washington were silent. Slowly, Katie met Mother Washington's steady gaze. "Mother," she began, a tremor to her voice and her eyes searched the older woman's for understanding. "You remember how you'se been tarrying long and hard, nearly ten years, to receive the baptism of the Holy Ghost? I spect if'n someone told you that God said the sure-fire way to receive the Holy Ghost was to bathe every night in tobacco juice, I spect you'd do jest that."

Mother Washington hunched forward in her seat, a puzzled look on her face. "That sound more like devil-worship." She folded her heavy arms around her, and frowned. "But I spect I might do jest that, if God said it. Ain't nothing too high or too low that I wouldn't do for the Lord. Why, God told Abraham to kill his only son... But what's the reason for you to bring that up now?"

"'Cause," Katie said, making a bridge with her fingers and pressing them to her chest, "when a person wants something they believe is gonna make them a better person, sometimes they do some mighty peculiar things."

"Now you hold on right there, Sister!" The older woman silenced Katie with an outstretched hand, eyeglasses dancing on her huge bosom. "I see what you is trying to do. But I ain't gonna sit still for it. No siree! You can't compare my wanting the Holy Ghost to your daughter dressing like Jezebel, breaking the dress code of the church liken she did, and you outright accepting that money for doing the Lord's work. Oh, no, it's two different things, mind you." She shook her finger at the air. "Two different things entirely."

She sighed deeply, pushed back in the chair, and stared at the ceiling. Immediately, Katie knew what to expect; she had seen Mother assume this position many times at church. Whenever Mother Washington had a particular point to make, she would stare at the ceiling and move her lips as though she was communicating with God, then deliver her revelations in the form of a riddle, parable, or story. With her eyes still focused on the ceiling, Mother Washington spoke in a slow, deliberate tone.

"The dove, full-feathered and white as snow, is the Christian symbol of simplicity and gentleness, whiles the Pharaoh Chicken, a naked, yellow-faced vulture, is the symbol of death to the Christian spirit. Now," she boomed, lowering her head and turning to face Katie, "some baby chicks turns out to be Doves—the gentlest—whiles others turns out to be Pharaoh Chickens—the thievinest. If a man steals, he is a thief. The way he done it, even the reason he done it, don't change the fact one bit."

"Now that depends," Katie interrupted, her face stinging. She had heard the deliberate malice in Mother Washington's voice and sensed an underlying evil in the story. She pushed forward on the sofa, the musky ointment piercing her nostrils.

"Depends on what?" Mother Washington snapped at the intrusion, and jerked forward in the chair.

"Why, on the situation, of course," Katie answered. "My pappy used to tell me to make sure that when I called a person a thief, he was jest that."

"Your pappy, indeed!" Mother Washington snorted, and bucked her eyes. "Well, if'n a person steals your chickens out of your barn, and you catch him red-handed, ain't that a thief?"

"I reckon there's some truth to that, but that ain't what I mean," Katie said, cutting her eyes. "Pappy used to tell us chillens 'bout a man what got all the chickens he wanted without even setting foot in the barn, or without laying a hand on one of em."

"Ha," Mother Washington cried out, and flung both arms in the air as though she was talking to a crazy person. "Now that's jest plain foolish talk."

"You obvious don't know much 'bout chickens," Katie said smugly, and slowly rubbed her hands together.

"No, but what is there to know 'bout chickens? Mother Washington snarled and screwed up her face. "Chickens is chickens!"

"Well, one thing for sure, if you knew anything 'bout chickens, you'd know that they will follow a straight line, even through fire."

Mother Washington glared at Katie.

"So if'n a fellow draws a line in the dirt and the chickens follows him, is he a thief?" Katie asked coyly.

Stunned by the cunning of the woman, and outraged that her perfect allegory had been reduced to a discussion on the behavior of chickens, Mother Washington rolled her eyes back and forth in her head, searching for a response. Suddenly, she leaned closer, placed her hands on the table, and grinned like a summer possum. "Well, white folks is liable to tell niggers anything; surely even you, with yo' blood mixed up liken it is, knows that!"

Something like fire bolted through Katie's chest, and she dropped back against the sofa dazed. Perspiration coated her nose, and a dry smile played about her lips as she realized that her earlier suspicions regarding the color of her skin had been warranted. In church she had overheard the tail-end of conversations about how they put up with Margaret because she was black, but Katie, with her lilly white skin… She had gained strength to carry on depending on Mother and Reverend Washington who had always stood behind her. Yet, now, the Mother of her church was one of them, and Mother Washington wanted to hear more than the simple truth that Katie loved God and would abide by the rules of the church. She wanted Katie to sweat, like Almeda and all the rest. She wanted her to reveal all her private life, expose her naked feelings, her desires, her beliefs about race, and, mostly, how she felt about her black mother and her white father. She wanted it all laid out before her like she was God himself. That's what Mother Washington wanted of her, and Katie braced herself, for Mother had implied that there had been a separation between her and her pappy.

"I ain't talking 'bout white folks, Mother," Katie said breathlessly. "I'se talking 'bout my pappy, and he, I assures you, ain't never thought I was no nigger."

Mother Washington groaned and dropped her head in her hands. Sighing loudly, she slowly raised her head, wove her fingers together and rocked. She flung her hands apart and counted on her fingers, her bass voice filling the room. "Fact number one is, he was a white man. And fact number two is, you ain't no mind reader, so how you know what he thought. It's all the same, white folks is white folks."

"No, no, it ain't quite the same," Katie said, sitting up and shaking her head. She uncrossed her ankles and placed her hands in her lap, the purse covering them. "White folks <u>is</u> white folks, that is if'n you is talking 'bout color, but your pappy is your pappy. There is a heap big difference." She spoke in a sharp, raspy voice and clutched the purse tightly in her fist. But the seed had caught root, and in the back of her mind Katie wondered if there was truth to what Mother said.

She remembered the last argument that her pappy and mammie had had—the night her mammie walked out of their lives forever. An argument that had started over a missing bar of store-bought soap, and ended with shouting and heated words. She was sixteen at the time and had clearly understood that the issue between her pappy and mammie had nothing to do with soap; although she had asked Pappy many times afterwards, he would never tell her what the issue had been. Pappy would turn red in the face and dismiss Katie with a shake of his head. Katie wondered, had Pappy called Mammie a nigger? What did Mammie mean when she said she "would not stand for that?" Had Pappy been ashamed of them? No, she thought, or he would not have kept his children—and later he was hanged… She had told Margaret the other night that Mammie had left on account of bad things, meaning bad things that other white folks had done to them. She shook her head and wondered if maybe she, too, was as naive as Margaret.

She gazed into the small, round eyes of the heavy black-skinned woman, the Mother of the church, the woman she had held close to her bosom (often calling her Ceola in private), and wondered, Did Mother Washington indeed know something about life that she hadn't grasped in her thirty-five years, or was this, like the Deacon's meeting, a test of her faith? She chose to believe it was a test. She would never believe that Pappy felt like that, never, even if someone brought documents of proof to her—why he had given his life for her sister Addie, but that was after Mammie had left. She shook her head and vowed never to think on it again. For if an inkling of what Mother Washington had said was true, Katie had worshipped a white man, sometimes placing him above God, while he had accepted and even expected her love not because she was his daughter but because it was a requirement—it was what niggers did! Niggers worshipped white folks. Suddenly her ears began to burn and something seemed to be crawling under her clothing.

"The fact is, Sister," Mother Washington said, "he still was a white man, and white folks do think different from us. But maybe you don't think you is one of us?" She shouldered back in the chair, fixing her eyes on Katie.

"What is you saying?" Katie shrieked, her voice high and unnatural, her heart pounding.

"Well, take that money, for instance." Mother Washington rested her head on the back of the chair and stared at the ceiling. "It ain't no way on this here earth I'd took that money, even if they begged me to, unless it was specified for the church. If Townsend had said, 'I leave this here fifteen-thousand dollars to Mother Ceola Washington to be used for the church,' then I'd a took it, being he done already stole so much from Negroes as it is. I might have been tempted, but I wouldn't a done it. Now, I was told by a reliable source that you stood and accepted that money, and that your daughter put on quite a show for them peckerwoods—parading 'round in a dress the color of hell fire. And you did nothing 'bout her display, jest stood and took that money. Outright, without so much as a second thought on why it was left to you in the first place." Mother Washing head, a look of righteousness on her face, her hanc bottom of her straining belly.

Katie chewed on her bottom lip and clutched the p her fist. Her breathing was rapid and shallow, like that [illegible]-born puppy. "Your source, as we both well knows," Katie said, glaring, "is Earline Simpson, and her mouth flaps constantly 'bout what she overhears at them white folks' houses. It ain't no way that she could have known I took that money outright without a second thought—Earline ain't no mind reader neither. Or is you saying that only pure-blood colored folks can read minds?" Letting her purse fall to the table, she waved her hand in front of her as though she was erasing a blackboard, leaned in closer, and growled, "I ain't took no money outright. God knows that! Besides, what went on up yonder ain't had nothing to do with the church anyhows."

"What? How in heaven's name can you say that?" Mother Washington gasped and clutched her chest. "Didn't that old pecker-wood put your name on his will cause you laid hands on him?"

"Well, yes…"

"And you is gonna stare me in the face and tell me spiritual healing ain't gots nothing to do with the church! You needs to be saved from your ignorance," she said, shaking her head and still clutching her chest.

The kerosene lamp, almost out of oil, flickered and burned low. The air in the room had disappeared, in spite of the open back door. They were both sweating and equally relieved to hear Sister Dunne's shrill soprano leading What a Friend We Have in Jesus. They listened for a moment to the words that were interspersed with the flap, flap, flap of the outhouse door. Mother Washington dropped her hands in her lap and looked at Katie. "Granted," she said, "Earline might not know the circumstances what made you accept the money, but that don't change the fact that you did."

"Oh, I see. We is back to 'a thief is a thief,'" Katie sighed, shaking her head and resigning herself to the lopsided logic of the Mother of her church. She raised her hands and stared at them as though she was reading a book, then slowly she let them drop to her lap. She rolled her eyes at Mother Washington. "My decision to take money, I assures you, ain't had nothing to do with my pappy being white.

"I see. Did you feel at that time it was the Christian thing to do—accepting money for doing God's work? Money that you obviously don't intend to give to the church? Or did you think you was given the power of laying hands on the sick by that white blood coming from that pappy you keeps throwing up to me?"

A warm sensation crept over Katie's body, and suddenly she felt unclean. She stood, snatched the purse from the table, and spat the words at her beloved Mother of the church, "If'n it came from any one of them, then it would be my mammie since she tended the sick. And my mammie was two shades darker than you is, old woman."

"Who you calling 'old woman'?" Mother Washington growled and struggled to her feet, her stomach leading the way as she advanced towards Katie.

"I ain't gots to explain to nobody 'bout my folks," Katie yelled, flinging her arms across her face. The purse, spinning from her hand, flew across the room, and landed in front of the kitchen curtain.

"You best watch what you say here, Sister. I ain't one that forgits easily," Mother Washington warned, her eyes blazing.

"All I'se gots to concern myself with is pleasing the Almighty," Katie said, and inched her way around the table to the other end of the sofa. She stood with her back to Mother Washington.

Mother Washington sucked in her breath and advanced until her knees bumped the corner of the table. She pointed at Katie's back, the flesh of her heavy arm quivering, her accusing finger almost touching Katie's shoulder.

"I suppose you is only thinking 'bout the Almighty when you is called on through the night to pray and lay hands. And I suppose you is only thinking 'bout the Almighty when your name rings out all over this here town, and even farther than the Reverend's. You ain't said nothing substantial yet in your defense; all you been talking 'bout is stupid chickens and your white pappy. Jest plain foolish talk, if you ask me."

Katie whirled around and faced the pregnant woman, her temples pounding, her throat raw. She wanted to strike out, destroy anyone and everyone who had mentioned the money. Instead, she stomped the few feet to the curtain, scooped up the purse from the floor, then turned and faced Mother Washington. She stood with her back to the curtain, fumbling with the purse straps, her face the color of fire. She dropped her hands to her side in a sweeping motion and fixed her eyes on Mother Washington's scowling face.

Ain't no ceptions with you, is it!" She screamed. Mother Washington flinched and dropped her heavy arm to her side. "Everythangs the same in your book. A thief is a thief, chickens is chickens, and white folks is white folks. I don't believes you wants to hear the truth." Katie caught her breath and prepared to lash the harshest words, and if necessary, blows at the threatening figure; but as she squared off, purse raised, her gaze fell upon the rapidly flashing light of the lamp across Mother Washington's shoulder. The lamp flickered on the wall at an accelerated speed—its waning light shimmering against the blood that oozed from Jesus' side in the picture—and for that infinitesimal moment, Katie thought she saw the blood move. Terror seized her body, and then agonizing shame. She bolted past Mother Washington and dropped weakly to the sofa, submitting herself unto the elder. "I goes where the Lord sends me," she whispered.

"So do we all, Sister," Mother Washington said with smug satisfaction and stepped back a few inches from the table. "We is all God's instruments, not God himself."

"But didn't Earline tell you everything that was said, didn't she tell you that the money was left to Margaret, not me? And that Townsend knew I wouldn't take the money, so he willed it all to Margaret. Didn't she tell you all of that?"

"I knows all of that. But as guardian of the money, you had the last say, and instead of making it clear it was against your principles, or that you was accepting this money for the church, you just stood and thanked that old slave-driving peckerwood for leaving it to you. Now I wants to know why," she demanded, glaring down at Katie.

"I accepted it for my daughter," Katie spoke to the floor. "So she could go to that college and become the teacher she wants to be. I accepted it 'cause it was the first time my daughter had gone against my word and it musta been mighty important to her. It was the first time in her eighteen years that she didn't do liken I said, and something strange happens to you when your chillens go against your word—you'll see. Margaret ain't no bad child." Katie faced Mother

Washington, a tremor in her voice. "She deliberately dressed up liken she did, and carried on liken she did so I would see jest what might come of her if I denied her that money."

Katie stopped, and her face went white as she grasped the meaning of what she had said. She had known all along that Margaret intended to defy her, but she had not grasped the significance of Margaret's display until now. She shook her head and mumbled, "My child, my child." And then she turned her attention back to Mother Washington. "I accepted it 'cause Charlie Hudnall, my pappy's oldest friend, said it was right, and that I oughta git Margaret away from this town. And he knows more 'bout life than me and you put together. I accepted it for her." She lowered her voice. "And I accepted it to save face, to keep them white folks from thinking Negroes couldn't manage their children. I felt ashamed. But I know now I couldn't have done nothing that God didn't mean for me to do. I mean, I don't make no decision like that, don't you see? He does. You is questioning me when you should be asking God, cause like you said, we is only instruments."

Mother Washington stared into Katie's face. In the gray unreadable eyes she thought she had seen a spark, but as she looked closer now, they were distant and cold, and a film separating the reality from the dream seemed to envelope them. Katie's word had always been honorable, but this money she had accepted for her daughter to receive learning outside the world of God; and Katie's explanation implied approval of her daughter's path. She had been moved by Katie's argument that it was God's decision, not hers, but it was impossible for Mother Washington to determine the truth.

And Mother Washington suddenly became tactful and sympathetic. It was like the transformation of the caterpillar to the butterfly —you had to see it to believe it.

"Sister Katie," she said calmly, her eyes soft and warm. "I will tell all this to the Reverend and see what he says. Frankly, I don't see the logic behind anything you said, but who am I?" She hunched her heavy shoulders.

Katie's eyes traveled down the print dress that draped about Mother Washington's body like a tent, and traveled back to rest on her face. She gazed deep into Mother Washington's eyes and thought she saw pity behind them. She shook her head slightly and looked about the room. She focused on the picture of the crucifixion, specifically the circle of light above Jesus' head. The kerosene lamp went out. And the picture now exemplified Mother Washington's convictions—everything was all black and white. She was suddenly deeply saddened. "Yes, Mother, I don't reckon you do, 'cause you is using logic, and you'll never see nothing that way." Calm surged through her body, and her headache seemed to ease. She nodded her head like she was listening to a voice that only she could hear, saying, "To see, you have to be like them chickens whose faith is unquestioning and who jest walk through the fire following that line in the dirt. And if you do that," she added and pushed her palms forward, "If you jest have faith and stop looking all the time for logic, you might jest receive the blessing of the Lord. You might jest receive the Holy Ghost!"

Katie stood, twisted the straps of the purse around her wrist, and walked to the door, leaving the older woman speechless. Katie opened the door and stepped onto the narrow porch. She turned and saw her shadow stretched across the floor, framed like a picture within the rectangular shape of sunlight that had been let in by the open door. She looked beyond the light to the pregnant woman standing by the pot-bellied stove. She did not see the Mother of her church; instead, she saw a heavy woman with flabby arms streaked white with stretch marks. A round-faced woman with cynical eyes and an inflated belly. A woman she had not seen before. Katie immediately thought of the caricature Margaret had created—the modern-day Jezebel. For unlike Margaret's creation, the woman who stood before her was the real Ceola Washington. At once, Katie knew that Margaret would never be a Ceola Washington. That Margaret would listen to her internal voice and get out of this backwater town. That Margaret would never attain a position of power and use it to strip ignorant people of their dreams, their heritage, their will to live free in this world. And that Margaret's many accomplishments would be acceptable (hallelujah!) in God's eyes.

She glanced around the room for the last time and stepped off the porch into the light.

Katie took the same narrow footpath on Riley Street, her head held high in spite of the anticipated trouble that the money was sure to bring. She turned off Riley Street to the footpath that ran alongside the church, instinctively heading for home. As she neared the big middle window of the Sanctified Church, she heard above the roar of the fan, the fiery voice of Reverend Washington delivering his text: "And the multitude of them that believed were of one heart and soul: neither said any of them that ought of the things which he possessed was his own; but they had all things common...But a certain man named Ananias, with Sapphira his wife, sold a possession—hear me now, children—and <u>kept back part of the price.</u>"

Katie stood for a moment, listening, and envisioned Reverend Washington's coffee-colored face glistening with sweat. She could see him mopping his face with a white-white handkerchief, then gesticulating, his powerful arms flying in all directions—and lastly, as he always did, hammering the pulpit loud enough to wake the dead. She turned and looked toward the road: cars and pick-up trucks lined the street. Everyone was in church, even those who did not attend on a regular basis. The throbbing in her temples had ceased. She walked swiftly up the path to the front door and entered the church, packed with people from end to end. There in the center pew, her back straight, her head high, sat Margaret, and Katie knew that her daughter was holding her own. She murmured, "Lord, this is Katie, your faithful servant, I go where you sends me."

DREAMS

It had been four days since the reading of the will. Four days Katie had spent going back and forth to work looking over her shoulder for the unexpected. And four days of dodging the expected, as she and Margaret were indeed the talk of the town. She was tired of avoiding people she usually stopped to converse with and tired of explaining about the money—how it had come to them and how she really didn't want the dirty money anyway. She was tired of walking home on her lunch every day to check on Margaret only to find on her return to work that she felt more ill at ease. Yesterday, she had hung around her house until Charlie finished nailing the windows and the back door and was late getting back to work. She had felt Miss Rosie's cold eyes upon her back. She had noticed how withdrawn Margaret had become with everyone except Luther. And she had noticed how Charlie seemed to complain more about everything and that he limped back and forth across the fields like an expectant father. She believed she had no where to turn and the old spiritual, "Where Could I Go But to the Lord," kept running through her head.

It was precisely her intention to carry her troubles to the Lord, and the Lord's house. It was Tuesday, the first night of their annual revival, when the doors of the church were open to anyone—even the lowest creature that walked on the earth. And she knew from past revivals that she would be treated with love and humility, not at all like it had been last Sunday when she entered the church, her heart racing, looking for Margaret. Only a few Saints acknowledged her presence with a curt bow, excluding Sister Dunne who had kissed her warmly outside, and she suspected their politeness had something to do with their needs being greater than pride and religion. Most of them had turned, glared, tossed their heads high in the air—the epitome of holiness shrouded with the vanity of evil—as the fiery words of Reverend Washington thundered back and forth across the room. And his eyes had raked over her face hard enough to draw blood. She had closed them out; she had asked the Lord to strengthen her will, and He had. But Margaret had been scourged: all the blame was laid at Margaret's feet and done so without ever mentioning Margaret's name—starting with an accusing sermon of thievery and deception among brethren, and ending with personal testimony of individual Saints who stood and questioned the good of white education for Negroes. But now that a few days had passed and the spirit of God moved them to ready His house for the glorious occasion, their attention would be on saving souls. Dressed in regulation attire, the standard long, white uniforms with long sleeves and white linen scarves to cover their hair, Katie and Margaret stepped inside the Church of God in Christ Sanctified, which was crowded with people from all over the state. Leaving Margaret at the front row pew, Katie walked the few feet past the podium to her pew, placed the Bible on the seat, set the thick cushion on the floor, and knelt in prayer. She remained on her knees with her eyes closed tight, her lips moving constantly as she talked to her God. She sang and danced that night for herself as well as for God, and never before had she danced so long, her feet pounding the wooden floor, her long dress swishing back and forth to the beat of the pulsating guitar. Never before had she sung so hard, praising God until the veins stood out prominently in her long white neck. She was wrapped in her vision of God's goodness and saw nothing else, for with His goodness and mercy, she knew that she and Margaret could survive anything.

The service lasted late into the night, and afterward, as she and Margaret neared their home—the tall house that stood on the pillars—Katie saw an outline of something stretched on the porch between the two swings. The darkness clung to the house like thick smoke, causing the overhead porch light to cast its own shadow over the figure, swallowing it up in the night. From the bottom of the steps Katie could see a round black spot resembling a bag of clothes. She craned her neck from side to side until she determined the lumpy shadow to be a medium-sized mongrel dog—a white, red-eyed bitch that rose to greet them with a low, menacing growl, threatening them with bodily harm should they step foot on its recently-claimed property. Margaret pointed a delicately gloved hand and cried out, "Mama, it's that dog again." The old fear was back in the pit of Katie's stomach, as the red-eyed beast bared its teeth and advanced to the edge of the high porch, daring them to come closer. A premonition of approaching disaster seized her brain—a strange white dog was the symbol for death in her eyes, or a warning of impending danger, and her hands shook uncontrollably. This was the dog that Margaret had seen the other night—the night when her mind was so filled with the past that she could not see what was happening in the present. Katie's first instinct was to run and rouse Charlie, but soon realized that would take too long, and it would be terribly inconsiderate. If she wanted to get inside her home, she had no choice than to remove the beast from her porch.

She crammed the Bible and purse in the bend of Margaret's arm, and picked up a broken tree limb from the ground. Instructing Margaret to stand aside, she proceeded up the steps cautiously, wondering if the dog's presence had something to do with her or Margaret, or if it was there to warn her of dangers that awaited them inside. The dog was thin, slightly malnourished, but alert—it moved closer, its growl deeper, its eyes glazed. When she reached the third step, the dog barked savagely until saliva hopped from its mouth. She raised her arm and brought the limb down with all her might across the dog's back. The dog's legs wobbled under the fierce blow, but it stood its ground, a deep growl rising in its quivering throat. She raised her arm again, determined the devil would not keep her from her door, until a howl erupted from the animal's mouth, a terrifying howl that sounded like a great wind caressing every corner of the old house. The dog bounded down the steps and past Margaret, urinated, and limped down the road into the night.

Katie, with fire in her eyes, pushed the front door open with one hard shove, banging it against the wall. She twisted the round knob on the wall, snapping the light on, her eyes instantly sweeping the room from top to bottom, her breath in her throat. Margaret stood cowering at the threshold of the front door, watching her mother rush from room to room to turn on all the electric lights—lights that were used stringently. Katie was in a frenzy, her gray eyes full and wide as she threw back the covers on her bed with one swoop of her hand and fell to her knees. If the dog stood as a warning, she knew they could not remain inside the house unless she prayed, for only prayer would drive out the evil spirits that might be lurking about. On the floor, she bent to peer under the bed and stared at the darkness. Using her arm as a broom, she made a clean sweep from the head to the foot, hitting only air and dust balls. It was as though she was sweeping years of ghosts from under the bed. And while she did this, she yelled, "Lu'Sha, Lu'Sha, be gone Satan."

Margaret had followed her mother and now stood in the doorway to the middle room. She expected her mother any minute now to give her a command to run. Katie sprang from her knees and stood in the middle of the floor with tears streaming down her face, her hands held high in the air, flexing them as though they had been dipped in ice cold water and she was trying to restart the flow of warm blood. She spoke in tongues, "Nign, nign nign, yes Lord, yes Lord, nign nign nign, thank you Jesus, thank you Jesus. Nign nign nign," louder then softer as she looked up at the wide-eyed, girl standing in the doorway. She said "Come on in, child."

Margaret had seen her mother praising God before, but it was never like this. Katie had never been in such a frenzied state. It was the strain of the past week, Margaret was sure. And although she had been affected by it, she now realized it was not the same. Her mother had now stripped naked before her, revealing inner fears that she had always managed to hold in check somehow. Margaret realized that the tower of strength—the picture that Katie projected—was just as human as she, just as scared as she, perhaps even more. Margaret knew that it was best for both of them if she slipped through the door into her room quietly, to allow her mother time to return to her usual self. She dropped Katie's purse and Bible on the edge of the bed, opened the middle door and stepped inside of her room.

As soon as Margaret disappeared behind the door, Katie did something she had never done; she walked back to the front door and locked it.

Her feet ached from the constant pounding she had given them at the church, and her throat was parched and raw from all the praying and crying out. She switched off the lights and fell upon the bed fully dressed, clutching the Bible to her chest. Its power was stronger than the evils attached to white dogs, and yes, even death. Its power was endless. It extended through time—back to her pappy and mammie, and his pappy, and even all the way back to the living Jesus. It made her feel invincible and lighthearted. She found strength from the vastness of its power, and also from the thought that it had belonged to her pappy. She lay listening to the pounding of her heart and to the noises coming from Margaret's room. She heard the squeaking of bed springs and knew that Margaret had retired. She felt divided, partially on earth and partially wrapped in the glory of God, and although she was content, she fought off sleep until she was sure that she heard sounds of labored breathing coming from Margaret's room—the sounds of sleep. The dim lamp from Margaret's side of the house flickered and cast its shadowy flame across the ceiling. She listened for another ten minutes as the old house popped and settled as usual; then sleep fell upon Katie like the closing of an open door, quickly, and removing all light. She twisted in turmoil as the dream wrestled from her subconscious and sent her back to her childhood.

She was back with Pappy and Mammie, her older sister, Addie, and her baby brother, little Robert. It was here on this same land, only everything was greener, everything was fresh and new. She was ten years old and her entire life revolved around her pappy, Robert Younger, a red-headed white man with huge, hairy arms. It was a clear morning, the gray beginning to leave the sky, just as Mammie's wash pot started to bubble, filling the air with steam. The tomato plants little Robert had planted had just begun peeking through the rich, red dirt, and the small-freckled-face, red-headed boy chopped diligently at the weeds that threatened his precious crop. Pappy walked off the area behind the chicken coop, measuring the spot of land he had claimed for his patio, something he had dreamed of having for years. Katie dogged his steps like a lost puppy that had found a friend. Addie, her coal black hair draping her thin shoulders, sorted the white clothes from the coloreds as Mammie watched her with a gleam of pride in her eyes. Addie filled the washpot with an arm load of white clothes and Mammie, her long, gray skirt sweeping the ground, walked over and poked the clothes down in the bubbling water with the butt of her shotgun. Mammie always carried her gun. It was a part of her dress. She never left the house without her shawl, and she never left the house without her gun. And since the talk of the night riders, she kept it constantly at her side along with a supply of shells which she hid almost any place unthinkable—even in the hen's nest. Katie could see the ground below, as vivid as though she rode in an airplane, as though she was separated from the family and yet watching herself, a small, thin girl with a dress much too large, trailing behind the tall man with the huge arms who would split a piece of green kindling with the axe, pound it down in the earth with the flat side of the axe, stop, pick her up, and place her on the other side of the wire he had strung.

A sudden cloud of red dust formed above galloping horses that came to a very fast stop at the end of the front yard. The dust settled slowly, revealing six white men on horses, with ropes and guns that glinted in the early morning sunlight. The men rode deliberately through the vegetables, crushing the tomato sprouts. Little Robert yelled for them to get out of his garden as they sat with rigid backs, laughing at his boyish attempts to push the horses out of the patch. Katie could see the look in Pappy's eyes, first a pain that expressed an agonizing defeat, then rapidly turning to flame, a passion of undeniable rage. He snatched the long-handled axe from the ground and walked the short distance to the men, his face blood red.

"Stop right there, Robert Younger," the one called Hall ordered. But Pappy kept walking until he stood in the patch of the garden with crushed tomato plants, looking up and beyond Hall's shoulder to the grinning man whose eyes were cold as a snake's. Mammie, a few feet to the left of them, braced herself for the inevitable. Her face became like chiseled marble—the deep-set eyes, heavy with lash and brow, froze, and immediately she kicked over the wash kettle, putting out the fire. A white steam hissed and mushroomed over her head. She stood like an iron jockey in the rain, her shiny black face glistening, her eyes cold and lifeless, the gun pointed in the air converging with the umbrella of steam.

"Git off my land, Hall," Pappy ordered. "I told you before never to set foot on my property."

"Now Younger, we don't 'low no niggers to have property, you knows that, and we treats nigger lovers the same," Hall replied.

"You tell him, Hall," the man with the snake eyes sneered. And suddenly Mammie's gun roared and the man with the snake eyes lay on his back at little Robert's feet, blood seeping through his flannel shirt. The five men charged Pappy and in desperation he hurled the axe, Indian fashion, into Hall's face. Hall's face turned a bright red under the rising of the morning sun. Katie ran around in a circle screaming and holding her head as Mammie's gun thundered and thundered, ripping through the early morning air, like cloudbursts. Suddenly, Charlie Hudnall was there, his wiry frame scuffling with the two white men piled on top of Pappy. The two men on the horses held the six men on the ground in a tight circle while the men on the ground fought to the death.

"Let go of him," Mammie yelled, and the gun thundered again.

"Somebody shut that nigger woman up," a voice yelled. The horses bucked and neighed, but no one moved from the circle for fear of losing ground.

"Watch it! He's got the god-damn axe. Smash his head, smash his head, smash that son-of-a-bitch's head," a voice yelled out over and over. The men scuffled on the ground that had now become mud from the wash water. The axe shone brightly as it rose and fell, rose and fell, and blood became diluted with suds and bluing. The horses neighed, the men grunted low, animal sounds. And blood flowed and bathed the earth as plentiful as rain water. The riders were three now and a voice called from the ground for help. It was Hall, and a man on the horse swept him onto his horse behind the saddle. Hall, blood running down his eyelids, pulled a gun from his shirt, squeezed the trigger, and Charlie fell face first into the mud, his leg twisted under his body.

"Addie, take the chillens out to the creek," Mammie yelled. "Run fast till you gits to the creek and hide yo' self. Don't come out till you hear me a calling you." They ran, but Katie worried about Pappy, turned around and started back towards the fight. She saw Pappy and Charlie lying on the ground, blood smeared over them, as Addie pulled her away. They ran and ran until Katie thought her lungs would explode. She ran until she could not breathe, and she screamed, Pappy, Mammie, Pappy, Pappy."

Katie awoke with a start, her face drenched with perspiration, the Bible yet across her chest. She took several deep breaths, as she realized it was a dream, a horrible, horrible dream. Her eyes slowly adjusted to the darkness of the room and drifted upward to where a streak of moonlight in the shape of a triangle lingered, illuminating the ceiling. Slowly, her eyes focused on the ceiling and gradually took in the room. Her heart stopped beating at the sight of the open front door. She flung the Bible onto the bed and sat straight up, her mind spinning, her brain screaming, "Margaret!"

How did the door get open, and just how long had it been that way? The thoughts raced through her mind. She searched for some logical reason. Did she turn the lock all the way? Had Margaret gotten up in the night and wandered out onto the porch in search of cool air? After all, the windows had been nailed practically closed, but she knew that Margaret always slept straight through the night, no matter what happened. And yes, she did lock the door, she could see it in her mind's eye, could hear the clicking cylinder. There was someone in the house! She was sure of it, and the creak of the worn floor boards coming from the kitchen convinced her it was not her imagination. She rose quietly from the bed, the pounding of her heart echoing in her ears. This was the storm she had been expecting ever since the announcement about the money had become public. But what if this was only a 'night stalk' as Pappy used to call them? What if this was only the trial run, where they come and go and keep you awake all night until you can't stand it any longer, until you finally close your eyes to rest and at that moment they come back for the kill? She had to get to Margaret. One thing she was sure of, whoever it was in the house, they were not professionals like the old night riders or the house would be in flames right now. The door. She had to close the door even though it was the only way out. She crawled on her knees the few feet to the bottom of the door and pushed it softly, shutting out the moonlight, and blanketing her side of the house in darkness. She rose to her feet, rubbed her hand alongside the wall until she felt the spring latch to the middle door and quickly stepped inside of Margaret's bedroom, latching the door quietly behind her. Her breath rapid, she walked slowly toward the small oil lamp flickering on the dresser—its flame the strength of a dying firefly—across the room. Working her way around to the head of the bed, she bent down and clamped her hand over the sleeping girl's mouth, while she listened to the footsteps moving about in the kitchen. Margaret struggled under Katie's grip and sat upright in the bed in alarm.

"Shush now," Katie warned. "There is somebody in the house," she added and feeling Margaret relax under her grip, she slowly removed her hand.

"But who?" Margaret whispered.

"Don't rightly know who, jest you git up real quiet, child."

Margaret moved quickly now. Katie eased back to the door and put her ear against it, straining to hear any movement from the other side. She heard the rustling of bedcovers and something heavy hit the floor. She recognized the sound; it was the Bible. She knew that they would be found, and soon—it would not be long before the intruders found the middle door that divided the house. They had to act fast. She turned from the door and began feeling for the hammer that had been lying on the table earlier.

"We'se got to git a window open." Katie said, her voice shaking with fear.

"But Charlie nailed them shut, Mama," Margaret said, flinging her arms in a hopeless circle.

"I know, but we gots to try. Help me find the hammer. Hurry, girl, hurry!"

A scraping sound came from the other side of the door and minute bursts of light could be seen through the splits in the panel. Through the cracks Katie could see that the intruders were striking matches. She stood frozen to the spot, waiting as if she were back in the dream. She, Addie, and little Robert had run to the creek and hidden in the wet grass waiting for Mammie to call them out. She could feel the cool water on her feet and the damp brush that Addie had thrown across her face-then the blaze of sunlight that almost blinded her when, after hours had passed, the brush was pulled away. She remembered it was like coming out of a dark hole. The trap door! Katie suddenly remembered that Pappy had cut a hole into the floor, for emergencies such as this one; it led to the outside and freedom, by way of the coal bin. She pulled Margaret to the corner, where Margaret's treasure chest sat. "Help me move the trunk," Katie whispered. Margaret obeyed without question. Like cats, they stole across the floor, dropped quietly to their knees, and pushed the trunk towards the wall—it made a swishing sound like a snake in the attic. Katie groped around on the floor until she found the iron ring, then took Margaret's hand and placed it alongside of hers, and together they pulled with all their strength. Margaret pulled with clenched teeth until her jaws ached, and her naked breasts bumped together constantly from the straining muscles that jerked back and forth at the unyielding door. They pulled, stopped and listened, pulled, stopped and listened, until finally the door opened with a squealing protest. They leaned, staring into the darkness of the hole, and in one swift motion Katie reached around Margaret's shoulder, placing her open palm into Margaret's back and pushed Margaret's torso towards the hole. Margaret breathed heavily and raised up on her knees, swinging her legs over the opening and Katie shoved her daughter's naked body through the door, through the spider webs and rust, just as the door to the room was ripped open and two huge shadows loomed towards them. One held a lit match over white hands, the other, quick like a demon, grabbed Margaret by the hair. She screamed and began clawing with her long nails at the face in back of her. Katie spun around, lunged at the figure, and dug her nails into the eyes of the man. He yelled and released Margaret's hair. At once Katie was on her feet behind him and wrapped her arms around his neck, squeezing and pulling simultaneously. She struggled with him until she heard the naked girl drop to the ground, until she heard the rustle of the coal beneath the girl's weight, until the girl's sobs of terror were distant and drowned out by her footsteps furiously pounding the dirt path as she ran to get Charlie.

The other man was suddenly there, pinning her arms behind her as the man with the scratched face got to his feet and punched her across the back of her head, buckling her knees. She reeled—a series of bright multicolored lights swam before her eyes—and slid to the floor. He squatted beside her, his hot whiskey breath on her face and commanded the other, "Go git that nigger!" The shadow tore from the room, leaving them. She heard the banging of the screen door, and heavy footsteps pounding the porch, but her only worry was that Margaret, may have lost her sense of direction coming from the dark hole, for she knew otherwise he would never catch Margaret. Not the girl who had three medals for being the fastest on the track team, and besides, she knew the short cuts to Charlie's house—it was her stomping grounds. Suddenly, powerful arms dragged her across the floor to the other side of the house, her body sliding over the torn linoleum until she was stopped by something in her path—Pappy's Bible. She was yanked to her feet, her head snapped backward and then toward the door where a triangle of light sat on the ceiling like a stranger afraid to come inside. The shadow was too close for her to see his face. He punched her in the stomach, grunting like a man lifting something heavy. The blow lifted her from the floor onto her toes. She reeled again and slipped on the pages of the open Bible, trying to maintain her balance. The dark figure holding her did not speak. He punched her again and again until she slammed against the wall, her hand falling against something cold and smooth—the axe.

"The blood of Jesus," she cried out and tightened her hand around the smooth wood of the axe-handle. She felt the blood trickle from her nose and spreading onto her lips. By the light coming from the slightly open front door in the front room, she saw his face and recognized him as the man from the diner-Roy Larkin. She watched him pace back and forth, obviously anxious about his partner's absence.

He walked swiftly to the front door and then turned. Facing her, he demanded, "Where did she go?" She watched the distorted shadow that stood before her and extended to the ceiling, its head a massive black circle above her, its shoulders a narrow strip jammed in the seams where the wall met. She watched through cloudy eyes as the dream floated in and out of her mind, the blood on the ground running in long streaks, mixing with bluing and suds from the wash water. Pappy, tall, vibrant, and unafraid, defeat in his eyes and bitter rage in his mouth; Mammie rooted to the ground like a giant black oak; and the screaming children who ran around in panic, too small to help. She suddenly felt very small. Small and naked like David, standing in Goliath's shadow. And like David she placed all her faith in the Almighty.

Carefully, she moved her other hand and gripped the axe handle in its center, and drawing to the right for leverage, she balanced herself firmly on the floor. The terrifying shadow stopped pacing and approached her, his hand drawn back to strike. Bringing the blade over her shoulder she swung in the name of the Lord. The blade whistled through the humid air, sounding like a fierce wind moving tree tops, and hit its mark with a solid, terrifying whack. The axe sliced cleanly through his arm and hit the wall banging, then severing several greeting cards in half. Roy fell back against the wall, sliding to the floor in front of the middle door-his eyes big, unreadable.

It was not a scream of anguish piercing the night air that she would always remember, for there was no scream, but instead a catch in the man's breath that seemed to last an eternity—followed by a moan so low, it was but a whisper, a whisper that even the keenest of ears could not interpret. And it was not the blood spraying her face and hair that terrified her the most, but the dream of a childhood memory long buried in her subconscious—a memory that was still black and chilling two decades later. A memory of blood spilling freely as water, of men—good men, like Pappy and Charlie, bloody and tussling in the mud, battering their fists into the faces of other men, as they listened only to the savagery of their hearts—forgetting God's Commandments—running headlong into that void of spiritual death. Perhaps the visit from the strange dog, and the reliving of the memory through a dream had nothing to do with her physical death as she had believed, but instead she, too, would fall into that void, that she would lose sight of her God.

The front door pushed open, and seeing the arm at Katie's feet, the other man froze. Katie stood, her eyes glazed, the axe hanging limply at her side.

"Marmy," Roy cried out in a weak trembling voice.

"My God, Roy, you're bleeding like a hog," Marmy exclaimed from the door, shifting his eyes from Roy to Katie.

"Marmy, man, help me," Roy begged.

"Jest you hold on," Marmy hollered and backed slowly out the door. He whistled and waved both arms above his head to a man in a pick-up truck sitting down the road under cover of the pecan trees. In a moment, another man appeared in the door; and together, their eyes never leaving Katie's face, the two men dragged Roy from the house. He clutched the air and screaming, "Don't leave my arm in that nigger's house. O, God, no, not in there!" She stood, listening to the blood drip onto the pages of the Bible and watching the arm move about on its own. Blood seemed to be everywhere. A long dark path of it ran out the door and down the steps behind the men who hurried towards their truck. She heard Charlie's old shotgun blast the air above their heads. The gun thundered again as the man brought the truck around. Marmy tied a belt around the stump of Roy's arm to stop the bleeding.

"Wait, Marmy, I can't go jest yet."

"Don't you worry none, we'll come back and finish the job, but we got to git you over to doc's right now!"

She heard the crunch of gravel and then Charlie's shotgun blast the air again. She crept to the door and watched the man wheel the truck around to the bottom of the steps—the brakes squealing. She saw the driver scoot to the edge of the seat, groping wildly for Roy's hand, then Marmy pushed Roy through the opening head first—blood gushing from the stump with every movement—until Roy's legs disappeared inside the truck. At once Marmy was on the running board and slapped his hand on the metal, yelling, "Move it!"

And she watched as the pick-up pulled off, leaving a swirl of dust behind it as it made the sharp turn heading towards town. In a few minutes, Margaret reached the bottom of the steps and took them two at a time, her wide hips stuffed in a pair of Charlie's old work pants. An old flannel shirt hung loosely around her shoulders, but she was still barefoot. With Charlie and Luther not far behind, she didn't stop running until she was in her mother's arms.

SCATTING

Simply because the houses stood in the huge shadow of the white stone mansion that belonged to the wealthy white recluse, Martha Monther, the gravel road that passed between them was called Monther's Alley. It was not taken into consideration that all these homes were privately owned, or that they stood miles apart from each other rather than crowded together like an alley because all the houses belonged to Negroes who did not pay rent for either the homes or the rich land around them. It was here, in Monther's Alley, halfway between Katie's house and his, that Charlie started the bonfire. He and Luther Dawson, who worked for Charlie and also resided in the alley, built the fire from scraps of wood, old clothing, and newspapers saturated with coal-oil.

The orange flames licked at the air, growing larger and larger as they ate their way upwards toward the sky. Charlie Hudnall, a yet wiry man in his sixties, and Luther Dawson, a young man of nineteen who swore he was twenty stood side by side gazing into the fire. Charlie stood leaning on his cane, dividing his attention between the fire and Luther. They talked in low, muffled voices, Luther with his head cocked back, until the blaze began to warm their shinbones beneath the heavy coveralls and Charlie determined the fire was hot enough to burn almost anything—even a human arm. Then he pushed himself to the left of the blaze, about ten feet away from Luther, to the pile of discarded old furnishings that had been donated by the residents. He searched among the stacks and stacks of tree branches; among the old faded clothes, including the bloody ones that Katie had worn earlier; and among a miscellany of other treasures—an old rocker with a tiny heart carved on its arm, a wooden half-moon with a staircase leading to the stars, and even an old white Mama doll with its rubber knees eaten through to the cotton stuffing—before he spied the package he sought—the package that contained Roy Larkin's arm. He stooped over and sifted through the branches with his cane, keeping his eye on the bold black print that announced a sale at Phillips Hardware on Buckeye's cotton seed oil. He rolled the newspaper towards him, using the tip of his cane like it was a poker, rolling and lifting it from beneath the other branches, until it lay at his feet. It reminded him of a giant sausage roll (like the one on display at Adkins' store) that had been crimped and tied on each end to retain its freshness—something that a young country boy could heft across his shoulder and carry for ten miles without tiring. But this roll had been wrapped hurriedly, in child-like fashion, and fingers protruded through one end of the bundle, looking like the knobbed end of a chair arm.

Slowly Charlie shifted his weight, and laid his cane on top of the branches. He cautiously picked up the package by the string, holding it close in front of him, hoping that Luther, who now stood on the other side of the fire, wouldn't become suspicious about its contents. Charlie held the package up and away from his chest as he inched towards the fire. With his back to Luther, he began to sway in and out. Quickly, he tossed the package into the flames, where it landed with a thump on top and instantly became an orange blur. And just as quickly, he and Luther jumped away from the fire as the flames suddenly expanded from the burst of air created by the arm. They stooped over and beat the flying sparks that flew onto their pants legs; their hands, brushing in unison against the stiff denim, sounded like the hooves of horses galloping at neck breaking speed.

Charlie picked up Katie's bloody dress from the rag pile near his feet, wiped his hands clean, tossed it into the flame as though it was diseased. And Luther, aware that Charlie was hiding something but respecting the old man's wisdom, pretended not to notice, and looked up and down the road. The fire sputtered momentarily, and, shortly, flames shot upward again, quickly digesting the dress and the newspaper, beginning it fiery assault on the new fuel—Roy Larkin's arm. Greedily, the fire licked at the air, cracking, while Charlie sighed, satisfied that Luther did not get a good look at the package. Although his conscience nagged him—whispering that it was no way he could keep a secret of this kind, that the law would eventually find him out—he knew he had no other choice but to try and cover up what had happened here tonight. He knew the white folks' laws, and Katie, Christian that she was, would not stand a chance fighting them on their terms, so what else could he do? But maybe they would not be discovered at all. It was a chance they had to take. Perhaps he could discover the identity of the other person driving that truck—it was not one of Roy's regular running buddies, Charlie was sure of that. But the jagged shadow that hung about the bed of the truck was familiar to Charlie, and the rattle of the gate hinge he knew he had heard somewhere, and recently, but where? The memory of the time and place would come back to him, he was sure, just as sure as he was that as long as the fire blazed, the men in the pick-up would not return tonight.

He pulled the Bible from underneath the rag pile and staggered backwards. "Confound it," he muttered, and flung the white leather-bound Holy Bible, stained from blood, into the raging fire, like he was pitching horseshoes. He leaned back on his cane, gazing at the fire and remembering his friend, Robert Younger, who many years ago had told him the Bible had been in his family for generations. He remembered how Robert's eyes would gleam with pride each time he talked about becoming a father, and how he had recorded each birth in that Bible. Charlie had been present when Little Robert was born where Robert retold the event around him becoming a father first with Addie, then Katie, and pulled out the Bible for Charlie to see their names as he entered the newest child. But mostly Charlie remembered his wedding day, when he and Anna Mae tied the knot—Robert had also recorded that wonderful day in the Bible. It was Robert's way of showing Charlie that he considered him to be a part of the family and not just a friend. But as miserable as he felt, Charlie knew it could never equal the agony that Katie must be feeling over having to destroy the book of memories her pappy had left to her. He shivered, remembering the anguish in her eyes when he told her it would have to be destroyed. The emptiness in her eyes cut into his flesh. A look he would never forget. His sigh was heavy, like that of a beaten man, and he shook his head at all of it. It just wasn't fair having to give up everything. Couldn't even keep your memories—and what good are you without them? He snatched his eyes away from the flame, walked the two feet towards Katie's place, and stared at the house in the darkness. He imagined he saw her standing there in the shadows with tears streaming down her face; he turned away, quickly blew his nose on his big handkerchief, and focused on Luther, who squatted a few feet away using Charlie's old gun for support.

"Better stretch them legs, Luther. We gonna be here all night," Charlie advised, cramming the handkerchief back in his pocket.

"I ain't tired yet, Mr. Charlie. Ain't tired a bit," Luther replied, his voice thick with concern, his brow heavy with wrinkles.

"Still, better stretch. A man thinks better on his feet. That's what my daddy used to say, God bless his soul, and he was usually right," Charlie said, approaching Luther, stroking his jaw like it was covered with grit. He leaned forward on his cane and stared down at the young man.

Luther's six-foot frame pushed up from he ground and stood almost one foot over Charlie's. The flicker from the flames exposed a thin face filled with outrage as hot as the sizzling fire, outrage that spread from his deep, black eyes and settled on his thin lips, creating a twisted sneer. "Why?" Luther spat the word so violently that the letters seemed to hang in the air above them, visible to the naked eye. "Why they beat on Sister Katie like they done?" he pressed, and leaned his head back to get a better view of Charlie's face.

"Why?" Charlie sputtered in amazement. "Now, boy, I'se knows you done heard 'bout that money Katie posed to git."

"Yes sir, I knows that. Margaret done tole me everything 'bout that money, and I spect everybody in town knows it too," Luther said quickly, dropping his head while he poked the barrel of the gun at the ground.

"Well, if'n you done been tole everythang, then why is you asking me that? Charlie questioned, twisting his neck around to look up at him.

"That ain't what I mean," Luther mumbled, still poking the gun barrel at the ground. "What I mean is, why is they like that?"

Suddenly aware of how impotent he felt, Charlie looked away. He wasn't sure just how to answer the question, for he had asked it many times himself. "Oh, you is asking the big question, the one 'bout white folks and the Negroes. Is that what you is asking me, boy?"

"Yes. I reckon that is what I'se asking," the words falling from Luther's lips as though he was unsure.

"Hump," Charlie grunted, and turned towards the drumming sound of water hitting inside a metal bucket at Katie's. He calculated the distance to be about fifty feet and realized that it was either Katie or Margaret pumping water in their back yard—probably to clean up the blood, he thought, and dropped his head. He looked over at Luther out of the corner of his eye and wondered where to start. He only knew what white folks did to Negroes and what they made Negroes do to other Negroes and sometimes even to white folks—like Katie cutting of Roy's arm. Should he dig through the fire and salvage the arm to show the boy what white folks had made a Christian woman like Katie do? Or should he insist that Luther go inside Katie's house and look at all the blood (he had not allowed Luther to enter after they arrive)? Or should he tell him about Katie's father, a white man who loved a Negro woman and died because of it? Or how a younger Charlie Hudnall had savagely beaten his pregnant wife to death because the white doctor had denied her medical attention. He could tell him of many instances of brutality and of the love that existed between the white and the Negro too, but why? He wasn't sure if any white person could answer that question—he wasn't even sure if Katie's God could answer it.

"That's a mighty big question for a man of my standing to try and answer," Charlie sputtered. "Why is they like that? I can't rightly say…" He stood up straight and peered across the grounds. "Maybe it has something to do with man kind…" He stopped and rubbed his chin. "The way I'se sees it is white folks act much like your mama and daddy does. You knows your mama and daddy is the boss of the house, and the chillens has to do what they say. Now they is all smiles and praising your efforts as long as you do likes you is tole. But when you don't they jest ups and pull rank. You know, laying down their laws and the sich. Only thing now with white folks being the strange folks they is, you might not jest know what they determines as being the right thang to do. But come to think on it, that's 'bout the same way your mama and daddy is, too. Oh, you knows the big important rules: no cussing, no drinking, no white womens, and you gots to call them Mister and Missis at all times. But it's them little rules they keeps changing on you that keeps you confused. Like your mama scolding you for walking on her fresh-washed floor one day, and the next time she is screaming, 'Boy go on cross that floor and bring me my egg money.' And white folks say very clear to you don't come over on this side of this place 'cause it's for white folks only, and later, after everybody done gone home, they yells, 'Boy don't jest stand there, come on over here and sweep this here floor.' Now take that there money been left to Margaret for x-zample. White folks left it to her legal—right? And now the same white family is trying to take it back. So there it is, you is bound to misunderstand them rules."

Charlie leaned closer, poking a skinny finger in Luther's chest, then rocked back on his cane and tucked his finger inside the wide strap of his coveralls. Luther shifted his weight, stood back in his legs, and nervously wiped at the tip of his nose, his dark eyes scanning every inch of Charlie's face. "But when you do misunderstand, ain't no compromise. You has done stepped out of place and you is not the sweet old nigger you used to be. They is your judge, jury and even your God. All you is, is one ignorant nigger child. Then it's time to make a x-zample out of you, so they does—much like your mama or daddy would—beat you till you can't sit down or stand up. Or they might jest take some privilege from you, like eating."

"But they ain't your mama and daddy. And they don't beat you the same way your folks do—it's different," Luther said loudly, jamming the nose of the gun hard into the dirt, his forehead coated with a thin layer of sweat.

"I knows that, but they don't know that. They thinks they is responsible for you jest like your parents do." Charlie waved his hand. "But you see, as long as they keep on thinking they is, and as long as they have these special rules to keep us in control, they will keep on doing whatever they feels like doing."

"Not to me they won't," Luther swore with conviction, gripping the gun until his knuckles ached, and Charlie looked hard into his face, suddenly feeling very uneasy.

The stench from the burning arm assaulted Charlie's nostrils and he spun away from Luther quickly, heading towards the pile of wood and indicating with his cane for Luther to help. Charlie grabbed an armload of old clothes and tossed them on the fire—hoping to disguise the smell as well as cover the area, should the arm be exposed. The rotten cloth burst into flames just as Luther returned with his arms loaded with wood, and just as a truck turned into the bend of the road. "Sssh, listen," Charlie commanded in a raspy whisper. "There's a truck a-coming up the road."

"Damn it, it's Sylvester," Luther reported, and dropped the wood at Charlie's feet.

"I was jest thinking them same words, boy. And you can bet your life he'll be a-coming over here to check out this here fire. Keep a tight lip," Charlie instructed as he grabbed Luther's shoulder and turned him around. "Head him off before he gits to the fire."

The battered pick-up truck that Sylvester Bodine called The Red Devil (he lifted the name from a can of lighter fluid) crept slowly up the road. Sylvester had only owned the truck for two years, but during that time it had somehow lost one of its doors—the one on the driver's side—and everyone in town agreed it was because he opened the door at every convenience to spit out the juices from the wad of tobacco that he kept in his mouth at all times. The fire, blazing again now, revealed the stark surprise as well as the intense curiosity on Sylvester's black, leathery face as he brought the truck to a squeaking halt alongside the road and climbed out. Charlie stiffened at the sound of the heavy footsteps, but continued piling the wood on the fire. Luther, remembering Charlie's instructions and how he felt about Sylvester, gripped the old gun tightly in his hand—he fought off the urge to shoot him on the spot.

Sylvester was the last person on earth they wanted to see tonight, even though he stayed on the far side of the alley and had every right to travel this road. He was despised by every Negro in town. It was not because he was nosy, or because he had filthy habits—chewing tobacco and scratching like he had lice. It wasn't even for his lack of bathing—many Negroes didn't have access to running water. They despised him for one simple reason: he couldn't keep his mouth closed. He told white folks everything he knew and everything he thought. He was an Uncle Tom. Luther walked out to meet Sylvester and stop him before he came across the gravel road. He held the barrel of the gun pointing downward at the ground as he walked with slow wide strides. He faced the stubby, wide-nosed man who stood under the shadows of the pecan tree in the middle of the road.

Uncle Toms were always a problem because they knew the rituals of their people, and Charlie had anticipated that Sylvester would understand the meaning of the bonfire—a signal Negroes used to warn others that they were being threatened by white people in one way or another. Usually in the worst way, with their lives in jeopardy. So just in case they faced dealing with Sylvester, Charlie's plan was one of confusion.

"What's the trouble? What's that I smell? What's going on here?" Sylvester rattled, stretching his thick neck to look around Luther's tall frame that stood purposely in front of him, blocking his view. His sallow eyes stretched to their limit, and he kept moving his head from side to side trying to see around Luther. "Ain't that Charlie Hudnall over yonder, boy? What in tarnation going on 'round here anyhows?" His brown hat, covered with layers of red dust and cotton lint, let Luther know that he had probably just now come from the cotton gin, and that if he could keep him from the fire, Sylvester wouldn't know anything to tell.

"Troubles over with now. Ain't no need to git all riled up and everythang," Charlie spoke matter-of-factly from across the road and poked the fire. The arm shifted down deeper under the wood. "Jest had a small case of scatting, that's all," Charlie added.

"Scatting you say," Sylvester yelled, and swallowed several times, his adam's apple bobbing up and down.

"Three truckloads of young white boys yelling and carrying on. You knows how they love to carry on," Charlie continued. "Didn't say, though, who they was aiming to teach a lesson, but we all figured it probably started on account of that there money Katie is due to git any time now," he added, steadily poking in the fire with his cane.

Quickly, Sylvester's huge eyes scanned all the windows in the alley, and he was confused at what he saw. All the houses had a lamp burning in their windows—he knew this was not the custom. The house in trouble was supposed to be blanketed in darkness, and all the houses had lights on. Charlie breathed a sigh of relief as he followed

Sylvester's gaze and realized that Margaret had not forgotten his instructions to leave her light on.

"Scatting, huh? Well, they musta said something. They don't jest come a-scatting and don't say nothing. What you reckon it was really 'bout? You reckon they coming back this way tonight? They usually comes back." Sylvester bombarded Charlie with questions as he tried to peek around Luther.

"Now jest you calm yo'self," Charlie said in a soothing, reassuring voice. Luther stepped to the side just enough for Sylvester to see Charlie's poker face, but not far enough for him to see what it was he smelled in the fire. Luther's instinct told him it was something Sylvester should not see as well as something that even he did not want to see or know about. He had taken his cue from Charlie, who told him when they first arrived not to come inside of Katie's house because Luther had "seed enough for tonight." Charlie was referring to Margaret's naked run to his house, when she burst in on Charlie and Luther sitting at the table eating cold beans.

"Mr. Bodine," Luther interrupted, "jest you go on home now and put a light in your window. Go on to sleep and git your rest 'cause we is gonna be here on guard all night. Any thing come up, we'll let you know first-hand, I promise."

"Luther," Charlie called from the fire. "Ain't you gonna ask Bodine can you pick with him tomorrow? You done forgot, ain't you?"

"I sho had," Luther replied, somewhat surprised, but not taking his face away from Sylvester's. "I hears you needs somebody to help you pick, Mr. Bodine. Wish you'd let me come with you. Mr. Charlie don't need me tomorrow, and I could sho use the money," Luther said.

Well, I reckon you'll do," Bodine said, eyeing Luther closely. "I leaves at five. Ain't you gonna be plumb wore out?" he said, sniffing the air and scratching underneath his hat.

"Naw, I'll git some sleep right here by the fire. Now you go on home, ain't no need for us both to worry all night 'bout nothing," Luther said, making a sweeping motion with his gun hand towards the flame. Bodine shuffled from side to side and reluctantly turned and walked the short distance to the truck. His shoulders stooped, and the huge brogans kicked up the red dust as he climbed inside, holding onto the steering wheel for support.

"Reckon old Bodine will turn in?" Luther asked as soon as the truck had cleared the bend in the road.

"Well, if'n he don't, you jest run over yonder and tell him some strange white woman was 'round here looking for him. He'll crawl under that house, and all you is gonna see is the whites of his eyes—Lawd, that man is scared to death of white womens," Charlie said, looking at Luther, who seemed on the verge of laughing out loud.

They both sat down by the fire. Charlie propped himself against the pecan tree, and Luther sat a few feet away with his knees pulled up. The blaze cracked and popped contentedly, while Luther, cradling his legs, rocked back and forth, smiling. "Mr. Charlie, I knows that feeling, believes me. I used to be scared to death of white womens, too."

"Yeah, how come?" Charlie asked, and turned to face him.

"It's all on account of the story Grandma Lil used to tell me when I was little," he confided and flushed under Charlie's scrutiny.

"Well, knowing your grandma liken I do, it probably is one of them tall tales of hern's," Charlie speculated, and rested his back against the trunk of the tree.

"Well, did she ever tell you the story 'bout womens shredding boys, and how it was common practice 'round these here parts?" Luther asked, stretching his eyes like an amused ten-year-old.

"Womens shredding boys!" Charlie said, amusement in his voice. "Now that's a good one, better than what I was specting to hear. Sure you ain't making this up yo'self 'cause you'se gots to go pick with that old spy, Sylvester?" Charlie asked, his eyes shining in anticipation of the story.

"Mr. Charlie, Mr. Charlie," Luther added, anxiously, "Grandma Lil used to tell me—I swears it's the truth." The gray smoke billowed about them and their shadows, thrown against the house at Charlie's back, were wavy—ghostlike. "Even swore on the Bible in my presence—that all white womens shreds little colored boys like they was cabbage, in a special machine.

Charlie threw back his head and roared, his head plastered against the tree trunk, his heels pushing long furrows in the dirt. He laughed until he began to choke, coughing and gasping for air. Finally, he settled down, but avoided looking directly at Luther for fear of another outburst. Luther laughed, too. Luther lay with his long legs stretched across the ground and his upper torso propped up with his elbows and yanked up the grass at his sides, tears streaming down his face—tears that seemed to leap from his eyes the more he laughed, tears that he did not bother to wipe away.

"Mr. Charlie, Mr. Charlie," Luther continued, his breath coming like gusts of wind. "Listen. You know why they does this? Grandma says they git awful white come winter time—awful white, and they use little colored boys' skin and blood to make them a special rouge for their cheeks."

Charlie shook his head in agony. He felt as if he were inside of a vise that threatened to burst him wide open if he did not laugh. He picked up his cane and slapped it against the ground several times, and it appeared that he had squashed the laughter. But when he envisioned his boss lady, Miss Clara, standing in the sun, her face bloodless, beckoning a long skinny finger to a wide-eyed colored boy to come with her into some obscure barn, he fell apart. His body shook. The cane seemed to be trying to jump from his hand. He and Luther laughed a long five minutes or so—each one pounding the ground and gasping for air like he had been swimming in the great Mississippi.

The laughter continued, sporadic and dying out, then erupting again, until they had exhausted themselves. Finally, they sat motionless, staring at the orange-red flames and listening to the splash of water that came in intervals, being tossed on the steps at Katie's house. A splash reminding Charlie that Katie and Margaret were still cleaning away blood, blood from the arm that now burned in the bonfire. He pushed the dirt with the heel of his shoe, made another furrow, and thought of the arm. Would it burn all the way? Probably not. Maybe he should have buried it like he started to, but no, he had to make the fire anyway. What would he do with the remains?

"I been knowing it wadn't true for the longest, Mr. Charlie," Luther interrupted his thoughts. "I jest played along like I didn't know nothing."

"Huh?" Charlie responded slowly and, remembering their conversation began to chuckle. But it was different this time, the moment of relief was gone, and the strain was back in his chest, a giant weight that pressed against his insides like a sharp crease on dress pants. The smoke thickened in a dome above their heads, dimming the stars. And Charlie's face seemed suddenly like stone—his thin jaws set in a grimace, his round eyes half-closed like a blind man straining to see light. It was insanity—here he sat laughing at a senseless story told by a boy, while the rank odor of burning flesh singed his nostrils.

"I knowed it was, 'cause she didn't want me messing 'round with no white womens, but for a long time, if I seed a white woman coming up the road, I'd run and hide. She told me this right after they done pulled that boy out of the river—you remember? The one that didn't have no eyes and no privates"

"Yeah, I remembers," Charlie responded, a sneer forming on his face. "That'll be Pete Sommers' boy. Lemme see. What was that child's name? Willie Lee, yeah that was it—Willie Lee. Surprise that you remembers it though, couldn't been no more than eight."

"I was x-actly eight. Wadn't till three years ago when they hung Reece Scott that I learned what it was white womens did to colored men ain't had nothing to do with no shredding. But Grandma is still telling that story, this time to little David—told him that the other day, and rolled her eyes at me, you know, daring me to spute her word."

"Boy, you old enough to be talking under women's clothes?"

"I'se twenty, Mr. Charlie. I reckon so. Anyways, it jest old white womens."

"You thinking on gitting married maybe then?" Charlie added, peering hard at Luther in the artificial light. "When a man gits to talking under women's clothes, marriage is usually the next step. You aiming to ask Margaret to become your wife?"

"Yep," he said, smiling, his thoughts wandering to some imaginary white house with a white picket fence where dark- skinned children with Margaret's wide eyes played in the yard and where Margaret sat in the swing brushing her long hair. And then her firm, naked body was before him—his mouth became very dry.

"Didn't know you and Margaret was courting," Charlie said, his heart swelling with hope. He genuinely liked Luther.

"Well," Luther hesitated. He lowered his head staring at the ground. "The thing is Mr. Charlie, Margaret acts like I'm her big brother. But I don't aim to let that stop me none."

"Well, what if she says no. What you aiming to do next?"

"Ain't gonna give up, Mr. Charlie," Luther replied, a soft light in his eyes. "I'm gonna keep trying until she says yes. I aims to visit her up yonder in St. Louis when she goes off to school. I aims for Margaret to see me with new eyes."

"Sorta wear her down where she see you for what you is?" Charlie questioned with a smile forming around his lips.

"That's the plan. I knows Margaret likes me more than she pretends."

"Well, you understand her, it seems. Margaret wants more than to be somebody's wife and mother—she wants a heap of things most women don't even think on." Charlie stared out into the night.

"Yep," Luther said sadly. "I knows my competition and it ain't no other man—well not yet, anyhows."

They were silent, the dogs yapped in the distance, and occasionally the splash of water would make them turn their heads. Luther looked half a mile up the road across the railroad tracks, toward the hazy lamplight that flooded Sylvester's window. "Reckon that old possum done gone to bed?"

Charlie looked towards the house, squinting his eyes. "Naw, that old spy ain't sleep yet. Probably got his eyeballs glued on us right this minute. That's why I volunteered you to pick with him tomorrow. I wants to make sure he ain't seed nothing. I wants you to stick to him like glue. Best run in the house and git your sack now." Charlie rose slowly and went back to the fire while Luther propped the gun by the tree and headed across the road to his house.

"Be back fore you can holler 'jack rabbit,'" Luther boasted. Charlie looked at the long shadow of the boy running across the road, then turned and looked towards Katie's house, towards the sound of splashing water, and continued stacking wood on the fire. It would be a very long night.

HOUSECLEANING

They had worked long and hard into the early morning; their efforts consumed with ridding the premises of Roy Larkin's remains—his blood and the main part of his right arm. They had divided the work; the women cleaned away the blood, the men guarded the bonfire closely as the arm burned. It had been a terrifying and grizzly ordeal, but they had set the place in order. And now, no one would ever guess this was the place where a young white man's arm had been deftly chopped off in the name of the Lord, then carefully burned with the neighborhood's trash in the name of survival.

The truck that delivered the cottonpickers to Lavilli Field pulled into the bend of the alley at four-thirty—its familiar rattling sideboards and slow putt-putt engine brought the alley to life. Viola Dawson, her daughters, Judy Rose and Zara Lee, the Hamptons, Big Oscar, Junebug, J.D., the Johnsons, Willie C, Bill, and their four year old brother, E.C., all stirred at the sound of the truck's engine. Lamps were blown out like birthday candles; gravel crunched and echoed as men, women, and children stumbled from their homes with disgruntled faces, remnants of sleep still glued to their eyes. Those who had no other work for that day yanked the long, canvas sacks from hooks on their kitchen walls, or mechanically produced them from onion or coal bins on their back porches. Those who were fortunate enough to have other work, such as Almeda Porter, Velma Williams (Katie would have been included in this group had this been a routine day), wrapped cold meat and bread and stuffed it in paper sacks, or made beds, even before the sun peeked through the curtains of gray, and before the rooster crowed twice.

The noise roused Katie from a narcotic sleep. She rolled out of bed, stuffed her feet into Margaret's cut-out oxfords, and stumbled in front of the mirror on her dresser. Standing in the shadow of the kerosene lamp, she gazed at her pasty white skin and the dark circles around her eyes. She was suddenly reminded of something she had overheard Margaret say to one of the Hampton boys—that he looked like death eating on a soda cracker. She thought that she, too, looked like death. Although the only visible bruise she had was a slight redness on her left cheek, a mark the size of a man's thumb print, she knew that she would not be able to work as planned. She poked her fingers under the bath towel wrapped around her head and flinched. She had a quarter-size lump on the back of her neck that throbbed with every move she made. Her stomach was bloated and felt dislocated, as if it floated, bumping into other organs, making her gait slow and awkward. There was no way she could move around Miss Rosie without arousing suspicion.

The burning kerosene lamp cast a yellow ball of light on the ceiling, like a tiny sun trying to break free of the early morning darkness that covered the house in a blanket of thick black sorghum—heavy, sweet and unfulfilling. The putt-putt of the truck continued and she wondered what was keeping it there. Old man Travis, the burly Negro, who worked for Townsend was strict about hands being on time. He had to deliver many field hands from all over town and rural areas before six, the time picking started, and Katie recalled that whenever Travis waited, it was for someone who could pick a good two hundred pounds a day, probably Cooper, as he was prone to oversleeping and picked enough cotton to make white men brag over their salted beer on Saturday nights.

She pushed up the sleeves on the long housedress and stared at her reflection once again—it had not changed. She frowned, sniffed the air—then, picking up the lamp, stepped across the threshold and into the kitchen. The house was humid, and in spite of the thorough wash down with strong lye soap and Pine Sol, she could still smell Roy

Larkin's blood—a wild, gamey odor that seemed to follow her from room to room. And it was no wonder, as it had been everywhere: on Katie's hair and clothes and under Margaret's feet. On the linoleum and soaked through the wood underneath. On the middle door, several greeting cards pinned to the wall, as well as the wall itself. On the light switch, under the space heater, on the outer door, the porch, the steps, the top of the mail box, and of course the axe. She set the lamp on the kitchen table, walked the few feet to the back door, and yanked it open—Charlie had removed the boards after the break-in last night. She inhaled the morning air, taking in the aroma of red dirt mixed with charred ash wood deeply into her lungs—anything was better than the smell of Roy's blood. She felt lifeless, and could not ever remember feeling so worn out. She closed her eyes for a moment, took another breath, and stepped away from the door to turn and face the long wooden table that was used as a wash-up area. The pots, large kettle and buckets—borrowed from neighbors—were stacked in rows of threes, reaching as high as her neck, and faced her like a stone mountain in Georgia. She fingered the lip of the large blue pail that belonged to Viola, the one she had used to wash Roy's blood from her hair. She hoped Viola would never find out what it had been used for and she saw again the red bubbling suds foaming in the pail, so like the red, sudsy water bathing the ground in the dream.

Slowly, the night came back to her—in swatches, like cloth cut and patterned for a fancy quilt. She saw Pappy's Bible being tossed into the fire, and she sobbed quietly into her hands. Now, she had nothing that she could touch to recall the days of her childhood—the life she had shared with her pappy and mammie. She would have to rely on her memory, which was now hazy and untrustworthy. Turning away from the table, she walked to the Warm Morning Cookstove, dragged a stick match across its apron, and touched the blue flame to the wad of newspaper inside. The wind rustled the leaves outside, carrying them high, high, high, aswirl, like the tail of a twister; and, for a moment, Katie heard the rustle of coal shifting under Margaret's weight as she dropped through the trap door, suddenly feeling Roy's hot whiskey breath on her face. Quickly, she slapped butter on bread and slid the pan into the warming oven. Then slid the coffee pot on the back burner to come to a slow-boil. She walked back through her room, opened the middle door to Margaret's side of the house, and stepped into her daughter's bedroom, stopping at the foot of the bed. A small kerosene lamp glowed on the night table next to Margaret's bed, and a faint ray of light crept around the window shades. She looked down on the sleeping girl, who lay on her back snoring. "Poor chile, Katie mumbled, then jerked her head towards the front door. The pounding of footsteps outside on the gravel made her start. She listened, her heart hammering in her chest, until she heard Cooper yell, "Here I comes, Mr. Travis, here I comes." She exhaled a sigh of relief, for she didn't want anyone within a ten-mile radius when Charlie came. She didn't dare trust herself around anyone until she knew that Roy was either dead or alive. She glanced at the bedside clock on the table, and knew that she could not wait for Charlie any longer—it was four-thirty-five. If she was to catch Alice on the road, she would have to hurry. She returned to the other side of the house, and hastily pulled a dress from the closet.

Standing again in front of the mirror, she unwound the towel from her head, clipped the sides with pins, and let it hang down her back like a scarf. She examined her cheek, applied a small dab of Mavis Talc to cover the redness, then clasping her hands together, said a quick prayer, walked to the kitchen, snatched the toast from the oven, and eased out the back door.

Charlie arrived at Katie's at five-fifteen, in a huff and smelling of fire. His lean face was spotted with soot and mud. His eyes were red and puffy. He looked around the kitchen suspiciously, turning his head slowly back and forth as he helped himself to the coffee on the stove. He propped his cane against the wall, picked up the cup, and looked around again. A weariness seemed to settle over his shoulders as he limped through Katie's bedroom (the middle room) and on to the front room where it had all happened. He stopped at the edge of the rocking chairs, marveled at the gleaming floor, then flicked on the electric light for a better view. He scanned the room with a microscopic eye, looking for incriminating evidence—blood splatters or pieces of Roy's clothing that might have been overlooked during their wild, desperate search last night. Satisfied that the women had been thorough, he slurped a mouthful of coffee, snapped off the light, and limped back to the kitchen. He pushed the dusty hat back on his head, set the cup on the table, and wolfed down a piece of toast. He leaned against the table, smacking his lips, his eyes hard and weary, his coveralls stained with grass and ash wood cinders. The sound of Margaret's labored breathing, coming from the other side of the house, filled his ears, and he relaxed. Katie had gone to work as planned. He would eat, nap in the chair for an hour, and head out to work for Miss Clara. Margaret would be up by then, and everything would be as usual. Just a normal Wednesday, nothing out of the ordinary to draw attention to them.

It had been a long time since Charlie stayed up all night, doing such strenuous work, and his body ached all over. Grabbing another piece of toast, and pulling out the chair, he sank down heavily, sighing with relief. The screen door squeaked open and Charlie jerked alert, his eyes big. "Drat, burn it, don't do that, Katie!" he sputtered, gasping for air and slamming the toast to the table. "You done justa 'bout scared me outa my skin. Thought you done gone to work.

"Can't work, Charlie," Katie said, stepping into the kitchen, flinging her hands in the air. "Jest ain't no way I can work 'round Miss Rosie. I'se too stiff, and jest plain wore out—liable to set myself on fire." She eased to the table, stopped at Charlie's chair, and looked down at the smashed toast. She looked up at Charlie curiously, then headed toward the stove for coffee. He listened for a moment to the liquid splashing in the cup, then turned around in the chair, facing the table. "I'se been up the road meeting Alice so she can splain to Miss Rosie that I can't work today," she said, talking to his back. "Ain't gots no other way to call 'cepting going over to the church, but I knows you is dead set against that. I been up since Travis come for the pickers. What kept you anyhows?"

He propped his elbows on the table, sighed and listened to the Rooster crow. "I knows you feels poorly, can't help but feel bad, but this here thing gots to be kept under the rug. You shoulda went on to work liken always," he finally answered. "What you say to Alice?"

She cradled the cup in her hand, her face pulled down in a frown. "Jest that there was sickness in my house. Didn't say no one in particular, but it's the God's truth, we is all sick! Me and Margaret took turns peeking in that crack in the wall for bits of a man's arm, and then you wrapped it in the sales paper and burned it and my pappy's Bible. And if'n that ain't sick, I don't know what is," she said in a crisp, sharp tone. She crossed the room and stood in the door, staring outside. "What I means is," her voice softer, "I can't hardly turn my head 'round, and Margaret done jest about suffocated herself, sleeping in that outing gown in this here heat to prove to somebody—me, I guess—that she ain't gonna be sputing my word no more. And you," she turned and looking down at his stained overalls, "you done stayed up all night doing God knows what… Oh, never mind." She turned back to the door and watched the chickens scratch the dirt. They were silent for a moment. The sun peeked through the gray sky and the quiet of the alley settled around them like a snug blanket. She turned and sat in the chair by the door, facing Charlie. She crinkled up her nose, sniffed the air, then announced emphatically, "You smells like fire."

Slowly, Charlie raised his head and glared at her, thinking, only a woman would say such a dang foolish thing. He wiped his mouth with the heel of his hand, picked up the remainder of the toast, and crammed it into his mouth. He chewed like a grazing cow, slowly and without effort, his gaze far away and dreamy. What the hell else would he smell like? He thought. He had stood over a fire until the flesh of Roy's arm had turned black as an old levee boot and until the bones became as dry as parched kindling. He closed his eyes to blot out the vision of the bones, but he couldn't get the hissing sound of blood spitting in the flames from his mind. He reeled in the chair and jerked forward. Instantly, his gaze found Katie's. "I'se all stoved up from stooping and pulling that rake, and my right arms feels like it's gonna fall plumb off," he said, and stretched his arm across the table until they both heard his aging joints pop. "You got any Miffling 'round hyar?" Needs to wash this soot offa me and rub these old bones fo' I goes do Miss Clara's yard."

She folded her arms, holding them to her chest, and studied his face. "Charlie, you needs rest. You look like you gonna fall over in a minute. And what if'n the law comes looking for you?"

He cut his eyes at her knowing she was sizing him up, checking how far she could go before he stopped her. "Then they'll find me at Miss Clara's cutting her grass, jest liken I does every Wednesday. He dropped his arm to the table, picked up the coffee and drained the cup.

Katie watched Charlie's hand trembling under the weight of the cup. Slowly, she rose from the table and walked to the shelf behind the stove's flue and removed the Miffling Alcohol Rub. "If you aims to wash," she pointed, "hot water is on Margaret's stove."

He sighed.

She set the bottle on the table, the liquid sparkling like captured silver, and suddenly she remembered the sheen on the axe. She could see its shimmering red blade winking at her, and the blood running towards her feet like hot, cherry syrup. She rubbed her eyes, then carefully bent over and unpinned the towel, letting her long black hair spill about her shoulders. She raised her head—the pain seeming to have eased—and brushed her hair off her neck. "I reckon you don't want Earline gitting a whiff of you like this first thing off?"

He raised his head and looked at her, his eyes mere slits now. "You sho right 'bout that," he mumbled and made an effort to hold his head up. "Must be pretty bad, huh? Any my coveralls over hyar?"

"I reckon, usually is," she said and sat back down, managing a weak smile. "Well," she said, "you gonna tell me or not?"

He pushed back from the table and shot her a warning look. She knew the rules—he would tell her in good time. Suddenly, he seemed refreshed. He picked up the Miffling, slapped it on the bottom with the flat of his hand, like it was expensive whiskey, and twisted off the cap with a snap. The pungent aroma filled the room as he poured it freely into his open palm, set the bottle down, then rolled it between his hands and wiped his face with two wide swipes. "The ways I figures, the less you knows, the better for us all. You knows how hard it is for you to tell a lie." He breathed hard, watching the disappointment in her face. "But I'll tell you this much, it's gone. Roy ain't never gonna see his arm no mo'. So you can put your mind to rest." He didn't believe that anyone would consider digging behind old man Cook's headstone. He turned away from her and spoke to the table. "Serves him right—low-life white trash ain't fit to breathe the same air as decent colored folks. Serves him right. I hopes he dies, and all the rest—Doc Smith especially."

The rooster crowed at that very moment and Katie gasped. She saw the pain in Charlie's eyes, and she watched his body swell with hatred, hatred for Roy's kind. It reminded her of old man Cook, whose body had swollen almost twice its size before he died. Doc Smith said it was from dropsy, while townsfolk said Cook's wife had put a hex on him. But with Charlie it was all hatred. Hate stacked on hate, hurt stacked on hurt, until the overpowering effect of it all became a disease that worked its way down to his bones. He had finally gotten his fill—it had taken thirty-one years, but it had happened. She had never seen Charlie so bitter, so unafraid, and it chilled her, especially so because his wish seemed to have been synchronized with the cock's crow—as if some evil force had confirmed it. Charlie had always been a man who reasoned things out, but now he seemed not to care about reason.

"Might be a possibility of some trouble, pends on what that black devil, Sylvester seed last night," he mumbled in a thick callous voice and twisted his face into a sneer.

She stiffened at the mention of Sylvester's name and wondered what else Charlie was keeping from her. She watched his eyes turn mean and knew that he was shifting gears, going from one type of hatred—the one he felt was justified, the hate-your-enemies kind—to another type of hatred—hatred of himself. For Katie knew when Charlie talked of Sylvester, Anna Mae's distant cousin, Charlie only thought of Anna Mae and the circumstances in which she died, and these heavy thoughts, whatever they were, made Charlie draw inside of himself like a snail, leaving only a hard, protective shell.

He stretched his arm again and yawned, filling the room with a loud, hissing sound. And it seemed to her that this expulsion somehow released some of the hatred that only moments ago had rolled around in his belly like sour dumplings. "I sees you is still gots more housecleaning to do," he turned and nodded in the direction of the pots.

"I aims to have Margaret return them soon as she gits up." She hesitated, propping her arms on the table and asked, "Charlie, you reckon Sylvester saw something?"

"Can't rightly say." He stared at the floor. "Jest you let me worry 'bout that. I told Luther to stick to that old musty, nigger's side like he was a sweat bee. Jest for a spell," he added, looking up at her. "Jest long enough to find if'n he knows something he can run to the law with. Told him we done had a spell of scatting. Don't know if'n he swallowed it. That's one old, crafty possum." He grunted and nodded as if he were remembering another time.

"What 'bout Luther?" She hunched her shoulders and studied his face.

"Luther!" Charlie almost shouted, and arched his sooty eyebrows. A bright light formed behind his eyes as he recalled Luther all a-tremble and gasping for air at the sight of Margaret's nakedness, almost choking on the cold beans they had been eating. He had yanked the old vinyl table cloth from the table and covered Margaret, while Luther just stood and backed himself against the wall.

Suddenly, the light disappeared from Charlie's eyes. He leaned back in the chair and rubbed the side of his face. "Don't worry 'bout neither one of them—that's my job. Jest you git yo'self together for Mista Wade Samuel's visit, wheres you can tell him to his longhead face he is gonna have to see me—me, Charlie Hudnall—'bout that fire, you hyar?" He pressed a bony finger to his chest.

"I hears you, Charlie, and so is everyone that didn't go to the field, if'n you don't calm down. Do you think it's gonna work?" She eyed him closely. Wade Samuels had a reputation for pounding anyone, including women and children, with his billy, but Katie didn't fear Wade for that reason—she feared the whirlwind of activity that always followed the law. That uncleanliness one felt after being examined like a germ; that uncertainty of wondering what would happen to you, jail or death. Oh, she realized what Charlie was doing—by taking all the blame for the fire, he was pointing the finger away for her. And considering what had happened—a Negro woman maiming, perhaps even killing, a white man, she knew very well she could go to jail and stay there for a very long time if she told what really happened. There was no such thing as self-defense when it came to Negroes hurting whites. But considering too that, if this was a part of God's plan, she could not offend Him by denying her role to any outsider. She whispered, "Lord, if'n it ain't a part of your plan, please don't let that man die."

"What you say?" Charlie asked, looking up and frowning.

"Didn't say nothing to you, Charlie." She stared at the table, avoiding his eyes.

"Well, then, to answer yo' question," Charlie said, eyeing her curiously. "It pends on several things whether it works. The first being Roy don't die, cause then old man Larkin is gonna nail Marmy's hide to the wall lessen he tells what went on. But I knows he ain't dead 'cause we'd a heard by now. News like that spreads faster than the bad disease. But if he was to die, it'd cause heap more trouble than that peckerwood ever been worth living. So as long as they ain't talking, we ain't neither, and they ain't gonna talk till J.T. says so. Ain't no doubt in my mind that this is his doing, sending them hyar to scare you and Margaret. Did you git a look at the other fella?"

Katie crinkled up her nose and shook her head, her hair stringing about her face. "No, the one what run after Margaret was jest a tall shadow, but you is right 'bout him being Marmy 'cause that Roy kept calling him that name, and the other one, I didn't see nothing 'bout him but his long legs" She sighed and folded her arms.

"That trash, Marmy Braswell, follows Roy to the outhouse, I spects. Wadn't hard to figger that, but that truck don't belong to neither one of them. And it ain't no Townsend vehicle either, 'cause I knows every thang they own." He shifted in the chair and stretched his legs under the table. "But I knows that truck; it has something to do with the way the bed is sit-u-ated, sorta fished to the left like it been hit or something."

Katie nodded her head in agreement, but her thoughts were on the white, hairy arm lying stretched across the linoleum. She could see it before her, bathed in the moonlight from the open door—it lay before her like an accepted oblation. She could see the blood trickling from the meaty, red stub that pulsated and twitched. She closed her eyes tight, then opened them to find Charlie staring.

"What 'bout my Bible? Anything left?"

He flinched and pulled up his legs. "Not a scrap. Couldn't be helped, blood was soaked plumb through it." He licked his lips and rested his head in his hands. They sat for a moment listening to the soft clucking of the chickens and the labored breathing coming from Margaret's room. Katie suddenly pushed away from the table and headed towards the pots. She began removing them from the table, making such a frightful noise that Charlie nearly bolted from the chair.

He straightened himself in the chair, shook his head, and although he could not see her face, he knew that it was pulled down in a frown, the same way her mama, Sarah, would do when she was hurt over something. But, he thought, Sarah would have chopped Roy to pieces and never blinked an eye. There had never been a fighting woman such as Sarah. She was tall and graceful and black as soot. She was the most striking woman that Charlie had ever known, including Anna Mae. Katie had always cried when she was hurt, but not Sarah. Sarah would fight anyone—even a Wade Samuels. He had to admit, though, that Katie had surprised him last night. She had defended Margaret and herself, cleaned the blood from her hair, and had not cried. Maybe, he thought, there was a Sarah there somewhere beneath all the holiness. "Best wake that gal, Katie," Charlie called above the rattle of the pots. "If she can sleep through all that racket, means you best shake her rough. It's going on six and I ain't never laid my head on a pillow or nothing. You is gots to start acting like you is sick, or who-sen-ever is sick 'round here best start acting like it. Send Margaret or Vie's youngen, David, to town for some medicine. Make it look good, jest in case that old spy Sylvester starts snooping 'round hyar with some foolish questions."

"What ails me can't be fixed with no store-bought medicine."

He squirmed in the chair and frowned, knowing that she was thinking of them eternally praying church folks. He pushed away from the table suddenly, his face ash-gray, grabbed the cane and limped into the middle room. He stopped at the pot-bellied stove and peeked through the grate as though he was still tending a fire. He felt like he was drunk on corn liquor, floating and rocking with every bend of the wind, only there was no wind. And he hadn't had a drop. He struck the floor with his cane and spun around to face Katie who trailed slowly behind him—a concerned look in her eyes.

"I said, tell that gal to git up right now! he growled, his face twisted in an ugly sneer. "We is gots to git this hyar thing together if'n we aims to live in this town. Why she ain't up anyhows? I'se up, you'se up. Why ain't she?"

Katie glanced at Charlie, seeing his haggard face she knew he was on the verge of collapse. She brushed past him, leaving him in the middle of the floor, swaying, and snatched open the middle door, leading to Margaret's room. She bent and shook Margaret roughly, and a loud moan came from the bed. Margaret rolled over, blinking at Katie. She bolted from the bed and staggered behind her mother into the middle room, collapsing in the chair at the foot of the bed. Charlie gazed at Margaret, her eyes mere slits as she tried to focus on Charlie's frame. "This," he said, turning to face Katie and pointing at Margaret, "is what happens when Negro children thinks they is free.

They thinks one night of big trouble is solved with a few buckshots scattered in the air."

"What's the matter?" Margaret yawned, looking from Katie to Charlie.

Charlie shook his head; he was tired, but knew he would have to deal harshly with Margaret. He realized the time had come to tell Margaret the shocking truth—that she was a nigger just the same as he and Katie. "Yo' mama," he said, his voice thick and raspy, "she didn't go to work liken we planned. She done met Alice and sent word that somebody is sick. Now, I jest wants to make sho when Wade gits here—and he's a coming, ain't no doubt to that—you stay in your room, and keep on sewing on them white folks clothes, or play tend to be sick. Jest keep your mouth closed."

"I know, I know," Margaret said, shaking her head as though she were irritated by all the fuss. "You don't have to keep repeating it. All this beating around the…" She embraced the bedpost, dismissing him.

Charlie's eyes blazed. He pulled his shoulders straight, and limped the few feet to the edge of the chair. "Now hear me good, Margaret Younger. I knows you is tired, but not nearly as tired as yo' mama and me. We is all tired, but you don't see us sleeping. Luther been gone to the fields high nigh two hours now. And you is still sleeping like you is Miss Anne or somebody important. You is the same as all of us. We is all niggers in the eyes of the law."

"Charlie," Katie gasped, and clutched the collar of her dress. Margaret jerked to attention and gaped, swallowing hard, her gaze searching her mother's face.

"I am not, and neither is my mother," Margaret sputtered. "Niggers are shiftless people who don't work, or on government relief and uneducated."

"Jest hush!" His words were thunder in the room. "Jest you hush." He snapped his fingers in the air. "I'se always been on your side cause I wants you to be somebody better than me and yo' mama, but I sees now you ain't gonna make it if'n you don't know who you is. Katie shoulda done told you long time ago," he said, and slowly twisted around to face Katie, warning her with a raised finger not to interfere. He turned sharply on his heel to face Margaret, his cane inches from Margaret's feet, his face a black statue. "Yo' mama had a white daddy and she still a nigger. I'se been a nigger ever since old man Thurman caught me in his apple tree. He let me know right off what I was. I was eight years old, and I done knowed it ever since. You'se one, too." He stabbed the air. "You jest done been pampered, polished, and protected till you thinks you is as good as them white folks you works for."

"I am…" Margaret blurted and froze at the frightful face he made.

"I ain't talking 'bout what we knows, I'se talking 'bout what is. Last night was the first real lesson you done had in this here race relations thing, and I can see right now, you ain't learned nothing yet."

"What did I do?" Margaret asked, cringing in terror.

"Jest hush, I said. That there is one thing right there, always wants some explanation for everything. And another, you still laying up in the bed, sleeping like you ain't got no reason to be worried 'bout nothing. Sleeping jest like everything is right, after what went on here last night."

"Charlie." Katie tried inching between them, but he barred her way, and warned her again.

"Why now, Charlie?" Katie pleaded. "Ain't we had enough…?"

"'Cause this sassy gal is gambling with our lives, and 'cause it's high time she knowed what she is up against."

"Mr. Charlie, I know a great deal more than you think," Margaret braved the words.

"You is a smart gal, ain't no doubt. But what worries me is you ain't smart enough to know how to act 'round white folks. You can't even stay quiet when told."

"But I know…" Margaret whispered.

Charlie's eyes went black. He reached down, grabbed a fistful of Margaret's gown, and yanked her face to his. In a hoarse whisper he said, "I wants you to be quiet when them white folks comes, little nigger gal." And feeling the bristling of Margaret's back, then the relaxing of her muscles, he knew he was getting through. She dropped back in the chair and nodded. He was calm. He released Margaret's gown, his heart heavy, and limped through the middle door, thinking, now the house was clean—everybody understood what had to be done. Katie would have to force herself to side-step the truth when talking to Wade, Margaret would have to acknowledge her blackness by keeping quiet, and he would have to stare Wade Samuels in the face and tell the biggest lie ever—that he set the fire to keep away scatters.

REMOVE THE DEVIL

What was them niggers really up to? Imagine the nerve! Old Charlie Hudnall setting a bonfire right smack in the middle of Monther's Alley, and that there holy-rolling white nigger, Sister Katie, acting like she pure as gold. Hell, they knows more than they's telling, you can mark my word on that!"

The last two days, Big Jim Davis, prosecuting attorney of Bennettsville County had listened quietly from his office across the hall while Sheriff Wade Samuels and his deputies, Shorty and Grahm, hashed over the details they had gathered from questioning the residents of Monther's Alley. Jim sat in the small, neat office, his elbows propped on the edge of the paper-laden desk, eyes closed. The sun streamed through the window and casting a reddish glow about the room, making his copper hair appear to be on fire. His mind was cluttered with questions, questions that he knew only intense probing would get answers to.

It was his usual routine to wait until the Sheriff's investigation was over before he stepped in and took over any case. This, however, was a strange situation—a huge bonfire in Monther's Alley that had raged throughout the night, and a young white man from the other side of town missing an arm that he refused to talk about, even to the proper authorities. And the complaints from the genteel townsfolk that bombarded his office, demanding that he not allow niggers to set fires, made it even harder for him to wait. He agreed with some of the points that Wade had made earlier—it was possible that the fire was connected to some Negro ritual. And he had lived just outside of Mother's Alley, and had seen, first hand, the old and young white men terrifying the Negroes in the middle of the night, then scatting away in their fast pick-up trucks before the Negroes could retaliate. But he could not ever remember, even as a child, the Negroes setting fires to scare away scatters.

What mystified Jim the most was Charlie Hudnall's directness—not only had Charlie set the fire, but openly confessed to the act. Why? Charlie had been talking around white folks for some sixty odd years. The absence of character analysis was apparent in Wade's report, and that also bothered Jim. Hadn't Wade surmised that Roy losing his arm maybe connected with the fire? Everyone knew Roy had been involved in scatting and other vile acts for years, and that Roy would do anything for money. And the fact that everyone expected J.T. to do something dastardly to change Katie's mind on accepting that money his daddy had left to her—shouldn't Wade be thinking alone those lines as well? Why was there no report from Doc Smith? Roy had to have had medical treatment before he was taken to Margestown, otherwise he would have bled to death during the fifty mile ride. Was Wade looking the other way to avoid trouble with J.T.?

Slowly Jim opened his eyes and sat up. He scanned Wade's report once more and determined the fire was set between Katie and Charlie's houses—perhaps, he thought, the answer was there, with Katie. He couldn't stand another day of excessive pondering and the speculation that drifted into his office above the odor of grilled onions and smoked ham butt as the three men from the Sheriff's Office toyed with ideas on how to produce enough fear to get them niggers talking straight. He grabbed his notepad from the desk, his straw hat from the wall hook, and headed out the door.

It was a hot sticky July afternoon. The cotton was thick and a-bloom, filling the air with its intoxicating scent. Jim pulled his pick-up truck into the sharp bend of the alley, drove two houses down, and brought it to a squeaking halt in front of the frame house that stood on tall, stone pillars in a dirt yard with a lone bed of dying roses. He got out, and walking with long, easy strides to the edge of Katie's walkway, paused to look around. Monther's Alley was nothing more than a graveled road which stretched from Main Street to Water Street.

The alley was unusually quiet for this time of day, and, Jim looked about for signs of field hands returning to the fields after supper, or heading home from half a-day work. He had the sudden notion that the Negroes had seen his truck turning in the bend and had hidden behind closed doors and drawn window shades—it would not be the first time. But this was different; it was as if an enormous secret ballooned high over his head in the guise of rumbling, dark clouds, or perhaps lay in the midst of the charred ground, a round spot that sat dead center, as though it had been paced off before torching, between Katie and Charlie's houses. A strong, piercing odor still lingered in the air, forcing him to hold his nose as he climbed the steps to Katie's door. From the porch he looked down on the massive spot—large enough to accommodate two shotgun houses, and shaped like a country flapjack all crusted over with thick, black molasses. He shook his head and wondered why Charlie would set such a fire. He rapped hard on the screen door, mopped his brow with the back of his hand, and waited, listening. He heard slow, almost dragging, footsteps inside, which came to a halt on the other side of the door. A moment later, the door creaked open slowly, and Katie peeked timidly around the frame.

"Afternoon, Katie," Jim grinned and, reaching up, automatically crimped the brim of his hat.

"Af-ta-noon,' Katie stammered, her eyes suddenly bright with alarm. Wisps of coarse, black hair plastered her forehead, and smudges of white flour streaked the sides of her slender face.

"Can I talk with you for a spell?" He pressed his palm against the screen, and squinted through the mesh, his eyes wandering curiously over her face.

"Spect it's alright, Mr. Jim," she answered in a startled voice—she had thought the questioning was over—and stepped back, dropping her eyes to the floor. The sun rushed through the open door as if it rode the wind and splashed a shaft of blinding light at her feet. Mechanically, she brushed the sides of her hair, suddenly aware of his presence filling the room. "Come on in. Jest in the kitchen finishing up supper. Margaret will be a-coming home soon and ready to eat.

You knows how chillens is?" She turned slowly as he walked past, and watched his spit-shined shoes cross the floor and stop at the edge of the rocker.

"Whew! Shore is a hot one. Dang near a hunnerd out there," he said, removing the straw hat, and raking his long fingers through his matted hair.

"That's the truth, and the rain we been gitting don't seem to be helping none at all." She pushed the door against the wall and stood across from him, gazing at his broad shoulders that filled the khaki shirt to its seams. She stuffed one hand in her apron pocket and waited as he wiped his face with a wrinkled handkerchief and crammed it back into his shirt pocket. "Can I git you something to drink, some lemonade before I finishes the supper?" She pointed toward the kitchen.

He looked into her face and grinned, his six-foot frame casting a lanky shadow against the sunlit wall. "That would do just fine, Katie. Something shore smells heavenly in the kitchen. We had missed that aroma from the Cafe these past two days. I hope you feel better soon."

"Thank you," she said meekly.

His dark eyes immediately scanned the room. It was immaculate: a brown sofa sat catty-cornered, facing him, with a small, dark, chipped ebony table on its left. A tall chest of drawers with several knobs missing was on the right, a small black oil heater stood on a square white rug above a highly polished linoleum, and two shiny black rockers, their arms almost kissing, sat near the window. His eye finally rested on the delicate handmade lace curtains that hung over the sparkling window pane.

Katie noticed his gaze. "Miss Rosie give me them last Christmas," she explained and flushed as she realized he had not asked her any questions—yet. He saw the color spread across her face and the light of fear behind her eyes. She waved her hand in the direction of the rocker near the window and he sat down, making the rocker creak under his weight.

She left the room, taking slow, awkward steps, as though she was afflicted with rheumatism—a common ailment for the populace of Bennettsville, being that that part of town circled a bend in the Mississippi River. He watched her, comparing her gait now, to the last time he had seen her—two weeks ago at the Cafe. It had been lunch time, and the Cafe had been packed with townsfolk from all over. He had stood at the swinging doors leading into the kitchen, watching her as she filled the orders, worked the grill, and prepared the supper plates. Two weeks ago, she had been agile and he found it odd that she should be so awkward now. He tapped the bridge of his nose, and absentmindedly rested the hat on his knee. She returned shortly, handed him a frosted glass, and walked back slowly to the kitchen.

A loud sizzle soon permeated the house, a sizzle that became a simmering roar—a sound he knew well: she was frying chicken. He relaxed, gulped his drink in one swallow, and meticulously placed the glass on the white doily on the table.

Thunder rumbled in the distance, and the whine of an engine straining its gears grabbed his attention. He twisted round in the chair and looked out the window to see two Negro men struggling to get an old truck out of the mud. "Sounds like we gonna git more rain," he called over the sizzle of frying chicken and the escalating whine of the truck's engine.

"It sho does. Probably won't hit us for a spell yet though," she called back, her voice bouncing through the room like an echo.

"Yeah, that's how I figure. East Ditch oughta be gitting one hell of a rain 'bout now. Storm probably hit us in a couple of hours." He leaned forward in the chair, calculating the distance between them. He knew from the sound of the splattering meat that she was still at the stove, and he remembered, from childhood visits, the large middle room that sat between the kitchen and the room he now sat in. Waiting increased his curiosity, and more questions flashed through his mind. Had something other than scatting happened here? Did Roy losing his arm have something to do with the scatting? Why had the door been closed on a hot day like this?

He stood, stretched his long arms, and quietly dropped the hat in the seat of the rocker. Looking up, he found himself facing numerous greeting cards. They lined the bumpy wall from end to end, and ranged from fluffy, down-like white Easter bunnies with pink and blue ribbons twisted in bright bows around their furry necks, to striped candy canes of tantalizing greens, whites and reds that stood on end dancing, from praying white hands pointed straight towards the ceiling, clasping the white holy book and its gleaming golden cross, to blue jays and fat-bellied red robins, scratching the greenest moss with padded, pointed razor-tipped claws. He found himself staring at a rosy-cheeked Santa with a split down the middle of his face—the result of the axe striking the wall. He flipped it over to see an amber crusting of glue that spread the length of the card. The scrawl at the bottom of the card was child-like and signed, "To Sister Katie with love."

The squealing of the engine died suddenly, leaving his ears throbbing. He stepped back quietly to the window and poked his hands through the curtains, separating them for a better view of the road. Immediately, he recognized the squat Negro man as Sylvester Bodine—the local Uncle Tom. The other man, slim and tall, stood on the far side of the truck out of his view. He watched Sylvester pulling at the straps of his coveralls while bending over the mud hole, apparently examining the reddish muck with great interest. The other man left the truck, the engine still running, and walked around to examine the same mud hole. It was Luther Dawson, Viola's son, and Jim wondered what they were doing in the alley this time of day—they worked on the other side of town. He also wondered what the hell they expected to find in the mud. He tried to raise the window, but it wouldn't budge. He soon discovered hammer indentations along the side of the frame, and shiny, new nails embedded in the wood—the window would open no more than an inch. He traced the grooves around the nails with his fingers and decided he had been right all along, there had been real trouble here—he would stake his reputation on it.

He kept a sharp eye on the men in the road. Sylvester on his knees, clawing through the wet mud, while Luther, standing above him, looked on, fascinated. What were they looking for? It was quick, like a flash, but Jim saw it. From the depths of the muck, Sylvester pulled out something that he hastily wiped clean on the side of his coveralls. It was a shiny, round object that refracted the light and became a dazzling swirl of prismatic colors—an explosion of reds, greens, yellows, and purples appeared instantaneously in the palm of his tar-black hand. In a moment, it was gone, Luther snatching the object from Sylvester's struggling hand and cramming it into his pocket. Jim was puzzled. What could it have been? Perhaps it was nothing, but a little voice inside said, "Check." He pulled out his notepad and scribbled, "See Sylvester about mud," looking up again in time to see the truck pull off with a jerk, kicking wet gravel high in the air.

He straightened up from the window and looked around again—his curiosity aroused. From where he now stood, his back facing the window, he had a view of the entire room, from the streaked yellow ceiling, to the gleaming, worn linoleum. Giving it all a good going over with a careful eye, he decided nothing was out of order. The cracked door in the middle of the wall adorned with the greeting cards was a sudden magnet. He had never been on that side of the house. The sizzle of the meat frying in the kitchen told him that he had time to look in.

He pushed the door open with the flat of his hand, waited for a second, then eased through. He didn't know exactly what he was looking for, only that if he saw it, he would be sure it was in some way connected to this investigation. The room was small but spacious, and smelled of ginger and lemon spices mixed with oil of cloves—a scent many women used for their body soaps. An exquisite piece of brown cloth, speckled with gold lame, was draped across a foot-pedaled sewing machine, and on the bed were pre-sewn pieces of the same cloth that would soon become the sleeves of an elegant party dress. The four-poster bed gleamed with richness that only comes from oak. It sat jammed against the wall, allowing entry from only one side, and was covered with a white satin spread fringed with pink crocheted bells. Matching plumped pillows lay on the headboard, and the same silvery curtains adorned the lone window. He rubbed the edge of the pillow case between his fingers—a gift no doubt (most Negroes could not afford such quality)—then walked to the window, pushed back the curtains, and yanked hard on the handle. It too was nailed. He nodded his head—everything was falling together for him—and looked around the room again. He remembered that Margaret took in sewing—this had to be her room. The sound of slow footsteps made him start, and quickly he stepped back through the door. He was standing in front of the greeting cards when Katie entered the room.

"Just been admiring your cards, Katie. Folks sure do think a great deal of you." He fingered the Santa Clause card, smiled sheepishly, and walking back to the rocker sat down.

"Thank you, Mr. Jim," she said, following him. "I'se right proud of them cards, every one of them. Why, some of them cards come from as far as New York. You ever been to New York?" She sat in the rocker across from him, her face now clean and shiny, her hair neatly brushed from her forehead into a sweeping pompadour.

He looked her over, fascinated by her high-cheekbones, rosy and yet pale. And at that moment, with only the sun peeking through the window occasionally and the stream of light from the open door, it was hard for him to believe that she was not white. "Call me Jim, Katie. The way you did in the old days, remember?" He placed the hat on the table beside him, scratched behind his ear, and grinned.

"We was chillens then, no more than thirteen or so," she reminded him and cleared her throat, then quickly looked away as though a memory had touched her heart. "We is grown up now, and that sheds a different light on things now, you agree?"

He nodded his head, paused, then said, "It just ain't possible for me to think about my childhood and not remember you. Being grown-up does change things, but that don't have to make us enemies. I know I haven't been to visit you in a while, but we have talked at other times. Oh, I don't mean when I questioned you about Townsend's death, that was different. But talk like we used to. In fact, two weeks ago, I tried to get your attention, but you were way to busy to talk."

"Musta been at work if I was too busy to talk." She cleared her throat again. "The last time you set foot in my house was three years ago."

"Yep," he smiled. "I came 'round here the day I got appointed to this job, and we sat talking 'bout old times and looking at them terrifying pictures of the four-headed beast in your pappy's Bible." He twisted in the chair and looked at the bare shelf on the wall, then twisted back, his eyes wide with surprise. "Where's your pappy's Bible?"

She winced at the mention of the Bible. She was suddenly warm all over. She did not know how to lie, because it had been against all the principles of her upbringing. Pappy had simply detested liars; and her role in the church—a faith healer of the Holiness Church of God in Christ—forbade it. But how could she tell him that the Bible had to be destroyed because it was soaked with Roy Larkin's blood? She avoided his gaze, staring at his brown shoes. "It ain't here no more," she managed and slowly crossed her ankles.

He sat with his head pressed against the back of the rocker, his curly, red hair damp with perspiration, making it appear almost black. He seemed to be in deep thought. He looked at her, studying her face closely, and after a few moments had passed asked. "Everythang alright with you and Margaret?" Ain't nobody giving y'all a hard time 'bout that there money, is they?"

"We is fine, thank you," she answered quickly, and turned her gaze toward the window. She did not want to talk about the money Townsend had willed to her. She did not want to remember those days she had been summoned to Townsend's deathbed, for that had been the start of all the trouble.

"Just wondering," he went on, carefully selecting his words. "I noticed you had the door closed on a hot day like this."

"Oh, that." She glanced at him, then turned back to the window. "Margaret musta pulled it to on her way out. Chillens." She shook her head.

"Yeah," he agreed. "You want it to stay open now?" he pointed in the direction of the door.

"Sho I do, purposely left it open the same way I always does when a man comes a visiting. It's expected, you knows that, of every woman living without her husband." She laughed, then caught herself. She must stay on her guard—this was the interview she dreaded. Wade Samuels had been easy to get around—Wade's focus had been on the setting of the fire and searching her house, something he always did whenever he investigated anyone.

Jim saw her suddenly look very sad, her eyes taking on a far-away look, lifeless and dull. He had the sudden impulse to reach across the few feet, gather her in his arms, and reassure her of all the goodness in the world. He leaned closer, inhaling the faint traces of lavender talc, and wondered what would happen if he kissed her firmly on the lips, like before when they were what she called chillens—they were never children to each other, never. What would she say? Would she scream, yell and kick—or kiss him back while she stubbornly insisted on calling him Mr. Jim? "Well, folks 'round here knows I'm the law," he blurted, trying to push the image of the kiss from his mind.

She turned and faced him, her mouth pulled up in a stern pout. "So, which one is at my house, Mr. Jim Davis or the law?" she asked, an underlying plea evident in her voice.

He straightened up, scratched behind his ear, and smiled. "I'd have to say both. I can't seem to separate one from the other." He waved his hands in front of him.

"Well!" she frowned, annoyed by his answer. "Why didn't you flash your badge like Wade Samuels done?" She spread her hands like she was measuring the empty space around her.

He dropped back in the chair, placed his hands on his thighs, and shook his head. Then, shaking his finger as though he was reprimanding a naughty child, said, "'Cause I ain't Wade Samuels." His eyes were dark, defiant. He resented being compared to Wade—everyone knew he was fair and that he pursued white lawbreakers just as persistently as he did black lawbreakers. He rubbed his eyebrows with his fingertips. He had developed a sudden headache, and she, sensing his distress but refusing to acknowledge it, folded her arms in a huff and gazed out the window. They were silent for a long spell, like old married couples who had been spatting over unresolvable issues. Finally, in a tired, dry voice, he broke the silence. "Listen, Katie. Wade is the type what believes flashing his badge and billy-clubbing people makes him big, you know, powerful and revered—manly. I don't approve of his methods, and I…"

"Well, I sho hopes you don't," she interrupted, her sharp voice slicing the air. "That man tore up this house something awful, even pulled the watermelons from under the bed. He left the biggest mess, watermelons rolling all over, and never told me what he was a looking for." Her face was filled with indignation.

He stared at her in amazement. "Watermelons?" he asked in a startled voice.

"Watermelons," she said, nodding her head.

His face was suddenly red. "I reckon I ain't never thought it necessary to flash a badge when I come by to talk with a friend.

She bristled. Did he still consider her to be his friend? She studied his face closely and recalled that he always flushed when he was sincere; but now the flush could simply mean he was embarrassed at Wade's peculiar attention to watermelons. She let her eyes wander over his handsome face, then turned her attention to the window. "Friends, yes, we was once friends," her voice strained. Unsteadily she placed her hands on the arms of the rocker as though she needed something solid to hold. "That was a long time ago. We was chillens and I was free, free as any whippersnapper on this earth, and Pappy was alive—that was a mighty long time ago," her voice waning down to almost a whisper. "That was long before I growed up and turned into a colored woman, and you into a white man."

"Hell, I couldn't turn no other color but white." He glared at her, his voice coarse, defensive.

"You knows what I mean." She snapped her head around to face him. "And keep that bad talk out of my house, law or not. I'se got sense to know you can't change the color of your skin. What I mean is—oh, I don't know what I mean!" She snatched her head away, angry that she could not find the words. She pressed her fingers against the bridge of her nose and, turning to face him again, said, "What I mean is, you has to remember where you come from, and that was jest a little ways down the road—the edge of Monther's Alley." She watched his face and could see by the softening of his glare that he understood—that present relationships often endured solely on past memories, or past obligations, and she was asking him to remember both: the secrets they shared, the kisses they sneaked, and how her white pappy and black mama treated him with kindness and love when other whites had turned him away, labeling him white trash. And how their division was caused by outside forces—his mother, and other whites who deemed her a Negro when she was just as white as they. She wanted him to always remember those times they shared, even though now the division had deepened, placing them in two different worlds. He was almost the same Jim, his copper hair and dark eyes, like night heat, making her restless looking into them. He was Jim alright, but he was also the law—and the law petrified her, for every time the law came into her life, it took away someone she loved.

He looked at her, his eyes soft. Then, nodding his head, he said, "I ain't one to forgit where I come from, Katie, I guarantees you that."

She stared into those dark eyes again, trying to see what lay behind them. But it was no use, she could not determine what was real. And she had long forgotten how to trust any man other than Charlie. She wove her fingers together, looked down at the floor, and in a voice laden with sorrow, mumbled, "Devil sho is busy."

"What devil is that, Katie?" he asked, his voice soft, curious. "White devils, black devils, or the one in your pappy's Bible?"

The mention of the Bible put her on alert to the present, and she sat erect in the chair, her head high, straining her neck until it ached.

He watched her closely. The suffering of the world was in her face. The effort to answer the question bloomed in her cheeks like lilies springing from the ground in time for Easter Sunday. He must act now and ask the question they both had been avoiding: "Katie, what was the bonfire all about?" the authority suddenly there, riding on the edge of his voice.

She cringed, and uncrossed her ankles. The question evoking images that she had tried hard to suppress—the pap, pap, pap of blood dripping from the gleaming axe onto the pages of the Bible; the arm, lying at her feet, jerking and bleeding. She swallowed hard, licked her lips, and crossed her ankles again. She could suddenly hear Charlie's warning, "Don't say yes or no to no question. Talk around it. Keep your senses." Slowly, she dropped her hands in her lap, lifted her eyes to meet his, and looked closely at Jim—his face somber, determined, like that of a hunter.

"Why did Charlie start that fire, Katie?" he repeated.

"Why in heaven's name is you asking me? Charlie Hudnall set that fire! Ask him!"

"'Cause," he said, pointing a menacing finger at her. "Charlie been acting like your daddy for thirty some years now. If anybody knows why he set it, it would be you. That and the fact that your house is no less than a hunnerd yards from where he set the fire." He stopped quickly and nodded like he had just made a sudden vital discovery, then drummed his long fingers, rapidly, on the arm of the chair. "To be honest, Katie, I knows scatting 'round in this alley is frequent. But I believe this wasn't your average bunch of scatters, and that fire had something to do with the real trouble what went on here. I think Charlie set that fire as a smoke screen for something else," he continued.

She tugged at the collar of her dress, watching Jim from the sides of her eyes. She could feel herself slipping back and forth in time.

She could see Jim's face clearly, but she could also see orange-yellow flames leaping in the air. And the thick, black smoke, draping across the false dawn light like a crepe funeral banner, releasing the stench of burning flesh into the air. A stench powerful enough to draw stray dogs from miles around, and particularly the white red-eyed bitch whose belly hung heavy with pups that ran the other strays away with her fierce determination to have the remains. She snatched her head back to find Jim's penetrating gaze upon her face. She slumped forward slightly and coughed into her hand—a haggling, dry cough that made him look away and frown.

"Well," she said, chewing on her bottom lip, her voice raspy and low. "I can't swear some of them things you say ain't true. All I knows is Charlie said there was scatting, and there was some ruckus outside. And like you say, we do git that 'round here a lots. Whenever them young devils wants to have fun, they come 'round here to scare the 'niggers.' They throw cans and rocks and yell, 'Go back to Africa with the apes,' or worsa things than that. Then they speeds off in them pick-ups and stays a spell, jest long enough for you to git comfortable before they starts all over. Sometimes we is up and down all night. Y'all calls it scatting, I calls it torture."

He rubbed his chin, watching her every move. He sympathized with her story, for as a child he had witnessed this foul atrocity, and yet he sensed she had been coached, that the words she spoke were, of course, true, but did not necessarily apply to the night in question. He rested his head against the back of the rocker, studying the ceiling as though he was estimating how many coats of paint it would take to bring the color to life. Then, almost absentmindedly, he drummed his fingers on the chair again, his nails clicking loudly against the wood, sounding like hungry chickens in a bag of corn. He looked down at the floor, clasped his hands together, and slowly turned, cutting his eyes sharply at her. "Katie, was there scatting 'round here Tuesday night, and if so, was Roy Larkin in the bunch? On second thought," he waved his hand to hush her, "don't answer that jest yet. Think on it for a spell," he drawled, placing great emphasis on the words. "I might as well tell you, Katie, I'm personally gonna wring the truth out of Roy. I promise you by sundown tomorrow, I'm gonna know what happened to his arm, and what happened around here, and if there is any connection." He turned his gaze toward the window.

She flinched; the flesh on her body trembled in fear. An electric tension filled the room. No, she did not know this man sitting before her at all, she thought. It was plain that the young freedom-loving, high-spirited boy she had known and trusted so long ago was not this man who sat before her.

'I'm jest gonna remind that boy," she heard Jim saying, "of the grave mistake he'll be a making if he don't tell me what happened. Roy knows very well folks in this town don't Cotton to his kind. They wouldn't care if he was to rot in jail or was run out of town on a jackass. And when he turns it over in his head a couple of times, you can bet he's gonna talk." He watched her—she sat stiffly like she was made of cardboard or bound with many heavy corsets.

A truck rolled by and they turned their attention to the road. Katie focused on the red dirt, glistening from sprinklings of rain, then clearly saw Margaret's footprints pressed firmly in the mud. She turned and faced Jim, and wondered if he had made the connection yet. Had he figured out it was she who had severed Roy's arm? Or was he trying to make her reveal what she knew?

Jim also toyed with ideas. He cleared his throat, propped his leg against the table, and spoke in slow measured tones. "Suppose I tell you what I think happened, Katie.

"What's that?" she gasped, her mouth falling open in amazement.

"Don't interrupt," he said, waving his index finger in the air, and she dropped her eyes to the floor, tugging harder on the dress collar.

He scratched behind his ear, smiled, and began, "The scatting, Roy losing his arm, and the bonfire—in that order—all happened on the same night. We either have three individual incidents, or a chain reaction to one. I say it's the latter, and Wade's a dang fool if he don't either. Hell, we all been sitting on eggs waiting for J.T. to do something to you, and I think he did, or tried." Jim looked up, but did not expect an answer. "You expected J.T. to do something, that's why your windows are nailed. And I'll never say you shouldn't took that money. Personally, I think you deserves it—Townsend was a powerful, but peculiar man and I don't think that I could have got down on my knees and prayed for him." Jim looked around the spare, hot room and shook his head. "God knows y'all could use it—these is hard times." He gazed at her. "But let's git back to Tuesday night. It makes sense to me that Roy and his wild bunch would be just the kind J.T. would hire to do his dirty work—scare the niggers." He held her gaze but flushed. "Just using your words, not mine.

"Anyhows," he continued, "Roy, and most likely Marmy Braswell—cause they are as thick as the thieves they are—come 'round here to do some special scatting for J.T." He stopped and sighed like a man weary from a long journey, and rested his head in his hand. He could hear her rapid breathing and was aware of the struggle she seemed to have controlling it. He lifted his head and let his eyes wander over her face—her sad, lonely, frightened face—and suddenly felt very uncomfortable. He cleared his throat, waited a few seconds, then continued. "I don't call it scatting either, Katie. I say they come 'round here that night to raise the devil, but something got out of hand, something happened they hadn't counted on. Now I knows 'bout the only thing in this world that matters to you is your daughter. Most mothers feel that way, but you and Margaret is 'bout the closest I've seen. So, out of the three of you," he waved his hand, and looking at his fingers like the solution was there in the palm of his hand, counted, "Charlie, you, and Margaret—maybe even all three of you banned together to teach Roy a lesson. It musta been something mighty awful to scare you so bad you keep your door closed on a hot day like this. Well?" he said, dropping his hands in his lap. He eyed her closely.

Unable to play dumb any longer, unable to talk around the horror of that night, she looked up and snapped, "Let it be, Jim Davis."

"Let what be?" he sat up and rounded his shoulders as though he would spring upon her. "Then you do know something? What is it you're holding back?" he demanded in a hushed command. Placing his foot on her rocker, he stopped the motion she had unconsciously begun.

"I said to let it be!" she yelled and glared at his foot, then at his face, demanding with steely eyes that he remove his foot from the rocker.

"Then there was something else going on. Something that scares you to talk about." He scooted to the edge of the rocker, his eyes dark as muddy pools.

"I ain't scared of nothing," she said in a shaky voice.

"Then why you want me to let it be? Why you asking me to leave it alone? J.T.'s been bothering you 'bout that money, ain't he?" he probed, rushing her, his foot still on the rocker.

"I don't know nothing 'bout J.T.," she replied, shaking her head violently, denying everything.

"What about Roy? Was he here the other night? Is that how he lost his arm, fooling 'round here? Who was with him? I know he wasn't by himself, he ain't got the nerve. Was he here, Katie?"

He was sweating profusely and leaning close enough for her to feel his hot breath on her cheeks. She leaned back in the chair, raised her eyes to the ceiling and with a loud, desperate cry, yelled, "Lord!"

Jim was insistent. "Was he here, Katie?"

"I wish I never set foot in Townsend's house," she said to the ceiling.

"Was he here?" he asked again, moving his head from side to side trying to make eye contact. But she was talking to her God.

"I don't want that tainted money, money he got from cheating the colored folks, Lord." She held her arms in the air, clenching her fists. "Lord, you knows I never wanted no parts of that money. Jest took it 'cause my child wanted to go to school. But Lord, you done heard her prayer, you knows why." She shook her head slowly, her face a mixture of pain and guilt.

He lifted his foot from the rocker, leaned to the edge of the chair and demanded in a hoarse, softer voice, "Well, then, tell me Katie, tell me that he wasn't here."

"I knowed it in my heart there was gonna be trouble when I went to the hill to pray for old man Townsend. Lord, you knowed it too, but I went anyhow."

"Just tell me he wasn't here, Katie," Jim growled.

"But, oh, Lord, it was your working, not my doing."

"Then maybe the Lord wants you to have this money, tainted or not, Katie. Did you ever think on that?"

He had broken through, for she gasped loudly, snatched her eyes from the ceiling to look him in the face, and with tears streaming down her cheeks, screamed, "That's blaspheem! You trying to say you personally knows what the Lord wants?"

"Katie," he sighed, sliding back in the chair, and gesticulating his arms. "I'm trying to help you, don't you believe that? I know you are hiding the truth from me, but it's cause you're plumb scared. I know Roy was here, and some way he lost his arm—them doctors over in Margestown said it was a sharp, clean cut, like he had been hit with a saw mill blade or wood axe."

She groaned loudly, as though something in the depths of her soul had cracked. She closed her eyes, trembling, and turned back to the ceiling, hurt and suffering in her face. She cried out, "Lord! in the name of Jesus, remove this devil!"

Jim turned a bright red, and rose slowly from the chair, his face filled with utter astonishment. He glared down at her upturned face and waved his finger by her nose. "I'm gonna find out, Katie. You might as well tell me. This is the last time I'm gonna ask you as a friend. The next time I come through that door," he pointed, "it will be as the law, you can count on it. Was Roy here?"

"Lord, I'se asking you in the name of Jesus…"

Thunder boomed and lightning streaked across the gray sky. The old house shook from the vibrations as the thunder blasted again and again. The lightning ripped through the sky like jagged hot irons. The rain fell outside in sheets. The two of them did not speak. Jim stood looking out the door, and she remained in the rocker, her head in her hands. The rain plummeted the tin roof like hot popcorn kernels bursting in rapid succession. And water gurgled as it soaked through the base of the window. The room dimmed until their shadows were black and disfigured against the rose-colored wallpaper. The front door slammed against the wall, banged closed, and then opened again. Margaret, wild-eyed and breathless bounded through the screen door and into the room, flinging water in every direction. Her skin glistening, and water rained from her hair, making rivulets that gathered at her pointed chin. She shook her long hair, wiped her face with both hands, and exhaled loudly. Looking up to see Jim standing a few feet in front of her, she froze. She sucked in her breath and gazed at him with fierce, dark eyes. Instantly, she looked around for her mother, and rushed past Jim to Katie's side, flung a protective arm around the rocker.

Margaret stood, shivering, and stared at Jim, her eyes filled with apprehension and distrust. And Katie, sensing that Margaret might suddenly lash out at him, struggled from the chair, grabbed the large white towel from the back of the sofa, and wrapped it lovingly around the shivering girl's shoulders. Gently, she scolded, "Margaret, child, you is soaked to the skin." Slowly, she led Margaret to the sofa, eased her down, and returned to the rocker. The two of them sat as still as statues. It was a ruling of the church that movement be minimized when God was about His work. And in Katie and Margaret's eyes, God was about His work—He was making a loud protest, and weeping uncontrollably for the sins of the world.

Katie sat with her hands clasped tightly in her lap, staring out the window, Margaret clutched the towel about her, keeping a sharp eye on Jim, and Jim stood at the door, his hands crammed in his pockets. They all seemed to be caught in a void, suspended in time. The rain and the constant bump, bump, bump of the pecan branch against the house beat out a song. Suddenly, as though a voice had spoken to him, it was clear to Jim what had happened here. Charlie's open confession, Katie's slow awkward movements, and Margaret's attempts to protect her mother when there was no need had brought all the pieces together for Jim. There had been a deadly confrontation that night and in the tussle, Katie had been battered. She had been beaten under her clothes where it could not be seen—an old tactic that he knew was often practiced by ruthless policemen and upstanding Deacons of the church. And acting in self-defense, or in defense of a loved one, one of them had attacked Roy with an axe. That would explain Charlie's confession, for Charlie would not shield himself: the old man had spunk, and the cunning of a Baptist preacher—all he needed to have said was that the fire had been an accident. It would also explain the fear that faced him when Katie opened the door, and again the same fear in Margaret's eyes. Oh, he had suspected that someone was shielding someone from something sinister, like the long shadow of J.T. or the law: but he was the law, and he had a job to do. He looked down at Katie, her head bent in silent prayer, and then over at Margaret who had stopped shivering but stared at him openly with, haunting eyes—eyes filled with abhorrence.

He turned and slammed out the door into the pouring rain.

Jim sat in the truck, slowly wiping the water from his face. He was soaked, but didn't seemed to mind—his thoughts were still inside with Katie. Hell, he thought, he did remember where it was he came from, he could almost see the old house he was raised in from here. He was not really as complex as the people around him made him out to be. He just didn't like the rules white society placed upon him. He was simply an individual who didn't seem to fit anywhere, except within the realms of law. He placed his hands on the steering wheel and listened to the rain pounding the hood of the cab. The sound, almost hypnotic, made him sort through the facts. Legally, he had no case unless Roy filled a complaint, and he didn't believe Roy would do that. But Roy's father would raise a stink. And as for the fire, no property, other than Katie and Charlie's had been damaged. That only left the matter of setting the fire. Charlie could be charged with a misdemeanor—and would get a fine. But how could he not act upon what he now knew as sure as fire burns. He had sworn to uphold the law.

A sudden pounding against the window of the truck brought Jim out of his trance. He rolled down the window, not sure what he would find, for all he had seen was a blur. The rain splashed inside, dampening his face. He looked closely at the window and saw Margaret. She was standing with the towel over her head, her small mouth in a pout. She did not speak as she poked the dripping straw hat through the window, turned quickly, the towel flying in the wind, and disappeared.

A chill went through him, but it was not from the cold rain—it was from somewhere deep within. He started up the engine, heading for town.

COLOREDS ONLY

As Charlie had predicted, Sheriff Wade Samuels had found him cutting grass at the Townsend's Mansion that same Wednesday afternoon. Wade had questioned, or attempted to question Charlie under the scrutiny of Miss Clara Townsend, but she would not stand for it. She ordered Wade off the premises, shouting, "If Charlie said he set the fire to keep the scatters away, then that is what happened." Wade had reluctantly swaggered away, red-faced and defeated. So when Katie informed Charlie of Big Jim's visit that same day, and that Jim had figured it all out, Charlie was not surprised. What he didn't understand was why no action had been taken. Four days had past and he had waited and waited. Instead of sleeping in his bed, he had sat at the table and dozed off, or sat at the window box, staring at the road and thinking of ways to murder Doc Smith.

And now he sat at the small kitchen table sipping Southern Comfort mixed with blackberry juice from a quart Mason jar. The alarm clock faced him like a watchful eye and read two a.m., but he made no attempt to retire. An oil lamp sat blazing across from him, sending a stream of black smoke up its chimney; and a copy of the Record, opened to page five, lay at his fingertips, a crease down its center where he had folded it earlier with shaky, angry fingers. The article he had circled with his number two pencil was not the one about Roy Larkin's accident with the wood axe, but the one about the hospital soon to be completed and that Doctor Thomas Smith would be its director. He glared at the picture of the smiling, gray-haired man—the man who had let Anna Mae die because he didn't have time for "niggers' bellyaches." He sipped the concoction, shuddered, flipped the paper over, and re-read the article about how Roy Larkin Sr. had found his son unconscious, bloody, and missing his right arm. The doctors over at the hospital in Margestown said, "It is a miracle that Roy is still alive." "A miracle my foot!" Charlie muttered and slapped the paper with the back of his hand, slamming it flat down on the table. "Anybody with a lick of sense knows Roy went to that blackhearted Doc Smith for medical tention." He flipped the paper over and glared at the picture of Doc Smith again. "A hospittle?" he shouted at the picture, as if he expected it to answer. Then sighed, picked up the jar, drained it, and set it back on the table. His insides were on fire, but he paid no notice. He shook his head and thought, "If only there had been a colored hospittle then… maybe…now I wouldn't be a lonely, old man with a bum leg and a head full of troubles. An old man who had to adopt another man's family so I'd have some place to visit, so I'd have someone to talk to and advise, so I'd have someone who would make sure that I was put in the ground properly." Katie and Margaret loved him—but they could never love him like a man is supposed to be loved, that magical bonding between man and woman that made a man a man. Charlie stared at the picture until it became a blur, and finally fell off to sleep with Doc Smith's face smiling up at him.

There in the small, hot room, his head down on his arms, Charlie had a strange dream. He dreamt of his wedding day, the day he and Anna Mae first kissed in public—to seal their vows. But instead of being at the Freewill Baptist Church, they were on the court house lawn in the bright sunshine. He held her close to his hard, vibrant frame with mock bashfulness; and with his right arm circled around her tiny waist, he bent to kiss her full, red lips. Suddenly her face changed from the beautiful smiling lady to a face grimacing in agonizing pain. She gnashed her teeth and a foul odor oozed from her mouth. He shoved her down on the damp ground and ran off into the darkness which had fallen suddenly. Then, he was on the levee, several miles away, where a mist blocked his view of the road and made it impossible for him to move without stumbling. He sat down on the levee bank with his head in his hands and wept. Tears flowed from his eyes and seeped through his fingers, while someone off in the distance, using his voice, yelled, "Doc, please sir, you is gots to help Anna Mae."

Charlie wiped his eyes with his handkerchief and discovered he was on the inside of a grand building. The ceilings were brightly lit and neck-strainingly high, making him feel small and helpless. A low, level row of windows circled the building, covered with black-out curtains that descended to the gleaming oak floors. White metal beds stretching away from him, even like two rows of cotton—sterile and white and covered with snowy white bedcovers and glaring over-head lamps. He stood at the door fascinated—never before had he seen the inside of a hospital. He shielded his eyes with his hands, the lights dazzling and breathtaking—a thousand white candles to each lamp. Anna Mae sat in the middle of the first bed—her breasts bare and full, her legs pulled up, making a tent under the sheet. She pressed a large acorn to the nipple of her breast, while she smiled lovingly at Charlie, beckoning with long, skinny fingers for him to come closer. He crept slowly towards her—a sudden foreboding awareness of impending disaster filling him. She smiled and continued to nurse the acorn, waving her free hand frantically for him to hurry. He glided across the gleaming floor until he stood beside her. Slowly, she pulled the acorn from her breast, and before his eyes it turned into a baby—a tiny complete baby with arms and legs and fierce, wide eyes that rolled back and forth as rhythmically as the pendulum of a grandfather clock. He groaned so loudly that the walls began to shake, and he trembled in fear as he fell on the bed across from Anna Mae, staring in amazement. He pressed his hand across his mouth just as something beneath him began to squirm. He leapt from the bed and yanked back the covers to expose two large, hairy white arms, one pointing an accusing finger at him, the other slowly and rhythmically flexing its bicep. Sweat flowed from Charlie's face. His breathing echoed throughout the room, sounding like thunder bouncing off the hard walls.

A ghost-like figure faded in and out before his eyes. A woman dressed in saintly white robes eventually came into focus and knelt at the foot of the bed next to Charlie. Katie, dressed in her baptizing robes, her hair hidden under a cone-shaped turban that extended almost to the ceiling, stood and stretched her arms violently, lifting her hands upward as if she were holding up the sky. Then, mechanically, she stooped over, grabbed a handful of lard from a five-pound, red bucket on the floor and began to smear it over Margaret's belly which, swollen with child glistened under the lights. He heard Margaret's muffled cries, "Help me, Mama, help me." Katie smeared the lard feverishly, but every time she would cover a spot, it would open and blood would seep through. Faster and faster she worked, moving around her daughter's belly, until it was coated completely. Still the blood broke through, slowly at first, then pouring, until the bed was saturated and the floor covered. All the while he stood, mouth agape, watching the flow of blood, Katie prayed to a great light in the middle of the ceiling. "Buke him, Lord. Buke him in the name of Jesus." He had a sudden realization that he must escape before Katie anointed him with the lard and began praying for him. He pushed his body forward, straining, feeling as though he were trying to walk through heavy maple syrup, until he reached the hall where the floor suddenly opened and he fell through a deep dark hole and landed in the middle of the same room he had just escaped. This time the room was empty, and the floors were gleaming again. An overpowering odor suddenly engulfed him—the smell of death, of rotten flesh and bursting guts, a foul sweet smell he knew too well. There was no other smell like it in the world. His eyes stung, and he began to dry heave. He jammed his fist into his coat pocket, yanked out his handkerchief, and buried his nostrils in the cloth.

He walked quickly to the window to pull back the black curtains. He stopped in his tracks when he saw his old friend, M.B., standing in the corridor, dressed in a long, white doctor's coat, grinning. Charlie brushed past him, almost stumbling to the floor, and flung back the curtain. He gasped at the sight on the grounds outside. Thousands and thousands of white people lay around the hospital, dead, their bodies twisted together like the links on a chain, as though they all tried to enter the building at the same time. They were not just white people, but very white people, with blue veins that had burst under their skin and left scone-shaped lesions on their faces. And there was no blood, only whiteness and blueness that emitted an eerie light like moonlight, all around. Doc Smith lay plastered against the fence, his mouth open, his silver hair gleaming.

Charlie whirled away from the window and faced M.B., his face demanding an explanation. How could there be so much death when the new hospital was there to prevent such a thing? M.B. smiled, flashing white teeth that illuminated his black face. And only when M.B. pointed towards the light outside the window and said, "I got the sign like you tole me," did Charlie understand. His gaze followed M.B.'s finger to the lamp by the side of the road. A large white sign with bold black letters dangled from a shiny chain—a sign that read, "Coloreds Only."

Suddenly Charlie awoke with a start, sending the Mason jar crashing to the floor. He jerked awake and looked about the kitchen—his face covered with sweat, his heart pounding. He looked at the clock—it was five a.m.—and shook his head trying to shake the remnants of the dream from his mind. His breathing was rapid and shallow, his mouth dry and foul. And suddenly he knew that the dream had been a warning, that he would die hating and cursing himself if he didn't take matters into his own hands now.

Daybreak found Charlie standing in front of Tom Lofton's dilapidated shack, confused and discouraged. The morning was still, sun squinted through gray clouds, making the beads of dew glisten on the skimpy grass, and the brown gravel sparkle like nuggets of fool's gold. He was dressed for working the yards; old jeans, a faded flannel shirt, and a wide, straw hat set recklessly on his head. He poked at the dirt, making round circles with his cane. The dream, he was sure, had brought him to this place, a place he had always avoided. He had feared and even hated Tom Lofton for many years. Besides sleeping with two women and keeping them in the same house—not two strangers but mother and daughter—Lofton was a two-headed doctor, a Hoodoo man who removed old spells, put on new spells, told fortunes, interpreted dreams, predicted the future, read the past, and often conferred with the devil. His services were available to anyone who had the right amount of money and enough nerve to face Lofton's imposing figure.

A giant, robust man with a soft melodic voice, Lofton could clear a crowded room in seconds. Even the uppity, rich, white folk gave him plenty of room. No one knew how old he was, and no one dared ask, but townsfolk judged him to be in his early forties because of the gray about his temples and the woolly, gray tufts of hair that poked out of his large ears. Most of the basic necessities that Tom needed were donated by local merchants—often, he would stroll into a store and help himself. It was only on rare occasion—when Tom insisted—that he was allowed to pay. Many a time, upon entering Hazel's, the only black owned Cafe in town, Tom had a dozen bottles of beer in front of him, beer that had been ordered by poor farm hands the minute they saw him coming up the road, and was carried to his reserved table by the owner the moment he stepped inside and fixed his wide, cat-like eyes on the cooler.

Charlie took a deep breath and stared at the shack that sat low to the ground. A three-foot railing circled the house, leaving an ample opening for entry or exit—not unusual for a Hoodoo house. He recalled the terror that Tom's presence had brought to the entire population of Bennettsville a year ago when Mrs. Callie Cook, a wealthy, and long-term resident, hired Lofton to get rid of Thadeus, her unfaithful, abusive husband. Not long after she paid a visit to Tom's house, her husband's body began to swell. Soon, Thadeus Cook took on the appearance of a man with an acute case of dropsy—later that of a very pregnant woman. After he died, the Cook's maid testified that, at the end, Thadeus' bowels groaned loud enough to set the dog barking and then issued forth a bushel of snarling, green garden snakes. She stated that it could be verified by Doc Smith, who had been called to the scene by Miss Callie. No one ever asked Doc Smith, however; no one dared. And it was not long after Thadeus' death that Lofton purchased, with three crisp one-hundred bills the shiny, black Ford.

At night, when the moon was huge in the sky, Tom's isolated shack looked evil—foreboding. A man would have to be blind or under the influence of strong whiskey to even approach the door. But in the early morning sunlight, it was just a run-down little shack that leaned precariously to the left, like it was held up by the wind. The box-like front yard was filled with rubble—old decayed and broken children's toys, wheelbarrows with no wheels, a rocking chair with no rockers, tires with no rims, and chicken troughs with no bottoms. In the middle of this rubble, facing an empty cowpen, sat the shiny, black automobile. Charlie inched closer and squinted at the weather-beaten shack. Its surface, a blend of whitewash and wood, created a color of its own—a slab gray or a brownish-white. Two round windows, one on each side of the plank door, were stuffed with blue, red, and green rags, and appeared to glare at him. They reminded Charlie of eyes; eyes like those described by his elders as belonging to Cris Cringle, the restless spirit who legend said, pushed around an empty wheelbarrow, searching for his head. His eyes, knocked from his head, and big as foghorns, guided the headless body floated above the torso like beacons. Charlie trembled slightly and looked about the shack carefully—spirits had been known to take other forms, and for him to discern the spirit of Cris Cringle would be too much of a fright for his aging heart to survive. He stepped under the awning that jutted skyward—a warped plank held up by two more warped planks—and reluctantly placed one foot on the bottom step. The front door creaked open immediately and his heart hammered in his chest as he looked into the darkness of the house. Suddenly, a melodious voice to his right said, "Shet that door, woman." Charlie jerked his head around to face Lofton, who had come around from the back of the house, noiseless as a cat, carrying a huge green apple in one hand. They stared at each other for a long second; then Tom, shirtless, barefoot, and wearing pajama bottoms, stepped over the low railing that circled the porch, and sat down quickly in the broken cane-bottomed chair. Cutting his jet-black eyes up at Charlie, he savagely bit into the apple.

Charlie stood like an intruder at the bottom of the steps, listening to the crunch of the apple. He watched the shiny, black man devour the huge apple in three bites—then, with a snap of his powerful wrist, sail the core into the yard. Mechanically, he looked up and smiled at Charlie, revealing four perfect gold teeth. Charlie's eyes fastened on the large bulge on Lofton's right hip that strained against the striped pajama bottoms. Charlie had been told that two-headed doctors had spare body parts and he wondered what could it be—another penis, one for each woman, or another hand for spell making, or... The sweet-sour aroma of apple floated across to Charlie as Tom rubbed his hairy chest and let out a loud yawn. He eyed Charlie closely, wiped his mouth and looked about the yard casually.

"You come to visit, or for business?" Tom's soft voice filled the morning air.

"Business," Charlie stammered, his voice thick and strange in his ears. He cleared his throat, making a loud, hacking noise, "Business," he said again, and looked down at the porch.

Gold teeth flashed as Lofton smiled and leaned back, folding his arms behind his head. Two clumps of kinky, knotted hair huddled like cottonseeds in his arm pits. He could see the indecision in Charlie's face, the look folks always wore when they finally came to him for help. Whenever they had exhausted themselves from trips to medical doctors and from sending countless prayers up to God, they would come to him with that same sick look that Charlie now wore. Oh, he knew that look well; the ash-gray skin, the bulging eyes that strained to hold in the evil that all men possessed. And he knew that he would not be shocked by Charlie's request, for there had been many like the one he was about to hear, and he had listened to them all—from bringing back their nature to outright murder.

"I was wondering when you'd git here, Charlie," Tom said, and let the chair drop softly to the porch.

"Huh?" Charlie gaped and watched Lofton watching him.

"Why, early this morning, I seed your face plain as day. You was drinking water black as tar, and fighting white demons," Tom said, creaking forward in the chair. His broad forehead shadowed his eyes.

"Well, I'se surprised to be here." Charlie swallowed hard and gazed down at the planks, wondering if he was still dreaming. "Seems like I was jest drawed over here," he heard himself say.

"Oh," Lofton said, resting his elbow on the window sill and leaning back to gaze into Charlie's face. "I assures you, Charlie, you is under your own power. But befo' you comes any closer," he leaned forward again and pointed a long finger at Charlie, "you'se gots to understand, you hasta come up here on your own."

Charlie wiped the sweat from his face with his sleeve, focused on the glint from the gold teeth, and nodded in Tom's direction. He understood: any transaction made with these kind of people had to be of his own free will or nothing could be accomplished. Lofton could not invite him on the porch, but once he was there he could not change his mind.

"Short time, or long time?" Tom asked, keeping his eyes on Charlie's face.

"Huh?" Charlie muttered in confusion, his right foot still on the bottom step.

"What I means is, do you want it to last a short time or a long time?"

"Oh." Charlie gripped the cane handle, hunched his shoulders and stammered, "Long time."

The sun danced around the windows, making the rags appear dazzling clean, and Charlie's wandering gaze fell upon a hole the size of a large fist below the left window. Before he realized what was happening, he was staring inside the dark shack at a candle-lit statue of Jesus, with a fiery, red wig on its head, sitting on a small, table. Charlie was not a religious man, but desecration of this kind was appalling, even to him. Shaken, he swiftly shifted his gaze to Lofton who sat comfortably in the chair, looking very pleased. Charlie had a sudden overpowering urge to turn and run; but his feet were like stone. He closed his eyes as tight as he could and remembered the reason for his coming—the dream. He saw Anna Mae nursing the acorn, and then the smiling face of Doc Smith floating up from the newspaper, taunting him. He stood there rocking back and forth, sweat rolling down his thin face, remembering all the times that he had murdered Doc Smith in his mind. And instantly, he saw himself, in broad-daylight, and in full view of the townsfolk, slash Doc Smith's face with a gleaming hunting knife, then pound it with a sledge-hammer that he had snatched from the on looking blacksmith, until Smith's eyeballs popped. Again he saw himself, this time in pitch-blackness and without any witnesses, dragging Doc Smith down Main Street on the bumper of a shiny, new pick-up, until Smith was skinless, pink, and bloody. And when the vision had left him, he realized he had neither the strength nor the nerve to do any such thing. He opened his puffy eyes and looked up the landing towards the strange black man who sat like a king in the broken chair. A promise of satisfaction and salvation seemed to be etched across the broad face, and Charlie knew that he needed more than just a service from this man—he needed to be free from the torment he carried within his soul, and he knew that only Lofton could release him. He focused on the crooked steps, sighed, and clumsily placed his other foot on the top step, pushing against the cane until he was on the porch. He breathed deeply; the pact was made—he could not turn back.

The front door creaked open again and two women—both dressed in red, one a tall, lumbering teenager whose name no one knew—the other a middle-aged woman with rolls of fat about the neck—stepped onto the porch. An unnamable odor followed them, and the older woman, Rubelle, stopped short when she neared Charlie, making a ridiculous dip in her fat legs that Charlie assumed was a bow. She had a long, slender face, and a keen nose. Her skin was remarkably smooth and satiny and reminded Charlie of the shiny, black automobile that sat among the rubble. She had one perfect eye—the right one. The other was covered with a milky-white film that clung to the ball like the white of an egg, draping like a watery curtain over the pupil which was but a dot. She announced in a high, trembling voice, "We is going to the ice house for ice." Then, she stood at attention, her large breasts rising and falling, waiting for Tom's approval.

Lofton came out of the chair as though he had been struck, his gaze fierce—bloodcurdling. "Un-fix that eye offa me, woman!" He said in a chilling voice. "Do it one more time and I'm gonna fix the other one the same." The woman cringed and covered the side of her face with her arms as if she had received a powerful blow; the teenage girl jumped up and down, rocking the wobbly porch, and making grunting noises as she snatched frantically for her mother's hand; Charlie drew back against the railing, dazed. He watched clouds of dust spurt from under the planks as the hefty, teenager's brogan shoes pounded the porch in a crazed dance. His back dug into the rail with every stomp of the girl's feet, and suddenly he understood the connection between them—they were all bound together by madness, fear, and evil. He shuddered as he realized that the things that connected these outcasts of society were the very things that had brought him here—for only a madman would remain and witness such a spectacle. But the fear of going to his grave without avenging Anna Mae's death, and the evil that lay beneath his breast-bone like a poison confirmed the union. He steadied himself with the cane, gripped the railing with his free hand, and twisted about to see Lofton fling a powerful arm in the air, turn away from the women, then point a long finger towards the ground, muttering words in a strange tongue. When Lofton finally reeled back to glare at the women, a silence hung in the air as thick as mist over the Mississippi River, broken only by the heavy rapid gasp of the women's breathing. Suddenly, Tom dropped into the chair and in a dry, crisp, deadly tone, said, "Now, git me my book, and git Charlie here a chair."

The door creaked open, slammed closed, and opened again, and a fine hardwood chair appeared instantly. Reluctantly Charlie pulled the chair across the porch and sat down, his back against the railing. He stole glances at Lofton, who now faced him, but he was watching Rubelle intensely as she timidly placed the brown leather book into Lofton's hands. She stepped away quickly, standing at attention at the edge of the porch. She did not move until Tom looked up, nodded, releasing her. Then, she stepped to the ground, only to leap immediately back onto the porch—a murderous look in her eyes—as she snatched the gaping teenager's hand. They moved quickly across the yard, their gestures awkward, furtive. The evident physical and mental deformities of the women repulsed and frightened Charlie, but still he sensed something beautiful about them—an aura of simplicity—something that he could not describe. As they walked towards the cowpen, the sun beaming down on their backs, he wondered, what did they think about? What did they talk about? Did staying with a man like Lofton offer them an identify that was otherwise denied by society?

He watched them take the path that snaked here and there all over the property, then connected with Russell Street, leading to the ice house some five miles away. No other houses sat on these ten acres of land, only weeds as tall as a man's middle and fruit trees that yielded continuously. Even now, Charlie could hear the fruit drop softly to the ground. Turning, he faced the Hoodoo man, whose attention was now focused on the thick, book spread open across his lap. A huge crow's feather lay pressed in the seam, and its stark-white pages were bordered with a fine, golden trim that contrasted sharply with Tom's bootblack hands. With an uneasy churning in his stomach, Charlie watched Lofton closely now as his hands slowly and methodically rubbed the pages. A familiar gleam radiated from his eyes. Charlie had seen that look on many a Preachers' face—a look they all wore when they opened the doors of the church for sinners to come forth and write their names in God's book. Tom flipped through the book as though it was the Holy Bible. He touched the pages carefully, as though they revealed some divine message, held the knowledge sought by all men. Finally, he lifted his head, his eyes steady, businesslike, and searched Charlie's face curiously. "Now, so's we understands one another, long term is gonna cost you more money." Slowly, he licked his thick lips, then wiped his mouth with the back of his hand. "You got money, ain't you?" he asked, a serious look on his face.

Charlie swallowed and nodded. "I'se got money," he said, letting his eyes linger on the black feather.

"Fine." Tom flashed the gold and fingered the feather, stroking it like he was giving it life. "Now, jest what is it you wants done?" He removed the feather and placed it between his fingers as if to write.

"I ain't rightly sure." Charlie hunched his shoulders and squirmed in the chair, suddenly aware that he was alone with Lofton in this desolate place on the other side of the levee. He looked for the answer in the planks of the porch. "Ain't never done nothing like this. Always done my fighting face to face; but I had this here 'sturbing dream last night and the next thang I knows I'se here. Had to do with my wife, Anna Mae. She been dead thirty-odd years now, long befo' you come here."

"If you is here on account of a dream, must be something eating way at your insides. Dreams often reminds us of our obligations," he said, and laid the feather on the page, its blackness gleaming in the sun as though it had been dipped in fine oil.

Charlie had begun to relax; his hatred for Lofton had eased, and he felt the words suddenly crowding his throat, choking him as they spilled out into the air. "I saw a whole lot of dead white folks sprawled on the ground outside a hospittle."

Tom eyed Charlie curiously and picked up the feather. "White folks, hum? When white folks is in a dream, they always represent death; but dead white folks stand for a prophecy 'bout to happen."

"Huh?" Charlie frowned, and looked to Lofton for an explanation.

"Turning back evil, Charlie," he said, pointing at Charlie. "You been the object of evil doing—somebody's spell-making—and now you wants to send it back."

Charlie nodded his head, although he didn't quite understand, and yet the pieces began to come together—evil had been consuming him ever since his first encounter with Doc Smith. "Doc Smith was one of em," he continued. "And I was surprised and happy at the same time to see him dead. And then I was shocked." Charlie waved his hands and looked towards the cowpen. "I means, all them dead bodies laying 'round and stinking worsa than catguts drying in the sun. God, what a smell!"

Tom smiled and closed his eyes—a serenity about him as though he had reached a plateau of some unknown altitude. He slowly opened his eyes and focused on Charlie's face. "Jest how many white folks is it you wants dead?" he asked, his voice steady, the sun splashing small, golden circles on his forehead.

Charlie looked at the planks, pulled in his bad leg, and rubbed it vigorously. "Jest one," he heard himself say in a bitter voice he didn't recognize. He looked up quickly, searching Tom's face for signs of reproval, but found none. He relaxed more—the air appearing calmer, less evil to him. He hadn't liked the way Lofton had treated the women, but that was not important now. What mattered was the dark secret that he had revealed to Tom—a secret that most men would not admit, even in play—and the fact that Tom had listened, knowing he was not selling wolf tickets, a declaration of vengeance that was never followed through. His hatred for Tom was softening, but the fear remained like an undigested meal in his stomach. He fished in his shirt pocket, pulled out his handkerchief, and mopped the insides of his hands.

There was no doubt that he still feared this man; Lofton's imposing figure and unusual life style caused many men to fear him, and Charlie knew of no one who confessed, even in play, to being Lofton's friend. He stared at the large, ugly man whose face reminded him of Susie's—his first plow mule—with its broad forehead and thin, prominent veins running beneath fine, delicate, tissue paper skin. Tom's long, slack jaw pulled his thick lips down toward his chin, and his flaring nostrils lay too close to the wide, cat-like eyes. When the sun beamed down over the porch, and the gold flashed from Tom's boxed mouth, his eyes seemed to disappear into his head. He shivered under Tom's hazy stare and thought, perhaps this was the head of Cris Cringle after all, located at last and attached in haste. Yes, Lofton was a frightful sight, but that was not all that bothered Charlie. Whoever he was—Cris Cringle, the Devil, or just an ugly man—Charlie had begun to note an unsettling bond forming between them, a bond that he feared would carry them to the gates of hell.

Tom leaned forward and scooted the chair back against the window sill. He steadied the huge book on his lap, gazed at the sky for a long second, then resumed studying the pages. Slowly, he removed three long strips of brown, crinkly paper and handed them across to Charlie. "Give me the name of this person. Say it out loud so it will ride on the wind, then write it on each paper—use this…" He removed the feather from the book and carefully passed it over to Charlie.

Charlie took the feather between trembling fingers and stared at it, admiring the sheen as the sunlight struck it—black as ink, blacker than tar, blacker than anything he had ever seen. He held it in his right hand like it was alive, his heart pounding and sweat rolling down from underneath his hat. "Doc Smith," he uttered slowly, like he was dreaming. Avoiding Lofton's gaze, he turned towards the cowpen, his eyes following the crooked alignment of the planks. Mentally, he straightened and nailed them properly; then, Anna Mae's beaming smile was suddenly before him. Her long, black hair rested on her shoulders, a soft, warm light radiated from the deep brown eyes, and a glow of peacefulness and motherhood was evident in her face. She nursed the tiny baby proudly. Then the glistening belly, under the lights, pushed Anna Mae's face into the background. The tap, tap, tap of a sharp fingernail on paper brought Charlie from his reverie. He stared down at the papers on his thigh and scratched "Doc Smith" on each one in a bold black ink that magically oozed from the feather's tip.

The writing finished, Charlie and Tom sat for a moment and listened to the low rumble of the gin across the levee—the rhythmic, hypnotic beat of the thrashers as they separated the seeds from the cotton—the heartbeat of the town. To Charlie it sounded like a thousand pairs of hands clapping in the distance.

The sun broke through the clouds and Charlie felt its hot beam on his neck. He cleared his throat and turned from Lofton's burning gaze. But there was no escaping the memory; it was as though Lofton's eyes commanded him to remember. His mind raced back to the horrible night that Anna Mae died. He heard the hoarse bear-like screams for mercy that had made M.B. and him shiver and dash inside. And suddenly, he could smell the fumes from the many oil lamps that had sat around Anna Mae's bed that night—an acrid smell that singed the hairs in his nose and made his eyes smart. He saw her there on their four-poster bed, wild-eyed, with gnashing teeth, and writhing in pain, her long, black hair plastered to a drenched forehead, then swirling in a crazed tousle about her head. Her full lips were stretched thin, ash-gray, and raw—blood oozing from gaping teeth wounds. He could not believe she was the same person he had left several hours ago to search for Doc Smith. She sat up on her knees, her belly distended, filled with blood, and rocked back and forth like she was in an invisible rocking chair sitting in a garden filled with full-bloomed daffodils—all that yellow, like sunshine, glaring up from the quilt at him. The bright colors from the wedding-ring quilt did a crazy dance before his eyes. He and M.B. wrapped her in the quilt, put her in the bed of M.B.'s truck, Charlie climbing in beside her, and headed for Margestown, praying they would make it in time, and praying them white folks would come outside to tend Anna Mae, when and if they made it.

Charlie shook his head, let out a low moan, and focused on the cowpen. He tried to straightened the boards again, but it was no use; he was powerless to stop the vision. It stood before him more vivid than ever—as if it had happened yesterday. Details that he had forgotten over the years were crisp and clear. And he saw the truck, the midnight blue pick-up with orange reflectors blinking from its tailgate. The wind was cool to his face as the truck streaked down the road; M.B. was flying, the gears screaming, dust swirling. The darkness enveloped them and he could only catch glimpses of Anna Mae in the flashes of light from lamp poles that guarded the intersections and railroad crossings. The truck swayed and dipped, M.B.'s tools and old work clothes slid back and forth, and Charlie strained to keep his balance, holding Anna Mae steady in his arms as he knelt next to her on the bucking truck bed. And Anna Mae fought: the quilt, the demons, and Charlie. Wracked with pain she ripped his clothes, scratched his face, wretched, spat blood against the wind, and then laid her head against the cab until the knife-like pains started again. Back and forth, up and down they went until Charlie, drained of strength and near hysterics started to cry. He knew they couldn't go on like this much longer. He began to pray for a miracle; he prayed that God would heal Anna Mae instantly, and he prayed that Doc Smith would change his mind, come to his house, and, following Josephine's instructions, would drive like a mad man to catch up with them. He prayed with all his fiber because he knew that was the only thing that could save her now. The wind whipped his clothing, and the tires sang, beating out a frenzied song of hopelessness on the blacktop.

Suddenly, Anna Mae sat up, grabbed Charlie by the shirt, and tried to stand. He had to wrestle her to the floor of the truck's bed, their faces almost touching as they struggled in the darkness. While holding her firmly to the floor, he became aware of light creeping above his head, and he knew they must be approaching a town. He looked up to see the sign that read, "Huntsville straight ahead; Margestown 42 miles." And when they passed under another roadside light, Charlie saw her face clearly. It was as though time came to a halt under the lights for Charlie saw all the horrors he had been told, as a boy, to expect in hell. He chilled at the sight of her. Her skin had a waxy yellowish sheen, her eyes were sunken, hollow, and glazed. She had bitten through her bottom lip, and her chin was smeared with blood. From her mouth came an odor of something long dead and it was plain to Charlie that she did not recognize him. She was a wild woman, insane from pain, making only animal grunts. He had to do something to stop this madness. He drew back his fist and struck her hard in the face. She grunted, shook her head, and stared at him with shock and surprise. He wilted, he could not bear that look—then wept openly, burying her head in his chest.

The truck spun into a curve, sending them reeling backwards, and something cold and hard bumped against his hand. He felt its strangeness, its coolness, and knew by its shape it was a tire iron. His hand gripped it tightly and a coldness enveloped him. He had prayed for a miracle, not this. But his thoughts were now on ending this nightmare. Anna Mae's sunken eyes told him that she would never make it to Margestown. And who was he kidding, thinking them white folks gave a damn. They would do the same as Smith had, wash their hands of it, the bastards. How many times had he heard Negroes talking about waiting outside for a doctor to come out until the person either got well or died? Anna Mae was not going to get well—he had seen it in her eyes, could hear it in her ragged breathing.

And now he felt the puddle seeping from under the quilt, warm and sticky to his hand and he knew it was blood. No, he would have to end this…, but he could not do it under the light, he could not bear to see those eyes reproach him again. He would wait for the next light and began timing them from then on. He sat, rigid, stone-like, caressing her hair and listening to the maddening song of the tires.

As he waited on Lofton's porch, Charlie's hands began to shake. He felt Lofton's gaze upon his face, boring into him, seemingly ordering him back. But he heard himself counting—one, two, three, four, five—as the streetlights slid overhead. The darkness came again, and he pushed up on his knees straddling his wife, the tire iron gripped tightly in his hand. His fingers searched her face as he estimated where to deal the blow. He cupped her left cheek, turning her head slightly to the left. The tires sang as he drew the tire iron back above his head and with all the rage and despair inside him, dealt her a fatal blow to her temple. She moaned, her head snapping and sliding to one side. She went limp. As they came under the light again, he saw her sprawled on her back, her head facing the east, and her belly glistening under the light. Bending, he listened to her chest—no sound. She was gone. He threw back his angry head and cursed the God who would honor his prayer for death, but not for life. He flung the tire iron out into the darkness, listening to its clanking as it bounced across the highway. He covered her completely with the quilt, and crawling on one knee to the window of the cab, he pounded for M.B. to stop.

Now, on Lofton's porch, Charlie tightened his grip on the papers and dropped his head. The horror of it all lay like a knife in his chest. He was afraid to meet Tom's steady gaze. Afraid that Tom would know what he had done. But how? He had never breathed a word of it to anyone, not even, M.B. The casket had been closed, and she had not been laid out on the cooling board—Josephine had told everyone how badly Anna Mae had suffered. Slowly, Charlie lifted his head to find Tom's eyes searching his face. They stared at each other for a long second, and in that instant Charlie was sure that somehow Lofton did know. He could see it there in those deep, hollow eyes; and yet Tom did not reproach him. Charlie cleared his throat and shook his head, but he knew he was not dreaming. He looked back at the cowpen, thinking that if Lofton knew what happened that night, then he knew why—that he had struck her to give her peace, that he had ended Anna Mae's life because she could not bear the pain any longer—thirty-six hours was beyond human endurance—and that his act was the greatest gift of love that he could have ever given her.

The tapping resumed and Tom's voice suddenly became businesslike again. "Well, since we understands one another, let's git down to the particulars." He ran his finger down the page, locating the hexes. "We gots, 'long-term revenge,' 'making them do your bidding,' 'public embarrassment,' 'stealing their spouses,' 'sudden accidents,' 'natural looking disasters,' 'driving them crazy,' and…"

"Stop right there," Charlie shouted in a hoarse, raspy voice, waving the papers in the air. "That's the one I wants, 'driving them crazy."

"Fine, jest fine." Tom smiled and crossed his legs, making a shelf for the heavy book with his thigh. He summed up, "We gots long-term revenge, driving this particular person, Doc Smith, crazy, right?"

"Right," Charlie said, glaring at the name on the paper.

"Now, how you wants it done? Day by day, over a long period, or instant madness?"

Charlie's brow was thick with wrinkles as he passed the papers over to Tom—their fingers touching—his fear suddenly gone.

Tom flashed the gold, folded each paper three times, and slipped them into a pocket inside the book. Charlie dabbed at his hot forehead and at the sides of his feverish face. He felt the sweat break suddenly from his armpits and fall inside his shirt. He knew it was the poison from within, boiling over, and leaking out. Oh, how he would love to see Doc Smith insane this very minute. He had killed Doc Smith a thousand times before in his mind, but this time it was going to be real. He sneered, leaned back in the chair, and envisioned Doc Smith foaming at the mouth, kicking the red dust for miles, bashing his head against the hard court house walls until it was mush. He saw Doc Smith being dragged through town from a bumper of a police car, his limp, battered body smeared with dog excrement. Then, suddenly, Charlie realized that if Doc Smith went mad instantly, It would be over in one day and Doc Smith would never know what had happened to him. No, Charlie wanted him to suffer! He licked his dry lips and raised his voice to the sky.

"Don't reckon it'll do no good if'n he was to go off clucking like a setting hen." He lowered his eyes to meet Tom's. "Naw, what that son-ah-bitch needs can't be found, even in hell. We is dealing with a man what don't even recollect his sins. Had the gall jest last week to ask me to come see what I could do for his ailing Red Hardies. Naw, what he needs is to feel the fear, the shame, the emptiness... He needs to feel liken I did when he refused to tend my pregnant wife. He needs to suffer every day he lives, jest liken I does. I wants his heart to swell so big wheres it pretty near bust his gut liken mine did. I wants his mouth to be dry like gravel wheres he can't even swallow his own spit. That's what I wants." Charlie chewed the words, blinked back tears and looked towards the cowpen, then snapped his head around to face Lofton and hissed, "I wants him to be so bad off, and look so bad, that won't no hospittle even touch him. You knows," he shook his head, "the same way they do all the coloreds!"

"Fine, fine, jest fine." The melodic voice floated on the morning wind. "Now, we gots long-term revenge, driving em crazy, day-by-day, right?"

"Yes, sir, that's right," Charlie said emphatically.

They sat for a moment, listening to the rumble of the gin—the clap, clap, clap of the thrashers and the roar of the dryers sucking the moisture from the cotton before the separation process began. It was a soothing sound; it meant money would be circulating throughout the town; it meant spirits would be high.

Tom closed the book with a thud, stood, and stretched one arm across the narrow porch. He yawned sleepily, then scratched the side of his face. Turning towards the door, he stopped, cupped his chin, and stared down at the planks. "Bring me some of his clothing, something personal, Charlie, and I'll make a potion and tell you what to do."

"Don't wants no potion," Charlie stammered. "I wants you to do it direct."

Tom looked down on Charlie's trembling straw hat, a twinkle in his eyes. "Direct. Now, that's gonna cost more if'n I does it direct, much more." He smiled.

"I knows your reputation, Mr. Lofton, and I ain't 'bout to ask for no services I can't pay for. And besides," he hesitated, pulling the hat down over his forehead, "this here ain't all I wants… I'se gonna need yo' help agin and soon. So I aims to pay yo' price."

Tom smiled, tightened his grip on the book, and looked at the sky, "Well, I likes work the same as the rest. Bring me them clothes, Charlie, and fifty dollars befo' midnight." He walked the few feet to the door; turned and looked at the sky again. "Looks like we is in for some rain." Turning around, he placed his huge palm against the door, stood for a moment studying Charlie's hat, then disappeared inside the shack.

Charlie lingered on the porch, listening to the creaking of the door and the brush of bare feet against linoleum. He stared at the plank door, wondering what secrets lay behind it, then turned his attention to the cowpen. He looked at the crooked boards for the last time, then pushed up from the chair, a feeling of satisfaction surging through him, making him feel young. He would get the things tonight, he thought, he was sure of that. He removed his cane from the railing and stepped off the porch, limping towards the winding path near the cowpen: one minute, the sun was beating down on his back; the next, a hard pouring rain.

FLIGHT

The sun baked the red earth by day, and the rain soaked it at night, resulting in muddy cotton fields, weather-beaten vegetable gardens, and an abundance of mosquitoes. During the day, the field hands grumbled because scale prices were calculated on estimations of what the cotton would weigh dry. And at night they argued that old man Townsend would have paid scale price and later deducted it from their yearly bill—at least that way they weren't cheated so blatantly. One month had passed since Townsend's death and the field hands were feeling the effects already. Townsend's funeral had been as grand as he had said it would be when he was alive—a procession of grieving relatives, friends, and townsfolk honored him with a turnout befitting a king. Even Katie and Margaret, although they did not attend the services as requested in Townsend's will, had gone down with Charlie and stood on Main Street watching the sleek, black hearse wind through town followed by cars and pick-ups trucks with blazing headlights, wagons loaded with Negro and white people from all over the county, and mounted police on gleaming, glossy-black horses, moving through and around the crowd with military precision. Shortly thereafter, J.T. took over, and during one of his visits to the fields he announced, to the hands' disappointment, that cotton scraping would begin two weeks earlier than usual. He contacted the land developers in St. Louis, seeking a deal to unload the sections of land that fell under President Roosevelt's new law—only so many acres of crops could be planted per year, making portions of the land useless—for a shoe factory to be erected in town. And by the end of that week, J.T. had purchased a shocking-red, single-engine airplane and housed it on the unused acres on the grounds of Lavilli Field—it sat like a huge menacing bird ready to swoop down on the field hands and gobble them up one by one.

Over the past two weeks a series of events had taken place—Roy Larkin had returned home a changed and quieter man. He claimed no memory of the night that he lost his arm. His daddy, some said, led Roy around like a two-year-old. Reverend Washington persuaded the Deacon Board to restore Sister Katie's status, that he had been wrong, stating that she had been the victim of Townsend's manipulation... Mother Washington had delivered an eight pound baby boy, but still had not received the Holy Ghost. And according to Velma Rice, who worked for Doc Smith on Tuesdays, the old man acting "mighty peculiar." She told every day worker in town that "Doc Smith come outside while I was hanging the wash, whipped out his old, wrinkled pecker, and peed like a castrated bull on top of several ant hills. He looked at me real evil-like and returned to the house."

During the day, at work, Katie chopped onions, mashed potatoes, shelled blue hulls, fried chicken, and baked pies. In the evening, at home, she fed her chickens with motherly concern, tended her vegetable garden with a shaking head of dismay, and paced the floor like a cat in heat at night, worrying about the consequences of the cover-up and Margaret. At home in the day, Margaret lined the floor with patterns, cut materials for dresses and linings, selected sturdy and fine threads, measured waistlines, busts, upper arms, and buttocks. In the evening she fetched water, brought in the wash, and carried in the kindling for the cook stove. But at night, she rode the swing like a witch on a scratchy broom, making the chains squeak and groan. During the day, Luther picked, hauled, and loaded cotton in wagons for ginning and watched Sylvester like a hawk. But at night, his thoughts were on Margaret. He wondered if he could make Margaret like him enough to become his wife. Charlie only worked one place now and that was for Miss Clara, and all his time in the evenings was spent with Katie and Margaret before returning home, worried. They all worried about the same thing: Had their cover-up worked?

Rather than the usual conversations with Alice on their breaks, Katie had taken to sitting alone and staring out the back door and one day while sitting in the kitchen of the Cafe, the dinner rush over, a sandwich before her, she had a vision. Suddenly, before her was an image of a winding circle of red bricks, slick and glistening from rain. A Negro man in a blue checked shirt and coveralls lay face down on the bricks, his long legs stretching across them and extending to the grass on the other side. Three policemen, one dressed in midnight blue, the others in beige khaki, clamored around the Negro, pushing and prodding him with their nightsticks. The policemen suddenly drifted away from each other—two of them moved to the right of the Negro man and began stomping the man's arm over and over, until it stretched and lay flat as the bricks, while the other policeman was preoccupied with something or someone on the left. Quickly, it began to rain—a sudden downpour that drenched them—but they remained as they were, their hats soaked and dripping water, their uniforms plastered to their bodies—their white skin suddenly visible through their soaked shirts.

At that point, the juke-box in the white section of the Cafe blasted out a country song, and Katie looked around to see Miss Rosie close the swinging doors. She turned back, brushing tears from her face—the vision gone. Her heart was very sad, because she knew that it—whatever it was—would come to pass, they always had. And although she had always felt helpless whenever she had these visions, today she thanked God, for this omen meant she was still in good standing with her God—that the dream of Pappy hurling the axe into his enemy's face was God's way of showing Katie how He would protect her. She shook her head, her heart suddenly filled with the spirit of God as she reasoned it out in her mind. After all, she had not gone looking for the axe; her enemy, Roy, had thrown her upon it—she hadn't even known it was there. Charlie, in his rush to board the door and nail the windows and return to work, had absentmindedly left it propped against the wall of the middle room door, a place where it had never been put. She felt relieved and sadden at the same time, for God had shown her the light while she stood the darkness.

Later that evening, after imploring Margaret to attend the foot-washing service with her, and getting nowhere, Katie went to church alone. The change in her daughter's demeanor worried her, Margaret had become quiet, dutiful, sad so unlike herself. As the service began remnants of the vision fluttered before her like a warning of something dreadful to come. But later as she sat in the Sanctified Church in her front pew listening to the Junior Choir sing "Glory Glory Hallelujah," her troubles seem to vanish. The young boys and girls, ranging in the age from eight to fifteen, stood behind the pulpit with jubilant faces lifted towards the ceiling as they swayed from side to side, clapping their hands and praising God. Reverend Washington sat in the pulpit, his deep-set eyes riveted on the choir, his hand clutching the neck of his guitar as though he would swing it upon his lap and began pounding it any minute. The Saints clapped their hands and rocked back and forth in their pews. Fierce bursts of "Yes, Lord!" mingled with "Sing the song, children!" erupted across the room. And Katie felt safe sitting there—barelegged, her stockings and garters tucked neatly inside of her handbag, in preparation for the foot-washing. The outside world seemed shut out. The spirit of the Holy Ghost seemed to fill the church with an electric and unexplainable joy as the youngsters belted out their song like professionals, stirring the hearts and souls of everyone present.

A cool breeze flitted through the screen door and caressed Katie's naked legs. Suddenly aware of the outside world, Katie felt a vision of impending danger loom before her, and she had the urge to run home, grab Margaret, and hide. She rose from the pew slowly, as though she was in a trance, and tiptoed around the long table lined with sparkling white foot basins until she reached the pulpit. She touched Reverend Washington lightly on his broad shoulder, and his head swiveled about to face her. She knew he saw the great fear in her eyes, the same fear she had felt at the restaurant when she was told about the will—that hot, white fear—and her knees trembled as though she carried a great weight upon her back. "Pray for me, Reverend. Please ask the Saints to pray for me—there is a great burden in my heart," she said in a desperate whisper. She knelt at the edge of the podium and clasped her hands together.

Reverend Washington studied her with intense dark eyes, quickly placed the guitar on the landing, and stepped down peering at her with concern. He was a tall, heavy man, but light on his feet, and as he approached Katie, he closed the space between them cautiously, as though he expected her to disappear.

Inspired by the spirit of God that oozed from every corner of the church and by the urgent request for prayer, he placed his huge hands on both of her shoulders, covering them completely, and shook her as though he was trying to snap her neck. He sprang backwards, his hands still on her shoulders, and lifted his burning eyes towards the ceiling, crying out in a loud, booming voice, "Heal!" The choir ended its song and gathered at the end of the pulpit directly above Reverend Washington and Katie. Reverend Washington raised his eyes and spoke, "Dear Father, we ask you to heal tonight in the name of Jesus." Sweat flew from his forehead, and he snatched his hands away from Katie's shoulders and spread his arms open, holding them straight and steady as though they had suddenly been thrust against a cross and nailed. The church was quiet. He looked long and lovingly at the congregation, a smile forming on his thick lips as though he knew the divine secret—a secret too glorious to speak out loud, a secret divulged through the meeting of souls. The words erupted from his lips in a thunderous baritone as he began to sing, "Heal, hee-al, hee-al, hee-al, hee-al."

Someone coughed and the scent of peppermint pushed through the screen door. Sister Dunne sprang from her pew alongside the wall. Tossing her arms, she joined in the song—her voice cracking, then finding strength. The Saints immediately took their cue and joined in, their strong voices ringing out the same word: "Hee-al." Mother Washington rose from her pew, shaking her head as she headed towards the other side of the pulpit, and pushed her mouth into a pout. Her eyes shut tight to fight back sudden tears, she shouted, "Yes, Lord, heal us tonight," and began to form the customary circle. A tambourine jangled and the choir began to sing and Mother Washington joined Reverend Washington and Katie at the foot of the pulpit. All the women began to wave their arms, white handkerchiefs fluttering in the air, and rose from their pews to fall in behind Mother Washington. Sister Dunne began to sing the word, "Hee-al," in a shrill soprano—everyone understood the message was for all of them, that they all needed to be healed. The women gathered to the left and right of Mother Washington—all crying out in a high-pitched frenzy until the room seemed to breathe on its own, and until the space around Reverend Washington and Katie was filled with the circle of love.

The Deacons began their raspy benediction—blessing His holy name as they formed a circle around the women. Brother Watson, a stout, bald-headed man, began his chant, rolling the words of the holy scriptures around on his tongue as if he had digested the words and they had become his own. His jaws puffed like a huge blow-fish and releasing the words with a rapidity that mimicked the staccato blast of a trumpet—he sounded like a man with a great hole in his chest—cried: "And I will lay sinews upon you, and will bring flesh upon you, and cover you with skin, and put breath into you, and ye shall live, and ye shall know that I am the Lord." Reverend Washington looked back at the ceiling, placed his hands on Katie's shoulders again, and took up the cry, "Oh, ye dry bones, hear the word of the Lord!"

Hands waved, and a loud sobbing filled the room. It was Katie. She cried out, "Thank you, Jesus!"

And Reverend Washington dropped his eyes, and as if he had given a command, they all began to sing again—the word: "Hee-al." Their voices drifted through the open doors and windows and were carried on the wind for miles. The atmosphere was heavenly—as close to heaven as anyone on earth could get—and this supplication sent up to God on her behalf created a calming effect for Katie, better than any medicinal powder or elixir she had ever taken.

Margaret, who had flatly refused to attend the evening service with her mother, also felt the need to be healed. She had carried all her troubles to the old, bulky, handmade swing. Margaret had spent many nights in that swing, wrestling with her conscience, or with the temptation to sneak down to Hazel's Cafe and dance all night, or wondering where was her father and why hadn't he contacted her.

Now she heard the voices of the Saints from the church across the railroad tracks and stopped the swing with her foot to listen. She sat there—her long, slender legs tucked under the wooden seat, her arms spread the length of the swing, clasping the chains tightly, and her head pushed forward like she was about to race the swing to the edge of the porch, leap off, and fly into the darkness. She was a shadowy figure, made even ghostly by the light from the street lamp bathing the corner of the porch and spilling long bars of light across her knees—highlighting the white cuffs of her pedal pushers—while the rest of her sat in the darkness. The song was a favorite of Margaret's and she listened intently to the crisp voices that seemed to travel on the wind. She had often wondered about the origin of the song—really more of a chant, since it consisted of only one small, but powerful word—a word of power that made people heal themselves—made them cry, made them shout, and made them believe in the impossible. A sad, but uplifting sound warbled in that way unique to Negroes that made your hair stand on end while soothing your aching soul. Hee-al.

She tilted her head to one side, straining to hear her mother's voice among the others. She imagined her mother with a long white towel draped across her shoulder as she walked towards the center of the circle to begin the foot washing. She could see her mother and the other woman designated to do the washing walk in single file to the table, select the wash basins, and place them gently to their chests. Gracefully, the women would stoop and fill the basins with the tepid water from the large galvanized tub that sat in the center of the circle, then place the basins in front of the person's feet they had chosen to wash. And the feet were always the same: the callused feet that were ashen and creased from tight fitting brogans; the smooth and oiled feet, obviously meticulously washed before the ceremony; the odorous feet filled the room with a sour smell, causing heads to snap and eyes to tear; the big feet with two-inch, claw-like nails that could puncture car tires; and tiny feet—baby feet—caked with sweet-smelling powder—all waited to be washed. Katie would kneel on the floor by the roughest-looking pair of feet there, remove the towel from her shoulder, and pass it over her head to the woman who remained standing above her. She would then slide her hand down the back of the heel she had selected, and under the foot until it sat crossways in the palm of her hand. She would lower the foot into the basin without letting it touch the floor. At this point Katie always cried, "Yes, Lord!' and Margaret wondered, when she saw this, if it meant that the foot needed washing badly or that her mother was just feeling the spirit. And soon the washing would begin, Katie submerging the wash cloth into the clear soapless water and running the towel from the hollow of the ankle under the heel and onward to the big toe. Then, she would wring the towel over the top of the foot, allowing the water to cascade from the ankle to the toes. Slowly, she would lift the foot and the standing woman would slip a towel underneath.

Margaret sighed, ran her hand through her long bangs, and leaned against the back of the swing. She began to squirm in the swing, wishing that she had gone to the foot washing; but recalling the controversy over the money, she decided it was better that she had not. She didn't want her feet washed, and she didn't want any advice on what she should do with the money. She brushed the buzzing mosquitoes away from her face and let out a loud sigh. She felt old and burdened with problems of the past weeks, problems that she hadn't dreamed would be placed upon her—being indirectly responsible for a man losing his arm and for the cloak and dagger atmosphere that hung around herself and her mother when anyone approached them. She longed for the time when dreams didn't seem to cause so much trouble, when, as a child, she would lay her ear to the railroad track and listen for the rumble of the approaching train. The same train that always jerked around the bend each Tuesday, puffing and straining like a fat old woman with arthritic knees.

That had been at another time in her life, a time when unfulfilled dreams could be easily resolved by a handful of sweet hickory nuts or a bar of Strick-O-lean candy from the traveling wagon store. Today, however, Margaret's dreams could not be solved so easily, because this money offered her the opportunity to board a real train that would lead to someplace away from Bennettsville, to an opening of doors, doors of learning and of real experiences in the world. Doors that were now closed to her and that kept her dreams confined to the old boxed swing.

The mosquitoes hummed near her ear, and the crickets suddenly seemed to increase the volume of their singing—as if a big foot had suddenly trodden on the dirt around them, perhaps even stepped upon their tiny homes among the tall reeds. She leaned forward, staring towards the dirt path that wound alongside the graveled road. She heard the shuffle of feet along with a swoosh-thack-swoosh-thack sound and realized that it could only be Charlie. The cane pushing between the rocks on the edge of the path made a swooshing sound—like the wind when it rushes pass your ear—and she could tell by the repeated stroking that he was in a hurry. She pushed the swing back until it touched the wall of the house and then picked up her feet, letting the swing carry her to the edge of the porch, where she planted both feet firmly on the wood floor to stop it. The swing rocked and shook underneath her like an old cart before finally settling to a halt.

"Margaret, Margaret, is that you?" Charlie called softly, and stood bobbing his head from side to side at the bottom of the steps.

"Yes, Mr. Charlie, it's me; who did you think I was, a ghost?" she replied, peering into the darkness.

"Well, I knowed it! I knowed it in my bones," he announced in one long gust of words as he mounted the stairs, pounding each step with his cane.

"You knew what, Mr. Charlie?" she asked cautiously, because it was most unusual for Charlie to rush, and because she had clearly heard the alarm in his voice.

"Told your mama I knowed something 'bout that truck," he said, stepping onto the porch. "Told her it was something 'bout that truck what bothered me, something I couldn't put my finger on, but it's been a pulling at my head ever since that night," he said, moving into the light, his forehead lined with wrinkles.

"What in the world has happened?" Margaret asked, slowly walking the swing back toward the house wall to get a better view of Charlie's face. The straw hat trembling on his head, as he repeatedly jerked his head towards the road.

"You mean you ain't heard, gal?" All hell done broke loose uptown," he replied, his voice rising until it became a shout.

"What are…" she stopped, and they both turned their attention to the road, to the crunch of gravel and the sliding, hurrying pounding of footsteps.

"Must be your mama and Luther," he said, peering up the road to the street lamp. I done sent Luther over to the church to bring her home."

He glared into the darkness—listening to the rustling of Katie's long white dress being whipped like clothes on a line by the violent thrusts of her legs, and to Luther's brogan feet scattering gravel and sending dust sailing. The blackness of the night hung thick around them, making it impossible for Charlie to see them on the road. When they reached the street lamp over the railroad tracks, they seemed to appear out of nowhere—Katie with a Bible clutched to her chest, and Luther, in dust-covered overalls, holding onto Katie's arm as they walked swiftly, heads down, on the watch for dips and treacherous holes in the road.

"What is it, Charlie? Why you send Luther to come git me outta service?" Katie gasped when she finally reached the steps. She held onto the railing at the bottom of the steps while her breathing settled.

"We best git on the inside," Charlie advised. He looked up and down the road as though he expected something or someone to suddenly leap from the darkness upon them. Margaret sprang from the swing, sending it backwards, jiggling and creaking. With Luther at her elbow, Katie mounted the steps like a school child late for classes, and Charlie turned, the cane pounding the porch, and led the way inside. Quickly, they all stepped through the door, following Charlie, and he, seeing the light on in the middle room, didn't stop until he was standing in front of Katie's dresser.

"What in heaven's name is it, Charlie?" Katie, trailing behind him, pleaded in a tiny, scared voice. She could hear her heart pounding above the footsteps of Margaret and Luther as they tagged behind. The naked light bulb that descended from the rope-like cord in the ceiling—set off by the crown of Charlie's hat—did a wild snake dance before her eyes. She dropped the Bible on the bed and turned to face Charlie, her face white as chrysanthemums. Margaret and Luther stopped at the foot of the bed near the middle door.

Charlie leaned against the dresser for support and gazed in the mirror. From this position he could look at four of them at the same time, and he watched their faces intently, not sure how to begin—how to break the news. They all stood behind him in a ragged line, Margaret on the edge of hysteria, Luther with blazing eyes that bore into Charlie's back, and Katie clutching the collar of her dress. In the mirror, he noticed that his own face bore a tight frown, the round dark eyes clearly emitting fear, even though he was trying to hold his jaw firm and straight. He pushed his weight down on the cane and slowly turned to face them. "Roy done filed a complaint. Told Wade everythang. But 'cording to Earline, he done named you as the one what chopped off his arm, Margaret."

"What?" they gasped collectively, and Margaret slumped against the middle door. Luther, turning quickly grabbed her firmly by the shoulders.

Katie stumbled forward with both hands stretched out in front of her as though she intended to grab Charlie by his collar, the white purse dangling on her wrist. "You done heard it wrong, Charlie," Katie pleaded. "You knows your hearing is poorly. You jest done heard it wrong, ain't you?"

"Ain't heard nothing wrong, woman," he snapped, glaring into her eyes and rocking forward on his cane. The straw hat shaking on his head signaled the struggle that was taking place inside of him—a struggle to deliver the message with the level- headedness necessary to keep down panic while stressing the urgency of the predicament that now faced them. His eyes swept the room and returned to Katie's bewildered stare. "Earline said Roy appeared, like a haint, in the door of the Sheriff's Office—all white in the face, telling Wade's bunch that he done suddenly remembered everythang what happened to him. And then he goes on to say that it was that uppity gal of Katie's what done it."

"Well, since he's remembering and all, did he tell the law that he beat up on Miss Katie some awful? Luther spat, stepping away from Margaret, his eyes blazing. "Nee mine. I don't wants to hear nothing that lying peckerwood said," he said, shaking his head and waving his hands in the air.

"Come tomorrow, boy, that's all everybody in this here town is gonna be talking 'bout. So you best listen anyhows, whereas you can see how that cracker operates—remember it was you what wanted to know. I already knows them crackers," Charlie said in a violent whisper.

"Nee mine," Luther yelled. Spinning around to face Margaret, he waved Charlie's words away. "I can't stand no mo' and Margaret ain't…"

"Charlie, is that the truth? Did Earline hear right? He named my child?" Katie asked, her eyes fixed on the brim of Charlie's hat.

Charlie sighed, raised his head and shifted his weight on the cane. He could see the rage consuming Luther's body. That reckless immature rage that demanded immediate retaliation—that eye-for-an-eye rage. He understood Luther's need to demand that they show some backbone, but this was not the time for wild displays of manhood. He cast a scalding gaze at Luther and pounded the floor with his cane. Margaret, dazed and speechless, seemed to float away from the door and into Luther's arms. "In all the years I done associated with Earline Simpson, I ain't never knowed her to git nothing wrong yet—jest talks too much sometime. She said that the law done even picked up Miss Rosie's boy, Buddy, for the one driving the pick-up that night."

"No," Katie cried out and clapped her hands over her mouth in horror. She turned from Charlie to Luther and Margaret, searching their faces for understanding. Dropping her hands to her sides, she asked, "That was Buddy in that truck? Lord, oh, mighty what did we ever do to him? And Miss Rosie gonna be fit to be tied for sho," she added, turning back to face Charlie.

"Ain't do doubt 'bout that, since she thinks the sun rises and sets in that boy. And to add coal oil to the cook stove, Wade picked him up at the Cafe during supper, with every long neck peckerwood in town gaping and grinning. It's a good thang for Wade that Miss Rosie was out yonder at Kennawa, 'cause Wade would had to fight for his life to take that boy of her'n out of there," he said, wiping his face with the back of his hand.

"And if'n he come 'round here, he gonna have to do the same," Katie said, her eyes suddenly flashing, her body trembling.

"What does this all mean, Mama?" Margaret asked, pulling away from Luther and falling upon the bed post, her long nails digging at the wood. She stood watching Katie and breathing heavily from her mouth; the tail of her blouse hung outside of her pedal pushers, and sweat trickled down from under her bangs.

"Lord, child, it means you is gotta git out of this here town tonight," Katie said, sucking in her breath like she had been kicked. "If'n I go and tell them it was me, not you, they won't believe me. They'll say I'se jest taking the blame to protect my child. Don't you see, you gots to go," Katie explained, slamming her purse onto the bed. She turned away from Margaret's incredulous stare and whispered, "Help me, Jesus."

"I won't leave you here, Mama. It's as simple as that—I just won't go," Margaret stated, embracing the bedpost, and talking to the side of her mother's face.

"Yes, you will!" Katie silenced her by throwing her hand in the air. "If'n we hurry, she can catch that twelve o'clock special to Chicago. You will go to your uncle Robert's house, and that's that!"

she said, turning to face Charlie, who stood with both hands wrapped around the top of his cane in deep thought.

"She best be gone fo' twelve,' cause that's' bout the time Wade and his bunch picks up colored girls, sos they can carry them over to the levee, fo' they takes them to the lock up. Lemme see," he said, squinting at the clock on the dresser. "It's 'bout a hour drive to Cairo, and it's high nigh ten now. We can make it by the skin of our teeth if'n we hurry. Boy, go git M.B. Tell him what done happened here, and tell him we needs him to take Margaret to Cairo to catch the twelve o'clock train. And tell him to hurry! Boy, I sho do wish you could run like Margaret," Charlie said, out of breath from the gush of words, and signal with his hand for Luther to hurry. "And tell him," Charlie stopped Luther in his tracks, "tell him to bring a gun." Luther stood with his legs in a tangle, one foot headed towards the door, the other twisted back in Charlie's direction. His broad shoulders pulled the buttons of the red flannel shirt that he wore on the outside of his coveralls. His dark eyes brightened with a new faith in the old man, and a wide grin broke across Luther's soot-black face. They looked at each other for a long second, then Luther turned quickly and was out of the door in a flash.

"Mama, please come, too. Don't stay here. Don't make me leave you this way—it's not fit for a person to leave this way. I should be the one to stay, not you, Mama. Oh Mama, please—," Margaret pleaded and grabbed Katie's arm, squeezing it as though she was trying to stop the flow of blood.

Katie didn't answer; instead she removed Margaret's hands from her arm with a quick jerk of her shoulder and walked to the curtain that lined the corner of the wall—the space she used as a closet. She flung the curtain open, yanked out the old, cardboard suitcase, walked back, and dropped it on the bed. Suddenly, as if she had been struck with a revelation, she spun around to face Charlie. "Money! She gonna need money. How much you'se got on you? And you, child, how much is you'se gots stashed away? Hurry, child, ain't no time to stand there hugging that there bedpost. M.B. ain't gonna take that long to git here. Grab some of the clothes you gonna need. Hurry, child—move!"

Charlie counted out thirty-five one dollar bills and tossed them on the bed. He, turned away, grabbed the kerosene lamp from the floor and pushed his frame into the front room where he placed the lamp in the window, removed the blackened globe, and carefully set the lumpy wick ablaze. Their talking had ceased; only the sounds of hasty preparations filled the house: drawers opening and squeaking closed as clothes were picked over, tossed aside, or stuffed inside of the suitcase; paper bags rattling as cold meat was wrapped for sandwiches; cleaner's wrappers cracking as dresses were pounded with a fist and folded carelessly inside the suitcase; hard-heel shoes clicking and the rubber tip of the cane on the wood floors as they scurried back and forth. Charlie thumped through the rooms, rolling down shades and lighting all the kerosene lamps. Katie darted back and forth from the closet to the bed and to the kitchen with clothes, shoes, food, a special lace hanky. Margaret filled the house with whispering low moans and loud cries of "no" as she grabbed at clothes and flung them in the direction of the suitcase. Finally, at the sound of the gravel popping under the weight of the pick-up truck coming to a jerking, spring-crying stop in front of the house, they all stopped in their tracks and looked towards the closed front door.

Charlie, knowing that they would not leave Cairo until Margaret was on the train, worried about Katie, who stood closing the suitcase and fighting back tears. "You, best not stay here tonight, Katie," he warned in his most authoritative voice. "If'n they don't find Margaret here, they might git awful mean. Wade picking up Buddy means only one thing—Jim don't know. Evidently, they don't plan to tell Jim 'bout Roy's complaint until they does what they wants. Cause its mighty strange that Roy jest ups and comes forth on his own—sound likes something cooked up by J.T.—Roy jest ain't that smart. They is liable to be boiling mad, especially if they believes it's you what really done it. They can be some mean son-ah-bitches."

Katie's eyes brightened with alarm at the mention of J.T.'s name. "I'se going back to the church. I'se gots to go back anyhows to call Robert up yonder in Chicago to tell him to be on the look out for Margaret. After I does that, I'll tell Reverend Washington everything that done happened, and you mark my word, he and the Saints is gonna stick by me. Wade Samuels might be crazy 'bout beating up on 'niggers,' but he ain't stupid. And he ain't stupid enough to be messing with Reverend Washington, you knows that yourself. Don't you be worrying none 'bout me, I'll be alright, 'cause the Almighty is gonna be a looking after me. Jest you git my child on that train, you hear me, Charlie Hudnall," she ordered with desperate eyes, then snatched her head back to the bed and hefted the suitcase to the floor.

He stared at her hands trembling from the strain of the suitcase and from the effort to conceal her nervousness. He knew that the rage seething through her body was created by the fear of losing someone she loved—as it had been when her pappy was killed. Only he knew how close she was to the breaking point, for as long as Charlie had known Katie, he had never heard her use the word "nigger." The front door pushed open and Luther, out of breath, his hat crumpled in his hands, advised, "We gotta move now, if we aims to make the midnight."

"You driving, boy?" Charlie asked, turning to face him—a question in his eye.

"Yes sir," Luther nodded. "Yes sir," he repeated, and winked at him indicating that he had not forgotten the gun.

Charlie winked back at Luther and pointed with his cane for Luther to grab the suitcase while he scanned the room once more. Luther headed for the door with Katie and Charlie trailing behind him. Margaret, the last to leave, walked grudgingly, like she was about to be delivered into the hands of Satan himself. She fumbled with the tail of the blouse, stuffing it inside of her pants, delaying. She looked around the room for the last time, and it seemed curiously foreign to her, as if she had already been separated from all that was familiar.

M.B. was leaning against the door of the truck—his long legs crossed comfortably at the ankles, his head propped against the hood of the cab, his cap pushed forward so the bill rested over his eyes. He leaned, pulling on his pipe, sucking the white smoke through his mouth and sending it out in long streams from his nose. He pushed forward when he saw them, knocked the pipe against the bed of the truck, and slipped it inside the blue checked shirt pocket. He watched them move slowly down the steps in single file. He saw Margaret lean back, reach over her head, and snap off the light, and during that quick glimpse, saw her tear-stained face, the look of terror that filled her eyes. She closed the door and stepped onto the porch, bumping the old swing with her thigh, causing it to creak, then dance like a marionette on a string. He cleared his throat, smiled, and approached her at the bottom of the steps. "Gal, I knows you ain't scared with all these here mens with you," he teased and patted her gently on the shoulder. She dragged her feet like she was walking through wet sand, stumbling aimlessly as he guided her to the cab.

Luther dropped the bag on the bed of the truck, then hurried around to the cab, where he waited until M.B. threw open the door and pushed Margaret by her shoulder inside. Luther got in beside her and took the wheel, the engine running quietly. He slipped it into neutral, and waited uneasily for M.B. and Charlie to take their places. Charlie hobbled to the back of the truck and slid the suitcase down the bed with one thrust, where it sailed freely like a fifty-pound block of ice and landed with a soft bump against the back of the cab. He gazed at the long grooves in the bed for a moment, visions of Anna Mae suddenly clouding his brain. He shook his head, dismissing old memories as he pulled himself up by the narrow metal bar, slammed the tailgate, and locked it. M.B. stepped in front of Katie and ease him the gun. He nodded, indicating he would be all right, and their eyes held briefly, both of them remembering another time—another desperate ride in the middle of the night.

The moon had slipped through the treetops and shone brightly in the sky as M.B. stepped back to the cab. Charlie sat with his arm draped across the sideboard like a field hand heading off for a days work in the cotton. His straw hat was pulled back from his head, and his cane, poking through the bend in his arm could have easily been mistaken for the handle of a hoe. He watched Katie fighting back tears, and knew that Katie would not touch Margaret, would not kiss her good-bye, did not dare, for if she did she would surely break down. But he could see the redness creeping into her face as she tightened the muscles in her jaws over and over during a powerful fit of swallowing. "You tell that brother on your'n when you call that I said hi and for him to see to Margaret real good, he told her. "We'll be back come early morning. Might stop off somewheres and git some corn." He chuckled uneasily.

"You best take care, Charlie," she said and turned her attention to the cab of the truck. Walking slowly, she slid her hand along the cool metal and stopped in front of the passenger's door. She looked past M.B.'s shoulder at Margaret, who sat like a frightened child jammed between Luther and M.B., her head in her hands. "Margaret, child,"

Katie called, "you write soon as you git there. Nothing fancy, jest a line or so. Look at my face, child! Child, I said look at my face. Don't go hanging your head. Let me look at you for a spell."

"I'll write, Mama, I'll write. I promise," Margaret cried out, as she stretched her body across M.B.'s to see Katie clearly in the moonlight. Her fingers squeezed against the glass on the partially open window, and her long hair brushed M.B.'s face. She held herself in this awkward position for as long as she could, then reluctantly sat back down between M.B. and Luther. She stared at the old house for the last time, the swing not even visible from this point, and suddenly she felt very sad. True, she had wanted to leave Bennettsville, but not like this. Not in the middle of the night like a common criminal. Not without proper farewells. She felt as if she had been thrown away, and that soon everyone would forget about her—forget that she ever existed. She shook her head; everything was happening too fast. Last month she had been a respected young Negro woman with dreams of becoming a teacher; tonight she was a nigger on the run.

"I reckon y'all better hurry, then. Don't want that child gitting to Chicago and Robert ain't there to meet her. Don't want her to be scared," Katie said, her voice slightly cracking. The truck, as though on its own, jerked then jetted off into the night towards the back roads that Luther knew as well as he knew his name, and Katie watched the whirls of gray dust that trailed the truck until they were out of sight. She wept loudly into her trembling hands, then turned with her shoulders sagging—a picture of Margaret's wide, questioning eyes before her—and walked down the gravel road in the direction of the church.

Midway to the church, she turned and looked back down the road toward the house. Standing against the darkness of the night, it looked to be cozy, brightly lit, and inviting. But she knew that it would be empty—as empty as her heart—without Margaret. Margaret was the music that made her heart sing praises, and now that her daughter was gone, she had no music, no song. She looked for a long minute, then turned and continued her walk.

As soon as Katie confessed to Reverend Washington all that had happened, he stuffed his feet into his shoes, stood, and announced it to the congregation. The strong-willed Saints, who defied the burning hell-fires of Satan daily, suddenly became meek and humble. The church was filled with sobbing, grief, pain, and fear. Sister McCree yelled out, "Oh, no, God, it's happening agin!" Brother Watson asked over and over, "Lord, Lord, when is it gonna stop?" Others cried in anguish, and an intensity of fear swept through the church until the children, too, became infected and began to cry.

The Saints scrambled to their seats like rabbits scurrying away from buckshot, grabbing their children or wringing their hands. Their reaction was the same as it had been three years ago, when Willie Thompson burst through the church doors, wild-eyed and half crazed with fear, yelling, "Pray, everybody pray, they is gonna kill everybody!" In one long breath, he had relayed the horror of what had happened to Reece Scott in the neighboring town twenty miles away. "Y'all pray. They done hung him and, Lord, then they tortured his dead body. It wadn't enough that they kilt him, they drug his body through town 'til wont a scrap of skin left on him nowhere!"

That day, three years ago, had been a nightmare, and now they seemed to be living it over again. Even though they knew that Margaret was safe for the moment, the feeling of desperation in the church, was the same as if she had been lynched like Reece Scott. Mother Washington's round eyes focused on Katie's, and this time there was no mistaking the misery and fear in them. She immediately took Katie to her bosom and held her tightly for a few seconds. This was not the time for "face washing" or laying blame; she knew too well what it meant for the law to be looking for your child, especially if that child was a Negro. She knew too well the immediate danger that hung over Margaret—Reece Scott had been her only brother's child—and that the rage that seized white people in times like this could be quickly transferred to any Negro in town at the flip of a coin. She pulled Katie to her pew below the pulpit, and they sat down like small children waiting for word from their leader—Reverend Washington.

Reverend Washington stepped up to the podium and raised his arms in the air for silence, his dark suit fitting his large biceps snugly, his crisp white shirt straining open slightly at the collar, his shoe laces spilling across the toes of his shoes. As the moaning settled he slowly turned his head from the left to the right, looking long and hard at each person in the church, his thin nose covered with beads of freshly-formed sweat. He held his arms in the air until the church was completely quiet, and nodded his head at Brothers Watson and Porter, who immediately took their positions at the doors. Mothers, with their children's heads tucked in the bend of their arms or mashed against their breasts by a guarded hand, rocked and stared with anxious eyes at the Reverend. Fathers, with stern poker faces to disguise their fears, sat rigid as boards on the pews or leaned forward cupping their hands. Fear was evident throughout the church, as though it rode on the crest of the hot air that occasionally floated in through the open doors. When Brothers Watson and Porter were stationed, Reverend Washington lowered his arms to his sides, looked quickly around at the upturned faces and addressed them with concern.

"Ain't no need for me to stand up here trying to pretend that everything is alright here tonight and that everything is gonna stay alright 'cause we are the children of God," he said in a thunderous voice. "Ain't no need for me to remind you about the many times we have had to face Satan. Just last year I was the talk of the town because I had to wrestle that crazy white man to the ground to keep him from killing me. Well, the law didn't bother me and none of the other white folks either. What I did they could understand—keep a crazy man offa me. Now, we all knows if that white man had been sane in their eyes, that I just might not be standing here now. But that's what makes Satan so powerful, he disguises himself in many forms. We all know that the sanest white man is probably the craziest creature that lives, 'cause he is able to rationalize, justify his place in this world, your place, and what oughta be.

"Then he turns around and murder the person that don't agree with him. I'm saying this to remind you who we are dealing with. Now, I knowed the first thing that come to your minds when I explained the trouble Sister Katie is having was what happened to Reece. And Lord knows that man went through a hell that kept sane white men smiling for months, while we suffered right along with everything but feeling his physical pain. I knows y'all ain't forgot all the trying times we went through, long after Reece was buried, dug up cause of the suit his mama filed against that town, and re-buried."

"Yes, Lord," Mother Washington cried out, and put her arm around Katie. "We is remembering it all."

"But I want to remind you that we are all still here!" he shouted, and pounded the podium with his fist. "Look around you. You'll see, excepting a few that the Lord done called home, we are all still here! Yes, Lord, we are all still here, and we are able to remember that time of sorrow. It ain't nothing that we'd likely forget, and it ain't likely that we would want to forget. But I think right now I'd better remind you—just in case some of you have forgot who you are! I want to remind you that we are all the children of the Lord Almighty, hallelujah!" he said, and his hands flew up in the air like he had touched a live wire. "I want to remind you that you are all sanctified and filled with the Holy Ghost and The Fire." He flashed a thankful smile at his wife, Mother Washington, who had just the other night spoken in tongues.

"Yes, Lord. Thank you, Jesus. Tell it—tell the truth, Reverend," the congregation cried out, rocking faster and leaning even closer. "Yes, we is still here," someone yelled. They came to life, sitting straight and shaking their heads as though they understood what they must do.

"I want to remind you that we all have to stay together and stick by our Sister in her hour of need. I want to remind you that her needs are also our needs. I want you to empty your hearts of everything but love—let God in. He is waiting. I want to remind you that time is very important here—we must stall for every minute we can—Sister Margaret's life is hanging in the throes of age-old sanctions—sanctions set by sane white men. I want to remind you that the devil is our enemy, and has been from the moment we were born into this world. And when Satan steps through that door," he said, pointing to Brother Watson at the front door, "I want to remind you, don't look him in his face. We will be like the wolf in sheep's clothing—hard to pick out from the flock. We will be like the Saints that's gonna rise on Judgment Day—many numbers. We will be every and anything that the Lord says we must be. Now let us pray, let us get down on our knees and call on Jesus, our Saviour."

In unison, they turned around, and facing the back of the pews they'd been sitting in, toward the open front door, knelt, with their elbows on the seats, and their knees on homemade cushions. They bowed their heads low, with faces partially concealed, and mumbled—some speaking in tongues. They prayed for God to remember his children, they prayed for God to deliver them from the jaws of death, just as He had delivered Daniel from the lion's den; and they prayed for Margaret's safety.

It was in this position, down on their knees, the Sisters' white scarves fluttering with every motion of their heads, and Reverend Washington down on one knee facing the door, his face bent towards the floor, his shoe laces still untied, that Wade Samuels found them.

The scent of fading talc, mixed with that of the sawdust lying on the floor around the pot-bellied stove and with the sudden mustiness created by fear, filled the room and hung in the air like an invisible wall—the same scent that hounds sniffed out to track down coons of all kinds. Charlie had been wrong; it was only eleven o'clock and the hunt had already begun. Wade Samuels stood in the center of the wood-framed church door, and although he did not have any horns, or even a tail, an aura of evil floated from his body across the room like a liquored breath. Upon seeing him, Brother Watson immediately fell to his knees and covered his face with his hands.

Dressed in a dark blue uniform and a blue policeman's cap with a shiny black bill that matched his round-toed black shoes and the thin black belt that snugged his waist and held the black billy club dangling from a loop, Samuels walked slowly down the center aisle to the first pews and stopped two feet in front of Reverend Washington. His face was burnt from the sun and fiery red. His massive two-hundred pound frame, cast a long black shadow down the aisle. He looked down and his cold eye fell upon the sea of white scarves that billowed like sails caught in a gentle breeze, and on the legs of the women as they knelt, covered with white stockings and long white dresses. He turned, walked back to his deputy, Shorty, a thin-faced man dressed in a khaki uniform and a ten-gallon hat, who stood outside the door, and whispered through the screen to him. Then he strolled back to the front of the pews, a smile curling his lips. He fingered the billy club intimately, making it twirl and dance about on the loop. Wade Samuels had never, in his ten years as sheriff, carried a gun. It was said by many people that he had killed more folks with his billy than others had with their guns. And everyone in church remembered the fight that took place between Samuels and his brother, who had suddenly appeared in town for a visit. They fought up and down Main Street like pack dogs fight for territory, a bloody, dismal fight that ended with Samuels smashing his brother's jaw with that same billy, over and over, until the cracking of bone was clearly heard by the crowd of onlookers.

"Reverend," the gravelly voice broke into their prayer. "Sorry to interrupt your praying; thought perhaps you just ain't aware that the law is standing before you, and you knows the law is got a big job, keeping the peace and all."

Reverend Washington pushed himself from the floor slowly and looked directly into Samuel's red, burnt face. "What is it you want here?" the Reverend asked calmly, although his insides were churning like butter in a mixer. "What is it you are looking for in God's house?"

"Well, now, I jest admires a man like you, Reverend, one what gits to the point: never did like hemming and hawing. All I want is Katie's gal, Margaret—I knows she is here, Reverend," he stated firmly, although he suddenly noticed how the words "God's house" had begun to affect him. He had never thought of this house-like church as being real; it was just a place where niggers gathered to keep up a lot of racket. But noticing Reverend Washington's mannerism and delivery, he sensed something else—unity and strength among these people who were subservient at their jobs, but now appeared strong when they gathered to pray. Samuels feared no human being on earth, even the Reverend, whom he had witnessed flip a two-hundred pound, raving, white maniac across his back like one would fling a sack of potatoes. It was Washington's strong convictions and power of persuasion that made Samuels wonder could this really be God's house? Wade didn't believe in God or the devil. He was, however, terrified to acknowledge or deny their existence—a fear stemming from childhood memories of his uncle being carried away to the madhouse in Farmington, screaming for someone to "Dig them devils outta my back!"

"Just turn over the gal," Samuels ordered, still holding his ground, although now distracted by a picture of Jesus that hung behind the pulpit. A picture of many colors, Jesus' fiery eyes focused on him no matter where he stood.

"She ain't here." The Reverend answered quickly to give the impression that he was lying.

"Now don't go standing in the way of the law, Reverend," Samuels advised. "Just turn over the gal!"

"Get behind me, Satan!" the Reverend said in a voice filled with hot anger, and raised his massive hand in the air like a barrier, defying Samuels to come past the first pews.

Samuels narrowed his eyes, shooting Washington a warning look. The screen door banged loudly as Shorty entered and beckoned with a long, skinny finger for Samuels, who swaggered back to the front door as if he owned the entire town and everything in it—as though he would be the one to say when church could resume. Quickly, Shorty stretched his neck, like the night weasel, and whispered into Samuel's ear. Samuels immediately turned his burnt neck sharply and stared in Reverend Washington's direction.

"I don't reckon you would know, by chance, where Charlie Hudnall might be?" Samuels asked in a long drawl.

"Why would Charlie Hudnall's whereabouts be of concern to me? He ain't one of my members."

"Jest thought since you said that Margaret ain't here, that she might be with Charlie. Everybody in town knows he is like one of their family," he said, closing the small space between himself and Reverend Washington who remained silent. "Well, tell me then, Reverend, is Katie here?" he said, and stopped at the front row of pews. "Perhaps she knows where her daughter is," he added, and moved his hand towards his billy as though he was going to remove it from its sinister loop.

The reverend did not answer. Instead he began to Pray. "Father, I ask you in the name of Jesus to rebuke and scorn our enemies."

"Did you hear that?" Samuels turned his head to Shorty and snorted. "Somebody oughta tell the Reverend the difference between the law and his enemies. Now, where is Katie?" he demanded, looking down at the front row of legs. Reverend Washington, standing in the aisle just past the first row of pews, firmly planted his hand behind the small of his back and pushed his chest forward, exposing his white shirt front.

"Everybody here knows devils and how they can easily possess a man's house. Now I knows I don't have to tell nobody here what a man's house is," he said, and walked toward Samuels with ease, as though he had just received the baptism of the spirit and was-walking on air. He ignored Samuels as he continued. "'Cause all the children of the Lord Almighty knows that his house is his-soul. 'What does it profit a man to gain the world and lose his soul?"' He spat the words in Samuels direction. "What does an evil man gain by cleaning up his- house? I say it's useless; I say it is a waste of precious time; I say an evil man has—no house in the first place, and I say it ain't no need to tell him something that he already knows. But everybody here knows me, everybody here knows I'm a preacher for God Almighty, and everybody knows that I always reveal the words of the Lord any and every time I can."

"Amen, hallelujah," several of the Sisters cried out, still on their knees, peeking up at the Reverend and at Samuels.

"So I tell you, children, 'when an evil spirit goes out of man, it travels over dry country looking for a place to rest. If it can't find one, it says to itself, I will go back to my house which I left,'" Reverend Washington paused, and then continued. "So it goes back and finds it empty—listen to me now—empty! And cleaned and all fixed up, and it is amazed and worried. Then it goes out and brings along seven other spirits even worse than itself; you sees, it needs extra power to mold his house. Now they all comes determined to get in, ain't nothing in the world gonna keep them out, and they live there. You know what I mean, children; they is sorta like twelve starving folks descending on a little scrawny pullet hen—greedy and determined to get what they need to survive. So that evil man who tried to clean up his house is in worse shape than what he was at the beginning. This is the way it will happen to the evil man who defies the church, who honors no one but man, hallelujah!"

"Praise God, Amen. Tell it—tell the God's truth, Reverend," the voices from the congregation echoed.

Samuels had not moved from the front row of pews. Washington had stopped him in his tracks with the Bible story, and his blood ran cold. Samuels, remembering his uncle, could not tear his eyes away from the picture of Jesus that faced him. The bold letters at the top of the picture, "The Coming in Glory," glared at him. Jesus sat on a throne that was hidden by the spread of angel's wings, a sickle in his right hand and a sword in his left. Samuels was fixed to the floor; he could not move or look away. The eyes of Jesus bore straight through him, daring him to flinch. He felt warm, and a thin coat of sweat formed on his wide neck, dampening the hairs at the base of his head and staining the collar of his dark uniform. He shook his head to release himself from the spell the picture had placed upon him, then turned quickly and walked out the door into a hard shower of rain.

Reverend Washington slowly turned, walked back to the front row of pews and knelt in the opening of the center aisle. Katie looked up at Mother Washington whose face was wet from tears, placed her left hand on Mother Washington's back, and began to rub it slowly, methodically, and lovingly. The church was quiet until they heard the car tear down the road, and until Reverend Washington called out in a deep voice, "Yes, I know he is real—I can feel him in my soul. Help Us Tonight, Jesus! We know you can do it! So, Lord, do it! Do it Lord. Lord do it. Help us tonight, Lord. Help Sister Margaret, Lord!"

"Yes you can do it, Lord. Yes, Lord," the Saints cried out and began to sing. "Heal, hee-al, hee-al, hee-al, hee-al." All the Saints placed a hand on the person next to them and began to rub their back slowly, methodically, and lovingly. The old song was ringing through the church. "Heal, hee-al, hee-al, hee-al, hee-al."

FOLLOW THE RED BRICK ROAD

Other than home, there were only a few places for any Negro to go—church, "The Back," under the "Wine Tree," or Hazel's Cafe. But after Wade and his deputies did not find Margaret at home or church, Wade had begun to suspect that she was on the run. Ordinarily, he would not have thought Margaret to be a runner—she was too sassy, too bold. But Charlie's absence made Wade suspect that Charlie had taken the girl away. The three-man police force had been busy: they had jailed Marmy and Buddy because Roy had placed them at the scene of the crime, and they had jailed Roy because Jim would have their hides if they didn't. Although none of the officers sympathized with Roy over the loss of his arm, they agreed that Negroes like Margaret were dangerous and needed to be taught a lesson—it had nothing to do with Roy at all.

The streets were quiet; only two Negroes were on the road, and three old-timers sprawled drunkenly under the Wine Tree—a scrawny, old ash wood where a few Negroes often gathered to drink cheap wine. The police car flashed through the darkness, flinging rocks and dust, and covered the two block distance from the church to Hazel's in seconds. Wade and Grahm were out of the car and inside the screen door in a flash. The Negroes stepped aside quickly, allowing the law all the room it needed. Everything stopped except the jukebox—a loud song about love being too strong rumbled through out the two rooms. Wade and Grahm looked about, their eyes searching the faces of the couples still wrapped in each other's arms on the dance floor. Neither Charlie or Margaret was in sight and they turned, their backs straight, and were outside in seconds—the aroma of strong tobacco, stale three-percent beer, and fried fish, clinging to their uniforms.

"Well, there's only one other option," Wade said, reaching the car and propping a long elbow against the door. "She could be off somewhere giving it up right about now." They laughed a deep hardy laugh, and Shorty, sitting behind the wheel, grabbed his crotch and drawled, "When we finds her, I aims to poke a hole straight through that gal."

Grahm pointed up the road beyond the shadows of the trees to an old one-door truck, belonging to Sylvester Bodine. The men crossed the space in minutes to where Bodine sat on the running board. His eyes widened when he saw the lawmen approach—he looked frightened to death. Wade leaned over Sylvester and looked down on his upturned face—he could have spit in Sylvester's eyes if he had had a mind to—and in less than ten minutes, Wade had found out that Charlie had not been in the area tonight, but that Luther Dawson, Viola's boy, who worked for Charlie, had passed by Hazel's half-an-hour ago in M.B.'s truck. Wade had Shorty call the specifications of M.B.'s 1938 Chevy to the Sheriff's Office, where Ludie Mae, the clerk, was to radio the High Sheriff's Office in Cairo for assistance in stopping a runaway. The police left as quickly as they had come, heading towards the back roads leading to highway 41, and leaving Sylvester greatly relieved.

The farther north Luther drove, the darker the highway became. It seemed he was heading away from all the lights, and even the moon seemed to hang over Huntsville, the small town that he had just driven through, like it was trapped in the tree tops behind him. The farmlands of soy-beans and cotton were dark and ominous and cast grotesque shapes against the drifting, creeping fog that hovered above the crops then rolled upward and outward, spilling onto the highway like a blanket of white death. Charlie had advised him to maintain a speed of forty-five miles an hour because the shadows made you see phantoms and forget the treacherous stretch of road that lay ahead. Margaret sat jammed between Luther and M.B. with Luther's sweat-stained hat on her lap. M.B., his shoulder pressed against the door, stared out into the darkness, his teeth clenched tightly on his unlit pipe, his switchblade in his breast pocket.

Sprawled in the bed of the truck, Charlie had given up on trying to keep Margaret's suitcase stationary. He had let it slide down to the tailgate as he sat listening to the humming of the tires on the blacktop. The tires sang a hypnotic song that reminded him of Anna Mae and of how he had prayed for Doc Smith to change his mind, but of course, no such thing happened. Suddenly, a dark scowl came across his face and he turned and pounded the back of the cab with his cane. The truck purred as Luther checked the speed and came to a stop on the side of the road, somewhere between Huntsville and Cairo. The truck idled quietly as they scrambled from the truck, Luther first, his eyes wide, a tire iron clutched in his fist, then M.B., looking cautiously around, and last, Margaret. Standing by the cab, she was unsure if she should approach the men who had now formed a small seclusive circle at the side of the truck.

"What's the trouble?" Luther panted, angling around until he stood in front of Charlie.

"Best let that gal relieve herself now; won't be no chance once she gits on that train. Then, I spects you best knock that speed up to whatever you can handle without killing us. But keep your eyes peeled to that road. Rain's in the air," Charlie warned, rolling his worried eyes towards the blue-black sky.

The beams from the truck's headlights stretched down the road, illuminating the weeds where thousands of insects swarmed about in a furious knot. The men huddled closer. Charlie, with his back to the truck's bed, rested his weight on his cane, while M.B. and Luther leaned towards him, hanging onto his every word.

"Thought you didn't wanna risk running off the road," Luther said in a calm voice, trying to stifle the excitement that tingled throughout his body.

"I changed my mind," Charlie growled and stopped to make sure Margaret was out of hearing range, signaling with his hand for her to make use of the bushes while they talked. "This time," Charlie continued, looking at M.B., "this time, I ain't gonna be depending on no white folks for help. So we best work out some plan now or we can jest turn 'round and go on back. What time is it gitting on?"

"Round eleben," M.B. slurred, his words distorted because of the pipe. "I done made this trip a heap a times, we gonna be there fo' twelve, I guarantees."

Charlie nodded, weighing M.B.'s logic and replied, "Jest hopes that damn train is on time."

"It's gotta work, Charlie," M.B. added, pulling the pipe from his mouth. "Besides, Samuels don't know we is gone."

"I ain't so sure 'bout that," Luther said, leaning in closer. "Remember Bodine saw us leaving New Town."

Charlie snatched his head around to face Luther, his voice filled with rage, "All they has to do is ask that loosed-lipped Negro and he tell everythang he knows. We best git our heads together and hit the road."

Margaret returned from the bushes, her hands crammed in the pockets of her pants. She walked quietly by the men as they headed for the bushes and waited by the open door of the cab. She had looked at the men with new eyes as they huddled like deacons in church, whispering. And from the bushes, she had heard portions of their conversation—phrases snatched, about time schedules, possible confrontations with the law from Cairo and Bennettsville, the need for the train to be on time. She had heard the anxiety and fear, even rage, in their voices as they discussed what was best for Margaret. It seemed they had forgotten the real Margaret who had stood only a few feet away from them. She had become an object that they manipulated and moved from place to place. She could not see them and suddenly felt they were people she did not know. The voices were familiar, but they were strangers. And she was someone different—she did not know who she was. Any other time she would be involved, she would inform them of their best strategies—but she was not that girl anymore. She was the stranger, not them.

The crickets sang and hopped at her feet and any minute now she expected something slimy to slither across her path. She raised her head at the sound of the men returning from the bushes. She felt alone and suddenly tears were streaming down her cheeks. She wiped her face with the back of her hand, hoisted herself up by the open door, picked up Luther's hat, and sat down.

The tailgate clanged and the doors on the cab jerked open, then slammed as the men quickly returned to their positions. She sensed that the air around her had changed. She wondered if they had seen her crying, but something told her not to utter a word. Perhaps it was the stiff, artificial grin on M.B.'s face, or the way Luther jammed the tire iron between the seat, then rammed the clutch to the floor, slinging the gears about as he pulled the truck off the shoulder in a swirl of dust. Her heart beat faster and she prepared herself for God knew what as the truck lurched forward, straining everyone's neck until the speedometer registered sixty and held.

Luther held it at sixty to make up for lost time, and he didn't check the speed until they came upon the snake-like curve leading into the massive steel bridge that stretched across the Mississippi River—the state line. Anyone who had driven over this particular stretch of highway knew that it was not advisable to take the curve doing more than ten miles an hour, but Luther swung the truck into the curve doing twenty-five. The steel girders surrounded the blacktop and straddled the great river like a decrepit, swayback horse. Its concaved center, sagging from years of use, made it impossible for two vehicles to cross at the same time. Many a collision had occurred at this point because people refused to yield or happened upon another vehicle suddenly and couldn't stop. Everyone leaned to the right, and then to the left following the bend in the road. Margaret and M.B. gripped the edge of the dash, leaning forward and holding their bodies as stiff as possible. Luther plastered his big chest against the steering wheel to limit its movement, and his hat, long forgotten, flew across the seat and landed between the accelerator and the hump in the floor. Outside, Charlie clung to the side board as the suitcase swished about from one side of the truck to the other. The truck's tires squealed as Luther's foot pumped the brake, the accelerator, the clutch, on and off, like he was plowing a rock field with a tractor. The truck whined and jerked, threatening to fall apart and fling them headlong into the great river. The north wind roared past them, filling their nostrils with the pungent musk of cotton in blossom, red-clay mud, and fat, river-bottom cat-fish. Then came the deafening clapping against their ears as the tires rolled over the steel grates. They all bounced up and down, like they had struck an embankment head on, their flesh quivering. The truck jerked, then slowed, and the road straightened out. They sighed with relief. There, before them stood the square, white sign with fading black letters, "Cairo. Population 5500."

Luther mopped his forehead with the sleeve of his shirt, turned to face a wild-eyed Margaret, and flashed her a toothy grin.

It was eleven forty-five. Margaret would make the train on time. The station was less than a mile away and she would buy her ticket on the train. They were silent, only the noises of the night could be heard as the truck whizzed past the huge magnolias that lined the smooth curved streets, leading to the mouth of the train station. The trees diminished the street lights, and darkened the road ahead, reducing the light from the truck's high-beam to weak streaks. As planned, Luther pulled the truck around and straddled the mouth of the station, blocking the only entrance, leaving a narrow space for walking on each side. The station, an old white-washed, barn like building with a roof extending over the driveway sat crouched like a peeping tom under a blanket of black clouds. A sign in the window read "Closed." The truck faced the station's door, the headlights glaring against the window. The yards were illuminated by a string of naked lights extending from the roof, brightening the red circle of bricks that covered most of the area. Behind the circle lay a long stretch of soft black top that extended across six sets of railroad tracks.

The doors of the truck burst open, and everyone scrambled out, anxious and fearful of what they might encounter. They took shelter under the overhang where they could see the tracks as well as the mouth of the station. Suddenly, the train roared around the bend, it's whistle shrill and ear-splitting. "Lord a mercy, look a hyar," Charlie yelled, pointing towards the tracks where The City of New Orleans slowed to a stop and sat belching smoke and filling the air with black cinders—its huge light gleaming down the tracks. "Boy, git that gal on board quick; they don't see nobody, liable not to wait." Charlie and M.B. waved their arms over their heads until they saw the lights on the side of the train pop on.

Margaret stood before them, her hair disheveled, her face streaked from crying, and her eyes filled with confusion. Now she felt even more alone, and soon she would be inside the train, on her way to a strange place. "Tell Mama I'll write as soon as I get there," she said, kissing Charlie on his sagging cheek. Shyly, she gripped M.B.'s hand, squeezing it gently. He nodded and clamped down hard on the pipe. She didn't know how to act.

"Git on now, and don't you stop till you gits Margaret on board," Charlie said to Luther. "And remember; if'n you hears me shoot the gun, you jest jump on behind her. They'll put you off somewhere down the line and we'll git you somehow." Luther nodded, offered an arm to Margaret, pulled her to him, and kissed her full on the mouth. Margaret was stunned, and Luther grabbed her hand, leading her towards the train. They ran across the red-bricked circle, the clatter of their feet echoing through the night, and finally onto the blacktop where the sound of their footsteps all but disappeared. They stopped at each coach, yelling, "Chicago," only to be directed farther down the line by Negro porters in dark blue uniforms. The train started to move, and there was no time left for talking, or proper farewells, or for anything but gasping for air and running. They ran along the stretch, panting like new-born puppies, and Margaret called to the tall, portly porter who stood on the last platform, "Chicago."

"Here, girl," the porter called back in a trembling voice. He leaned over and extended his arm, his eyes large and afraid. He had seen something that neither Margaret or Luther had—two white policemen in khaki, running rabbit-quick towards the train with guns in their hands. It was clear to him what was happening—he had seen many runs like this, they were all the same, sweaty, black faces grimacing with pain from exhaustion, running to escape the law. He reached down and grabbed the panting girl by her long hair—she screamed and clutched his legs—and yanked her aboard the train, just as Luther tossed the suitcase at his feet.

"Come on boy, jump," the porter yelled to Luther.

And for one maddening moment, realizing that he may never see Margaret again, Luther thought of hurling himself into the car and forgetting what Charlie had said. But he hesitated, remembering the old men depended upon him and the moment was lost—the train rumbled past, it's whistle wailing; and Margaret was gone.

He stood gazing down the long stretch of tracks where only seconds ago the train had sat, then, shaking his head, he turned, looking across the black top. He froze. Two white policemen had crossed the yards, and were now heading back to the end of the station, towards Charlie and M.B. who stood under the roof. Charlie was pointing the gun in the air—the barrel smoking. He had obviously fired the gun, but in the roar of the engine, Luther had not heard it. In their planning, Luther thought, the men hadn't counted on the noise the train makes. He should be on the train with Margaret and now, the porter's command, "Jump boy," registered—its urgency; he wished to God that he had. He was stunned. He watched the lawmen run, their tall, muscular bodies weaving in and out as they propelled themselves across the sets of tracks—a midnight ballet. They ran with ease, precision, and lightness. There was balance, even elegance in their motion. Suddenly, one deputy dropped to his knees and fired his gun, hitting the side of the station and sending Charlie and M.B. scrambling for cover. The blast, the eruption of dazzling blue-red sparks from the gun, made Luther shiver; he shook himself from his trance and bolted across the tracks, thinking, "Jesus this is it!"

The wind picked up, swirling the dust heavily about the yards. The trees and tall weeds that bordered the station swayed and bowed. Charlie and M.B. ducked behind the fender on the far side of the truck, their bodies crouched low. They listened to the rushing of the wind, the whisper of footsteps on the blacktop, and to the pounding of their hearts. They watched the police advancing—their pale faces coming closer and closer—phantoms the Negro dreaded, hated, and tried most of his life to avoid. They looked at each other briefly, realizing that this was the tightest spot that they had ever been in.

"Whatcha gonna do, Charlie?" M.B. asked, his voice barely audible.

Charlie pondered, his brow heavy with wrinkles, the gun held loosely at his side. "When they reaches the brick, I'se gonna toss out the gun whereas they can see it. Maybe then, if I convince them that I'm stupid, they'll jest lock us up," Charlie said in a non-convincing voice. M.B. shot him a disapproving look, and turned away. Yanking out his knife, he clicked it open. "Jest in case they ain't buying," he said, looking back across the yard.

A clatter of footsteps announced that the policemen had reached the brick, and through the separation between their bodies, Charlie suddenly saw Luther running behind them. Charlie gasped: he thought Luther had made the train. Evidently the deputies had, too, and could not hear Luther because of their own rapid foot steps. Charlie elbowed M.B., then pointed to the slightly arched figure pumping his long legs cross the blacktop.

"Damn," M.B. muttered. "I thought he'd made the train." Charlie shook his head and re-examined his plan. If he tossed the gun out now, the police might not see it—the trees cast long shadows across the brick. If he broke towards them, to warn Luther to keep a cool head, they would surely fire. As though he was reading M.B.'s thoughts, Charlie said, "I'se gots to chance it. I'm gonna toss out the gun, and you keep that knife out of sight. M.B. slid the knife up his shirt sleeve. Charlie flung the gun across the hood of the truck, where it skidded on the brick then stopped at the edge of the circle. The deputies slid to a stop, looked down at the gun, then towards the truck, their eyes peeled for treachery.

"We give up," Charlie hollered from the side of the truck; and raising their arms above their heads, they stepped directly under the lights hanging above the circle. The deputy picked up the gun and crammed it inside his belt. Satisfied that it wasn't a trap, they holstered their guns and pulled out their long, black nightsticks.

"You black son-ah-bitches!" One said, approaching Charlie and M.B. slowly. "Why you fire that damn gun? You black-ass niggers let us come past you thinking you were jest two old harmless coons. Niggers likes them has to be taught to respect the law," the other said, staring at Charlie.

And Charlie watched their pasty, white faces illuminated by the moonlight, the stern, cold, unfeeling eyes he knew it was no use to pretend or cow-tow. That it was all up to fate now. Besides no matter what he did, Luther would charge. Charlie recalled the night that he and Luther had burned Roy's arm when Luther swore, "Not to me they wont—they won't whip me like no child!" And so they stood, Charlie with one hand in the air, the other on his cane, and M.B. with both hands on top of his head. The deputies moved toward them, brandishing their nightsticks, when Luther cleared the blacktop and was suddenly upon them, leaping, crashing down on both deputies shoulders, separating them and sending them sprawling in different directions. The night sticks clacked noisily to the ground, and while one deputy lay stunned, Luther threw himself on the other. The deputy fought desperately to free himself from his surprise attacker. Luther's body covered the deputy as they scrambled over the red brick, their fists pounding each other. They grunted and muttered undistinguishable words as they rolled and struggled.

"Knock him senseless, and let's make a run for it," Charlie yelled over to Luther.

"Charlie!" M.B. cried, "Ain't no where to run, they car is blocking the truck." He shook the knife from his sleeve and raised it over his head.

"What? Charlie said, as he turned to look at the car. He swings back to see Luther and the deputy still struggling and a chill swept across his body as he realized that something ungodly was about to happen. He felt detached from the whole scene. It was like he was a spectator watching this madness, and yet he knew these were his hands and feet of lead that he pushed forward towards the men scrambling on the ground—their fists pounding each other. Suddenly, it began to rain, a light sprinkle that rapidly became a downpour. He had to get Luther away. What happened to him didn't matter. He was an old man who had lived out the biggest portion of his life. Yet, he did not want to die. He heard the squealing of car brakes and, momentarily, a bustle of footsteps pounding the brick behind him. He and M.B. turned to see Samuels and his entourage, Shorty and Grahm, charging them from behind. Charlie, only a few feet away from Luther now, hobbled faster. He strained every muscle in his body to reach Luther before Samuels reached him and before the other deputy awakened. Luther was holding his own, his rain-slicked fist pounding the deputy's face, but Charlie knew this would not last—could not last.

"Kill em, beat em to death if you has to!" the thunderous voice of Samuels sliced the air, and Charlie and M.B. were suddenly struck from behind and they all hit the ground—their bodies twisted in different position on the cold, slick brick. Every time one of them tried to get up, they all fell into each other—Wade on his knees pounding Charlie in the back with his billy, while Charlie dodged M.B.'s knife slicing through the air. The deputy from Cairo was revived suddenly and all over Luther. Charlie knew he would not reach Luther in time. The policeman from Cairo had Luther in a headlock. The other scrambled to his knees and, removing his gun, jammed it into Luther's side. He fired—the blast deafening and final.

Luther slipped from the deputy's arms like a rag doll, falling backwards, his head cracking against the brick. "Sweet Jesus," Charlie moaned, flinging his bony arms skyward. M.B. shook his head, grimaced, then sliced Shorty's pant's leg, ripping it open and drawing blood. All the noises seemed to close in on Charlie; everything was alive. The plink, plink of the rain on the bricks, the muffled groans that reached his ears from somewhere behind—like someone yelling into a hole—and their ragged breathing blended together and tore the air. He had the sudden urge to talk—to explain to Luther why he had tossed the gun away—but Samuels still on his knees was upon him... Something inside of him exploded, and he snatched up the cane and began spearing it at every white face he saw. The cane connected with an eye, a nose, a knee or solid bone on each swing, and resounded with every blow a loud THOCK, THOCK, THOCK. Loud groans, cries of black son-ah-bitches, red-neck plow boys, and the slosh of wet shoes upon the brick filled the air. Charlie inched his way to Luther, who lay with only the whites of his eyes visible, and blood pouring from a gaping hole in his side. In a ragged, raspy voice, Charlie cried out, "Dang it boy!" and shook his head in agony, unaware of the constant beating his back was receiving from Wade's billy until Wade delivered a searing blow to his kidney. He gasped and fell over Luther's long legs, where he gazed drunkenly into the young man's lifeless face. He snatched his head around and saw Shorty's white hairy leg, its shocking paleness stained with blood and M.B.'s old knife lying on the ground at his boots. M.B., held fast to the ground by a grinning Grahm, grimaced in pain as Shorty stomped his wrist over and over. Then a blow to the back of Charlie's head sent him sprawling head-first into a clump of grass pushing up between the cracks of the bricks, and with the smell of sweet clover in his nostrils, he closed his eyes.

THE SOUND OF VOICES

News always traveled fast in Bennettsville, and that of Margaret's escape and Luther's death whistled through town about the same time Charlie and M.B., battered and bruised, were tossed into the calaboose. At seven forty-five a.m., Clara Townsend, the epitome of white womanhood and the widow of the late founder of the town, Harrison Townsend, burst through the front door of the jail, wide-eyed and breathless, demanding that Charlie and M.B. be released immediately. She had driven the silver limousine the few blocks from her estate with a vivid picture of Charlie's face before her, drenched with perspiration and glistening in the hot sun as he planted the creeping myrtles that she loved so well. And with something else—something that she could not describe but that lay across her chest like a hot, smothering hand—guilt: she knew that her son J.T. was responsible for all of this, for she had over-heard him on the phone giving orders to Roy to file charges against Katie's daughter. That way the girl would not risk jail to collect the inheritance.

The last thirty years or so, she had walked in her husband's shadow—Harrison had run everything except the home. He'd even told her how she was to act and feel about certain issues. She had developed a thick skin on the issue of the Negroes and their living quarters, and had gone along with whatever Harrison had thought was best for them. And she thought she had gotten used to Negroes and the miseries that clung to them like silk cocoons—Negroes in rags, Negroes with broods of unkempt children, Negroes with gaunt faces and gnarled hands, even Negroes with sunken eyes and malformed bellies. But Charlie was not the same; she could not dismiss his troubles by justifying that he had got what he deserved. And now that Harrison was no longer living, she would no longer hide her feelings on any issue, especially the Negroes. She was, after all, a Christian white woman.

She felt transformed when she walked through the narrow hallway. It had been a very long time since she had taken matters into her own hands and made decisions about anything other than household duties. She had always admired and respected Wade Samuels when Harrison was alive, but when she heard Earline whisper to the Negro man across the fence that, "Wade had done took his billy and nearly beat Charlie and M.B. to death," she was filled with loathing for the Sheriff. Seeing his broad, rippling muscles straining the khaki shirt, and the look of satisfaction on his face as he sprawled back in the chair at the small desk, she was repulsed.

"Wade," she called sharply from the door, her voice filling the room with disapproval.

He came to his feet like he had been struck, and stood at attention. "Miss Clara," he stammered and gaped. "What in tarnation…?" Through the open door behind Wade she could see the cells and shadows of men cramped inside. She closed the space quickly, stopping at the edge of the desk. "I come to get Charlie and his friend out of this place," she announced, without batting an eye, and moved to the open area by the wall, blocking the breeze from the small overhead fan. The room was suddenly filled with a charge of electricity.

Wade flushed and immediately glanced over her shoulder to the wall telephone as though he expected it to ring and he would hear J.T's voice instructing him to do whatever his mother asked. He stood with his jaw slack and looked at her as if she had suddenly sprouted a three foot beard; she had crossed that invisible line that separated the men from the women. She frightened and puzzled him at the same time. The demand would not be unreasonable coming from a white man; he had released many prisoners to the care of their bosses when they came and asked that he let their nigger out, but white women were supposed to be fragile and sympathetic to the status quo—she was neither.

"Miss Clara," he stammered again.

"Don't talk, Wade. Just open that cell and let Charlie and his friend out of there this minute!" She stepped away from Wade and pointed across his shoulder.

Charlie stirred at the mention of his name and opened his eyes, staring at the ceiling, then turned his face to the bars where he looked across the room to the open door. Wade's back was to him, but he could see Miss Clara clearly. She glared at Wade, her pale blue eyes danced with anger, and her salt-and-pepper hair, partially covered by the blue scarf, trembled on her head as she ordered Wade around. Charlie saw Wade drop some papers to the desk, then gesture wildly with his hands, shaking them as if he would suddenly strangle someone. Charlie smiled; he hadn't expected this—God really did work in mysterious ways. And he had no doubt that he would be let out. He was witnessing a simple exercise that he had seen many white people engage in to measure their adversaries' and friends' stamina—but this was different. Wade didn't stand a chance against Miss Clara, for like all white men, fathers, husbands, brothers and sons, Wade had been raised to adore and protect white women, giving in to their every whim. What's more, Wade didn't dare risk reprisals from her son, J.T.

"In my custody. Isn't that how it's done, Wade? You think I don't know what went on. You think I'm just a silly, old woman. Well, you're wrong, Wade Samuels. You and your so-called keepers of the law hauled your asses over to Cairo and terrorized two, old colored men. I'm gonna see that you pay dearly for this, Wade. You take note," she said. It was the best tongue lashing that Charlie had ever heard a white woman give a white man. Wade shrugged his shoulders and snatched the ring of keys from the hook on the wall, swaggered over to the cell door and unlocked it. He jiggled the key as if he hoped it would break in the lock, and Charlie nudged M.B. awake. Charlie and M.B. hobbled by a red faced Wade, looking as though he could strangle a bear, but he just ordered them out of his sight with a wild jerk of his thumb. M.B. and Charlie stumbled forth like the walking dead—M.B. cradling his wrist in one hand and Charlie holding his head as they followed Miss Clara outside to the silver limousine. Charlie heard Wade swearing at the white men, Roy, Marmy and Buddy, in the other cell as they demanded, "Let us out too, Wade."

The noon whistle screamed and Charlie opened his eyes to find himself staring into blazing, black eyes shadowed by wild turfs of black hair. Charlie shut his eyes tightly then opened them slowly, only to find the same pointed, bushy eyebrows staring down at him—there was no mistaking the frowning face of Doc Smith and instantly Charlie thought that he had died and gone straight to hell. "Git away from here, you devil," he said in a trembling voice.

"It's alright, Charlie," Katie said in a soothing, motherly tone, and Charlie relaxed. If Katie was standing by his side, then he wasn't in hell. He looked about the room and discovered he was in his own bed, but he loathed the idea of Smith touching him. He waved his arm, batting Smith away, and Doc Smith sneered, baring tobacco stained teeth, moved back from the bed, and began probing his nose slowly and carefully as if grasping for something special.

"Tell that dang fool to git," Charlie commanded Katie.

With a nod of her head, Katie signal Doc Smith to leave, and Smith picked up his bag, looked around with eyes blazing, then left, banging the screen door behind him. Shaking her head in disgust, Katie turned back to Charlie and stooped to plump the pillow. She eased Charlie's head back until it rested against the red rubber bag packed with ice.

"It'll do you good to talk—the way I hears it, Wade just 'bout pounded the brains outta your head. Done slept enough; too much sleeping behind a lick like that could be bad. Liable not to never wake up."

His neck was stiff, his head throbbed, even the scalp of his head was tender to the touch—he ached all over, but he lay in his bed with a quilt draped over him looking like Charlie, ornery, contrary, and tough. "What you let that thang in my house fer? You knows how I feels 'bout that low-..." He struggled under the quilt and glared at her.

"Hush, now, Miss Clara brung him down here; you knows he wouldn't a come on his own. And besides you was so quiet and sick, and I was jest plain scared for you—I done even told the Saints to come over to pray for you. But I sees you is much better now," she said, and coming from around the bed, returned to the chair at the foot.

He glared at her again, suddenly feeling stronger, but avoided a fight by not telling her how he regarded the Saints, even though he was sure she knew—it was an old issue between them. He looked away, staring at the sunlight streaming through the window and suddenly realized that for the first time in thirty-five years he had actually let Doc Smith know how he really felt about him. And the spell was working, he was sure of that. The insanity had blazed from behind Smith's eyes, and the probing in his nose in front of them; convinced Charlie that the day-by-day spell Tom Lofton had put on Smith was surging through Smith's body with every beat of his heart. Charlie gazed down the bed at Katie's pained face. Traces of tears streaked her smooth, rosy cheeks, and a fear lay behind the wide eyes. He knew she waited patiently to hear him recount the details of the trip last night, to actually hear from his lips that Margaret made the train, and also what had happened to Luther. "Where's Viola?" he asked.

She looked up and held his gaze. "Up yonder in Cairo; ain't come back yet. She been up yonder since five this morning," Katie answered sadly.

"Hump," he grunted and looked away. "How'd she git up yonder?"

"Brother Watson drove her and Reverend Washington rode along with 'em. But she sent word by that youngen David that she is a coming over here tonight," Katie said, squirming in the chair and tugging at her collar. "Says she wants to hear first hand what happened to her boy."

"Them the words she used?" he said, raising his head from the pillow.

"Yes"

"Didn't spect no different from Viola. She's one straight-forward woman." He sighed and dropped his head heavily on the pillow. "Thought I heard a lots of folks talking outside," he said. "Musta been dreaming."

"Weren't no dream, Charlie. Whole town buzzing like honey bees in red clover, and been a-buzzing like that since early morning."

"Bout Luther, I reckon," he said and sighed with such a long trembling breath that Katie almost started to cry.

"Yes, some 'bout Luther, some 'bout Reece Scott's mama gitting all that money from the lawsuit."

Charlie's body trembled under the heavy quilt. "They done finally settled?"

"Seems so," she sighed. "News came through town early this morning, not too long after Miss Clara brung you home in that big fine car."

He felt his skin prickling all over as if he had been exposed to a sudden gust of artic air. He was exhilarated over the Negro woman's victory. A small black woman who came from the back woods of Mississippi, with a little bald-headed white man who refused to be bullied. Together they had acted, sued the city of Brocton for the murder and mutilation of her son. Together they saw to it that his body was exhumed from its dark grave and brought out for the world to see. Charlie swallowed hard, sat up, and pushed the water bottle away from his head, wedging it against the pillow. He tossed back the quilt and sighed, wishing that in some way he could have played a part in the victory. He lay there staring at the ceiling, his pants stained from Luther's and his own blood. He turned and faced Katie. "How much did she git?"

"Don't know the exact amount, so many thousands of dollars I can't pronounce it. Best way I can tell you is they said it's so much, Brocton gonna become a ghost town trying to pay it all."

"Glory, glory, that-much! Ha-ha," he laughed wickedly, and slapped his bony hands together, his pulse racing. He wanted to run all the way to Brocton to shake that Negro woman's hand and, if nothing else, nod a how-do to the little bald-headed white lawyer. Sudden rage consumed him and he sat up and cried out, "Hopes Viola do the same, hopes…" Then looking at the ceiling he shouted, "Why don't you jest tear this old heart from my chest sos it won't feel nothing? Why'd you give us hearts anyhows?"

"Jest you rest now," Katie said, coming to her feet and pushing him back gently on the pillow. "Ain't right you troubling yourself with this stuff now. Ain't right…"she mumbled, placing the cover back over him and retrieving the ice bag from the pillow stuck it back behind his head. She warned him with a raised eyebrow to leave it there. She returned to the chair, turning her head towards the window—a vision of Charlie's blood-stained pants in her mind's eye.

They sat with gloomy faces; the sun gleaming through the window brightened the small bedroom. "Charlie," Katie said after a long silence, "what makes colored folks acts like they knows everything when something happens?"

He poked his lips out and frowned as if she had opened an ugly wound. "I can't rightly say. But I spect it's 'cause colored folks is always dreaming of doing something big. You know, right all the wrongs. Most likely, though, it's 'cause sometimes the problems of other colored folks becomes they own, even though they don't knows why. Half the time, some don't even know what the problem is. Like if'n they sees a mob of Negroes kicking on a white boy, they jest join in and kick him, too. Later on they might ask what he done, then agin they might not never ask. Same thing 'plies when something good happens, they jest join in taking credit for something—anything."

"I guess you is right," she sighed. "It jest been a strange day. One like the Bible prophesies."

"What you mean?" his interest keened.

"'The sound of their voices went out over the earth, their words reached the very ends of the world.' Romans chapter ten, eighteen verse."

They were silent for a moment, the hot breeze floating through the open back door. The chickens clucked sporadically. "Before the sun come up this morning, something was constantly happening," she continued. "First, Margaret's escape, then the news 'bout Luther, bless his soul—losing his life over yonder in Cairo. Before a body can properly grieve for Luther, folks gits all stirred up 'bout Reece's mama gitting all that money. Then when I goes on the porch while you was sleeping, Mamie and Almeda is all up in the air 'bout the news what come on the radio 'bout that blues singer—you know the one you is always talking 'bout?"

"Bessie Smith?" he said and sat straight up.

"Yes, that's the one. Mamie said she dead. Said she was in a car accident and that the white folks in Clarksdale jest let her lay on the road and bleed to death."

"What…?"

"Jest hold on, there's more. It seems that the white folks up north done give the order that no white folks what says they is anybody is gonna set foot in Clarksdale till they learn how to treat people. Can you believe white folks is talking like that? And then to top that off, while I was still talking to them, the mailman brung me that letter from Tom Nolan 'bout that money what Townsend left to me and Margaret."

Charlie pushed his feet to the side of the bed and turned around, staring at Katie. He couldn't stand any more of this whirl of events. A surge of hope that something good was to come out of all this confusion pressed on his mind, and for a moment he forgot his pain. "When is the money to be picked up? We'se got to make plans to git it to Margaret cause she gonna need it up yonder in Chicago."

"Well," she stammered. "We first gotta make sure she done made it to Chicago; I ain't heard from Robert yet, and he is supposed to call Reverend Washington the minute she gits there. Reverend Washington ain't back yet, but Mother, she there. And then Margaret gots to be told what trouble this money done caused, somebody hasta to tell her 'bout Luther…' And besides I can't make head nor tails out of this letter, excepting I'se to be at Mr. Nolan's office day after tomorrow."

Charlie became very agitated, and shook his hands in the air, dismissing Katie's comments as though they were unimportant. "Listen, will you? She got on the train, Luther saw to that and I personally seed it with my own eyes," he lied—he had been watching the Cairo deputies who had come from behind, looked at he and M.B., then took off running in the direction of the train. "Train jest ain't made it, that's all. And considering all that done happened, I think we best make sure she gits that money. The way I sees it, Luther be sitting right here now if'n it wadn't for J.T. Anybody with a speck of common sense knows he's the one what sent them dumb hill-billies, Roy and Marmy, to yo' house. Anybody knows that! Sho, we'se gots to tell her 'bout Luther, but none of this here mess would have happened if'n J.T. had done like his daddy said. That money was left legal to Margaret, you the legal guardian. She ain't stole nothing, and don't you forgit it," he snapped, stretched his bad leg and wincing in pain.

"Listen, Katie," he said, softer, and rubbed the back of his neck. "That money means heap more to them peckerwoods than they wants to admit. Sho, J.T. gots plenty, but that ain't why he don't want y'all to have it. He don't want Margaret to live 'cause she had the gumption to stand up to him. He wants her to grow up and be like you and me, praying to God and pulling weeds. You can't even read that letter good enough to know what's in it, and I can't neither." He thought about the Negro woman and her victory and vowed to see it through. "Margaret gots to have that money to show them that we ain't gonna put up no mo' with this kind of mess. So we best git hold of M.B. to go over that letter and explain it, 'cause I aims to see this through."

"I ain't against you, Charlie, but I'se got to talk this thing over with the Father before I makes a decision. Besides, how we gonna git the money to her anyhow?"

He nodded his head, winced again, and said, "You leave that to me. I'll git it to her somehow. But while you is praying, you think 'bout how you had to chop off Roy's arm, and how Margaret had to run away in the dark of the night like a common criminal, and how bravely Luther fought and died over yonder in that dirty train station helping Margaret. Then you think hard on this here day—the one you say the Bible prophesized. And what done happened to bring all this news about on this day. Reece's mama gitting that money; white folks going against white folks 'cause a Negro blues singer was left to bleed to death on the roadside, and then think on me and M.B. all beat up, and Miss Clara, who ain't never hardly said "shoo" to a chicken putting Wade Samuels in his place and gitting us out of jail, and bringing that insane Smith into my house thirty-five years after Anna Mae's death. You think on them things, then tell me what you decide, you hyar?" he shouted, and was sorry immediately, for he knew that no matter how he reasoned, Katie still believed that if Margaret had not accepted that money, none of this would have happened, and certainly Luther would be alive.

A soft rap on the back screen door ended their conversation, and Charlie peeked around to see a huge shadow stretched across the floor in the square of sunlight. "Come on in," Katie called. "It's open."

Earline Simpson stepped through the door on her tip-toes. "Aftanoon," she whispered to Katie and sneaked a peek at Charlie who was now lying back in the bed, his arms folded across his face. Earline was a big woman, mostly top-heavy with slim hips. She had satiny smooth skin and pop eyes and moved with the grace of a cat.

"How you feeling, Charlie?" she asked, meekly, her honey voice warming the room. She took the chair that Katie brought from the kitchen and placed beside the other.

A long silence passed before Charlie lowered his arms and mumbled, "Ain't dead yet, Earline. Ain't going nowheres till ole Smitty dies and go to hell where he belongs," he growled in a weak voice.

"How you doing, Sister Katie?" she asked, still whispering. The blue and white checked dress strained at the buttons from her huge bosom, and her hair was plastered to her forehead in swirls from the heat. "I knows you sho is glad yo' daughter is safe up yonder in Chicago. Whew, this been one hot day and more than jest the heat," she sighed, and folded her arms about her chest.

"That's sho nuff the truth," Katie said. "I was jest telling Charlie all what been going on this here day. She cleared her throat, swallowed, then continued. "We was jest now trying to fit it all in our minds. But maybe he oughta rest now."

"Didn't you jest a minute ago tell me I needed to stay wake?" Charlie said in a puzzled voice. He didn't want to miss anything important. Earline always brought news on what the white folks was doing—they must be doing plenty today.

"You done had your dinner, Earline?" Katie asked, facing the woman. "We'se got a mess of fried cabbages and cornbread—plenty."

"Nome, thank you, Miss Katie. I et a sandwich over Miss Clara's—today I splits my time between the jail house and Miss Clara's. But yo' offer is mighty tempting, mighty tempting. I jest ain't had no mind fer eating much today."

"Me neither," Katie agreed. "Ain't had no mind for nothing with all this here news flying back and forth cross town and the world."

"Yes, Ma'am. Ain't that the truth? Did y'all hear what them white folks up north said 'bout white folks going down to Clarksdale. And Lord, them peckerwoods leaving that woman to die like that is enough to make yo' body sick."

"That's sho the truth. And we done heard everything, commencing with Miss Clara pitching a fit down at the calaboose early this morning to Reece's mama gitting all that money," Katie informed her.

"Well, did y'all hear 'bout Miss Rosie pitching a fit at the jail house too? She come to git her boy outta the jail."

"Lord," Katie cried out, turned to face Charlie, and quickly turned back to Earline. "What else is gonna happen in this here town today?"

Charlie perked up. He knew Earline had come to hear the details of Luther's death, and he was not ready to talk about it—he would not tell anyone until he had first told Viola. And the longer Earline talked, the longer he could keep it within, for if he spoke of it, then it surely had to be true. "Well, what happened? I hope she gave Wade hell; Miss Clara sho did," Charlie said.

Katie glared at him, but he stared her down.

"Well," Earline said, shouldering back in the chair and crossing her arms. "You knows they don't pay me no mind—I'se jest like a fly on the wall. I had gone back to the jail to take the lunch—ham butt sandwiches—like always, and do the dusting. It sho was fun seeing her tear into them rednecks, Graham was there then, but Shorty wadn't. Mista Wade had to call Mr. Jim back down to straighten it all out. It was a sight to see, I jest 'bout dusted the paint offa that old file cabinet, he-he," she laughed a little girl's snicker and clasped her hand over her mouth.

"I reckon Wade Samuels had to call Mr. Jim down after Miss Clara left," Charlie said, chuckling low.

"I didn't hear nothing 'bout that," Earline said and uncrossed her arms.

"Well, you said Wade had to call Mr. Jim back to the jail, didn't you?" Charlie asked, eyeing her closely.

"Oh, that weren't nothing to do with Miss Clara. Mr. Jim come down to that jail house 'bout the same time I got there this morning—round six o'clock—and he was madder that I'se ever seed anybody in my life. Naw, sir, Mr. Jim come down to put Mista Wade on spension."

Katie and Charlie's mouths dropped opened and Charlie pushed himself up in the bed, his eyes fastened to Earline's face. "Spension," they said in unison.

"That's right, spension," Earline confirmed. He done that long fo' Miss Clara set foot at the jail. I'd jest pulled on my apron and started cleaning the office likes always, emptying the trash cans, when Mr. Jim stormed through the door. Banged the screen so loud I jest about jumped outta my skin. He looked like he'd been up all night—eyes red and unshaved. His uniform was streaked with dirt like he'd been driving the back roads. His shoes was muddy and he was fit to be tied. He was trembling from head to toe. You see that little desk sitting in front of the door whiles you was there, Charlie? One what leads to the cells."

"Only glanced at it on my way out. Why?"

"Well, Mista Wade was sitting at that desk when Mr. Jim walked in and, like I said, he was mad. He chunked some papers on that desk and told Mista Wade he was the stupidest som-bitch he ever laid eyes on. I practically went through the floor, wadn't no place fer me to go, the door hadn't been unlocked where I could git in to clean, so I jest stood in that corner holding that waste can. I don't believe Mr. Jim ree-lized I was there anyways. He didn't see nobody but Mista Wade. Well, anyways, Mista Wade turned red in the face and stammered out something that wadn't clear and Mr. Jim yelled out then saying, "Who gave you the 'thority to call the High Sheriff in Cairo? Well, Mista Wade clammed up then. I guess 'cause ain't nobody give him the 'thority to do nothing. And fer one minute there, I thought Mr. Jim was gonna slammed that desk right into Mista Wade's chest. He was leaning hard on that desk and his eyes was blazing. He bared his teeth and lit into Mista Wade for a good long spell, and Mista Wade jest set there saying nothing, but you could see he was gitting mad too—his face was red as tomatoes in the sun."

"What did he say?" Charlie asked, sitting up from the pillow. He swung his feet to the floor and winced in pain.

Earline frowned and was quiet for a second, her brow heavy with wrinkles. "Well," she began, "Mr. Jim said Mista Wade was spended starting this coming Monday fer two months. Had to do with the High Sheriff in Cairo calling Ludie Mae to confermation the request for sistance to stop a runaway and he had to have this here confermation 'cause some-body from Bennettsville had got kilt by one of they deputies. Seems Ludie Mae called Mr. Jim at home and he got in his truck and drove over yonder 'round three-thirty, missing Mista Wade coming back to Bennettsville by a few minutes or so. Then, when he said that he had been to the train station and seed the body which he identified as Luther Dawson, well, I ain't heard nothing he said after that. My ears plugged up, and I gasped so loud that Mr. Jim turned 'round and saw me standing there holding that waste can to my chest.

"They stopped talking then. Mr. Jim waved his hand at them keys on the wall so Mista Wade can let me into the back where the cells is—I guess to git me out his way. I tells you," she paused and slowly shook her head. "I was ready to bust wide open. I wanted to run outside and shout it to the world that Luther was over yonder in Cairo, dead. Instead, I goes on inside the door still carrying that can, and what do I see, but one cell filled with three, straggly, red-eyed peckerwoods, and the other with two old Negroes what turns out to be you, Mr. Charlie, and M.B., stretched out like dead flies."

They were silent. They listened to the crunching of feet on gravel outside as people coming from the fields for dinner passed through the alley. Charley cleared his throat after a long silence and said, "Well, we was out like flies, but that's 'cause we fought them crackers with everythang we had. And that's all I'se gonna say 'bout it till I talks to Viola." He sighed, then made a great effort to push himself from the bed. The women seeing his weakness, hurried to help him, but he waved them away and remained on the bed.

Hot tears rolled down Katie and Earline's faces; but they didn't move.

"Well," he said, as if he had been talking all along, "did Miss Rosie git Buddy out?"

"Oh," Earline said, quickly wiping her face with her hands. "I forgot to finish. Miss Rosie made a deal with Mr. Jim. She told him she knew who it was what kilt old Boswell and if'n he let Buddy go, she tell him."

"What in tarnation…?" Charlie gasped, his eyes big. "Who was it gal? Tell me."

I didn't hear them. They went to whispering so soft, I couldn't make it out."

"None of it at all?"

"Nary a word," Earline said sourly, her lips in a pout.

Charlie stared at Earline and Katie, but Katie looked away, wondering how could Rosie know that; Rosie hadn't been nowhere in sight the day Boswell was killed.

"Earline," Charlie said, "I wants you to go down to M.B.'s in New Town. See if'n he's able to come up here for a spell as soon as he can. Tell him it's business."

Earline rose to her feet. "I'll do that on my way home, Mr. Charlie, aims to stop and pick me some sweet peas."

"I'd appreciate it if'n you does this first for me. I'se gots to figger this thing out," he said and looked into her eyes.

Yes, sir," she answered and rose from the chair. She walked through the kitchen and out the door, the screen creaking behind her, then snapping closed. "My, my, them cabbages sho smells good," she said.

HONEYBEES

Talk, talk, talk. For the next two days the talk continued. Within the confines of their homes or sitting in the swings on their porches, the townsfolk discussed the events that had rocked their world. The Negroes had several reactions: elation over Margaret's escape, sorrow over Luther's demise, pride—a strange new emotion—in their culture because one Negro woman had beat the white judicial system and made them pay for the death of her son. He wasn't just another "dead nigger." The whites had only one reaction: outrage. And they concluded that all the events occurred as a result of Yankee propaganda. Why else would Negroes defy and challenge the laws of the land? Differences on these issues were evident, and only one issue compelled the whites and Negroes to agree: that being it was indeed strange for their respected medical doctor to stop them on the street and demand that they "Kill a black chicken at the dark of the moon."

That night, however, Roy's papa, the owner of the Main Street filling station, was killed instead. The elder Larkin, unlike his son, was a hard working honest man who often worked into the wee hours of the morning. And about close up time old man Larkin's face was shot away during a robbery by two white men from Ohio. The town awoke to a din of confusion caused by a straggly posse, the sheriff and his deputies and Big Jim. Cars revved, gravel flying and men yelling as they gave chase, starting out on Main Street and ending up at the bottom of the muddy spillway, some eight miles away. There, spotlights created luminous moons on the sides of the river's dam. Men piled out of cars and struggled violently with the two intruders until they were bound, gagged, and secured in the back of Grahmn's squad car.

At the break of day, dirty, exhausted, and highly agitated, the posse crowded inside Jim's office. The room was stuffy and reeked of river water that had saturated the men's clothing during the struggle. They lined the wall across from Jim's desk—a disheveled bunch like the migrants who waited in a commodity line for handouts of cornmeal, dried beans, and soft apples. The electric lights blazed, creating an illusion of heat that made them sweat. Shorty limped back and forth across the room on a borrowed cane—his leg stiff from the thirty-three stitches it took to close the gash made by M.B.'s knife in the fight at the Cairo Station.

Jim stood behind the desk, his arms folded across his chest, his eyes focused on something far away. Shorty stopped at Jim's desk and said, "Jim, Graham jest found out that them two Yankee boys is from some place called Kettering, Ohio."

"Where in the Sam Hill is Kettering?" Jim asked, looking over at the men.

The men looked from one to the other until, finally, Samuels replied, "Some place them Yankee boys ain't never gonna lay eyes on no more."

Jim glared at Samuels.

"Some place in Ohio for sure," Samuels added and stood at attention.

"Well, thank you, Mr. Samuels," Jim growled and unfolding his arms leaned across the desk. "Where?" he demanded; his eyes wandered over Samuels' huge frame as though he studied a lizard crossing the road.

"Yep, that's where it is alright," a voice from the line said, and they all nodded in agreement. Jim turned away from Wade and yelled, "Shorty, git on that right now; find out everything you can about those two. See if they running."

Shorty, who had poked his head through the door, beamed. His face breaking into a bashful smile, proud that Jim had asked him and not Wade, he disappeared from the door. "And you, Samuels," Jim said, his eyes boring into Samuels, "Git on back to the spillway and find that gun. Ludie Mae," Jim yelled, pulling out the chair, and sitting down.

"She ain't here yet," Samuels said, and held Jim's steady gaze—the tension evident between them. "It's jest now six-thirty; she don't start till seven, remember."

Shorty limped into the room, a rolled up map tucked under his arm. The men pushed away from the wall, heading to the desk as Shorty placed the map in front of Jim, who unrolled it in a flash and weighted it down on both ends with a calendar and a cracked coffee mug. The men crowded about the desk, their eyes scanning the lines of blue and red ink. They watched Jim's finger trace along the blue curves and red lines that circled the state of Ohio—all eyes peeled, looking for a city named Kettering.

"There it is, right yonder," Lee Adkins' sharp voice pierced the quiet of the room. "See? Right below Dee-troit!" He tapped the paper with his finger, making a hollow sound.

The men were quiet. They straightened up one by one, looking confused. And, as if locating this one printed word on government paper confirmed that such a place existed, and that it sat above Bennettsville, running north, leading to towns that expressed different views on living—views that often condemned their southern life style, labeling it as antiquated and even barbaric, their anger seemed to rekindle, the barbarians were, of course, the people of Kettering—they had two of their animals in jail right now to prove it.

Lee Atkins, who hadn't been in town since the reading of Townsend's will—some six weeks now—stepped away from the desk, his eyes hard, and faced Jim, waving his hands in the air. "I saw it all," he said. "Them Yankees was cold as snakes. They had the money, but the tallest one of them just blowed Bob's face away. Guess my walking in on them and screaming the way I did put the fear of God in them." He rubbed his chin and stared at the floor for a long second. Suddenly, looking up, his eyes bright. "But we showed them dirty Yankees, didn't we? Imagine, trying to hide in the spillway. They musta thought they was in Texas and the spillway was a big outdoor bath tub." The men laughed, but Jim turned his back and stared out the window.

"Lee, give Shorty a full report on everything you saw," Jim said, pointing to the door, but never turning around. Lee nodded and walked slowly from the office; the men filed behind Lee in silence.

With the office empty and the silence disturbed only by the soft murmur of Lee's voice from the next room, Jim suddenly realized how tired he was. It had been three days now since Luther Dawson's death, and he hadn't slept a good four hours. And now, another killing. No doubt Judge Dalton would insist that this murder be given top priority. And that would put a halt to all ongoing cases—they were not equipped to handle such a load. He pushed away from the desk, walked to the window, and opened it with a hard yank. A rush of morning air brushed his face, filling his nostrils with the aroma of Sweet William. He looked out at the pavement, then paused and listened to the clicking of boots as the posse scrambled to their trucks. Walking back to the desk he looked down at the map and frowned. Rubbing his hair, he pulled at the clots of dirt embedded there and sighed. His desk was piled with papers, and an old box, the kind the cleaners used to pack shirts, sat off to the side. Reaching inside the box he fingered the objects that he had collected from cases he worked on. A gray rope, approximately two feet long, and a rusty piece of chicken wire that had been twisted into a V were objects left behind from Boswell's murder. Boswell had been found bound to a tree with the rope and the wire propped in his mouth. And a round metallic reflector, he had removed it from Luther Dawson's coveralls when he examined his body in the train station at Cairo—it gleamed, creating prisms of reds, yellows and greens in his hand. Just as it had gleamed that day when Luther snatched it from Sylvester Bodine's black hand. Dropping the reflector back into the box, he sighed—everything was a mess. Jim hated disorder, and there had been nothing but disorder ever since Roy's confession.

Jim sank heavily in the chair and pushed the box and papers to the side. He rested his head against the back of the chair. The whirl of events began to unravel. Roy had been charged, by his own confession, with breaking and entering a Negro woman's home with the intent to do bodily harm—even though Roy had stated he was "jest gonna scare her a bit." The confession was uncharacteristic of Roy, to say the least—usually Roy just made trouble and denied guilt of any kind. Jim didn't believe Roy to be capable of remorse, or even of having second thoughts, and he, like Charlie, suspected J.T.'s influence. J.T. would be the only person with enough power to persuade Roy to confess to anything. The idea that Roy had changed his mind when Katie screamed and roused the neighbors wasn't plausible, as Roy was notorious for his hate crimes. The only part of Roy's story that Jim believed was that Margaret had attacked Roy with an axe, but it was surely to protect her mother, and not as Roy implied, for no good reason at all.

The scraping of a chair against the floor in the next room brought Jim from his thoughts. He realized that Lee was leaving; and Jim sat up, stretched, and yawned just as Shorty walked into the room, dropping the report on Jim's desk.

"Going over to Rosie's. Want something?" Shorty asked, leaning on his good leg.

"Hell, I'm too sleepy to eat now, Shorty. Maybe later, "Jim replied. "You gonna be able to keep up with all these goings-on with that leg?"

"So far I feel okay. Just a bit stiff, but it don't pain much with them pills that Doc in Cairo gave me."

Jim nodded his head and Shorty limped from the room. Picking up the report, Jim flipped through it, then pushed it aside. He didn't want to read it just yet. He had heard everything: two white men from Kettering, Ohio, had broken into the gas station where they removed one hundred fifty-five dollars from the register; then, caught off guard by the elder Larkin walking in on them, shot and killed him. They were frightened off by Lee Atkins who stumbled upon them in the act and his loud screaming and they took off on foot running towards the back roads to the levee, where they were captured and brought to jail. What Jim wanted to do was petition Judge Dalton for a warrant for J.T.'s arrest for the murder of Boswell, but that could not happen now. He wondered if J.T. was somehow responsible for this Yankee intrusion. The strangers did seem to know how to get to the back roads—perhaps they even expected a boat to pick them up and were not as dumb as Adkins had said. But why kill old man Larkin? The land. That could be it. J.T. wanted that land for the new shoe factory. But if this were true, Roy would have to be in on it. That would certainly explain Roy's benevolent confession. However, Jim realized that if any of this were true, he would never be able to prove it. For once the Yankee's trial was over, the case would be closed. And the open hatred towards the northerners would prevent him from researching such a possibility of conspiracy between enemies for self-gain. He shook his head, dismissing thoughts of the Yankees. He concentrated again on Roy's confession. The only way Roy could be let out of jail would be to recant. And this, Jim was sure, would never happen. To recant would mean that Roy would have to deny that someone had cut off his arm. Was all the goings-on at Katie's a ruse to create a unchallengeable alibi for Roy? Perhaps it had nothing to do with the money at all?

The sun filled the room and streamed across the papers on Jim's desk, illuminating Shorty's childlike scrawl on the report. Jim flipped the pages again, and turned away, facing the window. He stared out across the lawn and, suddenly feeling drowsy, rubbed his eyes. But his thoughts would not let him rest, and he wondered why, after three years, when he finally had a witness, Rosie, to implicate J.T. in the murder of Boswell, would Yankees suddenly rob this place, of all places? He could see no further than J.T. Now, the things he had intended to do would have to be put aside until… He had intended to talk to Katie regarding Margaret's whereabouts; he had intended to recheck the procedure for grounds to terminate Samuels. But now he would have to talk to Lloyd about autopsy findings on old man Larkin, and he would have to rely on Samuels' experience to erect a roadblock to keep back the many spectators who would come to see the Yankees. He would have to talk to Judge Dalton, and Dalton, he was sure, would insist that he contact the Turner Brothers about lumber, plenty of lumber, for a scaffold, because as much as Jim detested Samuels' crudeness, he knew Samuels was right—the Yankees, running or not, would never see Kettering again. They would be hanged, and soon, probably within the next two weeks.

He gazed down at the calendar on his desk and swore. The scribbled note, "Meet Katie at bank" glared at him and he realized it was the day Katie was to receive the money from Townsend's will. He had to be present. He pushed up from the chair, and walked quickly to Shorty's office. He spoke to Shorty's back, "Git Ludie Mae on the phone. Tell her to git in here now! And wake me round ten-thirty." Shorty grunted over the ham-butt sandwich, and Jim returned to his office, closing the door softly behind him.

Tom Nolan, president of Bennettsville's bank, and executor of Harrison Townsend's estate, sat with his back to the window, his balding head gleaming under the stream of sunlight from the bay windows, his face red and sweaty. Across from him, Katie sat nervously twisting the straps of her purse and occasionally peeking at his face. The last fifteen minutes Katie had looked about the small office, pretending to be comfortable. She had stared out the window that looked down on Main Street and she had counted the eleven scratches, over and over, in the huge oak desk facing her. She had known Nolan most of her adult life, but had only done business with him on one other occasion—the time she borrowed money against her life insurance policy to buy Margaret's uniform and shoes for the track meet. He sat toying with his pipe, tapping it against the desk.

Jim arrived at Nolan's upstairs office at twelve-thirty—he had overslept. His eyes were red and swollen, and his gait was slow. Katie looked up and sighed with relief, and Nolan, just as relieved, laid the pipe on the desk quietly.

"Sorry I'm late; but I guess y'all heard about all the trouble," Jim said, walking over to the chair opposite Katie. He sat down.

"Everyone in town knows about them Yankees," Nolan replied and pressed a handkerchief to his forehead. Wiping his face with one swipe, he sighed, then let the handkerchief drop to the desk.

Katie nodded in Jim's direction and shifted in the chair. She looked across the desk and stared out the window behind him at the "Shoe Repair" sign across the street.

"How do, Katie?" Jim said, removing his hat and placing it on his knee.

"I'se fine, Mr. Jim, thank you," she said, facing him briefly, then turning her gaze back to the window. She had not seen him since the heated interview at her home regarding the bonfire. But she knew that he was still interested in anything she could tell him, especially Margaret's whereabouts. She wanted to get the money and get out of there fast, before Jim could ask any questions.

"Well," Nolan said, interrupting her thoughts. He wiped his face again. "My God it's hot! Seems like I'm going to melt right here on the spot." He smiled weakly and spread some papers across his desk.

"Now that everyone is here, let's get to the business at hand. Katie, do you understand why you're here?"

She looked up slowly and met his gaze. "At the reading of Mr. Townsend's will, Mr. Atkins said my daughter and I had been left some money," she replied and lowered her eyes.

"Why yes, that's true. But make no mistakes here, Katie. The money is yours. Harrison had an uncanny sense of people's character—he read them well. The will was correct as Atkins read it. There is only one exception. Jim and Katie looked at each other briefly, then back at Nolan.

"You, Katie," Nolan continued, and pointing a stubby finger across the desk, "can use the money in any way you want. It doesn't have to be used for your daughter's education. The decision is yours." He shouldered back in the chair, stuck the unlit pipe in his mouth, and drew upon it until his jaws almost touched. He removed the pipe and placed it by the file, then leaned forward in the chair. "We can set up an account here at the bank where you can draw upon it, or we can write you a check for the amount and you can deposit it someplace else—the latter will probably be the wisest, since J.T. has made his displeasure with this gift known."

Katie fumbled with the purse straps, then cleared her throat. "Ain't never cashed no check in my life, and don't aims to start. I aims to take all the money in cash, and that will do away with any problems from J.T." She leaned forward, managing a weak smile.

Nolan's mouth fell open. Jim snapped around to face Katie, his eyes big and questioning.

"You trying to tell me you wants all fifteen thousand dollars in cash?" Nolan said after regaining his breath.

"Ain't trying to say nothing, Mr. Nolan. You jest said I could spend the money any way I wants, so I reckon that means you is got to give it to me before I can spend it, and I wants cash!"

"Jim," Nolan said, pleading with Jim for intervention. "See if you can talk some sense into her—having all that money laying around. She's asking for trouble. Damn these people…" Nolan muttered under his breath.

They were quiet. Jim watched Katie with concerned eyes. But he knew from the angle of her chin, raised and trembling, that she had made up her mind and that neither Nolan nor he could change it. He pushed up from the chair and approached the desk. "Get the money, Tom. I've got a murder on my hands, this bickering is holding me up."

Immediately, Nolan came from around the desk and disappeared behind a side door leading downstairs to the main safe. Katie fumbled with the purse straps and stared out the window.

"I think he's got a point, Katie. It ain't wise having that kind of money on hand," Jim said as soon as Nolan was out of hearing range.

She did not answer; she turned her head toward the window where the sunlight blazed. It was getting up in the afternoon. Jim rubbed his chin, feeling the coarse stubble that was missed in his hasty shave. Walking to the window, he looked down on the street at the people coming and going. "Where's Margaret," he asked without turning around. She stared at his back—his broad and muscular shoulders sagged from fatigue—and suddenly felt compassion. It was a job that carried tremendous pressures and responsibilities—keeping law and order in Bennettsville. But remembering their last meeting, Katie knew she had to stay on her guard and that she would have to bury her emotions deep inside of her. And so she did what she had seen Charlie do many times when talking with white folk, she responded with a confusing question. "Where's Luther?" she said in a matter of fact tone. He spun around to face her, his face a mask of confusion.

"Luther is dead! Are you telling me that Margaret is dead?"

She was silent, letting his words hang in the air, and letting him agonize over the possibility. Finally, she spoke in that same slow tone, "I reckon she is. The Margaret I knowed for eighteen years don't exist no more. And I don't see her nowhere 'round my house, nowhere 'round my yard or my church. I reckon she is, in a sense, jest as dead as Luther." She heard his sigh of relief—a long, drawn-out gust of air. His relief angered her. Perhaps it was because he did not understand how she felt about her daughter's absence. He was relieved because Margaret wasn't physically dead, but didn't seem to note that Margaret's absence placed a cold hand against Katie's heart, a hand as cold as death. Perhaps it was because he had chosen to be a good boy and had obeyed his mother, severing their friendship because of her color, or because he had preferred to be a lawman, closing the door to any relationship between them. And, now, she wondered if Pappy had done the same to Mammie—closed a door between them by clinging to that part of him, his whiteness and that world that whites lived in. She dropped her head.

He was clearly angry, his face a deathly white, his eyes as black as the night. He walked from behind the desk and stood over her, glaring. The air was thick with something that emitted from their bodies—something that made his face suddenly strain red, and made hers pale. "Don't push me, Katie. I'll subpoena you like anyone else what stands in the way of the law. I heard she made the train the same night that Luther was killed."

She cut her eyes up at him. "You ain't gots to subpoena me. Don't you makes deals with colored women?" She watched as he raked his fingers through his hair, then shook his head in disbelief. She became bolder. "Oh," she said, twisting in the chair. "I knows 'bout the deal you made with Miss Rosie—practically everybody in town knows it, too. But what don't nobody know, but me and the Lord up above, is that I was on the levee road the day Boswell was killed. And I saw what happened to him. Now, if I was to tell you who it was what killed him, will you fix it so Margaret can come home?"

The downstairs door opened and Nolan plodded up the stairs carrying a small cardboard box advertising Phillips Fertilizer. Dropping the box on the edge of the desk, he looked to Jim, waved an arm towards the desk, and Jim, realizing he had no choice, reluctantly broke his gaze away from Katie and, crossing the floor picked up a handful of money that had been sorted and secured with thick rubber bands.

The sound of crisp paper flapped and the thumping of thumbs hitting against the oak desk filled the room. Periodically, Nolan would call out, "One hundred," and Jim would reply, "Check." Finally, after what seemed like hours to Katie, Jim walked away from the desk and nodded in her direction. Knowing that Jim was satisfied with the count, Katie rose from the chair and hurried to the box on the desk. Removing the scarf from her neck, she placed it over the box, tucking it neatly inside. She took the pen from Nolan's hand, scribbled her name on the paper, and, hefting the box against her hip, breezed out the door, leaving Jim stooped over the desk signing as a witness to the same paper.

By the time Jim reached the street, Katie had climbed into M.B.'s truck and it was moving slowly down Main Street. He stood at the curb frowning. He realized that he would have to subpoena Katie to get any information, for since their last talk, Katie had changed. Suddenly, he saw her as a child standing before him with three red ribbons in her hair and with much conviction, saying, "I will do as I please, thank you, Jim Davis." He knew that she was more like that girl than she had been for a long time—she was not afraid. He turned and crossed the street to his truck.

Twenty minutes later, Katie stepped sideways through Charlie's kitchen door—her temporary residence for three days now. Walking into the sunlit bedroom, she dropped the box of money on the foot of the bed. Charlie, who had been sitting with his head propped on three pillows, pretending to be sleeping, was suddenly sitting up and staring curiously at the box. Slowly, he pulled the box toward him and removed the scarf. He smiled. "Yes sir, best looking fertilizer I ever seed," he said.

"Best not git yourself all excited, Charlie," Katie said from the threshold. "You knows your head is still hurting."

"I feels fine," he declared, rubbing his hands together.

"You is lying, Charlie," she replied sharply, dropping her purse to the bed stand.

He cut his eyes at her curiously. He couldn't remember if he had ever heard Katie call anyone a liar. "No ma'am, I ain't lying. I feels fine," he lied.

"You tossed all night long in your sleep. You think I didn't hear you moaning and calling out for Luther to 'stop.' You think I didn't git up and look in on you? So stop your lying, Charlie, 'cause M.B. done tole me what went on up yonder in Cairo and my heart is very, very heavy." He stared at her, then casually looked back at the box on the bed. "M.B. ain't had time to tell you much. It ain't but a ten minute drive to town." She did not answer. They were interrupted by a hard rap on the kitchen door. Katie picked up the scarf, covered the box, and walked from the room to the back door.

"Hi do, Sister Katie," Helen Washington said, peeking through the mesh on the screen. Her black face glistening. "Daddy sent me to tell you yo' brother done called from Chicago. Said something 'bout the lines been down on account of they had a big storm up yonder.

Couldn't call 'fore now. Said Margaret made it jest fine!" she beamed. Katie stared at Helen, her thoughts still on Charlie and M.B's short version of how Luther died. Suddenly what Helen was saying registered—Margaret had made it safely to Chicago. She dropped to her knees and cried out, "Thank you Jesus!" Then there on her knees in the door way, she bawled. And Charlie let out a long sigh of relief.

SMART NIGGERS

Charlie cried too; but secretly, in the dead of night. Propped against the cushions in the rocker—the loaded shotgun at his side—he had cried for them all. He had cried for Luther, Margaret, Katie, and even Anna Mae. He took pains to make sure that Katie did not hear him this time. He had let the scorching tears flow freely down his face, but he had commanded his body to sit rigid and dared it to heave. Like an old Mama cat, he had sat guard over the money that night, rising early to catch J.D. Hampton, who lived three houses down the road, before Travis picked up the field hands. Charlie needed to see M.B. And once M.B. arrived, they had talked, and together decided that the money should be shipped by train to Chicago, and that the only person who could get through the barricades without incident would be Tom Lofton, the hoodoo man.

And for the sum of fifty dollars, Lofton had agreed to deliver the trunk to the train station in Cairo. Lofton and his woman, Rubelle, and the girl with no name, had rode through the mob of people and through the police blockades with ease. He had placed the trunk on the train after insuring it for the usual twenty dollars as Charlie had requested. It was common practice among Negroes and poor whites to ship clothing, tokens of love, and sometimes even food to relatives. But this trunk contained ten thousand dollars packed in a false bottom with heavy clothes on top, and two lace handkerchiefs that had belonged to Katie's mother. Charlie and M.B. had secured the trunk with a heavy lock; one that Robert would have to break himself, assuring them that no tampering had occurred enroute. Charlie trusted Lofton, for Lofton had always been a man of his word. If he said he would do a thing, he would, of course, do it. If he said a thing would be done, it was!

The shadows of night had fallen. Katie had gone to prayer meeting—she had been doing a "heap more praying" than usual Charlie thought. The moon had risen above the trees and the cicadas filled the night with their resonating songs. Sitting in the rocker by the kitchen table, Charlie unloaded the shotgun, and had rocked back in the chair when Tom Lofton raked his long fingernails across the screen door. The scraping sound, like music made with a wood saw, did not frighten Charlie. He recognized the signal and knew it was Tom. Charlie had observed Lofton closely during the two times they had met, and had concluded that what made Lofton different from others was that he refused to live within boundaries and this, along with his physical appearance, is what made people fear him—he was free. In Charlie's eyes most people accepted whatever they could get, never daring to take what they deserved. Only the unholy took all. And although Lofton took, he asked first. He asked that you make the decision to accept his assistance, not at all the usual taker. Takers were people who forced their ideals upon others, disregarding all who differed from them. Takers were those who conquered, something Lofton could easily do—he wondered how Lofton became a true human being. He thought of Katie and believed that she was beginning to see above the bounds of her religion, or perhaps from deep within it, but seeing still the same—that laws, and bylaws only worked for takers.

Charlie looked across to Lofton's shadow outside the door. Its huge frame blackened the threshold door where the moon light behind it seemed to be riding its back. A devil, some called him, but Charlie did not believe that now. At least not in the way the people meant. If Lofton could be labeled, then Charlie would say he was another Willie Dee. Willie Dee was a man from Charlie's past who also seemed unaffected by the drudgery of living. Charlie smiled, he hadn't thought of Willie Dee for ages. Like Lofton, Negroes and whites paid Willie Dee handsomely for services. This man was certainly no devil, and neither was Lofton—they had something powerful, something that made them resist the norms and this made other men tremble in awe.

"Come on in, Tom. Been 'specting you," Charlie said, leaning forward in the chair and watching the shadow looming in the doorway.

Lofton stepped into the kitchen, looking about the room until his eyes found Charlie's shadow. "Why you sitting in the dark?" Tom asked, the melodic voice filling the small room. He removed his hat and holding it in his hand stood with his back to the door.

"Light the lamp on the table, please," Charlie asked, his voice weak like that of an ailing man. "Matches right there." He pointed to the lamp, and leaned back in the rocker, resting his head.

The shadow of Tom stretched across the kitchen floor like the bogey man riding the moonlight that strained against the mesh of the screen door. He walked to the table, dropped his hat, struck the match, and ignited the wick of the lamp. Immediately a yellow circle of light danced on the ceiling and soon Lofton could see Charlie's face. They looked at each other for a second, as though each was waiting for the other to speak. Charlie nodded toward the chair by the table and Lofton return his nod and straddled the chair, gripping its back with his hands and the chair creaked under his weight.

"Everythang go all right?" Charlie asked.

"Fine, jest fine. It was, to my surprise, a nice ride," Lofton added, pressing his chest against the chair. "Everything all right here?" Lofton asked.

"Oh," Charlie said, removing five crisp ten-dollar bills from his shirt pocket and passing them over to Lofton.

"This was the easiest money I've made in a long time," Lofton said, rubbing the bills with his long fingers, then jamming them into his shirt pocket. "Making potions and laying spells ain't as easy as folks think." He folded his arms on the back of the chair and leaned forward.

"I reckon it's so if'n you says it," Charlie said, dropping his head. The lamp oil gave off a pungent odor of coal oil and tar that permeated the room. He looked up at Lofton, parted his lips, and hesitated.

"Something you wanting to ask, Charlie?" Tom said, his voice soft, encouraging.

There was something different about Lofton, Charlie noticed. It was as though the night brought out another side of the man—a non-threatening, almost pleasant side. Or they had formed the bond Charlie had felt at Lofton's on his first visit. "Anythang intresting happen?"

Tom nodded his head, smiled—the gold barely visible in the lamplight. "Same as always. Them police took one look at the three of us and flung them saw horses aside to let us through.

"Ha," Charlie laughed. "Didn't have no trouble then."

"None," Lofton added. "They treats me just like I was President Roosevelt or poison."

"You jest smarter than they is and they knows it," Charlie said, leaning forward.

Lofton acknowledged the compliment with a slight nod of his head then, continued. "We went straight on to Cairo. Only had to stop twice. Police is all over town and the highway is filled with them clear up to Huntsville. Oh," he stopped and pulled a wrinkled receipt from his pocket. "Your receipt for the trunk. Insured it like you wanted." He passed the paper over to Charlie who laid it on the table.

"I ain't seen that many white folks since... Well, let's just say it's a scary thing to see, even to me. Although can't none of them individually kill me, a bunch of them can do me great harm."

Charlie's eyebrows shot up in surprise. He was stunned to hear that Lofton was vulnerable to anyone. "Any news on when they aims to hang them white mens up yonder in the Big House? They done practically finished that scaffold, and I hear tell the trial is gonna be quick. Something 'bout prisoners rights to a speedy trial," Charlie said.

"Trial my foot. That's the same as saying Doc Smith got a chance of living after my spell been laid—Smith will be dead in a month, and them Yankees will be dead in a week or so. Only smart-mouthed niggers and Yankees get lynched that fast."

Charlie chilled at the mention of Smith's death. He stared into Lofton's hollow eyes, and suddenly remembered the extent of this man's power. But there in the soft lamp light, he seemed human, even warm. He wondered if Lofton had ever been different, and if he needed Rubelle the same way other men needed women.

"Smart-mouth niggers and Yankees are a threat to everybody," Charlie heard Lofton saying. "They both are always talking about what they can do, or what others should do. But men who understand other men, like you and I Charlie, usually live very long lives."

"Reckon you is right. I knows my life will start up agin once Smith is dead."

"Perhaps then we'll do more business of some nature. It has been a long time since I found another man's conversation enlightening."

"Perhaps," Charlie chuckled, warming to the compliment. "You know you'se reminds me of another fellow I usta be 'quainted with."

"How so?" Tom asked, a curious look on his face.

"There was another man I knowed when I was young—he was one smart nigger. Not a smart-mouth one. He knew the white folks' ways. You reminds me a lot of him. But he wern't from around these parts. He was from Alabama, and for all I knows jest might still be there somewhere."

Lofton rested his chin on the curve of the chair and closed his eyes. "Tell me about him," he said softly, but to Charlie it seemed more of a command.

"Well," Charlie said, straightening his shoulders and swallowing hard, "Like I said, we was in Alabama. This here fellow's name was Willie Dee Macon. We all stayed on this farm; it was several Negro families along with me and my first wife. We hired out to work cotton, beans and the like—jest common folk trying to make do. But not Willie Dee. Weren't nothing common 'bout him. Oh, he worked jest as hard as us, but he was different; he was talked about all over the county. Some said he was the smartest nigger alive."

"What made him so smart?" Lofton asked in a easy voice, never opening his eyes.

"Some say," Charlie said, and cleared his throat, "some said it was 'cause he was born with a veil. What does that really mean?" He gazed over at Lofton. "I seed something once; a woman's child had it over her face. It was a thin piece of flesh. That was years before the winter of the turn of the century. But what does it really mean?" he repeated.

"Means more than I could explain in a few seconds, Charlie. Much more. Go on with the story."

"Well, anyhows, Willie Dee sho knowed white folks. He could tell the time of day a white person was gonna step foot in the cove—that was the shaded area where we would rest a spell 'fore we'd go back to the field. He told one of the white bosses when his wife was gonna die, and he told the Negroes 'bout a albino horse that the same white boss was gonna buy, even before the boss man laid eyes on this horse."

"Yes," Lofton mumbled. "I know this power well. It is most prominent in New Orleans, however."

"I'se sure you knows more 'bout this power than me. All I ever know was what I'd seed him do.

"What did you see him do? Lofton asked.

Well, the main boss what owned all the land and his bunch decided they was fed up with folks claiming Willie Dee was so much and put him to the test. He told Willie Dee to prove once and for all if he could read minds and they demanded a demonstration of his powers, and guaranteed him that if he couldn't do what folks said they was gonna slick him down with honey, then hang him under the 'simmon tree, and let the possums suck his bones dry. They gave him three things to do, the first was to tell them what they had put in a krocker sack, what it cost, and where they got it. The white bosses took off on their horses so fast, a trail of red dust was all you could see. They was to meet back at the cove straight up noon, and Willie Dee better tell them the three things they wanted to know.

"Now all the Negroes was worried 'bout Willie Dee, 'cause don't nobody relish the thought of being sucked to death by possums. Even though they knew Willie Dee was usually able to read minds, they still worried. So they all was saying to him 'Git Missy Daisy to make you a potion to look in the future, can't hurt none.' But Willie Dee jest shook his head, laughed and said,

'Don't need no potions
Don't need no spells
No crystal ball
'cause I'se got the veil.'

Lofton smiled.

"Well," Charlie continued. "Everybody went back to work but Willie Dee. He went up to the mountain like he always done when he wanted to see into the future. Come noon, everybody saw this cloud of red dust swirling towards the cove. It was the white bosses returning from town. So we dropped everythang and come running.

Well, Willie Dee come down from the mountain jest as cool and calm, not a drop of sweat on him nowhere. He sat down on the ground, crossing his legs Indian fashion, and didn't say nothing to nobody. 'Well, nigger,' one boss man said, walking over to Willie Dee. 'What's in the sack?' Willie Dee jest waved his hands over his head, the same way Missy Daisy done when she was making spells and said, 'Corn, taters and blue hulls. You gots them from old Sly's garden, and all it cost you was them torn breeches and a hard ride from buckshot.'"

Charlie looked up at Lofton whose position hadn't changed. "Go on with the story, Charlie, or I'm gonna git ahead of you," Lofton said and placed his hands over his forehead. Charlie, seeing that Lofton was listening, but sensing that Lofton was somehow tapping into his memory like before, proceeded slowly.

"Well, sho enough, one of the white bosses' pants was tore, and they horses was still in a sweat. And when the krocker sack was opened, there was corn, taters, and blue hulls jest like Willie Dee had said. The Negroes cried out, 'Lord, Lord, Willie Dee done it agin,' and they started clapping their hands and dancing round in a circle. But them white bosses put a stop to that right quick. The big boss walked up real close to Willie Dee's face and said, 'I'm gonna kill me ten niggers come tomorrow, if you can't tell us what it is that we bring in the buckboard.' And they was off, kicking up that dust agin.

"Now, I had to ask him, 'cause I could be one of the people what gits kilt. 'Willie Dee,' I says. 'How come you to know what was in the sack?' And he jest smiled that great big smile of his and said, 'seed the knick in that horse's ear. Knowed old Sly is the only farm round these parts what uses buckshot that size; and that's all he ever crops is corn, taters, and blue hulls.' 'But what about tomorrow?" I asked. 'Ain't you worried, ain't you gonna need help?' He jest smiled and said,

'Don't need no potions
Don't need no spells
No crystal ball
'cause I'se gots the veil.'

"Well, they done that kind of thing for two days straight, and every time Willie Dee knowed what they asked. But on the third day, they promised they was gonna kill everyone if he didn't know, and if'n he did they was to declare him a fortune teller.

"Well, come the next day nobody could hardly work, being so tensed and all. And Willie Dee went up to the mountain and didn't come down until the swirl of dust was seen. Now, I looked over and I could see that Willie Dee wasn't his usual calm self. He was all in a sweat, like he'd been running or was scared of something. And I gots to tell you, this time I was scared clean down to my bones. But he jest sat on the ground and waited. The three white bosses got down from their horses and laid the cotton sack on the ground—a twelve footer—and it was packed from end to end. Grinning like an old pole-cat what done pissed in the gravy boat, the boss man says, 'Well, nigger, what's in the sack?' Willie Dee's eyes roamed all over that sack before he waved his hands in the air and says, "Gideon Bibles; black pitch and duck feathers; one hunnerd feet lynching rope; short handle hatchet; and three-year-old Mulberry Wine. The Bibles comes from Reverend Beedle; pitch and rope from Garvey's; feathers from farmer Reed; hatchet from the woodshed out yonder; and the Mulberry from John Tuck's stock. Whole thing comes to three dollars —a dollar a gallon for the wine. After y'all tared and feathered us, you aimed to hang us till we was dead, cut us down and read the Psalms over us, then drink the wine to celebrate your victory.'

"Them white bosses was outdone, turned red as the dust on the ground, but kept their word and declared Willie Dee a fortune teller. And they was off, kicking up that dust agin.

"Now, I had to know how it was Willie Dee come to know what was in the sack," Charlie said, scratching his chin, and leaning towards Lofton. His eyes squinted. Lofton nodded his head and Charlie continued. "But as I started over to him, he got up from the ground in a rush and headed towards the mountain. I was puzzled, 'cause usually after one of his tellings, he would head for his old cabin to rest. Naturally, I followed him, keeping my distance, of course. But I jest had to see what he was up to. Well, inside the mountain was a cave that led clear through to the other side and into town. That cave was filled with horse tracks leading in and out, and Willie Dee was standing with his back to me cussin that albino horse for running off and leaving him. Then Willie Dee suddenly stops cussin and goes to whispering something in that horse's ear. I crouched behind a rock till I was sure Willie Dee didn't sense my presence. Then I looked around that cave and saw a pair of old ladies shoes, they was black with the high instep. A long black dress laid on a bench and on the floor near by was a long heavy black veil—the kind what widows wear."

Charlie slapped his knee and laughed so hard his body shook. Lofton dropped his hands from his face and stared at Charlie. Then in a very soft voice asked, "Do you know why you are laughing, Charlie?"

Charlie sat up straight with a frown on his face and pondered the question for a second. "I reckon I'se laughing 'cause I found out that Willie Dee didn't have no more power than them crackers, but he fooled them into declaring him a fortune teller. I reckon that's it."

"But don't you see, Charlie? This Willie Dee did have the power." Lofton waved a long finger in Charlie's direction. "He had the ability to take physical evidence and draw a conclusion that saved his life and yours. He had the ability to read what was in a man's heart and not what was in his face. He had the gift to communicate with other species—the albino horse. And he had enough smarts about himself to seek out the information he needed to be accurate to the degree of shocking his enemy. Oh, he had the power all right!" Lofton declared, and stood, pushing the chair to the table. He waved his arm as though he were offering Charlie a seat. "Power," Lofton continued, "is knowing what you're up against and not letting on that you know. Feats that seem impossible can easily be accomplished, especially if mystery surrounds the person who must perform them."

"Like you?" Charlie dare, ask.

"Yes, in a way, like me," Lofton replied, his eyes bold, but not hard. "What men do not know is astounding—even educated men with many degrees. It does not take a lot of fuss to accomplish great things. But first one must be sure of what it is he wants. Then he must set out after it, not in a rage, but with the coolness and calmness one goes to his porch to relax in the swing. It should never be the fluster and bluster that accompanies work, but always with the ease of relaxation. This attitude alone creates the mystery—your enemy can not read your action, therefore he can't read your thoughts. He sees instead, the quietude as acceptance and is satisfied that you are what he thinks you to be.

"It is no doubt that Willie Dee had the power—the veil over his face at birth confirms it. As you said, a veil is simply a thin piece of flesh—that is what the naked eye sees. But a veil is not just flesh; it is your mother's flesh, your father's flesh and their mothers and father's flesh. It is timeless generations of cells that have united and now lay upon the infant's face like an interceptor what picks and chooses only the most powerful, the most God-like cells to nurture the babe. A interceptor that absorbs nutrients, characteristics, culture, and blood of blood, then fills that child with remarkable abilities. Among them is an automatic understanding that the usual approach to life only rivets men to the ground, rendering them alike, dull, awkward, and predictable—the latter being the killer of all men. To have power over other men, one must be unlike them in many ways. Remember that, Charlie, you must challenge the enemy with the unexpected."

Lofton removed the hat from the table, patted his shirt front where the money bulged, then smiled. "It has been most pleasurable doing business with you, Charlie. I know that we will be seeing each other again. There is yet something I must do for you." He turned and eased out the screen door, the moonlight splashing across the floor. And Charlie suddenly feeling stronger, knew that Lofton was right.

SHADOW OF THE VALLEY OF DEATH

Sunday mornings in Bennettsville were usually quiet and lazy days. But the town was still buzzing; there hadn't been so many going-ons since the quake of 1811 when the river swallowed parts of Bennettsville and flooded the nearby counties. The townsfolk were preoccupied with death. The whites strived to execute the two Yankees in a timely fashion, and the Negroes were pressed to get Luther buried.

White men armed with rifles stalked the mouth of the spillway. Negro men stalked the mouth of the graveled drive-way to Robbins' Funeral Parlor, waiting to claim Luther's body. White men sped back and forth across town in trucks, hauling freshly cut lumber. Negro men sped back and forth across town in trucks, hauling fried chicken, baked hams, and boiled sweetmeats for the repast. White men braved the glaring, hot sun for hours, sawing, planing, and hammering the lumber into a crude scaffold behind the jail. Negro men plowed hot fields, wearing two sets of clothing—coveralls over Sunday-go-meeting suits. The Yankees clutched Bibles, seeking solace from white, uncaring ministers who gathered facts from police records. Negro ministers clutched Bibles, selected scriptures, and gathered facts about the deceased. White police officers called neighboring towns for additional police assistance. Some Negro men dropped pistols in coat pockets, others sprinkled goober-dust in the air, damning the white man's soul. White funeral directors ordered graves to be opened, and Negroes grave diggers opened them—one for Luther, two for the Yankees from Ohio. White women juggled babies on their hips, carried water and hot meals to their men, and watched with passion. Negro women pressed shirts, hot-combed hair, gathered their best white hankies, juggled babies on their hips, baked pies, cakes, creamed vegetables, and made Viola Dawson a dress to wear to her son's funeral. White children, armed with BB guns, rolled about in the mud, shooting imaginary robbers, shot marbles on the levee bank, and held spitting contests. Negro children spit-shined shoes, curried horses, polished chrome bumpers, stacked hay, gathered eggs, kicked frogs, and chunked rocks at fat chickens. And Viola Dawson sat staring out the window.

She was a thin woman with bony arms, razor-sharp elbows, and legs that resembled pressed kindling wood. She could spit chew four feet in any given direction, and walk ten miles without so much as a grunt. She was fifty-eight years old with wooley-gray hair and eyes as black as soot. If Viola had lived during slavery time, her master would have undoubtedly categorized her as a "field nigger." She dressed in men's clothing—long pants, heavy jackets, and two-tone shoes with no laces. But today she wore a handmade sack dress of Indian head material that the Sisters of the Sanctified Church had hastily sewn from a crude pattern.

The borrowed, stiff, black hat shadowed Viola's face, and veiled it in a mask of grief. She sat in the rickety chair in the front of her three-room shack, staring out the window, her shoulders hunched, her hands clasping the chair arms as if she were about to rise but couldn't make up her mind. Flanked by Katie, Mother Washington, and Almeda, the rattle of their crisp, white dresses a constant reminder of why they were there, she stared with mean eyes at the weeds that bordered the gate to her front yard. She had sat that way, off and on, ever since her talk with Charlie the night her son, Luther, was killed. All morning the bell had tolled—ten minutes of non-stop ringing, followed by a twenty minute silence. During these intervals, the jarring quiet was silenced by the hammering and buzzing of saws in the distance—a lulling sound of men working, and Viola would listen quietly to the building of the scaffold. But once the tolling of the bell began again, she would cringe and press her hands to her ears.

At ten forty-five precisely, the sleek, black limousine rolled to a halt in front of the shack. Two pasty-faced white men approached the door, knocked, and soon escorted Viola to the waiting car. Katie, Mother Washington, and Almeda followed them, but joined the other people who had gathered by the car, falling into lines of fours, creating a train of white uniforms, black suits and dresses and very sad faces. They were joined by others-who suddenly appeared out of no-where, or emerged from behind picket fences along the winding alley road. It was a humble and quiet procession that headed to the Freewill Baptist Church, and not the usual singing, glorifying God, in the highest procession.

They walked the few blocks to the church where a large crowd of people gathered outside and huddled in knots by the black shiny hearse. It was a sea of hats with feathers of all colors, bow ties, white hankies fluttering with every wave. The sun beating down on faces with eyes brimming with tears and with angry frowns. The limousine crept to a stop behind the hearse parked in front of the church door, and an usher immediately began leading people inside. The hearse door was opened, displaying the cherry wood casket, and someone yelled, "Oh, Lord, Lord, Lord!"

The Freewill Baptist Church was built by free black men and slaves, and sat on the corner that marked the beginning of the new addition called "New Town" like a black God. An ebony richness enveloped it from its pointed steeple to its hand-carved doors. The walls inside were a pale gray, and a singular cross of plain wood hung above the pulpit. A wide center aisle separated the pews and led up to the altar just below the pulpit. Behind the pulpit sat a beat-up piano on a raised platform enclosed by a wooden banister that separated the choir from the row of chairs for the ministers.

The people stood by their seats facing the door, watching for the casket. Suddenly, the casket appeared at the mouth of the aisle, the family trailing behind—Viola, her daughters, Judy Rose and Zara Lee, and little David. The choir, as though suddenly stung by the same bee, sprang to its feet, leading the congregation in the traditional hymn:

If I walk in the path of duty
If I work till the close of the day
I shall see God and His bright beauty
When I've gone the last mile of the way.

When I've gone the last mile of the way
I shall rest at the close of the day
For I know that my love ones will be waiting
When I've gone the last mile of the way.

The men rolled the casket down the aisle. The family was seated while the attendants busied themselves preparing the body for viewing. Then two muscular ladies in starched white uniforms folded Viola like she was stiff cardboard into the middle of the front pew next to her youngest son. Katie and the Saints occupied the fourth row behind the family on the left, while Charlie, M.B., and most of the men, sat on the right. The atmosphere was thick, pressing down heavily on the congregation. Stifling scents of Mavis Talc, cheap perfume, Royal Crown Hair Dressing, and ammonia floated through the church, slowly removing the air. The entire Negro community had turned out for the funeral: Mamie, the town whore; Vernell Boswell, whom folks had deemed crazy as a loon before she was twelve; Sylvester Bodine, the despised Uncle Tom; and even Tom Lofton's family, Rubelle and the girl with no name sat in the back.

The large church was packed—a sea of hats with large feathers and white scarves. There was a fixed and ceremonial atmosphere throughout the funeral, starting with the invocation and ending with prayers offered by the visiting ministers, Reverend Washington of the Sanctified Church and Reverend Hodges of the AME Methodist church. As the funeral progressed, many people fainted and a blur of white uniforms moved between the aisles helping them. A young woman lay slumped against the pew while the ushers slapped her wrists and snapped ammonia capsules under her nose. People cried out for Jesus to help them bear the strain, even Charlie had cried out Luther's name. Tears fell on shirt fronts as well as on dresses, while children wiped their noses with the sleeves of their coats. However, all of this was but a small measure compared to the final viewing of the remains. Viola reached across the casket and slapped Luther across his forehead and mumbled, "Done gone on and left me." And the family, Viola, her two daughters and little David collapsed in a heap on the floor—screaming.

At the end, stony-faced, eyes red, with hats pulled off, and ties untied, the people filed out behind the casket, heading to the cemetery. Once they reached the cemetery and were all situated, the atmosphere changed. Suddenly, everyone was livid with rage, for across from Luther's final resting place, two freshly dug graves gaped at them—graves that had been reserved for the two white murders. Even now they could hear the hammering, sawing, and buzzing, coming from uptown, two miles away, of the white folks tools as they hurried to erect the scaffold. Reverend Washington stepped forward, raising his arms in the air for silence, shook his head in dismay. In a voice filled with trepidation he jolted the congregation back to the reason they were there—to bury Luther. "Be on guard against the yeast of the Pharisees—I mean their hypocrisy. Whatever is covered up will be uncovered, and every secret will be made known. So then, whatever you have said in the dark will be heard in broad daylight, and whatever you have whispered in men's ears in a closed room will be shouted from the housetops." The scripture seemed to mesmerize everyone except Charlie, for suddenly Charlie snapped to attention and twisting his neck around, stared long and hard across the road at Tom Lofton who was suddenly there watching with great interest. Charlie's gaze found Lofton's and like a story unfolding before him, he again saw Lofton at his house on their last visit. He saw Lofton twisting in the chair explaining how power works. Lofton's words were like magic, explaining how power is created. An "aura of mystery" that Reverend Washington's scripture on covering and uncovering the truth had touch upon and shown him the way to tell the white authorities they could not disgrace the Negro community by burying scum in their cemetery. It was suddenly very clear to Charlie what had to be done. He would need Lofton's services once again. He would ask Lofton to defile the graves with—three-eyed coconut shells, snake skin and bat wings, a mixture guaranteed, so he had been told, to keep souls on the prowl. And if the white law broke the seals on the graves anyway, he and a few good men here today would dig the coffins up in the dead of the night, and roll them alongside the curb on Main Street. And if they re-buried them white murders in the Negro cemetery, they would dig them up again and again for as long as it took to make these upstanding white folks understand. He would select men like himself—meek in appearance, but downright stubborn. Men like M.B. and Brother Watson, Zack Porter, and sleepy-headed Cooper would be the backbone of the unit, while men like Reverend Washington, Reverend Taylor, and little David would be the eyes—they would keep up with the whereabouts of the law. And the men would become men—the men they should have been years ago. Crawling around on their bellies in the cemetery mud, exhuming, or extracting in this case, the filth from the upstanding Negroes' final resting place. He gazed back at Reverend Washington, who now was leading the congregation in the old song. "This little light of Mine. I'm gonna let it shine."

The song ended and Reverend Washington signaled for the grave-tenders to come forward to start filling in the grave. Viola screamed and twisted around to look at the coffin once more before the attendants from Robbins'escorted her and her family to the shiny limousine. The mourners crammed hats on their heads, blew their noses, dried tears from their faces, and scattered in different directions. Only Charlie, M.B., Reverend Taylor, and Reverend Washington remained at the grave-site—the custom was that someone should remain until the dirt had been packed into a mound. Katie stood across the road watching and waiting for Charlie. Finally, Charlie placed his hat on his head, turned, leaving the men, and limped across the road to where Katie stood. They looked at each other, then slowly began walking up the footpath by the Sanctified Church. It was almost noon, and the sun bore down on them as they ambled along in silence. The crunch of gravel under their feet was their only connection to the world. It told them that they were still alive, even though their bodies were drained and lifeless.

When they finally reached Charlie's door, Katie sighed with great relief. She removed the scarf from her head, jammed it in her purse, and stepped inside to the solace of the house. The air was as thick as it had been in the church, but the sun filtered through the curtains, basking the walls and furniture in warmth and softening the sternness of the room. She felt at peace; there was eternity in this room, she thought. Two old, bulky, handmade rocking chairs that had belonged to Charlie's parents, and one fragile, cushioned stool patterned with roses and lilies that had belonged to Anna Mae marked the generations. She had been too preoccupied earlier to notice the simplicity and sternness of the room, and the order in which the sparse furniture was arranged. The rockers sat at the back of the room near the windows, signifying sturdiness and wisdom, the stool sat in the center of the floor, signifying loneliness—the tender part of Charlie's life. Yes, she could see it all now, before she had been too distracted. She sighed again and spun around to see Charlie straightening up from the floor with a letter in his hand. From across the room, she could see the glaring special delivery stamp. "It's a letter for you, Katie; a letter from Margaret," Charlie said, his voice filled with surprise. Walking over to the rocker, he sat down, loosened his tie, and looked at the letter again. Katie dropped the purse to the table and took the rocker by Charlie. It was the first direct communication from Margaret. Although it seemed like ages to Katie, Margaret had only been gone for a week and three days. She took the letter from Charlie's shaking hands and hugged it to her chest. Then, cautiously, she held the envelope up to the sunlight, tore off the left corner, then the right corner and, carrying it to her mouth, blew until the envelope ballooned so she could withdraw the letter. Unfolding it, she read, "Dear Mama." Suddenly she felt alive—more alive than she had since Margaret's frantic departure. She read the words again, only softer: "Dear Mama." Looking up at Charlie, she smiled, and a tear slid down her cheek.

He swallowed hard. "Gone read the letter, don't be stopping on my account," he said, slipping the tie from his neck and tossing it on the table.

Katie nodded and continued. "It seems like years have past since I saw your face, although it been just a week. My only comfort is that in Uncle Robert I see something I recognize as you—his mannerisms or expressions. I hope you miss me as much as I miss you." Katie smiled. "Give my love to Mr. Charlie and Luther, also Mr. M.B." Katie's voice broke and Charlie grunted.

Katie let the letter drop to her lap, tears suddenly streaming down her face. She thought of Viola and her children suffering as she sat reading a letter from her daughter—the very person for whom Luther had given his life.

Squaring his shoulders, Charlie rested his head on the back of the chair and grunted again. They were silent for a while and finally Charlie said, "Best finish the letter so we can git some rest fo' we goes to the repast."

Katie wiped her face with her hand. "Mama, everything in Chicago is strange; so strange that I feel I'm on the outside of a window peeking in on other people's lives. It is an exciting, but unfriendly place, not at all like the south. I miss that the most; the friendliness of the people. The people up here are cold, they walk right past you and do not even speak, and if you speak to them, they look at you oddly. They refer to Chicago as 'the city with big shoulders.' Why I'm not sure, unless it's because there are so many different kinds of people spread throughout this massive place. But I was glad to see it—the ride was long and dirty.

"When I stepped off the train inside the Illinois Central Station, I was overwhelmed. Imagine a building large enough to house four trains at one time and still accommodate thousands of people. The trains stretched from end to end, belching and snorting like four-headed demons, while these men in dark blue uniforms with shiny gold buttons down the front and red caps on their heads, scurried about with bags and trunks of all sizes. These redcaps (as they call themselves) carry your bags to the waiting taxis outside, for a fee that is—they expect money from people. I told you it was strange here. People down home do that sort of thing just being neighborly.

"When the taxi pulled in front of Uncle Robert's home, I was stunned at the size of the building. It looked like a mansion that you see in magazines or like Mr. Townsend's house back home. But it's still not home. Mama, I want to start school this fall, just a month away, but I am stuck here in this strange place and time lays upon my hands like a heavy glove. Please send me the money to register for school as soon as possible. I need to feel like myself again—this place is distant and cold, even the nice people here, such as Uncle Robert, and Aunt Mindy have walls about them—they are warm and friendly, but aloof and brisk as well. The fall is upon us and I feel I must remind you that if I am to attend school, I must act fast. I would like to be away from here as soon as possible.

"I will close now, it's getting late. The street lamps have popped on and people will begin coming out and going places, not like home at all. So Mama, until we meet again, I will remember you in my prayers, and pray that you remember me too. Please write me soon and tell me everything that is going on with you and the folks back home.

Love, Margaret.

P.S. Tell Miss Viola and Zara Lee I said hi.

P.P.S. Uncle Robert said that we all benefit from the sweat and blood of others—it is our inheritance.

Katie folded the letter into a neat square and tucked it up the sleeve of her uniform. Charlie watched her closely; he knew that she would read it over and over before retiring. He also expected Katie to cry off and on all night—She had lost her child, the letter was evidence of that. Margaret had escaped physical and maybe even spiritual death, and now although she was free, had to surrender all that she held dear to exist in an alien land—one that separated her from everything she had known and loved.

THE SMELL OF OIL LAMPS

Two weeks had passed since Luther's funeral and the hanging of the two white men from Ohio; and all things postponed because of people's interest in seeing justice—this legal murder—were now being acted upon in the order of importance. A court day had been selected for Roy, Marmy, and Buddy. Charges had been dropped against Charlie, but not M.B. M.B. had been charged with assaulting a police officer and was to spend thirty days in jail. Katie had been subpoenaed to testify at the inquest—either to confirm or deny Roy's charges against Margaret. Margaret had been charged with the attempted murder of Roy, and Big Jim had petitioned Judge Dalton for a warrant to arrest J.T. for the murder of Boswell.

Katie dusted the flour from her hands, slid six apple pies into the oven at Rosie's, and turned to stare at the clock again. Her face was as pale as the flour on her hands, her eyes filled with concern. Staring at the numerous red dials on the huge oven, with her thumb pressed against her lips, she thought about Margaret and how if all this mess had only concerned Negroes, a decision would have been handed down by the judge the following day, not a month later. But when white folks involved Negroes in their wrongdoings, the law had always been as slow as cream rising on buttermilk. She had left the courthouse two hours ago—right after her testimony. Right after she swore before God that it was she who had cut off Roy's arm, and right after Hal Buck, the defense attorney for Roy, Marmy, and Buddy, leaned over the smooth conference table, popped his eyes, and ordered her down. White faces glowered at her from all directions—the bench, the tables, and the sections designated for spectators. After arguing among themselves, the Judge, Big Jim, Hal Buck and J.T.'s private attorney from St. Louis allowed her to return to work. It was more of a dismissal. Much like the time when Charlie had testified against the Halls on her pappy's behalf. The court had argued that Charlie couldn't have possibly seen anything from the distance of the trees, and so Charlie's testimony had been disregarded, characterized as nothing but loyalty to a white friend. Reluctantly, she left the courthouse and had made her way to the cafe where she immersed herself in work—the preparation of the noon dinner.

The noon whistle screeched: a familiar sound and yet today an intrusion. She turned automatically and looked out the window, facing the cotton gin where soon the workers would leave trailers and muddy fields and come piling through the doors of the cafe for dinner. And she would be expected to handle the orders as though it was a routine Monday, as though the possibility of her going to jail and Margaret being labeled a criminal wasn't affecting her. She told herself that she had put it all in the hands of God and would resign herself to the outcome; but silently she prayed that Margaret be allowed to come home and visit if she wanted, and that could only happen if Margaret's name was cleared.

Through the window, she saw Dick and Sam Johnston, two Negroes who worked at the cotton gin, cross Main Street, heading for the back. The Negro section would soon fill up, and she strained her neck up the road for a sign of Alice, who was, as usual, late. Katie turned away from the window and snatched the colander from the table. She wondered what was keeping them. She expected Charlie or Big Jim to come by and tell her the outcome of the inquest. She stooped over the sink, turned on the water, and stiffened at the sound of Miss Rosie's high-pitched voice drifting through the kitchen above the thump-thump of the jukebox up front. Rosie was back—that meant that the inquest was over. The low, muffled sound of a man's voice mingled with Rosie's, and Katie recognized it as Jim's. They just had to have believed her. How could they not when she was a pillar of the church. She whirled around to face the swinging door that separated her from the white section of the cafe, and fixed her eyes upon the space above the door, her body rigid. Every muscle in her screamed as though she was being pulled apart on a rack; and every nerve tingled sending hot flashes to the soles of her feet. There was something familiar about the slowness of Jim's walk—his footsteps dragging across the smooth tiles like something heavy weighed him down. And suddenly she remembered the time when, as a boy, Jim lost the sack race competition to Paul Rankin, the town's best athlete. When Jim walked away, his feet flapped the red dust until it mushroomed around his ankles. And she sensed that today echoed the same, that Jim had not only lost his case against Roy Larkin, but also against J.T.

She swallowed hard as Jim approached and folded his long arms over the top of the swinging door. She looked past his gaze, listening to the laughter fill the front room like bursts of cannon fire, ringing deeply and repeatedly as though timed for a festive occasion. It was obvious; the court had freed Rosie's son of all charges. And obviously from the way Jim's dark eyes flitted across the kitchen, never quite focusing on Katie's, the court had found Margaret guilty. Margaret would never be allowed to return home without facing the prospect of going to jail—there would be no more chats around the kitchen table, and everything that was to be between Katie and her daughter would be done in secret and in unfamiliar surroundings. She snatched her face away from his—there was nothing he could say that didn't show in his face—and walking back to the counter, picked up the large knife and sliced the head of cabbage as though it was someone she personally disliked. J.T. had won, after all. Margaret had gotten the money, but had been deprived of her roots.

The music and chatter from up front grew louder as Jim pushed inside the kitchen and stood there, looking as out of place as a watermelon in a strawberry patch. He suddenly felt intimidated by the vast assortment of skillets that hung from metal hooks above his head. Square skillets with dividing sections, round skillets with bottoms as deep as roasting pans, and tiny skillets that could hold only one small hen's egg, at most. On the counter to his right lay an assortment of knives. He stooped under the skillets, taking care to protect his hat, and stopped at the edge of the counter that faced Katie's back. The smooth motion with which she sliced and tossed the cabbage into the foamy water flowing from the faucet into the colander reminded him of the times he had, as a boy, watched the experienced field hands pick cotton. Their deft black hands seemed to roll the cotton from the bolls and slip it into the long sack that was umbilically connected to their bending bodies. The liquidity of their movements was spellbinding, compelling him to watch in awe. He inched closer, reached over the counter, and toyed with the stalk of a bruised green onion. He watched as she brushed the last of the shredded cabbage into the sink with a weak sweep of her hand. "Katie," Jim said.

She did not turn around; instead, she drowned out his voice by turning the water on full force and dunking the cabbage up and down in the sink like she was rinsing clothes. The swinging door burst open and, like a small boy caught playing with grown-up things, Jim quickly laid the onion back on the counter. Rosie rushed into the room, automatically producing an order pad with the flip of her wrists and said, "Good Lord, Katie. What's holding things up?" She stretched her neck, peeked into the Negro section, and with venom in her voice said, "Alice ain't here yet?"

"She on her way, Miss Rosie," Katie replied, leaving the cabbage, she dried her hands quickly. "Can I help?"

"I need two burgers with everything," Rosie snapped, stuffing the pad in her apron. She hesitated for a second, then turned and smiled at Jim. "Lord, Jim, you ain't got no idea the weight what's been lifted from these shoulders of mine. I feel like I could fly away," she said as she left the room.

Katie and Jim listened to the flapping of the door and Katie, wishing Rosie truly would fly away somewhere, turned and faced Jim, who toyed with the onion again. He avoided her gaze. She walked to the grill and slapped the meat down, pulled out the hamburger buns from under the cabinet, and popped the cellophane with a large knife.

"Is that apple pie I smell?" he asked, slouching lazily against the cutting table.

She cut her eyes, then pointing said, "It sho is, Mr. Jim. And over there is cabbage soaking, and we'se got hamburgers sizzling on the grill, and these right here that I is now pressing to this grill is what they calls hamburger buns." Her shrill voice cut into his flesh.

Automatically, he strangled the onion in his fist. The onion bulb scooted above his fingers as though trying to free itself from his grasp. What was it about her that always pushed him to the edge? Carefully, he laid the onion on the counter and glaring at her, said, "It just wasn't the right time, Katie. Don't you see? If it hadn't been for that there hanging, everybody what was involved would have got what they deserved, especially Roy."

"Lord have mercy," she moaned above the splatter of the meat, her heart threatening to explode in her chest. She shook her head as she realized none of those people in the courthouse had taken her serious. They had made up their minds even before she took the stand—she was just a nigger trying to protect her daughter. She felt lightheaded, as though something had stolen all the air from the room—like she had suddenly inhaled the smoke from a thousand oil lamps. Silently, she prayed that she would not stumble or faint in the presence of this white man. And when the dizziness passed, she hissed, "What time would a been right for Margaret? Or should I say Negroes."

"Katie," he sighed, feeling helpless. It became apparent to him that Katie had expected him to do something—anything—that would guarantee Margaret's freedom, but she didn't understand that he too was a victim of the system. "I ain't talking to you about Negroes or whites. Listen to me, will you?" He pushed his hat back on his head and stood straight. "What I'm trying to git you to see is how people react to guilt. Suddenly after committing such a heinous act, blocking the streets and yelling for the blood of the Ohioans, even throwing rocks, they cooled off and was ashamed." The music up front thumped louder and Jim held one ear, trying to drown out the noise. It was not only the jukebox, but gravel popping, car doors banging on the front, and the crinkling of paper bags on the back as the Negroes practically laid upon the door awaiting entry. "It ain't got nothing to do with color," he continued. "It was like they all had the 'galloping fever'—everybody got it at the same time. And after they had participated in the hunt, their blood was up for the kill. Now that the excitement has died down, and their thirst for blood is quenched, Roy's crimes don't look so bad as they first did, especially since he lost his pa, and his arm to boot. They feel old Roy's been punished enough."

"Still sounds funny to me," she said, flipping the burgers over. "If it ain't got nothing to do with whites or Negroes, why can't Margaret come home? Looks like to me I've done suffered enough too.

He removed his hat, raked his long fingers through his hair, and placed the hat back on his head. He suddenly seemed agitated, as though something that he could not grasp kept him from saying what he meant. "Didn't nothing happen to Charlie. Ain't he a Negro?"

She sighed and turned to peek at him over her shoulder while she pressed the burgers with the long, steel spatula to the grill. "Well," she hissed. "Everybody in town knows Miss Clara ain't gonna 'low nobody to mess with Charlie. M.B., on the other hand, gots to do thirty days in the Big House on account of them lawmakers. Don't seem like no one is forgiving him either."

"They didn't believe you, Katie. It's as simple as that! They felt you was acting like any mother would to protect her child," he said, leaning against the counter.

"Well, how comes they believes Miss Rosie, then? She did the same. Testified for her child." She turned to him, her face hard, demanding, her eyes bold. She felt cold even in the midst of all the steam from the grill. She realized that feeling this way could only mean God had removed her fear and replaced it with a calm—a thinking, calculated, questioning calm.

"Hell," Jim snapped. "Rosie testified she knew it was J.T. what hired Roy and his bunch to break into your house. She also furnished a reason as to why her son participated in the break in—Buddy was afraid to go against someone as powerful as J.T. Rosie's testimony showed conspiracy, the connection needed to tie J.T. to this crime and to Boswell's murder. Try to understand, Katie," he said.

"Oh, I understands perfectly, Mr. Jim," she announced with an air of judgment, piled the hamburgers on the platter and rang the silver bell. "When I was in that witness chair, didn't you ask me if I knowed who killed Boswell, and didn't I say outright that I saw J.T. do it? Me and Miss Rosie said practically the same thing, and any fool knows J.T. is the only one who would hire somebody to scare me and Margaret. It's jest like I said, one test-ti-monee was white and the other colored."

"Now that ain't so, Katie. If you compare the charges, you'll see the difference. Both Buddy and Margaret are good kids," he said, bending the fingers of his hand backwards. But Buddy was charged with abetting—he drove the getaway car—while Margaret was charged with attempted murder—hacking off Roy's arm. Also, remember that Buddy was in court to swear that his testimony was true. Where was Margaret? Somewhere up north, dodging the law."

She swallowed hard, trying to remove the dryness from her throat. It was useless, she thought, trying to make him see the law as it was—against Negroes, against the Ohioans, against all, but the lily white. "Suppose you jest tell me outright when Margaret can come home."

A horn blared outside and somebody yelled, "Ain't nobody taking no orders yet?" The juke-box up front thumped loudly, and someone shook the handle of the back door. Katie did not move. She watched as Jim wiped his mouth with the back of his hand then looked down at the floor.

"She can't set foot in Bennettsville ever again, Katie. Not as long as Clem Dalton is the judge, and, well, I reckon that goes for me too. I have to obey the law even though I might sometimes feel the punishment don't fit the crime. Katie I know you ain't no liar, but I also know you'd do anything for your daughter. At times I doubted that you maimed Roy. But I believed you in the end and what was left for me to do? Insist that you be charged instead of Margaret. The matter already seemed to be solved," he spoke softly and brought his eyes up to meet hers.

At that moment, Rosie burst into the kitchen again. "Gimme five burgers with everything, and three Blue Plate Specials." Katie looked up, scooped up three meat patties, and slapped them on the grill. Pulling out three platters, she turned her attention back to Jim.

"Is she gonna be hunted like a dog?"

Jim scratched his chin and waited until Rosie had cleared the room before he answered. "If you mean will a wanted notice be issued to other states, the answer is no. There will be no further action taken against her, but if she is caught back here, she will be picked up, charged, and dealt with according to the law. The dismissal of a warrant was the only thing that I could get Clem to agree on."

Katie closed her eyes and breathed a sigh of relief. At least Margaret wouldn't be tracked down and put in jail. At least she could live a fairly decent life somewhere. "It's on account she took that money, ain't it?" Katie asked, her voice softening. She dipped peas evenly onto the plates.

"Hell, Katie. That's a possibility. But if she had been here, I would have fought for her just the same as I did for Buddy," he said, exhaling a long gust of air, as though his pride had been pricked with a long needle and had torn away a surface that exposed a deep shame for his people, a surface that hid his true feelings behind some abstract principle that he should, but at the moment could not remember. He turned and looked out the back door at the crowd milling there. The Negroes that had formed a line stood gazing through the locked screen door.

"But they all knows what a big liar Roy is," she said in a desperate voice.

"Katie, I told you their decision had nothing to do with Roy. It was their own skins, or better yet, their souls, they was trying to set right with God. And they justified it by saying, liar or not, a man oughta know who maimed him."

"Hump," she snarled, ringing the bell. "What 'bout Marmy and Buddy? They knows what happened."

"Sure they do, but they didn't add nothing pertinent. You said so yourself that they was on the outside of the house when it happened, that they didn't actually see the fight, that made it your word against Roy's."

"My word against a known liar. Oh, Charlie was right! Your word don't count for nothing important, jest for stuff like when the dinner will be ready and the like. It don't count for nothing when it goes aginst white folks, even the lowest." She looked across Jim's shoulder, her face glistening with perspiration, her eyes lifted in shock as she realized she would never be considered anything but a nigger, no matter how she lived. "It don't matter to none of them," she shouted. "Maybe not even to you that I'se always told the truth, treats all folks the same like the Good Book says. No sir, that don't matter at all." She did not allow Jim to answer. "Margaret ain't never been in no trouble. She jest headstrong, but what youngen ain't?" She watched Jim's face turn from red to white, then back to red. She knew he was struggling with his thoughts, she knew he strived to make her understand his point of view for she had seen that same look on Margaret's face when they differed over issues. She walked over to the oven, removed the bubbling pies, and sat them on the cooling rack near Jim's elbow. She looked at him, her eyes blazing. "Well, all I can say is Roy Larkin best not come 'round my house no more. Not as long as he lives—not scatting, not standing, not for nothing 'cause we aims to protect ourselves. Won't be no turning back. You best tell him that!"

He winced. The violence was evident in her voice. Tears collected in her eyes, and he did not know how to ease her pain. In fact, he agreed Roy could benefit from an undetermined amount of buckshot. "I lost too, Katie. J.T.'s fancy lawyer made me look like a fool. I wasn't allowed to even question him, and J.T.'s made so many enemies since his pa's death, it's a wonder he wasn't hung right alongside them Ohioans. Now, had you come forward instead of being subpoenaed, things might have gone better for Margaret, but you kept fighting me, and avoiding the truth."

"Avoiding the truth!" she spat and, turning around, looked directly into the whites of Sam Johnston's eyes as he stood with his head straining against the screen door. She gasped and spun back around, then headed back to the sink where she dumped the cabbage into a large bowl and sprinkled a handful of sugar on top. "It seems to me that avoiding the truth is a way of life when it comes to dealing with the law. And I'd do it agin. Do you have any idea what it was like sending my child away from me to save her from what Wade and his bunch intended to do to her? You do knows what they does to colored girls before they brings them to the jailhouse. Do you have any idea what it's like to say to your child, 'Run, Run,' even though that child ain't-done nothing wrong? Is you gots any sense at all? Don't you think that child is gonna look through new eyes at me for the rest of her born days? Don't you understands what it means to be free all your life then suddenly you ain't free no more? No," she answered for him, "you wouldn't know nothing 'bout that 'cause you always been a free white man."

"Hold on there, Katie," Jim shouted and stretched his arms in front of him. "I remember a whole lot more than you is giving me credit for. Yes, I know what it means to be a <u>free</u> white man. I found that out the day my ma told me I couldn't take up no more time with you. I found out just what it meant to be a free white man—I could have everything, but what I wanted most—you." He held her with his eyes, and seeing his face flush, she quickly turned away, fumbling for the spatula. He raked his fingers through his hair and turned toward the door to see Alice, who had entered the side door and stood watching them, her mouth agape.

Rosie entered the kitchen again. She stopped in her tracks, looking first at Jim, then at Katie, and finally at Alice. "Lord, Katie. You is a wonder to behold," Rosie said, breaking the awkward silence. She glared at Alice, promising a harsh reprimand, then turned and sniffed the air like a bloodhound. "Them pies smell heavenly." And deciding that all this talk should be over by now, she approached Jim with an outstretched hand. "Lord, Jim ain't you ready for your dinner? You must be starved—over there at that courthouse all morning arguing with that fool-headed Hal Buck. Lord, that is one stubborn man."

"Yeah," he agreed, cramming his hands in his pockets and letting her lead him from the room.

"Katie," Rosie said, steering Jim towards the swinging door. "Fix Big Jim something to eat." Turning on her heels, Katie reached for a platter and placed it on the counter. With a crack in her voice, asked, "You want the usual?"

The hollowness of her voice seemed to echo across the room and Jim closed his eyes, then nodded, and followed Rosie through the door. As they walked through the narrow aisle, Katie heard Rosie say, "Lord, Jim on top of all this mess, I heard tell this morning them Yankees' caskets was found outside on the courthouse lawn. Is that the truth?"

And Katie heard a long sigh escape Jim's lips and his low whisper, "Yeah. Shore is—it's the damnest thing I ever seen.

Charlie stood in the doorway of his kitchen staring out into the yard. His emotions were mixed. The events at the courthouse this morning had left him elated, soaring high at moments, and at times down at his lowest—on the verge of tears. Every time Charlie would recall Hal Buck's announcement, "Due to grave illness the witness, Doc Smith, will not be able to take the stand." Charlie's heart pounded as though it would leap from his chest. It had taken all his will power to remain seated in the courtroom; he had wanted to jump and shout "hallelujah!" But, instead, he slapped his thigh and grinned.

Over the years he had grudgingly accepted the fact that he would die long before Doc Smith, carrying his bitterness and grief to the grave. Somewhere in the back of his mind he had harbored the image of an old, broken man, head white from age being lowered into the red mud. However, now he stood in his kitchen door looking out at his garden—the second crop of tomatoes heavy on the vines, rich and red, the okra green as jade, and the blue hulls mouthwatering even in their shell—and Doc Smith lay in his bed on the other side of town, dying. Charlie was often drawn to the garden, and excepting Anna Mae loved nothing more than digging in the earth. The garden had always been a reminder of her. It had been the source for many of their playful arguments: she would chastise him for spending too much time 'fooling 'round in that garden,' and he would come back with something sassy that would make her turn away and giggle, then catch her mouth for giggling too loud.

But Anna Mae had died, died—oh, my God, he remembered. She died because the same Doc Smith who had suffered a stroke earlier this morning would not help her. She had died by his hand in the bed of M.B.'s pick-up truck, wrapped in a red-and-yellow, wedding-ring quilt. She had died a horrible, horrible death, and he had had to live with the horror of it all. And now today in the midst of "white folks mess," he received the news he had waited years to hear. Hal Buck had stood and announced it as though it was just a part of everyday life—the normal order of existence. Charlie thought about the spell that he had had Lofton put on Doc Smith and knew that it not coincidence. And if Lofton wanted to take credit, it was fine with him—hell they would both take credit. Why not? All he needed to hear now was those long awaited words "Doc Smith is dead." He prayed to hear those words. In fact, he promised himself that should it come to pass, he would attend church this coming Sunday. He would sit down in his old seat in the pew among the deacons. He would bang his bony hands together and sing louder than anyone else. He would get happy because the Reverend's sermon would be specifically aimed at him and his long-awaited return to the fold. He would shout and shout to the heavens, over and over, "Thank you, Jesus! Thank you, Jesus!"

And there on the spot—the threshold of his kitchen door—Charlie lifted his eyes to the heavens and yelled, "If'n you is up there on yo' thone listening, let that white bastard die like a dog!" Tears streamed down his face, and he brushed them away like they were poisonous black spiders that lived among you, learned all your secrets, then spread them about like flimsy webs for everyone to see. He stepped out the door, down the steps, and cornered the house winding up on the front. He sat down on the bottom step in the shade. Suddenly, something drew his attention to the road— Katie, entering the mouth of the alley.

A dejected, downhearted Katie walked with slumped shoulders and her head, down. The purse she always carried pressed to her bosom was now hanging at her side. The early September breeze played with the brim of her straw hat and the tail of her long dress. Slowly, she raised her head; her eyes, shiny with tears, swept over the alley, then rested on his face. Her pain was so great, it seemed to leap ahead of her and sock him hard in the chest. He shook his head as she stumbled closer. How well he knew that feeling—that feeling of losing someone you loved to the unknown. But Margaret would be better off in a world other than theirs—a world that they would be as much out of place as Margaret had been in theirs. At least in this new world, Margaret could survive—maybe even question, speculate, and plan her future instead of leaving it up to the whims of people like J.T. She was better off in the north, he thought. Here she would only die, like Anna Mae.

He saw a strange light in Katie's eyes. He promised himself that he would make her smile again, and soon. If Big Jim wasn't white, he could make Katie smile. But unlike her mother, Sarah, Katie would never cross the color line—she had been straddling the road all her life, afraid to openly show love and tenderness toward whites, and afraid to show honest anger toward Negroes because they had grudgingly accepted her. She hid all these feelings under the cloak of religion, for if she were a Saint, it would be expected that she treat everyone equally.

Katie stared at him. She was close enough now for him to see the tiny roses at the hem of her dress, and it was as though she looked directly into his soul. He felt her eyes probe deep inside him, questioning about the life they had to live. He had seen that look before in his own eyes, and in the eyes of other Negroes. That look of utter surprise. A look that stretched the eyes to their limits, and gaped the mouth to incredible proportions, as though a mighty blow had been delivered to the back of the head, snapping the neck, and catching one completely off guard. As though a light had finally seeped into the cortex—that impenetrable cortex that only Negroes have—and opened that unyielding door. Revealing the magnitude of the whites' power over them, forcing them to see the picture in its entirety, the flower in full detail, not just its delicate perfumed bloom, but its ugly brown stem and the cow shit that constantly feeds it. And after all is brought out into the open, show the Negro how powerless he is—that the world in which he struggled to live is in reality the mere fantasy of white folks.

Yes, how well he knew that look. The look that questioned beliefs, and asked why are they so hard to change. He had once seen a young Negro man shame himself because of his belief that if his feet were swept with a broom, he would have bad luck for the rest of his life. He had seen him hop around on the ground, holding the foot the broom had touched, and sweating with fear. It was a sight: a grown man jumping around like a two-hundred pound black frog, spitting on a broom to reverse his luck in the world. This was well beyond the realms of superstition: it was, in his mind, a curse that would beat him down to the ground much quicker than his already destined fate—Negrodom.

And he had seen a young white boy of twelve defy his mother's instructions to come inside from play. The lad was too young to understand fate or superstition; but freedom, he knew. And knowing full well the beating he would get from his mother, he had stood back in his legs and yelled, "Didn't I tell you I'd be there tereckly?" Charlie had understood that his actions demonstrated more than the usual hardheadedness displayed by stubborn children. This child knew he was free and saw no sane reason for his mother to allocate his freedom in time frames. He clearly understood he was free and that he alone should decide how his time would be used. He knew that no one should try and make him jump.

Oh, yes, he knew exactly how she felt. She was just a babe even though she had grown up today; she still had bushels to learn about white folks. He pushed up from the steps, walked across the porch, and reached inside the door for his cane—the door banged loudly behind him, like a scatter gun at night, and the curious Dominique hens retracted their long necks, squawked loudly, and ran away like bow-legged, old ladies. He walked to the bottom of the steps and, stepping over the million three-prone chicken tracks that covered the yard, hobbled down the road to meet her—to touch her, to console her, and to be a part of her.

They met in the middle of the dirt path leading to Charlie's front yard and she collapsed against his shoulder. "Lord, Lord, Charlie. I feels like I'se been throwed away. I walked out, Charlie. Jest couldn't take no more. Walked right out in the middle of dinner—left everything like it was, and Miss Rosie standing with her mouth wide open."

"Serves 'em right," Charlie spoke to the ground. He avoided looking at her face. "Serves 'em right," he repeated and cleared his throat. He could not stand to see her tears. "Jest you come on inside and rest," he cooed, while he gently put his arm around her shoulder like she was a porcelain doll.

"I ain't ready to go inside jest yet. My child ain't inside, and I wants my child, Charlie. I needs to see her face. I want to see it now."

"You gonna be seeing Margaret agin," he said, patting her shoulder as they walked towards the steps. "Don't you be a thinking you wont. We'll be a going up to Chicago real soon and stay long as you wants. We can have M.B. drive us, soon as his hand heals, or if'n you wants we can ketch that Greyhound Bus or even that City of New Orleans train and stay up yonder long as it seem fit. I can come back and tend to everything here. Won't be no need for you to worry, even if'n you wants to stay a month, even two. Yeah, you'll be going back and forth so much you'll be saying you is tired of Margaret—tired of looking in her face. Yes, ma'am, you wait," he said, and pulled her to the steps on the porch into the shade.

They sat side by side on the steps, Katie holding her head in her hands and Charlie staring at the tomatoes in the garden. The sun was hot and golden against the red dirt, the chickens clucked softly. Their world was going on all about them. A world that had long been without Anna Mae was now without Margaret.

Katie gazed across the alley. A steamy haze rose above the rocks. She wiped the sweat from her brow, suddenly aware that the earth was very still, as though it had stopped. She knew this was an indication that she was about to have a vision. And she braced herself, focusing on her house in the distance, aware of how lonely it looked. The house faded, and suddenly she saw a large field a-bloom with cotton—white tufts dotted the land throughout. On a hill, a few feet away, sat a bright, red airplane, gleaming. And then she saw him: the same tall man in the sleek chauffeur uniform who had come to take her to pray for Townsend. He was stooped over the plane removing something from the engine. His hands dripped with oil. The plane shifted slightly, then settled, and the man grinned. And suddenly he faded and the plane was airborne, buzzing in the sky. Its engine whining, whining, until it spun crazily and its nose dove towards the ground. Then her house came back into view. She frowned, shook her head—she had no idea what it meant. And so, she let it go. God would make it clear in time.

A gentle pat upon her shoulder made her look around. Charlie's eyes were bright with plans and he said in a tone so sincere as though he had figured everything out, as though their world had new meaning, "Yeah, we'll go to Chicago so much, you'll be tired of looking at Margaret's face.

She turned away from him and looked about the yard; her eyes following the chicken tracks that circled the house. "I go where the Lord sends me," she said, and rested her head against his shoulder.

THE END

Printed in the United States
70779LV00002B/523

9 781418 440152